PORTRAIT OF POLWERRIS

Portrait
of
Polwerris

Enid Mavor

UNITED WRITERS
Cornwall

UNITED WRITERS PUBLICATIONS LTD
Ailsa, Castle Gate, Penzance, Cornwall.

British Library Cataloguing in Publication Data:
A catalogue record for this book is
available from the British Library.

ISBN 1 85200 078 3

Printed in Great Britain by
United Writers Publications Ltd
Cornwall.

For Jimmy

Chapter One

I was painting. Silas Jenkin stood beside the small table, one gnarled hand resting on its polished top, uncomfortable in his pose, stiff in his best suit and tight-lipped with the effort to be still. Much better that he had let me paint him working alongside the harbour, intent on mending the nets, with the reflected light off the moving water chasing patterns across his face. But no, he wants a stern, dark portrait for his parlour wall; something for his children, and theirs.

But I had stood him beside the table so that I could get a part of the corner window onto the canvas, with a glimpse of the harbour where the masts of the fishing boats rocked gently in the blue air.

They often do not approve of what I see, but because I am a woman and of a different background, and perhaps because of my accident, they accept me. And good craftsmen themselves, they respect my skill and take canny advantage of my desire, my hunger, to put them onto canvas.

So I was lost to all but the smell of the paint and the lines which ran from the corners of his mouth down his seamed chin. A narrow mouth, hard yet not cruel, and there were those other lines too that hinted at an easy frequent laugh. If only he would relax that glazed unnatural stare. . .

I tried to get him to talk, but it was not until I mentioned the war that I got the response I needed.

'War, is it? Which war would that be then, Miss Millbrook, the war in France or on the Peninsula or the one with America? You got to say that for our leaders, they don't do things by halves! Nowhere to sell our goods in Europe, no imports from America, and then they say that it is our bit of trading on the side with the

Frenchies behind their backs that is what is keeping Napoleon's armies goin'!' Had he been on the harbour wall he would have spat his contempt into the sea. As it was he clenched his teeth and slowed down his breathing with an effort. 'There's our factories going bankrupt in the Midlands for want of trade and all the government can think of is tryin' to control more lands. Time they took a good look at our own country before we rise up like the French did.'

'Not such a bloody uprising I hope Mr Jenkin!'

He shook his head. 'No. All that slaughter. . . No. Not like that. If it had been done different though, I do believe it would have spread over here and our rulers would have had to give a thought to the way most of us live - nothin' but work from cradle to the grave. As 'tis, they're too frightened now to give us an inch.' He paused, gave me his sudden smile and said, 'It'll come though, sooner or later, you'll see.'

I could have told him. I could have told him something of what it was like in Paris during the Terror almost twenty years ago; of the horrors I had seen with my disbelieving seventeen-year-old eyes. Of the crowds in the streets, the noise and the smell. That dreadful smell of fear, of hate, of blood. But I said nothing. The villagers knew I was part French, but I never spoke of my French mother, nor of my childhood spent roaming Europe with my parents. Most of all, they did not know, and must not know of the disastrous marriage which had been my means of escape from the stricken city. . . That marriage from which three years ago I had fled with such dire consequences. So many times, relaxed with these people amongst whom I lived, I had almost crossed that line of mutual trust, but always I drew back, aware of the abyss into which not only I would fall if my secret were to be revealed. So now I took a deep breath and shut out my thoughts and concentrated on the figure of the man before me.

He was silent again, but now his face was relaxed and his eyes gazed steadily into a future where freedom and the rights of man were more than simply the slogans of a rebellion.

I painted steadily, aware of nothing but the need to capture just that look, when suddenly my palette slid from my left hand and struck the wooden floor with a clatter. Colour splattered across the smooth surface and a brush rolled through the resurging silence with a small scratch.

Silas looked at me where I sat immobile in my chair, at my left hand, bluish and stiff as a claw, and in his sunken old eyes was a compassion I did not wish for. So I cursed, fluently and succinctly, and was glad to see him wince at my novel and catholic choice of words.

He hid his embarrassment by stooping to pick up the palette and brushes and he even used a rag from my box to wipe up the stains, something he would never have done in his own house for a woman of his own.

'Thank you,' I said harshly. 'I'll go on with it whenever you have time to sit again.'

He crossed the room to stand beside me, eager to examine what I had done. I hate them looking at my work, half finished and raw. But I have learned to bear it, just one small thing more.

'Well?' My voice was still rough and angry. 'What do you make of it?' As if I cared what he thought. And yet I always did. . .

But he mumbled a little, unsure of what he saw, even more unsure of me, a virago who smouldered in her chair and would swear like a tooth drawer when upset. So he was polite and cautious and soon he left and Gladys came to give me tea and chafe my numb hand.

That was on Tuesday. I slept little that night and before the next day's dawn I had hoisted myself from my bed and shuffled round the room several times, leaning on the furniture to convince myself that my arm was functioning again. Perhaps the recurrent numbness is only evident when holding my palette for a prolonged period. If so, I will still be able to paint. And I, who never pray, lay prostrate upon the bare floor pleading with Providence to leave me that much at least.

Then I pulled myself up into the big, heavy armchair, regretting my moment of weakness, cursing once more the God who had done these things to me. It was this same surging anger which had brought me back from the edge of death three years ago and it must now sustain me through whatever else might be in store.

I looked down to where my legs were hidden beneath my nightgown. The accident had left me completely paralysed for some time, but now I could hobble about for short periods. I smiled wryly, remembering the fierce joy such movement had brought me. I, who had danced and ridden, strode lightly across the moors with the men on a shoot. . . But that was in my other life. And it struck me then that apart from the separation from my son, this present life, despite my infirmities was in many ways more satisfying than the old. Here I was respected for what I was, for my talent and skills, not the accidents of birth and marriage that had taken me to Trevingey, to the great house that lay in its rolling park at the other end of the county. At the other end of the world, for me. . .

But the thought was comforting and when Gladys came in a few minutes later with the ewer of hot water, I greeted her with a smile and after breakfast I was eager to be out in the warm spring sunshine.

Gladys wheeled me down to the harbour, for the steepness of the narrow street was too much for my uncertain legs, and the chair which the carpenter had designed was tailored for the hilly lanes hereabout. There was a stiffish breeze, and she fussed around me for a while, my friend Gladys, once my maid, in whose home I have found my peculiar refuge.

After she had gone, I tossed off the smothering shawl and propped my makeshift easel against the low parapet which ran along one side of the harbour wall. I liked it here, with the moving sea against the wall on one side and the small sheltered harbour basin on the other, and the warmth of the sun shining on the clustered houses which tumbled down the hillside in such blithe accord.

There were a number of people about, but after the first greeting and politeness, they went about their work and left me to mine and I settled down to wrestle with an unlikely and tantalisingly foreshortened view of a battered pinnace, the survivor of some old wreck, which rubbed its barnacles against the granite wall below.

I was aware of the slap and rush of water against the wall to my left, and the occasional murmur of voices from the working men, but was soon lost in concentration. Time passed. At last, warned by the threat of stiffness in my hand, I put down my brushes and stretched, flexing my neck and shoulders gratefully.

As I turned my head I could see the masts and sails of a fishing vessel, plunging and rearing gaily as it approached the narrow entrance to the harbour, faded red sails brilliant against the encircling cliffs. Gulls shrieked in its wake and as if galvanised by the increasing chorus, the working men looked up and several girls came running along the wall with baskets swinging easily in their brown hands.

Morwenna, Silas Jenkin's daughter, ran with them, her bare feet light as butterflies on the sunlit grey stone. The swinging brown skirt was too short and showed inches of slender leg, but no more so than the dresses of the other girls, for they were all equally poor. Only her looks set her apart from the others and of this she appeared to be quite unconscious. But today there was a new light in her face, a burning eagerness that wakened my curiosity.

Just then there was a shout from the boat and sails came rattling down. Like a reined horse, the *Liza Jane* paused, plunged and slid through the gap in the wall and into the calm of the basin.

And as she passed through, I saw Zeb Martin, high in the prow. He waved and called and picked up a coiled rope. With horrified realisation I saw what he was about to do, but before I could even draw my breath in a gasp, he made a leap for the wall upon which we waited. Had the ship remained poised for a moment longer, it would have been an easy jump, but even as he leapt, the deck dropped beneath him and for one heart-stopping moment I thought he would crash against the wall and be crushed by the passing boat, so narrow was the gap.

Some of the girls screamed and a man ran forward, but in the same instant Zeb landed on his toes, crouched on the very edge of the harbour wall. I can see him now, frozen in that moment of precarious balance and I know there was no vestige of fear on his face. Like a cat, he tipped himself forward, and spun and rolled and was on his feet at once, the rope still in his hand. In two easy strides he had looped it round a granite bollard and as easily caught a second rope thrown in a snaking lunge from the passing deck. He said something in a laughing aside to one of the girls as he made fast the rope.

The girl was Morwenna. Her blue eyes were dark pools in a face white with shock and her hands clutched her basket against her breast as if for mortal support. He said something else over his shoulder as he turned back to the ship and the other girls came

11

closer, giggling and jostling. I saw the colour gradually return to the girl's pale face, and with it a hint of anger at his recklessness.

And I saw how, even with his back to the girls, he was always aware of Morwenna. He stood, waiting as the ship was made fast, apparently intent upon the business of docking, but whenever he turned, it was always to where Morwenna had moved. And I saw how the girl too, never took her eyes from the lithe, restless youth.

How old were they? Eighteen? Nineteen? Old enough to be safely married in this village. I wondered why they were not; the attraction between them was smoulderingly evident. Then I remembered what Silas Jenkin, Morwenna's father, had said to me yesterday when I had first been trying to relax him, to unstiffen those taut shoulders. I had asked after his children, especially Morwenna whom I have painted more than once. And he told me he had hopes for her, George Thomas, a steady young man, just right for his girl. . . Now I shook my head; there would be trouble if Silas tried to force that match.

But now the fishing boat was safely berthed and Zeb leapt back onto her deck, flashing a farewell smile at Morwenna. And as the girls turned to go, picking up their baskets, Morwenna's face was once more aglow.

They came towards me, a laughing carefree group of girls, apparently content with their poverty and the narrow boundaries of their lives; with a future that would hold little but child-bearing and endless hard work. And I felt once more that guilt which so wracked me when I remembered the life I had once lived, a life of indolence and indulgence, built upon the toil and poverty of people like these. So I smiled my stiff smile when they paused beside me to chatter and exclaim over my painting. Just then one of the girls turned and pointed.

'Look! Who's that then, on the deck of the *Liza Jane*?

We all turned to look and as I did so, I felt the familiar frisson of fear. A stranger! Had I been discovered? Was this man an emissary from Charles? And then I saw the trunks and boxes upon the deck. No. This man was not concerned with me; my threat would come from a silent shadow, a quick thrust of a dagger in the night, not in a public place like this. And the sunshine on my back warmed away the gooseflesh of my fear.

So it was with relief that I joined the girls in their inspection of the man who now stood beside his luggage on the deck.

A man of medium height and build but set apart from the other men by the clothes he wore - a leather jacket with fringes, dark trousers and hat with a brim so wide it hid most of his face. Who could this be? My artist's eye followed him as he crossed the deck, liking the way he moved and noting the strength of the shoulders beneath that well-worn jacket.

We were joined by another girl who had been talking to her father. Excitedly she poured out her news.

' 'Tis Mistress Matthews' nephew! Comed home from Canada on the packet boat to Falmouth. And now he've come to live here in Polwerris!' And the girls shrieked and chattered like a flurry of birds as they chased this scrap of information gaily between themselves.

And then, perhaps drawn by their shrillness, he looked up and I saw his face. A handsome man, in his thirties I supposed, with wide set eyes and a small beard framing his jaw. He smiled at the bevy of girls around me and removed his hat in a salute, revealing a head of thick black curls. And then our eyes met.

How long did we gaze at one another? A few seconds only I suppose for it takes no longer to read the heart, to see interest, admiration, desire. I felt something within me, long frozen, pulse into life. My throat was tight. . . And then one of the other men on board took his arm and pointed to the luggage that was being lifted to the harbour wall and reluctantly he turned away.

I gripped the painting I still held between my hands, confused by the sudden upsurge of emotion. Not since my accident had a man looked at me like that; always now the admiration in their eyes was marred by pity, or perhaps, distaste. But what had he seen as he looked up? A cluster of girls surrounding a seated woman. The chair which proclaimed my state would be hidden by the parapet. I was wearing a bright tabbard over my blouse and my hair was tucked away beneath the old hat which kept the sun from my eyes while I worked; an old hat, but flattering none the less for I wore nothing that was not becoming, vain that I am. And why not? Why should I not make the best of what was left? And I was glad he had seen me, that it was I on whom his gaze had rested; glad that the heady wine of open admiration and instant attraction had been mine, for however brief a moment it might prove to be. . .

But now the stranger had followed the skipper down below decks again and with an effort I turned away. Morwenna lingered beside my chair, her eyes still on the boat and I thought with wry amusement that the sturdy little vessel was an unlikely steed to bear not one, but two men who in the space of the last few moments had unleashed such strong emotions in both our breasts.

Amongst the group of girls was a child I had not seen before, a small skinny girl with lank hair and grimy skin. But it was the look on her face that brought me out of my reverie, for as she gazed at the painting on my lap her eyes were alight with pleasure. Such a look I had so often seen on my son's face; for he alone could share with me total understanding of what I had portrayed. And now, here was the same look on the face of this waif, for that is what she seemed to be.

She appeared to be about to speak then changed her mind and looked away. The other girls exclaimed and chattered, obviously bewildered by the composition but impressed by the adroitness of my brush. Morwenna said nothing, still too aware of the nearness of Zeb to give more than cursory attention to a mere painting. She suddenly spoke to her companions.

'You go on. I want to see Miss Millbrook.' And without evident curiosity, they went on their way, squealing with delight over something one had said. Only the strange child hung back, reluctant to leave, but intimidated by Morwenna's greater age and status she slowly followed the others.

Morwenna came nearer to my chair.

'Father was some proud of his picture, Miss Millbrook. You know him, he doesn't say much, but last night that was all he could talk about. He says you made him look like a man of worth.'

'A man of worth!' I smiled thoughtfully. 'Well I hope I did. I think that sums him up, don't you?' And I was secretly pleased. But I knew the girl had a different reason to stop and talk to me.

She had sat herself down on the parapet.

'Yes, I suppose you're right.' But there was a sudden rebellious look on her face and her eyes returned to the activity on the deck of the berthed vessel.

'Would you like to push me home, Morwenna? I've just about finished here.' For suddenly I knew I did not want the stranger to see me here in my chair; for just a little longer I wanted him to keep his illusions, however trifling they might be.

And she turned to me eagerly. I had been right when I had sensed in her the need to confide.

'Oh yes. I'm back early from selling the butter anyway.'

And I realised that the girls had already returned from the early morning walk into Helston where they sold their wares to the shops and hotels of the busy market town.

Now, at last, she looked at the picture with awareness.

'You're lucky,' she said in a small voice.

'Lucky?' I grinned wryly down at the rug which covered my legs and I thought with a sudden wrench of anguish about the man on the deck. . .

She nodded gravely. 'Yes. You know what you want to do.' And she slid off the wall, her back to where Zeb worked, and stared out towards the horizon.

I packed my things away slowly, and with an effort tried to find something to talk about, something to take my mind off the stranger. So I asked about the child.

'Who was that skinny little thing, Morwenna? I've never seen her about the place before. She looks too young to be going to town with you.'

'Aw, that's Jinny Pellow. She's only eleven. She's come to live with her grandmother. You know, the one who lives at the end of Frog Lane.'

Yes I did know of Mrs Pellow who lived in a hovel on the outskirts of the village with a seemingly endless brood of children. Not her own, for she was long past childbearing but numerous grandchildren, some legitimate, some not, were housed with her while their mothers worked. She was much talked about, for the greyness of the washing spread to dry on the bushes in the gully beside her tiny cottage, for the neglect of the children in her care, the lack of food, the raggedness of their clothing. They told how she had regular money from her daughters but was too mean to spend it on the children.

I was surprised that the child was able to mix with the other girls so easily for there was a strong feeling of class even at this stratum of society. As if in answer to my unvoiced question, Morwenna went on, 'Her gran asked my mother if Jinny could come with us to town to sell some jars of lemon curd. She's afraid to let her go on her own. I don't know why. I think it's something that happened when Jinny was living at her aunt's place. Anyway, Mother told me to look after her and not let her get lost.'

And she pushed back the hair that blew across her cheek and turned to pick up my things. Suddenly she grinned. 'Just think, all those grand people eating lemon curd from that house! I bet they wouldn't eat it if they knew we all had boxes of lemons from that wreck last month! But they do say that old Ma Pellow's is the best there is! Pity she doesn't spend a bit more time on proper food for the children.'

But I could see the subject was of no more interest to her; Morwenna's concerns were much closer to hand.

'Come on then. You can have a cup of tea with me.'

'Thank you,' she said with sudden gravity. 'I want to ask you something.' And she gathered up my painting bag while I held the wet picture carefully on my lap and then she pushed me back along the wall and up the steep cobbled street where we exchanged greetings with some women who were standing in their doorways for a moment's respite from their chores. And glancing over my shoulder, I was glad to see that the stranger had not yet reappeared to witness my slow progress and thus we came to the door of my cottage with its green paint peeling in the sun.

Chapter Two

In the kitchen Gladys was making bread, the smell reminding me that I was hungry after my morning in the open air. She grinned cheerfully at Morwenna, who was one of her favourites, and nodded that she would bring some tea into my sitting-room.

I needed to be helped from the chair, then I could make my way round the room using the furniture as a prop. We sat at the round, polished table, and I could see our joint reflection in the mirror over the fireplace. Morwenna, head bent, twisting the belt of her dress. I felt a moment of satisfied vanity that at the age of thirty-seven I was not eclipsed by the young girl's beauty, for despite my infirmities, I had kept my looks. After my accident and during the long weeks when I lay in pain-racked fever, the waist-long black hair that had been my particular pride, became so matted and tangled that in a fit of desperation I had taken the scissors and cut it off in handfuls. The relief was instant, and as I recovered, Gladys had cut it more neatly. Since coming to the village, one of the men trimmed it for me regularly and it now swung free just below my ears, a gamin look that secretly pleased me. I had found too, that my full skirts and petticoats were cumbrous in the extreme and I had made for myself several pairs of baggy trousers, drawn in at the ankle, such as are worn by Turkish women, and seeing they had so little wear, on my feet some satin slippers. It was an exotic look that contrived to set me still further apart from the women of the village; emphasising my foreignness, though I feel sure my French mother, so correct during her lifetime, would have found my appearance eccentric in the extreme.

Morwenna looked up. 'I do like this room.'

She had been here often, but still she gazed around in frank curiosity. I had given the furniture some thought because this was my only living-room; here I had to work and sleep. So I had shown the village carpenter a sketch of a cupboard bed, the sort I had seen as a child in cottages in Normandy. Jack Saunders had worked well; fine wooden doors now concealed my bed which was flanked by large storage cupboards, the space above useful for storing my various canvases. This splendid piece of carpentry took up the whole of the back wall. For the rest, there was the round table at which we sat on two kitchen chairs, a small sofa with a drop end where I could rest during the day, and a wing chair before the fire. The front window faced the street and in the fireplace wall there was a narrower window which looked down towards the harbour, through the still bare branches of the lilac tree which seemed to grow out of the foundations of the house.

I smiled. 'You didn't come here to discuss the furniture, Morwenna.'

Her eyes met mine and the smile on her face died away.

'No,' she agreed. She folded her hands round her teacup and her head drooped. Then she looked up, eyes miserable.

'I don't know what to do, Miss Millbrook.'

I said nothing, waiting for her to go on.

'You see, it's Zeb. He won't marry me.'

'You don't mean . . .' But before I could finish the question she shook her head, giving me a wan smile.

'Oh no. It's not a baby. In a way that would make it easy . . .'

Once more she fell silent, her eyes following the spoon with which I stirred my tea.

'He's the one I want, the only one. From the day he came to the school when he was eight and his mother and brother had just died, I knew then, from that minute, that he was the one for me. The teacher put him to sit beside me and I held his hand, and not one of the other children teased us or said anything. Right from then I knew. And he knew as well. We were always talking about the house we would have, the things we would do.' Her voice broke and there was only the faint tinkle of my spoon against the saucer.

'He wants to go away. To make some money, he says. Four or five years it will take. I must wait four or five years until he comes back.'

'Won't he marry you first, Morwenna? I know he's mad about

you, everyone knows that.'

'No.' She shook her head slowly. 'He remembers how it was for his mother when his father was away at sea. And how they nearly starved when his father was drowned.'

I recalled what I had heard about the small boy arriving in the village all alone when his mother and brother had died of typhoid. An eight-year-old making his way the length of Cornwall to reach the granny his mother had told him he must find.

'What do your parents say?' I asked diffidently, guessing what the answer might be.

'Father says it's all daftness. He says I must marry George Thomas who's got something to offer, not day dreams.' She raised her eyes to mine again. 'But I'm not going to Miss Millbrook! I can't stand him. And anyway, it's Zeb for me, or no one. But my father says I can't live at home any longer if I won't do as he says. I shall have to go into service again.' And there was apprehension in her eyes and voice as she spoke.

'You were up at the Hall for a time weren't you Morwenna?'

'Yes,' and she shuddered. 'Those awful young men, the sons, thinking they could . . .' She left the sentence unfinished.

I smiled. 'I heard you gave them more than they bargained for?'

She nodded, head downcast. 'Of course I was sent home to my parents the same day. They were very nice about it though.'

I could just imagine the reaction of Silas Jenkin to any attempted philandering with his daughter. However, I could see his point too, regarding Zeb, a penniless suitor with only dreams to offer. And there was George Thomas, ardent and steady and waiting with his neat little smallholding alongside their own few acres.

'So whatever can I do, Miss Millbrook?'

I rubbed the surface of the table, gazing into its polished surface as if an answer might appear there. Why did the child have to come to me, of all people? She only had to look at me to see I was the last person from whom to seek advice. But of course, she did not know that it was my own actions which had brought about the events leading to my 'accident'. Only Gladys knew, and my secret was safe with her. . .

Presently though, an idea stirred.

'Would you like to work in a school, Morwenna? A girls'

school, in Plymouth.'

Her gratitude was instant. 'Oh yes! But do you think I could? What would I have to do?'

'Hold on a minute,' I laughed. 'I don't know if there is any post there at all. It's just a thought. I could write and find out.'

But Morwenna was sparkling, clutching at the idea with delight. 'That would mean I could leave home and be independent. And save some money too!'

'My dear child, I haven't even written yet! Now drink your tea and then go away and let me think. I make no promises, but I will do what I can. If that fails, then we must think again.'

And soon she left, her face alight with hope.

When she had gone, I sat at the table and thought. The letter must be written as if from one of the girls who had shared those years I had spent at Woodlands. It could not come from me; the web of secrecy I had built around myself these last three years must be protected. But presently I smiled to myself and began to write.

Later, I sat back and looked at the letter I had just completed.

A barely decipherable scrawl at the top could have read, 'The Empire Hotel' with the date more clearly written beneath, Twenty-seventh March, eighteen hundred and thirteen. Then it began. 'Dear Bobbet,' The nickname meant that the letter must have come from someone in our inner circle, for Miss Roberts was only 'Bobbet' to a handful of friends. A popular teacher, she had later gone on to run the school after the retirement of the old head. She had become a dear friend, and she was one of the people whom I truly missed in this new life of mine. 'My old dresser has a daughter who would like to work at Woodlands. She is reliable and intelligent and could help with the young ones, as well as sew and cook. I am off to Europe for a few months. If you want her, write to her mother at Trevince Cotts, Polwerris, Cornwall.' (I had printed this address in capitals.) 'I keep saying I will come and see you, when I get back I will. Remember when Sally Winters tried to elope with the Music Master and he reported her to Madame!' At the bottom of the letter I had signed the name Lena, with a flourish. I had added a postscript, 'Her name is Morwenna Jenkins.'

I felt the letter to be suitably arrogant in tone to ring true. And I knew from personal experience how a casual reference from an acquaintance almost guaranteed the applicant a post; for the constant changes in the large workforce, especially among the young women, meant vacancies were always arising. The reference to the Music Master gave, I felt, the necessary touch of familiarity. I only hoped I had not misjudged Lena St. John for she seemed to be the least likely person to keep in touch with her old school. All in all, I was pleased with the missive.

I folded the letter and placed it in an envelope. Tomorrow I would give it to the carter's boy to post.

Writing the letter had stirred a host of memories. I limped out to the kitchen to sit with Gladys for a while, but the pain in my back was particularly intense and I went and lay down on the sofa in my own room. Gladys followed me with a cup of camomile tea, a tisane which sometimes helped me to sleep. I sipped the beverage and then lay back and closed my eyes. My friend drew the curtains across the windows and then left me to rest in the darkened room.

And for the thousandth time, I wondered what I would do without Gladys. And my thoughts went back to the summer when Guy and I were staying with the Tregales at Polmennor Court, and that first dramatic meeting. . .

I was walking with my son. We went briskly through the woods for Guy was looking for an open space where he could kick the new ball he had been given for his tenth birthday a few days before and I remember the shout of pleasure he gave when we emerged from the shady gloom into a sunlit field.

I settled myself down with my sketch-pad while Guy raced up and down the field after the ball, both of us enjoying the freedom from the formal constraints of the great house where we were familiar guests when suddenly I came leaping to my feet with a scream of warning!

Guy was running down the field, racing after the ball which bounced far ahead of him. But what he had not seen was the strange figure which was hurtling towards him from the wood farther down the hill. A female figure, short and squat, skirts held high above the pounding legs, running fast, faster than even my terror-stricken legs could take me. Running straight at Guy!

He had turned at the sound of my scream, but the impetus of

his downhill rush kept him going and he could do no more than swerve away from his antagonist. I could only run, and scream, much too far away to save my son from whatever the madwoman intended. For madness there seemed to be in that fleet, ungainly form.

Then she reached him. I saw her launch herself at Guy, saw the tangle of their bodies hitting the ground and rolling over. . .

And then I was there, pulling at the cloth of her dress, trying to free my son.

She sat up, grinning. Then, still pinning Guy to the ground, she pointed down the field. I was on my knees trying to release my son, but I turned my head involuntarily. And then I gasped. Not ten feet away from us the ground ended and space yawned. I got shakily to my feet and looked again. Guy and the girl too stood up, she still gripping his hand. She took us carefully forward, stopped us with a warning finger, and showed us the quarry that lay at our feet.

A grey quarry, not now in use, stunted alder and sallow growing in clumps in its basin. Great boulders strewn across its base. And Guy's ball, lying in a little pool to one side, far below.

I drew them both away from the edge, and sat down a little way up the field, for my legs were weak with fear. They sat down with me, Guy taking my hand and telling me it was all right, concerned no doubt by my pallor. The strange girl sat, saying nothing, her round face beaming with pleasure.

I sat with my head leaning against my updrawn knees, trying to compose myself. At last I looked up.

'Why on earth didn't you just shout to us?' I asked the girl.

She was looking at Guy, smiling, and she took not the least notice of me. Despite my gratitude for her action, I felt a stirring of anger and repeated my question grittily.

Guy also said something to her and she peered intently at his face and shook her head. Then she touched her mouth and her ears and I understood. Mute! The girl was a deaf mute.

I closed my eyes and mentally saw again the racing form, the wild need to reach him before . . . 'Thank God,' I whispered, 'oh thank God the child was in time.'

Now the girl stood up, indicated to us to stay where we were, and trotted off round the lip of the quarry. 'She's going to get my ball,' announced Guy matter-of-factly. And so she did, using a path that zig-zagged down to the bottom.

Soon she returned, and taking Guy's hand she led us back through the woods and so to another field, large and flat. Grinning all over her face, she took the ball and kicked it high into the air. With a shout of delight Guy joined her. I sat down again, my legs still shaky, and watched the two of them play. The girl must be about fourteen, I thought. She was square and sturdy with a plain round face and mousey hair pulled back into a bun. She wore a striped dress which seemed familiar and, with a start of surprise, I realised it was the uniform worn by the kitchen staff at Polmennor Court. If I found the girl did indeed work there, I would see what I could do for her; some gesture that would show my gratitude.

Presently we walked back together through the woods, Guy chatting non-stop to his benefactor, regardless of the fact that she could not hear a word. Although, indeed she seemed to understand much of what he was saying, communicating in the mysterious way of children everywhere.

When we entered the formal gardens of the manor, the girl gave Guy a playful punch by way of farewell and then turned and plodded off, head down, along one of the paths that led to the distant laundry.

Guy wanted to go with her. 'Mother, I've had more fun today that I ever have when we stay here. There's no one to play with and it's always so dull!'

And I wondered guiltily whether his father was right, that he should go away to school instead of having lessons with the vicar's boys at home. All my instincts were against it, my French upbringing causing me to revolt at the English way of sending one's children away at the earliest opportunity. No, at ten he was far too young, and I gripped his hand and promised him that tomorrow we should go for a long ride.

But a shudder went through my body as I thought that had it not been for the girl's swiftness of action, for Guy there would have been no tomorrow. . .

And when next morning I saw where the child was working, I decided on the spot to take her with me back to Trevingey, and not all the protestations of my friend and hostess, the Honourable Lady Lucinda Tregale, could shake my resolve. 'But my dear, whatever will Charles say when you turn up with that creature? I mean, what can she do? We only took her on because my mother-in-law insisted we do something for her old dresser's grandchild. But the housekeeper tells me she keeps running off . . .' And so it went on.

Indeed, the thought of Charles's cold contempt disturbed me. But I was determined that she should move into the old nurse's room across the corridor from Guy for I had been appalled at the conditions in the laundry - the heat and steam, the slippery floors and constant traffic of maids carrying cauldrons of boiling water. And the child unable to hear any shout of warning. . . Yes, I agreed with Lucinda, I was stubborn and impulsive and all the rest. And yes, I agreed it was important that the girl should be able to earn her living. In fact that is what I would insist upon. But I owed her my son's life and that was worth much more to me than the toss of a gold coin into her lap and if I lived to regret my gesture, well, so be it.

Learning that the child's only relations were her dead mother's parents, I had the grandmother sent for and I explained to her my intentions. She wept with gratitude for she loved her handicapped ward dearly and I learned with surprise that she had taught her to read a little, and to print messages. She had not wanted to send Gladys away from the little holding where they lived, but both she and her husband were aging and she felt the child must learn to earn a living independently. Her grandfather had devised a form of sign language and Guy was quick to make himself familiar with this, but for the time being I relied upon my pencil and sketch pad to make little cartoon drawings to show her our plans. And so it was that Gladys came with us to Trevingey, and if during our journey home I many times regretted my impulsive gesture, each time I remembered the quarry, the gaping space and Guy, running heedless with the ball. . .

I do not know when my thoughts slipped into dreams, but sleep I did, and when I woke, stiff on the couch, I found my cheeks were wet with tears. I mopped my eyes hastily before Gladys should come in and find me weeping, and made a determined effort to stop thinking of the unchangeable past. But the ache of longing to know how my son fared grew stronger, not weaker through the years. And I regretted once more, selfishly this time, the death of

Gladys's grandmother who had given me those few rare and precious snippets of information about my son during the first few weeks after the accident.

It was writing the letter that had brought everything back so vividly. The letter! Suddenly I sat up, oblivious of the pain of movement. If Morwenna did get the Plymouth post, then perhaps I could use her as an intermediary! I twisted my hands together, planning, scheming, the future suddenly full of possibilities. And when Gladys came in, I had no need to fear her seeing my tears, for I was aglow with excitement. Just to hear how he was, what he was doing, that much at least I should surely be able to contrive!

b

Chapter Three

Next day the sun shone again and I sat outside to paint. Instead of using my chair, I was seated on a cushion on the ramp which the men had made for my wheelchair - a level ramp which ran from the top of the steps at the front door, across the house beneath the kitchen window and so to the cobbled street. I often painted from here, my 'bread and butter' pictures, for the street was an intriguing hotchpotch of houses and buttresses and unexpected alleys, and the light was trapped and reflected in ways that demanded all my skill in the execution of my work. I was wearing a smock and had spread an old shawl across my knees for protection against both spilt paint and insidious cold and my materials were within reach along the ramp at my side. I pinned a fresh parchment onto the board before me and set to work with a sigh of pleasure.

Several people passed up and down the street but apart from giving me the time of day as they went by, no one stopped and interrupted my work. So I was surprised when at length a pair of feet paused nearby.

'Now that's what I call a beautiful picture!' The voice, full of laughter, had an accent I did not recognise.

I looked up and found the stranger standing and looking at me with open admiration in his smiling eyes. Theobald Pentire! From where he stood he could not see any part of my painting and my lips twitched into a smile as I accepted his compliment.

'You are a connoisseur, I take it, sir?'

His smile broadened and blue eyes danced.

'Of the highest order, madam. And I state with authority that the picture I behold would grace any gallery in the land.' And he gave a little bow, flourishing his hat.

I straightened and flexed my back and pushed my own hat

back off my brow as I smiled up at him.

'And would you have the subject hung in oils or water?' I was aware of the slight trace of my French accent as I spoke.

'Oh, not oil! Definitely not oil. Water, I think. Or, no, I think it should be asses' milk. Yes, nothing less than asses' milk for Cleopatra.'

A little laugh escaped me. It was so long since a man had flirted with me and my whole being responded to the lightness of tone and the inconsequential nonsense which sprang so readily from his lips.

But someone from down the street was calling to him.

'Come on Theobald my handsome! Pasties is all ready and Mother's dyin' to see you again and hear what you bin up to.'

He doffed that raffish, wide-brimmed hat once more.

'Duty calls. I must tear myself from your side, dear madam. Only duty would drag me off so soon.'

'And the pasty too, no doubt,' I smiled.

'Perhaps. The body will often overrule the mind. Even when studying beautiful art.' And at the smiling challenge in his eyes, I laughed again.

'So long,' he was turning away.

'Au 'voir.' He gave another little bow and I watched him walk away down the street. He greeted his cousin Pauline with a great hug and as he swung her round, behind her back he was waving at me!

The cheek! My body bubbled with laughter and when Gladys came out later to help me indoors to eat, she looked both puzzled and pleased at my sudden gaiety and high spirits.

Since his arrival in the village we had learned a great deal about the handsome stranger for his cousin, Pauline Thomas was a close friend of Gladys and the previous evening she had called to share her news with us. She told us that his parents had left Polwerris for Canada when the boy was five years old and he had grown up in the backwoods where his father worked as miner and small-holder, much as he had done in Cornwall. It was a hard life by any standards, made harder when his mother died when the boy was ten. To all intents and purposes, the child was then in charge of his own life, for his father had been broken by the loss of his wife

27

and lasted only a couple of years more before drink finally killed him. The young boy earned enough to eat by caring for horses in the small town, clearing paths, doing odd jobs for the elderly, anything that would bring the price of some food. He learned to hunt for the pot, using a catapult with deadly accuracy, and giving his small catch to some housewife in exchange for a meal.

Pauline told us he had been taught in a little school before his mother died, and when he was thirteen, one of the ranchers took him under his wing to help with the book work, such as it was, as well as working outside and he became a valued part of the rancher's family. And when he was twenty, he married a local girl. Sadly she became ill and was bedridden within the year. He took her to the city of Montreal for treatment, but nothing was effective and there followed years of hardship, paying for someone to be with his wife while he worked to earn the money for her medicines and care. Eventually he set up as a shipping agent, finding cargoes and organising the transport of goods across a wide area of that great country.

He prospered. But during the last year his wife had died. His cousin Pauline looked excited as she went on. 'Now he've come home to Cornwall to find himself a young wife. He wants to settle down and have a family. He's some nice man, Miss Millbrook. He've got a few relations round here. Mother was his uncle's little maid. I hope he'll find hisself some real nice girl. He deserves it if anyone do.'

I had been both moved and interested by his story and I found myself going over idly in my mind the girls in the area who might suit him. There were plenty of young women, but most of them were offered for by the time they were sixteen. I had once worked out that in the village itself, half of the men had been widowed at least once. Not only childbirth took its toll, for that was dangerous enough in women poor and rich alike, but for the working woman the sheer hard toil, damp cottages and sometime lack of food, brought a woman to such a state that any slight ailment could carry her off. . .

That afternoon Pauline dropped in again for a cup of tea and told us more about her cousin. He was going to Penzance to an auction. Several ships, French prizes were to be sold this week.

He was going to look them over and perhaps buy one to use as a trading vessel up and down the coast. 'And', she went on excitedly, 'He's thinkin' of having a steam engine put into it! He've seen them at work on Lake Victoria for years.'

I had read about steam vessels and had listened to the men talking and arguing over their merits as they worked at their nets; one view being that they were an unnecessary fire risk, the other that they had to be the way of the future.

But Pauline was not interested in the future of steam. She leaned forward and smiled at me. 'He asked after you, Miss Millbrook, about your painting and such. We told him you was our mystery woman,' and here she laughed a little self-consciously. 'But we said as how you were as good a neighbour and friend as we could want. And that's true enough.'

Gladys followed Pauline's account with intense interest, and then Pauline returned to the matter of her cousin finding a wife. 'After all,' she said, ' 'tis only natural to want children and a home of your own like all the rest of us.' And her words suddenly hung in the air and as she heard them, she reddened and looked from Gladys to me and then away. I filled the awkward silence with a question about her mother's health and she responded gratefully. But both of us had seen the look on Gladys's face as she had read the words 'children and a home of your own' on Pauline's lips. . . I had never thought, never anticipated that Gladys too, would want a family of her own! In my selfishness I had thought it enough in those years at Trevingey to train her one day to achieve independence. I had taught her and fed her lively intelligence largely for my own satisfaction. And she had repaid me with total devotion and selflessness. Suddenly I shuddered despite the warmth of the kitchen where we sat, for I was remembering the dark waters of a distant millstream closing over my head and remembering also that I too, owed my very life to the courage and resourcefulness of my friend on that fateful night.

Pauline prattled on, directing her talk towards Gladys for it must have been evident that I was lost in a world of my own. Then I tore my thoughts from those dark memories as I had grimly trained myself to do. The present. Think of the present. But the present brings thoughts of the future, and now that too held its dread, for if Gladys should marry, then what would become of me . . ?

I forced myself to join in the conversation, to sip tea and try and cover with a veil of words the abyss that had opened beneath me. But Pauline's simple chatter was now itself full of threats to my peace of mind, for as she spoke of Chapel and the preacher, I remembered that it was only recently Gladys had started going to the Wesleyan chapel up the hill. Chapel! The centre of the social world of the villagers and the neighbourhood. A place where her evident worth would soon set her apart, where some young man would see that despite the handicap of her muteness, Gladys would make a perfect wife and mother.

And then I would have to start my life again. And I thought wryly of Theobald Pentire, who was also seeking the comfort of marriage and family. And like a knife thrust I felt the loss of my youth and health, that I must now only experience love and passion vicariously through the lives of the people amongst whom I lived. That while he would find a wife and children and contentment, and that while Gladys would, indeed must, have a family of her own, I would remain a lonely, increasingly eccentric woman, deprived of the slightest news of my only son. For even if Morwenna should get a post in Plymouth, how could I get word of Guy's welfare without betraying, and thus endangering, the life I had so painfully rebuilt and the dark secret which only Gladys and I now shared?

I tried that evening to lose myself in a book from my small collection, but the nagging worry in the pit of my stomach prevented the solace of forgetfulness. Gladys was aware, as she always was, that I was out of sorts and we both knew that the inflammation of the nerves of my back would get worse as it did when I was depressed. And indeed, I was forced to my bed for a day or two; lost in that familiar world of agony blurred with heavy doses of laudanum. But I remember that even in the midst of the pain and ignominy of total helplessness, I had felt a sudden flare of satisfaction that at least Theobald Pentire was not in the village to hear of my sickness and indisposition.

But life went on in the way it does; my back improved and I was able to get up again and start work, even if it was a little feebly at first. And it was at the end of that week that Morwenna's mother had her surprise letter from Miss Robertson: if Morwenna cared to present herself at Woodlands Seminary for Young Ladies in Plymouth, Miss Roberts would assess her suitability for a post.

Morwenna was in my sitting-room eagerly watching as I read the proferred letter. Her excitement was palpable; tendrils of curling brown hair had escaped from under her cotton bonnet and framed cheeks peach-pink from her hasty walk to the village while her wide eyes sparkled with delight. 'But what it I don't get the job, Miss Millbrook?' And the dancing lights of a moment before quite fled away leaving her eyes huge and sombre.

I smiled at her, wishing for my sketch-pad though knowing from experience that I could never capture the girl's translucent loveliness.

'Don't worry, Morwenna. When she meets you Miss Roberts will certainly take you on. Mind you, if there were young men around I think she might hesitate! But she keeps them at arm's length, looking after her girls!'

Then I had to tell her all about the place while she sat, all eyes, drinking it in.

'But remember, Morwenna,' I leaned forward in my chair, 'when you are asked about your mother's contact, you must say you never met her. Say your mother bumped into her old employer as she was coming out of a hotel in Falmouth - she's off on a cruise or something. If she asks you her name, look confused and say your mother always referred to her as "My Lady". And you know nothing of *me*. Never mention me, my painting, my accident, anything.' I took her hand and gripped it. 'Promise me.'

Morwenna's eyes were dark and serious. She put her other hand on mine. 'I promise. It will be hard, though, because you are my friend, but I won't mention you to anyone.'

I sighed and sat back. 'I'll miss you, you know. I like it when you call and see me. But still, you can write and tell me all about it. It'll be a change to get a letter now and then. But what does Zeb say about all this? I saw him down by the harbour yesterday so he hasn't gone off on his travels yet.'

'He was very surprised when I told him.' Morwenna smiled a little smugly. 'It's all right for them to go off, but when the boot is on the other foot they don't like it, do they?'

'Well, see it from his point, Morwenna. Here, he knows you

31

are safe. You're not likely to meet any handsome young men in this place. But Plymouth! Well, you never know!'

She laughed. 'Serves him right for going away. He's sailing tomorrow with that horrible Tom Spinks, the one who owns that boat with the patched-up sails.'

I remembered. All the local boats had sails patched to some degree, but Spinks's had patches of all colours and his ship appeared quite unseaworthy. An odd man who came occasionally to the harbour and about whom there were rumours and whispers of strange dealings. I could see why Morwenna did not relish the thought of Zeb being involved with him and I wondered again where this 'fortune' of Zeb's was to come from.

But the dye was cast. Zeb sailed off next day and the following week Morwenna and her father left Polwerris Cove on a small cargo ship which was on its way to Plymouth. I had been surprised at her father's insistence in accompanying her, but when I saw the light in his eye as he waved from the ship, I could see he was using the excuse of chaperoning his daughter as a rare chance of escape from his daily routine.

I missed her when she had gone, but I tried to resume my normal pattern of life, painting in the open when the weather was clement, indoors when it rained, and listening eagerly to the scraps of gossip that came my way. From the first I had taken a keen interest in the incidents that made up the lives of my neighbours, and although I was still treated as a stranger - not one of their own - they confided in me freely. I seemed almost to hold the position of parish priest. But perhaps that was because although I received much information, I never passed on or discussed what I had heard with anyone else.

Thus it was that I heard Zeb had sailed off with Tom Spinks, but that Spinks was now in Falmouth and there was no sign of Zeb. 'Good thing too,' my informant muttered. 'Better have nothing to do with that one. I 'specs he's gone to Plymouth after Morwenna,' and the old man leered meaningfully.

I smiled and held my peace while eagerly awaiting a letter. But there were now two other interests in my life; the first was my burning interest in the affairs of Theobald Pentire, and the second was the daily appearance at my side of the child, Jinny. I know that had Theo, as he was known, been present in the village more often instead of travelling up and down the coast starting up his trading venture, I would have ignored the child. But I was unsettled by Morwenna's leaving for Plymouth, and was glad enough for the girl to stay and watch me work whenever she turned up, something no one else had ever shown a desire to do.

There is one incident from that time which stands out in my mind. It was soon after Theo's arrival in the village. I was painting with Jinny perched nearby when Theo climbed from a dinghy to the harbour wall where I sat, smiling as he greeted me. Then his eyes had taken in the nature of my chair and the smile had frozen on his face. He stopped abruptly, was about to speak then bit back his words and strode past me with the briefest of nods.

'That's funny,' muttered Jinny, 'I thought he was going to stop and chat.'

But I sat, chill as stone. So he had not known of my infirmity! I had been glad enough that he had not seen me in my wheelchair, but I had assumed my disability had been talked over by Pauline Thomas at least.

It was some while after he had gone before my hands stopped shaking enough to continue my painting. I was annoyed with myself that I should be so distressed at his reaction, for he was nothing to me, could be nothing to me. Quite apart from my frailty, I was not the choice for a man seeking a young woman to raise him a family. But I knew I would miss the gaiety of his flirtation and the flattery in his laughing eyes.

But at length my hands could hold the brushes steady and I went on with my work. And later he came back down the hill and stopped to chat for a moment, cheerful and seemingly unconcerned, teasing Jinny by tweaking her hair.

Despite the hollow in my heart, I was grateful for the way he drew the child out. With me, after only a couple of days, she was now relaxed and happy, fascinated by the techniques of the brush, but when others were about she relapsed into that painful reserve, her thin hands twitching nervously.

'I must go. I'm helping Jack Symons get his steering gear repaired. Talking to you ladies won't feed the cat.' He bowed gravely to Jinny then turned to me. 'I'm sorry about that,' he indicated my chair. 'But it makes you more, not less, doesn't it?' And without waiting for my reaction, he waved a laconic goodbye and swung himself down the ladder to the deck of the ship which lay below the wall.

And thus with a few simple words, did Theo clear the way for our friendship to continue; on the surface a light and cheerful friendship, but I was constantly aware that he, like me, was fighting to stifle the powerful attraction that lay between us. And all the while his cousins sought to find the girl who would become his new wife. . .

Chapter Four

It must have been about a week later that the weather broke and we had several days of drizzle, the dreary days that I hated, when I longed and fretted for a glimpse of blue sky, a break in the massed grey clouds that pressed down upon the surface of land and sea, smothering and claustrophobic.

I busied myself painting the small landscapes which I sold to a small gallery in Penzance. They did not take very long to complete, and although the fee was not large, it at least paid for the cost of my paints and canvases and there was a little over which I gave to Gladys who ran the financial side of our lives. Strange when I remembered how I had managed Trevingey, but here it was she who made the weekly purchases and I was glad that I could make a contribution to our household expenses however small it seemed after the prodigal spending I had always known before.

But time dragged. I had caught only one glimpse of Theo early in the week when he made his way down to the harbour. He was to sail to Plymouth to attend another auction of captured French vessels and I waited impatiently for his return. I had not missed the searching look he directed at my window as he passed by, nor the lightening of his face and the gleam of his smile when he had seen me. And though I recalled that glance many times, it was not enough. . . I tried to console myself by looking forward to a letter from Morwenna and concentrating on my work, but I was irritable at being confined to the house and my back troubled me more than usual so that I was often forced to to lie on my couch for hours at a time.

Another damp, depressing day passed, a day when I had lain upon my bed trying with a dose of laudanum to blot out the pain in my spine for most of the daylight hours, glad only that Theo was not around to hear of my indisposition. I roused myself when Gladys came in to settle me for the night, and when she had gone to bed I found myself wide awake and comfortable for the first time for days. I sat up gingerly, afraid of triggering the knife-like stab of pain, but when it did not come I climbed out of bed. The fire still smouldered in the hearth, banked up for the night and I stirred it gently to life, lit a taper and set it to the wick of a new candle. Then I fetched my journal and sat at the table to write.

Suddenly there was a scuffle of running feet on the cobbles outside, and the next moment I heard someone at my open window! There was the thump of the sash being fiercely closed, the curtains parted and a wet, panting figure burst through.

I opened my mouth to scream, recognised the figure as Zeb, and sat, frozen on the chair.

'They're after me! Can I go out the back way?'

But even as he spoke, we heard urgent feet running up the street. He was very white and clutched a bloodstained sleeve. I pulled the cord that would tug at Gladys's pillow and looked round desperately for a hiding place, for I could see the boy was at the end of his tether.

Gladys came stumbling down the stairs, a white wrapper clutched round her shoulders. She had no more than entered the room and was staring open-mouthed like myself at Zeb, when the pounding on the door began. 'Open up in the King's name!' a voice yelled.

Despair was written on Zeb's face. He moved as if to find his way out to the back door but I beckoned him back.

'Quick! Under the mattress!'

Gladys, always so aware of my intentions, was beside me in a flash. She lifted the feather mattress which rested on the under-palette of flock, and bemused but unprotesting, Zeb climbed across and lay down against the back wall. We quickly covered him with the feather overlay and I got into the bed, tucking the sheet and bedspread in around Zeb's hidden form.

The pounding on the door continued, then I heard a woman's shrill voice, 'Give them time, the maid's deaf and the other one's a cripple!' And even through my fear, the words cut to the quick with their stark truth. But the pounding did at least pause momentarily.

Gladys stood back and inspected the bed. She nodded, and at my indication, she went to open the door. And as she did so, I saw the wet patch on the wooden floor where Zeb had stood! I bit my lip; if the men outside the door spotted that, all their suspicions would he confirmed. But it was too late now, for she had already pulled back the bolt. I took a deep breath and prepared myself to face whatever was to come.

The door was flung open and half a dozen men burst through. The fear on both our faces was real enough; total panic on Gladys's Dutch doll features and I myself bloodless and near to fainting.

But even through my terror, I saw that the newcomers had obliterated Zeb's footmarks with the trample of their own wet boots.

When the leader came towards me, Gladys ran across the room and flung herself against the bed to face him, arms akimbo. I pulled myself up on one elbow and touched her, drawing her down to sit beside me. She drew her thin wrap tightly round her body, and pressed herself close against the bed.

'What is the meaning of this outrage!' I was surprised at the arrogance in my shaking voice, and the man too was for a moment taken aback.

'Why did you take so long to open the door?' he demanded. 'Come on, we know he came in here.' He had come to stand beside the bed and I held Gladys's hand to restrain her for she was ready to defend me, physically if necessary.

'Can't you see? She's deaf. I heard you, but I can't move very well without help. I had to summon her down from her bed and then tell her to open the door. But what is all this? Who is supposed to have come in here?'

'A likely story!' he sneered. 'Men, search the house. Goby, see if Tremayne needs help out the back.' He turned back to me. 'And how,' he asked with heavy sarcasm, 'do you summon a deaf person from another room?'

I indicated the cord which hung at the head of my bed. 'That goes up through the floor. If I need Gladys, I pull it - the end is tied to her pillow. But you have not answered me. How dare you burst into my home in this manner?' I was overcoming my fear and my voice no longer shook but was icily cutting. The man looked at me more closely, my reaction not what he had expected. He had pulled off his hat when he came into the room - his childhood training perhaps - and his hair was sparse and ginger. A man of medium build, compact and tough; a dangerous adversary.

'Zeb Martin,' he snapped. 'Known smuggler. Ran from us tonight when challenged to stop. Injured one of my men when escaping.'

'Zeb!' I repeated as though bemused. 'But I thought he had left the village.'

Part of me was listening to the tramp of heavy boots overhead, to the sound of furniture being pulled out and overturned. I turned Gladys to face me and began to spell out to her what was happening, using our sign language instead of words.

'What are you telling her?' the man demanded.

'I'm telling her as much as I know, as much as you've told me. The poor girl's terrified.' I reached for a crocheted shawl which was draped over the chair by the bed and drew it round her shoulders, over the thin wrap. Along the length of my left leg, I could feel the chill of Zeb's wet clothes as the moisture seeped through the bedclothes. I moved a little, glancing along the bed as I did so. All appeared normal, the eiderdown a little crumpled as one would expect in an occupied bed. We had shaken most of the feathers of the overlay mattress away from the side which covered our fugitive. I hoped he had enough air. . .

I turned to the leader again. 'Why do you say he is here?'

'He was seen climbing up your window, that's why. You can't deny he came in. You were still awake.' And he indicated the candle which was still burning beside my bed.

I gave a wry smile. 'That doesn't mean I'm awake. I was writing a letter and I must have dozed. That often happens.' I gave what I hoped was a puzzled frown. 'Perhaps that was what woke me - just before you started beating at the door.'

One of the search party spoke from the doorway.

'Nothing upstairs sir, we've looked everywhere, under the roof, the lot.'

'What about outside?'

'Tremayne says no one came up the back lane after he got there. I don't see how Zeb Martin could have got there before Tremayne. We were heading him away from there.'

38

'Then he must be here, in this house.'

I felt a fresh wave of terror-induced nausea sweep over me, wondering at the outcome of this disastrous affair, not only for Zeb, but for myself too. Gladys could be exonerated. Must be exonerated.

'Right. Come and search this room. You'd best get up, Madam, and take your girl into the kitchen with you,' and he turned to us waving his hand at Gladys as though to shoo her away.

I hoped he would read the discomfiture on my face as embarrassment for this would be our last chance.

'Then will you all leave the room while I get up.' I spoke clearly. 'I am a cripple, but I am also a woman, with the usual woman's problem, and I cannot be helped from this bed in front of any man.' I kept my gaze steady on his face as I spoke and saw the dull blush spread up from his collar.

'Then stay where you are.' He muttered brusquely. 'But don't complain when my men start searching your things. We've got a job to do.' And he stalked over to stand beside the door.

I drew Gladys onto the bed beside me and moved closer to the wall. I could actually feel Zeb's head as I took my weight on my left hand. I wondered if he could hear what was going on. If he were still conscious, if he were still alive. . .

'All right, go ahead and search the room. But be careful of the paintings in that cupboard.' I indicated the door at the head end of my bed and saw their triumphant exchange of looks.

The men went straight to that cupboard but could soon see that there was indeed, nothing but paintings stacked inside.

'Careful with that picture,' I snapped. 'That's for one of the Bassets. They won't be very pleased if I tell them how it got damaged.'

The mention of the well-known and highly influential name brought them up sharply, as I had thought it would. Tom Basset, a local smallholder, would chuckle if he ever heard he had been mistaken for one of the wealthiest landowners in Cornwall.

Then they pulled out the contents of the other cupboard, piling the assortment of clothes and paintings all together on the floor. One climbed onto a chair and searched the overhead cupboard where Gladys and I kept our sewing materials and wools. In a great cascade of colour, down they came to fall in a heap on the now cluttered floor.

'Was this man actually seen to enter this house?' I

demanded suddenly.

The leader turned back to me, face tight with suppressed rage. 'What do you mean?'

'I just wondered if Zeb - that's if it was him - opened the window, closed it again and ran off up the street. There are plenty of doorways where he could have hidden and watched what you were doing.'

All four of the men now in the room became still.

'Well?' The leader fired the question at the youngest, whose face I recognised as one of the Thomas boys, a lad from the village.

'Yes, I saw him!' He looked defiant. 'He opened the window as I come runnin' round the corner and I saw him start to climb in. Tha's when I turned back and shouted for you. I just went round the corner and came straight back and he was gone, inside the window. He could'n be nowhere else.'

'You fool! You must never take your eyes off the quarry, never! We were coming. We were behind you. He's tricked us. He's not in this house, that's for sure. And Tremayne says he didn't come out the back. Wait there.'

And he went out through the kitchen and we heard the street door open and the cold damp air came swirling in. A few moments, later the leader of the posse returned, his ginger hair bristling. 'Come on, let's get out of here.'

'But sir,' the young one began, only to be roughly cuffed by one of the others. 'Just get movin', boy. You done enough damage for one night. Just get out.'

And out they went leaving behind lumps of mud on the wooden floor and the smell of their wet, woollen garments. And Gladys and I sat, not daring to move until the echoes of the heavy boots on the cobbles died away into the silence of the night.

We sat for a while, gazing at one another, stupefied by the aftermath of the search. Then, at last, Gladys cautiously stood up and she was just helping me from the bed when another knock sounded on the door. Before we could move, Mrs Fisher's reassuring voice called to us.

Gladys helped me into my wrap and we both went to the door. Our neighbour from across the street was all consternation when she saw the chaos of the rooms behind us. While standing in the doorway, I glanced briefly up and down the street and noticed the houses were all in darkness, although I had no doubt there were figures crouched in every window, watching the movements of the posse. I could not blame them for their discretion for hardly a house would not contain smuggled goods of some sort. And I realised with surprise that the men had said nothing about the several bottles of wine and one of brandy that stood on the kitchen dresser. Mrs Fisher offered to help straighten up the place, but I shook my head and thanked her for her kind offer, reminding her of Gladys's jealous guardianship of our home.

'We will soon sort it out. Go back to bed Mrs Fisher. We shall not sleep any more tonight anyway. But thank you again.' With great relief, we locked the door behind her reluctantly retreating form, and Gladys fastened the window and bolted the back door also. Only then did we dare to turn to Zeb.

We drew back the mattress and his face was so still and pale that I thought for one heart-stopping moment he was dead. But when I touched him I found his skin was damp and hot. Gladys went off for a bowl of warm water and it was only when we began to bathe his face that he muttered something and stirred into consciousness. He suddenly sat up and gazed wildly about.

'It's all right Zeb. You're safe,' I spoke quietly and he turned his face and looked at me, recollection in his eyes.

'Oh my God. They came, didn't they? How did you manage it? I heard part of it and then. . .'

'Don't talk. We've got to get these wet clothes off you first.'

Together, Gladys and I began to pull off the wet, clinging garments. He had lost his boots and his bare feet were scratched and muddy. He clutched at his left arm when we moved him. 'I think he got me here,' he said. And we saw that the dark material of the jacket sleeve was heavily bloodstained. His arm was so swollen that it was necessary to cut the seam of the sodden garment in order to remove it, and as soon as we did so the bleeding started again. When we uncovered the wound, we found a deep gash - from Cecil Thomas's knife according to Zeb as he told of the scuffle in which he had been injured.

Gladys lighted a lamp and set it on the table beside the bed, then went to fetch some more hot water and I gingerly bathed the wound. Then I rummaged through the littered debris of the room to find the box which contained our sewing things. When Zeb saw me threading a long, curved needle, he grimaced, but did not flinch when I began to work on the wound. Gritting my teeth, I drew the edges of the gash together and proceeded to stitch the torn muscles back into place. Outwardly I was calm, remembering how I had watched my favourite horse being similarly stitched when I was a child. The groom who had then performed the operation had assured me that it hurt the animal far less than I thought, and that it had to be done. Now, I kept telling myself the same, and Zeb never moved or cried out, only letting out a long sigh of relief when I finally put the needle down. I smeared the arm with one of Gladys's salves and bandaged it tightly, glad to see that the bleeding had almost stopped.

As soon as I finished, Gladys went off and made some hot tea for us all, which she laced generously with brandy. We drank gratefully, and I was glad to see some colour returning to the boy's face as warmth and relief seeped through his body.

'I must go,' he said presently, putting down the cup. 'Can I have my clothes back?' indicating the wet garments which now hung from chairs before the fire.

Gladys could see his intentions, and shook her head. To me, she signed that there was someone watching the back lane - she had seen a figure through the window when she was making the tea. She then doused the lamp and looked through the front window. A man stood some yards up the road, leaning against the wall of one of the houses.

I bit my lip when she passed on this information but I was not surprised, for although the posse had thoroughly searched the building, it made sense for them to keep a close watch in the area where he had last been seen.

I turned to Zeb. 'There's nothing for it but for you to stay here until we find some way to get you out. You wouldn't get far in this state anyway.' And it was true; the young man looked to be at the end of his resources. I wondered how far he had run, and swum too, from the white salt marks on his clothing. 'I don't think they'll come here again tonight so you might just as well stay where you are and get some sleep. I'll rest on the couch,' and I indicated the old chaise-longue. I could see he was about to protest, so I forestalled him by pointing out that the place where he was had already proved to be the best hiding place we could wish for.

Gladys began to restore our cupboards to a state of order and presently the room looked pleasant and comfortable once more. But I insisted that she leave the muddy floor until morning, and looking at Zeb's drawn face she nodded her head in agreement. We decided that if the excise men should return, Gladys would quickly come downstairs, and I should leave the couch and go back to my earlier place alongside Zeb before she answered the door.

I myself lay down, huddled under the spare blankets, my stomach churning as I relived the terror of the search. I could not get the leader's face out of my mind; there was a doggedness about the mouth that warned me we had not seen the last of him yet. I turned and lay on my side, facing the glow of the fire that would slumber on until Gladys came in the morning to rekindle it. If only Theo were in the village I could send word to him, and pass to him the responsibility that I knew instinctively he would willingly accept. I tried to settle myself, glad at least to be temporarily free of pain and contemplated the long night that lay ahead. If only I could sleep. . .

And I did. To my astonishment, when I next opened my eyes, Gladys was placing a tray on the table beside me. Reflected sunlight poured through the chinks in the curtains as she gave me her usual wide grin, her face cheerful and unperturbed.

I sat up stiffly, disorientated in my strange bed. Then I remembered and looked anxiously round. Gladys put her hand on my shoulder and informed me in her usual manner, that Zeb was still asleep and looked much better, that the sentries were still in place outside, and that my porridge was getting cold.

Chapter Five

The neighbours were sure to call and when they did I wanted the room to look open and innocent; no closed doors on the bed cupboard today.

Gladys had anticipated me. Over the lean-to scullery at the back was a half-floored loft area where we stored my old trunk and some of the furniture which had belonged to Gladys's grandmother. The Excise men had rummaged through this but Gladys, with flying hands, gleefully informed me that the old bed spring which was propped against the wall had not been moved for there were still cobwebs over the end. And although the frame was almost vertical, the old wall bulged outward shaping a space at the bottom which was large enough to conceal Zeb's slim form. Gladys had already prepared some bedding for him there and we decided to move him as soon as we could.

I went over to the bed and looked down at Zeb's sleeping face. Certainly he looked better than when we settled him last night, and as I felt his forehead he opened his eyes and started with surprise.

'Why, Miss Millbrook!' Then memory surfaced and he glanced fearfully around.

'It's all right. You're quite safe. But they're still watching the house, so you cannot think of leaving yet. Gladys will give you some breakfast and then we're going to find you a different bed.' I smiled reassuringly at him but I was concerned at the glassiness of his eyes and the cracked dryness of his lips.

I gathered some fresh clothes for myself and went out to the scullery to wash and dress myself while Gladys tried to get Zeb to take some nourishment. When I returned after my swift toilette Gladys was bathing his face. She shook her head at the tray and I could see Zeb had taken nothing apart from a little weak tea.

I checked the wound on his arm and was relieved to see that the stitches were holding and that the bleeding had not started again. The flesh round the gash was not unduly hot, but I would be surprised if the boy did not run a fever before the day was out.

With Gladys supporting him, we made our way to the scullery where Zeb sank into an old chair, shaking his head in bewilderment at his weakness. I reminded him that he had lost a considerable amount of blood and asked if he could manage the ladder which led to the loft. He set his jaw grimly and said to just give him a minute to catch his breath and he'd be up there in a trice.

I signed to Gladys that I would stay with him for a while and she fetched my chair and left us together, closing the door which led from the kitchen as she went. Clever Gladys! She knew that anyone who called would imagine I was washing and we would not be disturbed. As soon as Zeb was ready to essay the climb to the loft I would fetch her to help him.

'Take your time, Zeb. If any neighbours call there will be plenty of time for you to hide. They'd never come in here, anyway.'

He looked at me uneasily. 'They'd not give me away, Miss Millbrook. Not anyone in the village.'

'I don't think they would deliberately, Zeb. But people talk and I don't know who has been watching you and who put the Revenue on to you last night. So we won't take any risks. What they don't know they can't tell. Right?'

'Right.' He looked at me and grinned weakly. 'I suppose you want to know now what all this is about.'

I smiled back. 'I'll settle for a good bottle of claret if that's what the cargo was!'

He shook his head. 'It's a lot worse than that, Miss Millbrook. A lot worse than a few barrels and a bit of perfume. . .' There was a stretched moment of silence while he bit his lip. Then he turned to me. 'I expect you'll think what we did is wrong. We helped two French prisoners to escape.'

My stomach lurched and I felt the blood leave my face. But this was treason! I clutched the arm rests on my chair and willed the room to stop spinning. Treason!

'There, I knew you'd be shocked. You must hand me over if you have to. But let me tell you Miss Millbrook - even if I'm caught and hanged for this, I'll go with my head high. There'll be no shame in it for me.' He leaned forward as he spoke and took my hand in his, willing me to listen, to give him a hearing. His face was tight, his eyes angry. I took a deep breath and told him to go on.

'Just ordinary lads they are. They don't care about navies or governments and things. They just want to live their lives and do the best they can,' and his voice caught, almost in a sob.

Ordinary lads no doubt. But prisoners of the King. And if we were caught, there would be no sympathy from the villagers and no mercy from the State. I thought of Gladys. But we would see that she was not blamed. As for myself, I had long since crossed the Rubicon. And I remembered once accusing my husband Charles of not knowing the meaning of justice or fairness or decency, of seeing only the letter of the law. But treason. . .

Once more I stood at a crossroads. Not that other one, in darkness and fear of pursuit. And I closed my eyes to the sudden memory of horses' hooves and the crack of gunshot. . .

'Don't worry, Zeb. I'll try to understand. Go on, tell me about it. I myself have French blood. And I have already broken many, many rules.' I squeezed the hand that held mine. 'But I need to know what it's all about.'

'All right. That's only fair. I didn't want to tell you before - I thought the less you knew the better for you. But you deserve to hear it now. Then you can make up your own mind what to do.'

He settled himself back in the chair and told me a strange story.

'It was Tom Spinks' plan, of course; his way of repaying the villagers of St Eoy in Brittany for saving his life when some of the fishermen had plucked him from the sea, as a twelve-year-old midshipman, the only survivor from a wreck. For there he had stayed, nurtured by the villagers and growing up to speak Breton and French as fluently as his native English. And last year he had returned for a visit and discovered that two of the local boys had been pressed into the French navy and captured by the British. Spinks wrote letters and discovered that one lad had died, but the other, the only child of the man who had been like a brother to him in his youth, was being held at Clowance, an estate not thirty miles from Polwerris.

46

'Tom put his boat up the river at Devoran to be re-masted, and went and got himself a job as one of the guards at Clowance. It was a while before he was able to track down Jean-Louis, but when he did he told the boy he would get him out in a few weeks. There was a sycamore which stood a bit higher than the other trees in the woods nearby; he told the boy to watch for a signal rag in that tree and what to do when the time came.

'A couple of weeks later he got himself sacked for being drunk and firing a musket on duty. His boat was ready by then, and that's when he came and asked me if I'd like to make some money. He pointed out the risks, Miss Millbrook, don't think he misled me.' And here Zeb leaned forward again and said very earnestly, 'I never thought before that those gangs of Frenchies we see working on the roads, are just men like us, with families and things. . . But Tom Spinks, well, he's got a way with words and it just made me mad that one of his folks was imprisoned for years, and not for anything wrong. So I said yes, of course I'd help, money or no money.'

(Just then we heard someone at the front door and we both stiffened with fear. But soon there was the reassuring sound of the door being closed and Gladys poked her head into the scullery and signed that Mrs Jenkins had called to ask after my health and would come back after I'd dressed!)

My heartbeat slowed to normal and I saw a little colour return to Zeb's pale cheeks. 'Go on, Zeb. You must go and rest soon.'

He nodded. 'Well, Spinks wanted to give me good cover, so after we had laid up a dinghy in the cave under Gurnard's point, we sailed into Falmouth harbour and there I laid low aboard ship while Spinks went ashore and let it be known in the pubs that I was an ungrateful pup who had found himself another berth. Then, two nights ago, we rowed ashore in the dark and walked across country until we came to a skinners' camp.' Here Zeb let out his breath with some semblance of his old vigour 'The smell, Miss Millbrook! Tom said you get used to it, but when he made me leave my clothes in a bag and put on some of the things they gave us, well, I was sick as a dog.'

'Spinks knew these people, I take it?'

'Oh yes. He'd got it all planned. We were to use their horse and cart piled up with stinking skins. There was a crate underneath them, with our good clothes and space for the prisoner and more clothes in another bag for him.'

Zeb's eyes were becoming fevered as he told his story and when I fetched a mug of water from the ewer, he took it gratefully and gulped it down.

'When we got into the woods near Clowance, I was scared, Miss Millbrook. I don't mind telling you, I was scared stiff of being caught. Through the trees, we could see the prisoners working in groups building a great boundary wall. There were several guards lounging about; they had guns but you felt they weren't too bothered. 'Cos where could the prisoners run to? The locals would turn them in for the reward, so they didn't need to be very alert. But all the same. . .

'Tom pointed out the sycamore and I scrambled up and tied a piece of old shirt as high up as I could get. It looked like a piece of rag the wind had blown there. Then we had to wait.

'That was the worst time, that waiting. A couple of hours and no birds singing, only the sounds of the working gangs, sometimes a shout from the guards and sometimes a gabble of French. We were back a bit in the trees and now and then we would see a prisoner ask to go to the edge of the wood to answer a call of nature, begging your pardon, miss. Tom winked and whispered that our boy would do the same and then hurry along through the trees to where we were waiting so we must be ready to move.

'And then, at last, we hear twigs snap and into the clearing comes not only Jean-Louis but this other lad, stumbling along, hardly able to walk! Tom Spinks doesn't turn a hair to find it's two men we have to shift instead of one. Quick as a flash, he raises the crate under all those skins and nods for me to help them in. I lift in the sick one, Pierre he was called, while Jean-Louis is trying to kiss Tom and tears are running down his face. Well, I'd cry too, if I had to lie down under all that stench!

'Anyway, in no time at all, we're leading the old horse out of the wood. And that's when I get my biggest shock, because we are going straight towards the gangs and the guards! Tom is wearing a hat pulled down over his eyes, but I doubt anyone would recognise him as the guard they sacked because everyone turns their heads away from the smell of the cart as we cross the field to the road. And once on the road - a good road too, built by the prisoners - the old nag puts on a good turn of speed, knowing she's on the way home.

'An hour later we reach another skinners' camp, a bigger one this time with some tents and a fire and women and children. Here we get the lads out of the crate, and very grateful they are for fresh air at last. We burn what they've been wearing and put on our own clothes again and share out the togs Tom had brought for Jean-Louis. When I ask why he'd brought so much, he grinned and said he didn't think Jean-Louis would leave a mate behind.

'We borrowed a little pony from the camp and a young lad to take it back. The skinners didn't mind, they got a bit more gold for their pains. And then we crossed country, me and Jean-Louis on ahead, Tom and the boy leading the pony with Pierre swaying on its back. If we met anyone, we were sailors making for Falmouth a bit the worse for wear.

'Well, to cut it all short, Miss Millbrook, we got as far as Goonhilly Downs and then the skinner's boy took the pony back and we rested until it was dark. It was raining by then, but I know those paths like the back of my hand and so I led them across the moors to Gurnard's Point and that Pierre scrambled down under his own steam like a new man, with the smell of freedom in his nose.

'We got the boat out of the cave and dragged it down almost to the water when the shouting started! And the next minute we could hear feet scrabbling over the rocks towards us. "Quick!" I says to Tom. "Get them away! I'll draw them off."

'And off I run up the beach, yelling up at the cliff as if warning someone to get away. And the posse on the beach broke up, some chasing me up the cliff path and some firing towards the boat, but half-hearted like, thinking the real action was up the cliff.

'And as I got to the top, I looked back and could just make out the smudge of dark in the white surf and I knew the boat was out of range and safe. And the next minute that Cecil Thomas grabbed me and that's when I got this, Miss Millbrook.'

Zeb looked at me as he finished his tale and I could see that talking had exhausted him and that the fever I had feared was already flaring in his cheeks.

But he had one more thing to say.

'I don't regret it mind. I don't regret it at all.' And the fierce jut of his jaw belied his physical weakness.

49

c

'Don't worry Zeb. I'm with you all the way! But where was Spinks taking the boys?'

'There'll have been a Breton fishing boat up and down the coast every night since Tuesday. Spinks was to signal when he was ready and they'd come and pick them all up. Then they were to put Tom down in the dinghy off Carrick Roads so he could row back into Falmouth harbour and no one'd be any the wiser that he's been away!'

I smiled. 'A resourceful man, your Tom Spinks.'

'Yes he is,' Zeb tried to stand unaided. 'I think I will have to climb up there and rest for a bit, like you said. But as soon as it's dark, Miss Millbrook, I'll be on my way.'

But it needed all Gladys's strength to help him up the ladder and into his new hiding place. And after admitting several neighbours into my sitting-room where they avidly questioned me about the behaviour of the Revenue men, I pleaded a migraine and drew the curtains. And Gladys, relieved of answering the door, was able to climb up to the loft and sponge and sooth the restless, tossing youth.

And in my darkened room I pondered what I could do to get Zeb safely away. It seemed to me that my only hope lay in the cunning of Tom Spinks. Surely he would soon hear what had happened in Polwerris and would take some action to discover Zeb's whereabouts.

For Spinks had laid his plans well; if he got away there would be nothing to link Zeb with the escaped prisoners of war. If he was caught, however. . . And I shuddered and knew that even if Theo returned to Polwerris in time, I could not, must not put his safety too, in danger by asking for his help.

Chapter Six

Next morning, to my great relief, Zeb was much better; his fever had abated and although he was still very weak, he professed himself ready to have some breakfast and then he would have to go.

We assuaged his hunger with bread and ham and tea. As for leaving, he was safer where he was until the hunt had died down; we had learned from the neighbours that the Revenue men were still combing the countryside, for the fact that Zeb had attacked one of their party was a serious matter to the authorities. They had redoubled their search and offered a twenty guinea reward for his capture. Several men from the village had set up a search party of their own, and when I heard of this, I was sorely tempted to contact them and enlist their aid. Only the fear that someone had alerted the Excise to the unexplained presence of the dinghy in the cave under Gurnard's Point, made me hesitate and finally decide to say nothing. After all, we had not been troubled by any further search, so surely it was better to wait until Spinks made contact. Resourceful and cunning, he would surely find a way.

But for how long must we wait?

The sun shone that morning, and I forced myself to go outside and paint, perched on a cushion on the ramp beneath the kitchen window. I found it difficult to involve myself in the work which was an order for the Penzance gallery, for I was nervous and jumpy at each approaching footstep. But at last I settled down and completed the first of the pictures. It showed the corner of a buttressed and thatched cottage, its quaint porch enveloped in an ancient climbing rose whose sweet scent drifted through the more mundane smells of fish and drains. The second painting would be of the same cottage but from a different angle. I did not need to leave my seat for this second view, for I had done the painting several times before and could recollect each of the tiny windows and the curve of the thatch, while the steps and the glimpse of cobbled street were from a different house altogether! Sometimes to these pictures I would add a cat lazing in the sun, or in winter, a robin perched on the bare stems of the climber rose and sometimes a small child dressed as no village child would be dressed, angelic in a cloud of white.

I was halfway through the second painting, when Mrs Snell came down the road, basket over her arm. My heart sank, for she was an inveterate talker, but now she merely nodded at me, and then, without turning her head, muttered out of the corner of her mouth as she passed, 'Watch out, HE's coming again.' I started to turn and look, glimpsed the red-haired Excise man climbing the hill, and turned away, my heart pounding.

This was what we had feared! Zeb was still snug in his hiding place; for we had impressed upon him that he could put our safety at risk if he did not lie low until we were sure we were not longer under suspicion. But since the Excise men had not returned yesterday, I had begun to think we were safe. Now I struggled to appear calm.

'Good morning Miss Millbrook.' He had approached so quietly and quickly that even knowing he was there, I jumped.

'Oh. Good morning Officer,' I coldly replied.

'Are you well? You seem to have recovered. An admirable painting if I may say so.'

I shrugged my shoulders. 'Have you come to turn my house upside down again?' My voice sounded nervous and brittle.

'No madam.' His gaze left my face, and came to rest on the smudge beneath the sitting-room window where someone had tried to clean off the bloodstains Zeb's arm had smeared on the limewashed wall.

I too regarded the smeared wall. 'A long reach for an injured man, Captain.' For due to the steep slope of the street, the sill of my sitting-room window was some five feet above the cobbles, a factor which gave my room considerable privacy from the gaze of passers by.

He looked at me and said nothing. Just that level, assessing look.

I turned from my painting and busied myself washing out the

brushes in order to disguise my shaking hands, drying them carefully on a clean rag. Then I returned his look, schooling my face into calm.

'Yes, a very long reach,' he said at last. 'But for a desperate man . . .' He let his words tail away.

I said nothing, folding up the rags and cloths as though I had finished.

'We know he was here,' he said quietly. 'I don't know where you sent him, but we know he was here.' He looked pointedly again at the smudge on the wall.

'The men are out searching for him this minute. If they don't know where he is, how do you expect me to know?' I tried to stem the tremble in my knees. I knew my face was pale. 'They say he's badly injured, that he'll die if he's not found. Do you think I'd let the boy die rather than say where he is?' My voice was shaking but I lifted my shoulders in another shrug and sighed. 'Look captain, I care about the boy. His girl is a protégé of mine. So yes, I do hope, whatever he has done, wherever he is, that he survives, that he gets away. But I have sent him nowhere. His safety must lie in other hands than mine.' My voice was now steady and I was able to look the officer straight in the eyes as I spoke.

He stared back at me for a long time, his pale eyes boring into mine. I held his gaze, chin up, defiant.

At last he let out his breath in something of a snort and gave me a slight bow, his heels clicking. For a moment he looked past me at the cottage and I feared that my bluff had failed, that he had noticed the 'sent him nowhere' and would once more search, and this time find, the fugitive. But with a curt, 'Good morning Madam,' he turned and strode back down the steep cobbles towards the quay.

I sat immobile for a long time. Two or three of the women came out of their houses and walked past, giving me nervous smiles, but they did not stop and ask what had passed between the two of us, nor would they while the Excise vessel lay tied up alongside the harbour wall.

No longer able to concentrate on my work, I went back indoors and warned Zeb of the development. Stronger now, he once more talked of slipping out of the house and away and I had to remind him forcefully that with search parties scouring the neighbour-hood, he would soon be spotted and there was no saying whether it would be by the villagers or by the Excise.

So the day dragged on. I sat near the little window which over-looked the harbour, watching and waiting for some movement. And then, late in the afternoon, on the ebbing tide, the Excise vessel raised anchor and moved slowly out of the harbour and out from the shelter of the steep cliffs that held the cove within their protective curve.

For a long while I sat, gazing out to sea, to where the masts of the Excise cutter had disappeared and I was still there when another ship came round the headland; a ship that was instantly recognisable by the patchwork salts that billowed gaily in the sun. Tom Spinks had arrived at last!

In some excitement I prepared myself to go down to the harbour. Gladys pushed the chair and I sat with my large sketch-pad on my knees. She settled me out of the wind against a wall and tucked the rug more securely round my legs. But just as she turned to leave, she swung back and squeezed my arm hard in warning.

I looked up. There was no one about except a young boy, Timmy Pascoe who was strolling down the street, whistling. He passed us, nodded his head and went on, then hopped from the harbour wall onto the deck of one of the boats which lay there. Just a boy. But what Gladys had spotted was an air of self-consciousness about him that I too could now see. From the corner of my eye, I watched him climb onto the roof of the wheel-house and sit down. Gladys pressed my arm again and I nodded my head. Damn! A lookout. But for whom? I could do nothing but wait so I sent Gladys back to the cottage, fearing that Zeb might make some rash move in our absence.

I busied myself with a series of sketches of the boats at anchor, thinking hard all the while. Perhaps I should risk writing a note and passing it to Spinks if he came by. But then they would watch his every move. Damn Timmy! And damn whoever sent him to spy on me.

It was more than an hour before Tom Spinks left his outlandish vessel and made for the shore. He had anchored the ship some way out in the bay and now rowed himself into the harbour. Then, slowly and nonchalantly he made his way along the harbour wall stopping to talk to a couple of old men who sat oblivious of the cold wind, and bored by the lack of activity in the harbour since all the normal work was in abeyance while the search for Zeb went on.

And it was while he was chatting that I had an idea. My plan would need only a moment of his attention and if he was as acute as everyone said, I saw no reason why it should not work. I worked swiftly with my pencil. But when I looked up to see if he was coming towards me, I saw that he had stopped, and beckoned to Timmy of all people! Side by side they came along to where I sat and I bit my lip in frustration. What chance would I now have to pass him my message!

I stared hard at the man as he approached. He was as shabby as his ship; he wore patched knee breeches, an old shirt and sleeveless waistcoat, and a battered black hat was perched on his unkempt grey hair. As he neared me, chatting, with the boy at his side, he tipped the hat and gave me a little bow.

'A cold day for sitting out Madam.'

'Yes. I'll be glad when Gladys comes back for me. I think it was a mistake to come out so late in the afternoon.'

'Ah sure it's not. Just see the fine ships you've captured with your little pencil. Look at them Timmy boy. Don't you wish you could draw like that?' I wondered if his Irish accent were real. But I obligingly turned the pad so that they could see the sketches. Spinks leaned forward as if to inspect them and I was enveloped in the smell of tar and tobacco. And then he contrived to knock my tin of pencils from my lap.

'Now there's a clumsy oaf it is I am!' But while he made as if to bend stiffly down, Timmy went down on his knees to gather up my scattered belongings. And there was no doubt about the urgent question in the man's eyes as he looked down at me.

In response I turned back the corner of the page to reveal what I had drawn there; a small likeness of Zeb, with his curly hair and wearing a huge sling on his arm. Then another of him standing, with a dress over his clothes, head swathed in a shawl, a slim moon overhead and a ship with patched sails standing off.

Now Timmy was on his feet again, and my sketch-pad was flat and innocent on my lap. Had Spinks had time to see my drawings? And if so, did he understand my message?

'That's good. Very good if I may say so.'

I took the pencils from the boy and saw that he looked keenly against my pad. 'Can you draw?' I asked, merely for something to say.

He shook his head. 'I'm going to be a sailor I am.'

'A sailor it is!' Spinks slung an arm across the boy's shoulder. 'And him a mere eleven.' Was there a slight emphasis on the 'eleven'?

'I'm twelve!' the boy said with some annoyance.

'Twelve is it? Ah, but eleven is the age I liked the best. Eleven for me.' Yes there was no doubt now of the emphasis. 'And now we have to find Samuel and see if he wants to go fishing tomorrow morning. Mind you the tide would be right this night, and the boy here would like to come, but his dear mother won't allow him out at night. So if I want company to fish tonight I shall have to find someone else. Good-day to you my dear Madam. I'm honoured to have seen your talented work. A clever lady indeed if I may say so.' He raised the battered hat once more and strolled off.

But a few paces away he turned. 'There's a good place, down there on that bit of beach at the bottom of the wall. You wouldn't feel the wind there, you wouldn't, my dear lady.'

'But she wouldn't be able to see the boats from there, would she?' Timmy sounded important.

'Well no, and that's a fact. ' 'Tis a smart lad you are and no mistake; Come along then, find this uncle of yours for me.' And off they went.

I sat in a turmoil of excitement intermixed with doubt. If my reading of his meaning was right, Zeb must wait under the harbour wall at eleven o'clock tonight. The tide would be right, he said. I chewed my lip in anxiety. Was I right? Then I recalled that fleeting moment when the boy was on his knees; the man's eyes worried and questioning. The way he had absorbed the content of my cartoon sketches. The instant response with his coded message.

I watched them walk away and as I did so, the man turned and raised his hand in salute. And for a moment the fist was clenched in a gesture of victory and there was no mistaking the gaiety and delight in his wide and toothless grin.

I sat shivering with cold and excitement until Gladys came for me. Sometimes when the weather turned so chill, I would ask one of the men to push me back up the hill. But today, cold though I was, the time fled by as I worked out exactly how we were to get

Zeb safely out of the house.

Just as Gladys came hurrying down the street, it began to rain, steady drumming rain that sent the old men on the harbour wall scurrying home for shelter and by the time we had reached our front door, we were both soaked through.

Safe indoors it took all Gladys's energy to make me change out of my wet clothing, for though my teeth chattered with cold, I was aglow with triumph and impatient to call Zeb down from his hideaway and let him know that the time had almost come for him to make his escape.

It became dark early for a spring evening, and the rain poured down from the leaden cloud mass. I could not keep still and hobbled to and fro in restless anxiety. For not even Gladys would go down to the beach on such a night, and if we were still being watched as I suspected was the case, anyone leaving the house would be immediately suspect.

But just after ten o'clock the rain stopped. It was very quiet, and most of the cottages in darkness, with only the glimmer of candlelight behind a couple of windows where perhaps a woman watched over a sick child or sat up late mending clothes for work on the morrow.

Gladys and Zeb were both impatient, anxious to go. She was wearing a heavy cloak which once had been mine, the hood pulled up to conceal her face completely. It gave her a furtive look, as she fretted in the kitchen waiting to play her part in our dangerous game. Zeb pulled on the muslin dress we had made over his own clothes which were now clean and mended. Around his shoulders was slung a hessian sack, common wear in the village. With a shawl wrapped round his head and neck he would easily pass for a woman in normal times. But I was only too aware that times were anything but normal. The tension I had been under ever since Zeb's dramatic arrival was becoming unbearable and his eager impatience to be gone seemed to me to be reckless folly. What had I done? What was I doing?

Gladys swung towards me and indicated that she was going now, this minute, though the clock hands were only pointing to ten thirty-five.

'Yes, I'm going too.' Zeb drew the shawl tighter round his

face. I'll be able to hide below the wall - it'll be even darker there. And I'll hear if there's anyone about and be able to warn Tom off.'

'And what will you do then?' I asked with acerbity.

'If I get away, I'll lie low and then slip in your back door when I'm sure they've gone.' He pushed back the shawl and I could see his face was pale. Then he took my hands in his. 'It'll be all right. Don't you worry. And if they do get me, I'm wearing nothing they can connect with you.' It was true, for we had made up the dress out of layers of butter muslin, dyed to a muddy grey with a brew of leaves. 'I can't thank you Miss Millbrook. But one day I will repay you.'

I pressed his hands. 'Just take care. And remember, you must never let anyone know what you were doing when they nearly caught you down on the beach. It's better if they think it was smuggling. Not anyone mind, Zeb. Not even Morwenna. If word ever got about, Gladys and I would have to leave this place. Even if the authorities could prove nothing, the villagers would never understand that we could help the French. Promise me.'

He looked into my eyes, his own a little startled at my vehemence. Then he pressed my hands in return and slowly nodded his head. 'Yes. I didn't think of it like that. You're right. You have my word.' He turned to Gladys and hugged her for a moment. 'Thank you,' he mouthed. She pushed back her hood and grinned at him happily, giving the thumbs up salute which she used to express her delight. Then she turned to me and signalled that she was off, and for Zeb to wait five minutes while she checked that there was no one about. If she didn't come back, then he was to leave for the beach by the back door.

I nodded, my mouth dry. She opened the front door and the cold night air blew in. Then, pulling the hood forward again she let herself out quietly, Zeb concealing himself until the door closed behind her. I don't think either of us spoke during that endless five minutes. We strained our ears for the sounds of feet, of voices, of anything that might mean someone else was out there, waiting, watching.

At last, Zeb turned to me. Hugged me without a word. Went to the back door and slipped away into the night. And I had to wait in agonising suspense until Gladys returned to let me know how our plans had fared.

Chapter Seven

And later, much later, this is what Gladys told me with mime and darting hands. . .

She walked down the street, almost invisible in the black cloak, darting glances all around, but seeing no one. She reached the harbour and set out along the wall, leaning into the stiff breeze that now blew from the sea. She wondered how Spinks would come ashore, and wondered how long it would take to get back to his ship in the teeth of this unfriendly wind. Her eyes, accustomed now to the darkness, combed the harbour but she could see no moving thing apart from the transitory white shapes of small waves that raced before the wind. How long, she wondered, would Zeb have to wait, out here in the open, in great danger should the Excise men have been alerted.

She walked slowly back along the harbour wall, standing for a while to peer down at the boats tied up alongside. There seemed to be no living being apart from herself. She continued along the wall and then down the steps towards the little beach that lay on the outer side of the harbour wall.

The tide already lapped the foot of the steps and she paused, not wanting to get wet. It was while she stood there, a silent shadow, that from the corner of her eye she sensed rather than saw a movement. She froze. Then, slowly she turned her head and made out the shape of a dinghy bobbing against the wall, with the darker shadow of a man's form seated on the thwart, oars shipped, waiting. She drew back and looked about for Zeb.

Then she saw him; his silhouette - a woman's shape in dress and shawl - showed for a moment against the pale shingle. Then, no doubt in answer to some low signal that she of course would never hear, he came nearer. He paused for an instant at the water's edge, then hoisted the skirts of the dress and waded out towards the dinghy and swung his leg over the side with practised ease.

She leaned forward now and saw the dinghy move mysteriously away, its oars still shipped. Amazed she craned her head and then saw the faint splash of a rope. Cunning Spinks! He had fixed a line to one of the buoys that marked the safe channel to the harbour and was hauling the boat away so that no creak of oars should alert listening ears. Once outside the harbour they would have a good start on any pursuit. She watched until her straining eyes could no longer discern the darker blur of the dinghy against the moving, white-flecked sea. They had gone! They had got away!

She sat down on the step, smiling to herself, imagining Zeb's joy in the night air, with the wind on his face, and the surge of the sea beneath the tiny craft.

The tide was now creeping up towards the step where she sat so she climbed slowly back to the top of the wall. Not wanting yet to go back indoors (for Gladys would all her life prefer to be out of doors) she walked along to its seaward end once more and stood leaning against the balustrade peering out into the darkness. She could see no movement, no sign of the departing boat but she imagined it moving steadily towards the ship that lay waiting. Her vision, perhaps to compensate for her lack of hearing, was better than most people's and she could make out the crescent of the cliffs that encircled the bay. But peer though she might, she could see no shape of mast or sails and she wondered if Spinks had already moved his ship round the headland to the next cove under the cover of darkness.

She stood, watching the water heave against the wall beneath, the splash of white now and then where the swell broke against the stones, liking the feel of the salt-laden wind on her face. Presently, satisfied at last that they were safely away, Gladys turned back for home, hugging her cloak tight around her, against the cold she was now beginning to feel.

But hardly had she taken two steps, when out of the darkness she was grabbed and her arms pinned to her sides. Terrified by the onslaught she fought and struggled, helpless in the all-enveloping cloak. A face a few inches from her own yelled something; she smelled his breath on her face and recoiled in disgust. Now other hands too were bruising the flesh of her arms and, still struggling, she was flung down onto the granite paving, a heavy body on top of her, pinning her down and crushing the air from her body.

There was more breath on her face and she knew the man was shouting. This was her recurrent dream, a sudden onslaught out of her enfolding silence; this was the reason for her constant backward glances. Only tonight, in her concentration on Zeb and the boat, had she failed to keep her guard. And now she was at the mercy of the men who had attacked her.

The man who had flung her down now shifted to one side and the other hauled her roughly to her feet. The hood of the cloak had fallen forward and a hand now yanked it back, jerking out the pins which held her hair so that it fell around her shoulders, thick and heavy.

There was no mistaking their astonishment. She knew they swore: the spittle from their chagrin settled on her face. They released her so abruptly that she almost fell again. One of the men was the Excise captain himself. He took her face in his hands and mouthed words at her slowly and she could feel the tremor of rage in his very fingers.

'What are you doing here?' The shape of the words was clear enough at such close quarters.

Gladys stared back into the eyes so close to hers. Her own terror was evident. And her helpless gibbering was unsimulated. Tears of pain and fright began to pour from her eyes and after a few moments the captain released her, fury and disappointment in every inch of his body. Then the two men turned away and hurried along the wall towards the village leaving the distraught girl alone at the end of the windy pier.

She sat down with her back against the balustrade, head on her knees. She needed to regain her strength and give them time to be gone before making her way to home and safety.

And so it was that I waited a long hour alone in the cottage kitchen, until at last I heard the click of the latch and Gladys came home, tear-stained and dishevelled, but still able to give me her indomitable grin of triumph.

I missed Theo even more in the days that followed Zeb's escape. I knew he was deeply involved in setting up his trading venture but longed to see him again, to see a face that was unreservedly friendly. For there was a change in people's attitude to us in the days that followed Zeb's escape. Some, like Ned Kellow, were openly grateful. Once, when Gladys was pushing me up the hill in my chair, Ned came along, gently put her to one side and wheeled me home, lifting the chair and me, bodily onto the ramp and saying, 'Thanks for what you did for Zeb. He's my mate. I won't forget.'

From others, however, there was a marked coolness. I was not sure why this should be until one afternoon I saw Francis Turner, one of the oldest men in the village, sitting beside the harbour wall.

I called a greeting to him, for I enjoyed his reminiscences, but he replied with a curt nod. When I had put away my work, I rolled my chair along and stopped beside him.

'What's the matter Mr Turner?' I asked. 'What have I done to upset you?'

He looked a little discomfited at the directness of my approach, but removed his pipe from his mouth and paused a moment before answering.

'We've all got along in this village for years, Miss Millbrook. Then you come along, and in an emergency, you act as if you was the only one able to help one of our own. And you turned down our help when you was offered it. I'm not saying you never did a good job. You did. Got the boy away and we still don't know how. But tha's what we don't like. You don't have any faith in us.'

I felt a sickness in my stomach. The wind from the sea was cool and there was rain in the air. This was the place we had made our home and I could not bear the thought that the easy relations we had built up over the years should now be lost.

'Mr Turner. As you said, it was an emergency. There was no time to get help from anyone. And after the Revenue men had left, it was obvious from what Zeb told me that someone in the village had set a trap. And he didn't know who it was. So what could I do other than keep my own counsel?'

The old man turned his frowning gaze towards me.

'A trap? He said that? Zeb?'

'Yes. The others got away but Zeb was very lucky not to have been caught. Or killed.'

'The others. . . Funny that. Spinks don't usually work with more'n one or two. And we heard there was a boatful.' He looked at me enquiringly and I felt the need to dissemble.

'I don't know about that. Zeb told me the less I knew the better.' (I did not add that I had persuaded him to change his mind about that.) 'But he did tell me there was a trap set on the beach.'

Francis Turner looked at me and now there was less hostility in his gaze. 'An informer eh? And you've got no idea who it might be?' The sunken old eyes were like gimlets, probing mine.

I hesitated and then spoke reluctantly.

'I don't know. But several women came to see us the day after the Excise came. I knew some were offering help, but I couldn't risk telling the wrong one.' I looked at him fiercely. 'I've seen the poverty, the hardship some people live with here. I can understand the temptation to get hold of some money. I don't blame them.' I set my jaw. 'But I couldn't risk Zeb's life.'

He shook his head. 'Times have always been hard for people like us who live off the land and the sea. 'Tis too chancy. Storms wreck the boats, ruin the crops. We all has our share of sickness. And death. But 'tis a hard thing to find one of our own would do a thing like that for money. He never gave you an idea who it could be?'

I sat for a while, going over in my mind what Zeb had told me. And remembered. 'He said it was Cecil Thomas who fought him when he got to the top of the cliff. Who stabbed him. Zeb knocked him out. And,' I went on, 'I had a feeling that young Timmy Pascoe was watching me last week, the day Tom Spinks came. I could be wrong because he went off with Tom Spinks for a while, but he was soon back, just messing about on one of the boats in the harbour and seeming to watch what I was doing.'

'Young Timmy is a cousin of Cecil Thomas, the one you say hurt Zeb. Cecil joined the Revenue last year. Can't blame the boy for that, 'tis a job after all.' He knocked out his pipe and began carefully to cut a fresh chunk of tobacco. 'Did Mrs Pearce come to your place by any chance?'

'Oh yes. She came several times. Brought me some cakes once. I must say I was surprised. She's never been particularly friendly before.'

He nodded slowly. 'Yes, well you see m'dear. Her sister married Cecil Thomas's father who was killed over to Mabe stone quarries. And young Timmy is her grandson. It seems like we know who our informer is.' His face was grim.

'What are you going to do?' I asked uneasily.

He sighed. 'We shall just go along and tell her what we think. See what she says. I 'specs 'tis like you said, all about money. And the boy in the Revenue will be looking for a bit a success. Nothin's simple in this world, my dear." His mood changed and he gave a sly grin. 'Did they get away with a good cargo then?'

My heart missed a beat. 'Cargo? Why yes, I should think so. Spinks is a canny fellow after all.'

He nodded. 'Aise, my sparrow. We thought all along 'twas Spinks behind it all.'

I gave him a challenging look. 'Are we going to be good neighbours again? I'll tell you how Zeb got away, but then I would much rather forget about the whole affair. It's over and done with I hope.' And I briefly recounted the story of Zeb's flight wearing a dress, and Gladys's successful act as a decoy.

He was an appreciative listener, chuckling at the picture of Zeb climbing into the boat with his skirts about his waist, and nodding his head at Spinks hauling the boat out against wind and tide on the rope.

Presently he reached forward and patted my hand. 'Fair enough my girl. You did a grand job. And you know how to keep your mouth shut, that much I do know.' He looked at me keenly again. 'So fair enough.' And he shouted to one of the men working on the boats to give a hand and take this lovely lady home, you lucky chap!

Chapter Eight

I was about to write 'So life returned to normal', but how could it be normal ever again after the evening when Theobald Pentire called on me. . .

He had been spending some time in Polwerris in the weeks following Zeb's escape, for the ketch he had bought in Devonport was being fitted to his requirements and he already had several merchants ready to join his trading venture. He was in the village now to finalise the purchase of a house, a house I had often admired when out with Gladys in the trap. It stood half a mile up the hill from the village, a rambling old place with a pear tree trained against the wall and a bench in the porch which must offer an idyllic view of the woods spilling down the valley to the sea. . .

I knew that all he now required was the wife to share his new home and several of the village women had taken pains to tell me he had been seen talking to this young woman or that; to Elspeth Treloar, to Anita Parsons, to Gwendoline Matthews. . . And each time I would smile cheerfully and say how nice, while my heart yearned for the rumour to be untrue.

On this particular evening I was reading in my room with Gladys crocheting in the chair beside me, and I was aware of the sudden leap of my pulse when I heard the sound of his voice call a greeting from the front door.

I felt the warm colour flood my face as I called 'Come in!' and a moment later Theo entered the room. Gladys pulled forward the chair she had just vacated and beckoned him forward. I urged her to stay but she shook her head and smiled and bustled off.

He sat down and smiled at me, without the challenging flirtation in his eyes. 'You'll wonder why I came. I hope you don't mind, but I would like to borrow something to read. My stuff hasn't yet come from Canada and I guessed you'd have something more than the Bible and three volumes of the Reverend Samuel's sermons.'

I laughed and indicated my book shelf.

'You may find some of the novels there a little lurid, but help yourself by all means.'

There was little to choose from on my shelf and I thought wistfully of the library at Trevingey. 'I also have a few magazines - I indulge in one every month. Have a look anyway.'

He crossed the room and picked up now one book, now another, while I watched him. I study people, all people, with the eye of a painter, aware of the set of a shoulder, the carriage of the head, the bones of the face. But I recognised more than artistic curiosity in the hunger of my gaze upon his back, and I knew I must veil my feelings before he turned around. But for the moment I was safe to watch him browsing and I let my hungry eyes feed upon him. The now familiar leather jacket was well worn and had moulded itself to the shape of his broad shoulders and my eyes dwelt upon the dark hair which curled where it met the collar. Then, sensing he was about to turn, I quickly averted my face towards the fireplace.

'I'll borrow this one if I may,' and I saw to my surprise that he had a copy of Scott's narrative poems which was my latest acquisition.

'Oh yes. It's very good. I read the review in my magazine and sent to London for it last month. I know you'll enjoy it.'

At my invitation he sat down again and leaned back. Then he gave a sigh. And I heard in the gentle expiration of air all the hopelessness of the attraction between us.

I gave a wry smile. 'Yes, I know,' I said.

He looked up sharply as I spoke and was about to speak but I put my fingers to my lips.

'Let's just leave it at this, shall we?'

Then Gladys banged against the door prior to pushing it open with the tea tray she bore in her hands. I was glad of the interruption and insisted that she joined us. So she too sat down and Theo amused us both with his attempts at sign language and I watched his hands, sail-calloused and brown and strong and yet extraordinarily graceful as he tried to follow Gladys's instruction.

And I wondered how those hands would feel upon my skin. . . I shivered and dragged my thoughts back to the light conversation the pair were laughingly attempting.

He stayed an hour or so, then went off carrying the book and I was left to think and remember all the unspoken messages which had flown between us. And I wondered if Gladys too had read the very different wordless language that flowed between us in that delightful hour.

I shook my head. This attraction must not develop; the hurt would be all the more when it came to an end. As it must. And yet, and yet. . . I did not want it to end. Did not want to lose this sudden awareness of every nerve ending in my body, the warmth that radiated from the centre of my being. Did not want to stop going out each day, ostensibly to paint, in reality to fill the time until he must come, walking down the hill from the house he had bought for the bride he had yet to find. Or climbing from a boat, his movements controlled and deliberate. It did not matter that he had work to do. Just a grin as he passed, tipping that ridiculous wide-brimmed hat was enough. And if he did have time to stop and talk that was a bonus, and our casual conversation would be gone over and over in my mind for hours, as I remembered each glance of his eye and every intonation of his voice. And neither did it matter if there were half a dozen girls around me, all vying for his attention for I knew that the smouldering gleam in his eyes was for me alone.

And I thought back to the men I had known, to my husband Charles whose love-making had been perfunctory and offhand, and whom I later found had kept his passions for his numerous women of the night, believing that no 'lady' should seek or desire love-making, that the conjugal bed was solely for the procreation of an heir. And then there had been Richard, young and ardent as we coupled in the woods; our bodies responsive and sated, but our hearts and minds untouched by our union.

And now Theo. . . Theo who was already seeking his wife-to-be, who would soon have to stop our seemingly casual meetings, who should not have called here tonight. But call he did, and the book of poetry he had borrowed would do nothing to dampen the flames that were flickering about us.

It was a long time before I slept that night. A long time before I acknowledged that I did not want this sweet anguish to end. I knew, and Theo's sigh had told me that he too, could not bear more years of tending another dear invalid. And if I allowed myself foolishly to dream of spending the rest of my life in his arms, I woke to the harsh reality that inevitably the love in his eyes would turn to pity as my condition worsened. So I knew that one day soon, Theo would raise his hat and smile from across the street and the pain in my heart would never be cauterised by the flame of our passion.

But even so, I knew that until then, I should go on watching for his coming, and that no thought of the future would cloud my gaiety when we exchanged our pleasantries and when our eyes sought each other and met in what was, almost, an embrace.

But mine was not the only heart to beat unsteadily in our cottage at the sight of a certain man, for Gladys was being courted by Will Thomas. He was a quiet young man, but at first I regarded him as suspiciously as any parent protective of her young. His mother had recently died and I was afraid he was merely seeking a replacement housekeeper for himself and his father. But in this I misjudged him for the aunt who had come to nurse his dying mother had stayed on to care for them both and had no plans to leave. And when I saw the shy adoration in the boy's gaze reflected in my Gladys's blue eyes, I fought down my jealousy; if Gladys was to marry, she would do very well with Will. My only reservation was his diffidence, for it seemed to me that Gladys was the one who would have to make all the decisions in their home.

But thoughts of their possible marriage raised several problems for me and for the first time in my life I began to worry about money. Gladys brought me the suede pouch I had tossed so blithely into my valise on the night of my flight; the purse which then had bulged with golden sovereigns but which was now sadly depleted. From it we had bought the cottage and such pieces of furniture as were needed, and though my paintings brought in enough for our daily needs, that was our only source of income and from time to time we had dipped into our dwindling nest egg.

Now I had the future to think of; the not so distant time when Gladys would marry Will for I had seen the brief courtships in Polwerris when there was no mother to delay sending her son into another woman's arms. When that time came I must find another home, with rent to pay and the cost of hiring help so that I could still be free to paint. Gladys could see my concern. With extravagant gestures she conveyed to me that this cottage was my own, and my home would always be there; that Will agreed, that he would never think of my leaving. I calmed her down by giving her my smiling thanks, but I had no intention of remaining with the young couple once they were married.

I thought of my mother's legacy to me, of the steady flow of income from France that had once been mine. It would of course be Guy's upon his coming of age, but in the meantime Charles would have the handling of those funds. If only I could find a way to get some of what was rightly mine. . . And news of Guy. . . Surely I could think of some way of using Morwenna's presence in Plymouth. . .

But as always the thought of Charles sent a shudder of fear through my being and I knew I dare not risk involving Morwenna. If only I could find another way. . .

I had had several letters from Morwenna since her move, the latest telling with delight of Zeb's arrival in Plymouth. He had found himself a job with a ferry company on the Tamar, and to his joy it involved working with engines as the firm was experimenting with steam power. He had always been interested in steam engines, but preferred the sea to the mines where so many of the engines were found. Now he had the best of both worlds, and would be able to save a little money besides. Morwenna was sure her father would get over his disapproval of Zeb now that he had a steady job. She offered me her grateful thanks for helping Zeb and I was glad of the careful way she phrased the letter to say nothing that would incriminate either of us.

Jinny was sitting beside me when Gladys brought me Morwenna's latest letter and when she heard that Zeb had met Morwenna in Plymouth she clapped her hands and crowed with pleasure. She liked to talk about the older girl whom she greatly admired and Morwenna's letters gave us a pleasant picture of her busy new life. She was teaching the little ones to read and Miss Roberts had promised to increase her retainer at the end of the next month. Zeb's unlooked for arrival had added to her happiness.

I had sifted carefully through the gossip which came my way in the weeks following Zeb's flight from Polwerris to find out if any mention was made of the escape of the French prisoners. But thankfully there was none. Spinks had covered their tracks with care and no connection had been made between the village and the missing prisoners from distant Clowance.

So, buoyed up by the delight of seeing Theo so much more often, I worked hard and completed a whole new batch of paintings, both water colours and oils and Lambeth Weekes came and collected them to take to the gallery in Penzance.

I did not like Lambeth Weekes. Nor did I trust him; the monies he brought me for my work were sufficient to cover the cost of the materials and for our normal simple needs. But I was never given a written account from the gallery to show how the sums were arrived at, and when I first mentioned this to Lambeth, he blandly stated that Mr Swain was like that; he did his business that way. So because it was due to his suggestion that I was selling my work at all, I said no more.

Today I wrote my usual note to Mr Swain of the gallery with instructions for the type of frame for each picture and a list of the new paints and brushes I required. Lambeth stood near my shoulder as I wrote and I could not help wrinkling my nose. Like most of the village men, he reeked of strong tobacco, but in his case there was too the reek of dirt and neglect, the smell which fell through his cottage door in an almost tangible cloud if one passed on the rare occasions when it was left ajar.

He made two trips from our cottage to his own with the pictures. He had fashioned a wooden cage with slots to keep the oils separate for some were not yet quite dry. Sometimes he rode the cliff path on his cob, with his packages precariously strapped on to both horse and rider. At other times he hitched up the cart and followed the track. It seemed he had a number of customers like myself who needed someone to carry out their business but a more unlikely looking agent it would be hard to find. He was unpredictable and often arrived several days late when his excuse would he 'Bein' a agent, yore at ev'rybody's beck and call, yore life idden yore own, I can tell 'ee Miss Millbrook.'

As he left today he announced, 'Well me dear, I'll be bringin' you yore money next week. Got a couple of jobs to do over Penryn way.

'Very well, Mr Weekes. I'll get on with some more work.' But I hoped I would not run out of my blues. It was a nuisance being so dependent on this man and I wondered once more if I could get someone else from the village to act on my behalf.

And then, with a start, I had another thought. Perhaps I could use Lambeth Weekes as the intermediary I needed to make contact with Charles! For whatever his shortcomings, he was a man of discretion; never had I heard him repeat gossip or indeed talk about anyone else's affairs. I sat for a long time staring into space. It would need very careful planning but perhaps in the days to come I would be able to think of a way which would not put both Gladys and me in danger. . .

Chapter Nine

In the following week Gladys was baffled by my changing moods; elation when I had spoken with Theo, grim determination to earn more money from my paintings for the gallery, and long silences when I gazed into space with a set face, trying to find how I could safely make contact with Charles. . .

Only when I was painting was I calm. Quite often these days when I painted I had a companion, for Morwenna's little protégé, Jinny, liked to slip away from her home as soon as her chores were completed and would come and find me if I was working out of doors. Until now I had rarely had an audience, my obvious concentration and lack of conversation hardly encouraging to anyone who might like to stay and watch. But Jinny was different; she neither spoke herself nor looked to me for comment but was content to sit on a nearby wall or step, or upon the ground, ignoring the chill breezes that forever searched and hunted along our coast, small hands grasping her knees and her huge eyes following my every move.

Today, I paused and put down my palette to stretch my arms and free my stiff shoulders, and as I did so I noticed the child's arms were bare and goosefleshed, her thin cotton dress the only buffer against the wind. I myself was wearing a woollen jersey like those used by the fishermen, one I had purchased from a neighbour whose son grew faster than the garment on her needles. Although Gladys clicked her tongue in disapproval, it was warm and windproof and far more snug than any shawl or movement-restricting jacket.

Over the back of my chair lay the wrap which Gladys liked me to wear to cover this unseemly garment while she pushed me through the village and now I picked it up and handed it to the child. 'Here, take this. You'll freeze.'

Diffidently she took the shawl and wrapped it round her huddled shoulders and her face broke into a smile of pleasure at its soft thickness. I myself had crocheted the wrap during the previous winter evenings, a waist length cape-shawl in mixed shades of green.

I looked at the child. The colour complemented her grey-green eyes. 'Keep it Jinny. It suits you.'

Her pale face reddened and paled again and suddenly she spoke, her voice rough with emotion. 'You would'n give me nothin' it you knew what I done.'

I gave her my full attention, startled by the tone of her voice. 'Jinny, child, it doesn't matter to me what you have done. You're cold. I'd like you to have the shawl.'

But there must have been something behind my brusque dismissive words that reached the child, for clutching the shawl tightly to her shoulders, she began to talk.

'I stabbed someone, Miss Millbrook. I nearly killed him. I would'n a cared if I did. I tried to. I meant to.'

I turned back to my box of paints, shocked by the look on the child's face, and keeping my voice neutral and unjudgemental while I sorted through my colours, I remarked, 'From what I've seen of you Jinny, he must have deserved it.'

'He did,' her voice was eager. 'He's my cousin, Miss Millbrook. Da sent me to live over his brother's place when Ma died. I was eight. Aunt Ida made me do all the work, I must earn me keep, she said. I didn' mind the work so much, 'twas Job.' She paused briefly and then went on. 'I was give the linney to sleep in.' I nodded my head and thought of the upstairs room beneath the sloping roof of our own cottage, the place where Zeb had taken refuge.

'Right from the start, Miss, that Job, he was climbing the ladder every night to my bed.'

My own voice was tight. 'How old was he, Jinny?'

'I s'pose he was 'bout thirteen when it started. The other boys was still too young. Three years I stuck it. He was big and fat, Miss.' And I could hear the revulsion in her voice.

'She knew what was goin' on, Aunt Ida did. She knew all the time. And then one day I heard her talkin' to the girl who came for the cream - 'bout babies and things. The girl said, "What if

73

d

Jinny do have a baby?" So she must a knowed all 'bout it too. And my aunt said, "She'll have to get rid of it. I don't want no bastards in my house." And I thought I better kill myself before that happened. When my work was done that night, late, I took the big knife up to my room. Everyone was asleep, they always was time I finished my work. Everyone 'cept him.

'I wadden sure how best to do it, I did'n want to linger, like. And then, whilst I was standin' by the bed, holding the knife, he came. I heard the step creak like it always did, every night. And I went all cold and when he come over to me and started pulling at my skirt, I just pushed the knife into him. He screamed like a stuck pig and fell down and they all come runnin'.

'My uncle, that's Da's brother, he were the first up the ladder. He never even had a candle but there was moonlight enough coming in the little window. He yelled for Aunt Ida to bring a candle and he grabbed the sheet and pressed a handful of it against Job's stomach. There was black stuff everywhere, over me, over Job's nightshirt, running over Uncle Simeon's hands. At first I couldn' make out what it was, black like that in the moonlight. But when Aunt Ida came screechin' up with the candles, I could see then that 'twas red blood.

'She screamed and screamed when she saw her precious Job. She would have gone for me like a mad thing only Uncle Simeon stopped her. "Give a hand here quick if you want to save him," he said. And they did save him, 'cos Uncle Simeon is like that, good with sickness and animals and such. But 'twas a close thing, his fat saved him, Uncle said. All the time, I was crouched down on the floor, there where the ceiling came right down to my head. Then, when they got him comfortable on my bed, 'cos he were too weak to move, Aunt Ida said I should hang for this. But Uncle Simeon said do she want the neighbourhood to know what her dear boy been up to and the next day he brought me home to Gran and told her he was sorry. That he never knew.'

She paused. I saw that while I had been listening, my hands had carefully tidied and straightened my paintbox. Now I looked up and met those haunted eyes, eyes too old for a child's face. 'I s'pose you won't want me round you now you know.'

I reached out to her. 'My dear child.' And slowly, tentatively, one of her clenched fists released the shawl and met my outstretched hands. I took the icy little paw and held it briefly to my lips.

And Jinny looked at me, her eyes wide with wonder at the tears in my own. 'You don't mind? You don't think I'm wicked and will burn in hell fire like she said?'

'No Jinny. No. The fault was with the mother, who knew and did nothing. Not with you. Just you be glad that it's over. That you're free.'

And without another word, I turned abruptly back to my work. And with a long sigh of release, Jinny settled down to watch, enveloped in the comfort of the woollen shawl.

From this time I was more aware of Jinny when she arrived at my side. Since Morwenna had left the village, she was ignored by the other girls and no one else seemed to bother much with the child. But the thought of the horrific abuse which she had suffered haunted me and I cast about for a way to help as unobtrusively as possible. In the end it was so simple that I marvelled I had not thought of it before.

'Here, Jinny. Try and paint that boat.' I indicated a dinghy drawn up on the shingle of the tide-drained harbour.

Biting her lip with excitement, the child took the brush and board I handed her and made a few tentative strokes. Soon she began to get the feel of the water colours which that day I was using. The many hours she had spent at my side, intently watching, had not been wasted and she was soon making work-manlike attempts at some of the techniques she had seen me use. A passable picture was emerging. I was pleased, not only that the girl showed talent, but because the concentration on her work removed all trace of the twitching nerves from her face and body.

She was almost twelve but her thin body showed little sign of budding womanhood. Her skin had the greyish pallor which spoke of the need for soap and water and her mousy hair was scraped back into an uncompromising pigtail. But now, caught up in the painting, lips parted and eyes alight, the child was far from plain.

I sat relaxed in my chair, enjoying my new role of tutor, watching her progress. She had almost finished her first painting when two younger children came puffing along the wall. 'Gran says you got to come home right this minute!' the older of the two announced smugly.

Jinny looked round at the two and glared. 'I'll come when I'm good and ready!' Her mouth was set and her eyes had filled with tears of anger.

I held out my hand for the brushes. 'Run along Jinny. You need to let that dry before you do any more or you'll spoil it. It's good, Jinny. I'll keep it safe for you and you can finish it next time.'

Her truculence fled and she handed me the board with sparkling eyes. 'Can I come again this afternoon?'

'Whenever you like, child. But don't upset your grandmother.' She looked at me keenly, saw the sense of my remark and turned gaily to the young children.

'All right. Race you home then.' And the trio scampered away, the young ones squealing at Jinny to wait for she was going much too fast for their little legs to keep up with.

I sat for a while after they had gone, thinking about the child and wondering if I were doing her any favour by giving her my encouragement. The life ahead for a girl from such an impoverished family would hold little opportunity for painting, of that I had no illusions. And without a wealthy patron, no artist, let alone a female one, could expect a life of other than the direst poverty. For I knew that without the small reserve of capital which still remained after we purchased the cottage, I would have been unable to pursue my painting hobby which had so soon become a means of income thanks to the intervention of Lambeth Weekes.

So I bit my lip thoughtfully and grew cold and stiff by the time Gladys came. She pushed me back to the foot of the steps and helped me from the chair until I could grasp the handrail and pull myself up the steps while she wheeled the chair along the ramp. And indoors, I walked round the kitchen a few times to restore my circulation before sitting down to enjoy my meal with Gladys.

But at the back of my mind an idea had formed and I was impatient for Lambeth Weekes to call again so that I could sound him out and see if he was prepared to make a journey on my behalf.

Chapter Ten

Will Thomas was now openly courting Gladys. She had taken to going to Chapel with Will and his father and aunt and had even tried to persuade me to join them. But I had smiled and shaken my head. Although brought up as a Catholic, I had nothing against the Wesleyans; indeed I admired what the brothers Wesley had done to tame and control the unruly miners all over Cornwall. But I had no wish to join the Chapel community; I felt myself too alien, too far apart. . .

The Thomases were all good, respectable people and Gladys was blooming with her new happiness and love. My sole reservation about Will was that he was dominated by his father who owned the boat from which they fished for their livelihood; my fear being that Gladys would always have to be the stronger partner and leader, and though I, of all people, had no doubts about her strength and resolve, I was disappointed that Will showed no initiative and seemed content to let life take its course with little direction from himself.

Then one day Gladys announced that she and Will wanted to go to the fair at Helston in our pony trap. (When we arrived at Polwerris I had insisted that Gladys keep her pony Jem - our one extravagance in our new life.) On the way, they would pick up his sister Grace from the farm at Polbrean where she worked so that she too would be able to spend the day with her young man who was an ostler at the Angel Hotel. I was pleased for Gladys; it was high time she had a day off on her own. Then came her surprise. 'Why don't you come too and bring Jinny?'

The suggestion left me speechless for a moment for I had not left the vicinity of the village in the three years I had dwelt here. I was nervous even of the strangers who came ashore from those few ships which put in to Polwerris Cove, sometimes with a cargo, more usually to shelter from the stormy seas that claimed so many vessels around this wild peninsula.

But the thought of Jinny's delight appealed. And as I considered the invitation, the idea of being amongst a gay crowd was tempting; the variety, the colours, new faces, and new ideas for my brush, for sitting in my wheelchair I would be able to use my sketch-pad and thus take full advantage of the day. And what settled the matter was that Theo had gone off again to Devonport to see the alterations which had been made to his ship. And I smiled to myself that had he been working in the cove, no outing, however delightful, would have drawn me away!

So now I looked up at Gladys's excited face and laughed my acceptance of their generous offer.

Gladys went with Jinny to ask her grandmother's permission for the child to go with us, Jinny acting as her interpreter. The old woman agreed that she could go but said the child had nothing smart to wear and she had no money to spare for new clothes. Gladys smiled and indicated that she could cut down one of her skirts for Jinny. And it would be best if Jinny stayed at our house on both the night before our trip and when we returned, for we would be leaving early and could not be sure at what hour we might get back to Polwerris. Mrs Pellow agreed to this suggestion also and Jinny's excitement was boundless.

That week we spent some pleasant hours making a green and white striped cotton skirt and a blouse of white muslin for the child which went well with the cape shawl I had given her. We bought her a straw boater from Widow Peter's shop which was in reality her front parlour. Mrs Peters was a woman who could concoct an attractive bonnet from a handful of gauze and ribbon and she nodded her approval when I chose some artificial daisies to decorate the boater, and these she swiftly stitched into place.

Now we had to think of shoes, for Jinny possessed not a pair and though she would happily have gone along barefoot, Gladys and I were both getting great pleasure from dressing the child and from the glazed delight in her eyes. So next we went down to the store beside the inn on the harbour front, an Aladdin's cave where sacks of flour and bags of oats rested alongside bolts of cotton and muslin, where barrels of tar stood at the foot of the wall from which hung cards of bootlaces, paintbrushes, men's heavy jackets and bundles of skipping ropes, and where the owner, Septimus Trebilcock could put his hand on anything he was asked for in the wink of an eye.

Here Jinny chose for herself a pair of wooden clogs, not even looking at the few pairs of leather boots that Mr Trebilcock produced for her inspection. Gladys sighed with exasperation, wanting her to be properly shod, but I could see that the child was looking ahead and knew she would still be able to wear them when they were well outgrown, as did so many young girls.

The night before the trip, Jinny bathed in the wooden tub in the scullery while Gladys washed the child's hair and twisted it into ringlets which she deftly tied with rags. Gladys too, knew Jinny's secret; the child had asked me to tell her but no one else, although I think she knew there was no danger of my betraying her confidence. Perhaps it was this knowledge that made Gladys so wish to please the child, or perhaps it was her own latent mothering instinct, but watching the two of them, I could well imagine Gladys sitting with a baby on her lap and a toddler at her knee. But soon Gladys shooed Jinny up the stairs to her bed in the room opposite Gladys's and we settled to put the finishing touches to the undergarments we had made to complete Jinny's new wardrobe.

Early next morning I looked seawards and found the harbour was almost invisible in mist, but there was a translucence about it that hinted at the nearness of the sun, and we prepared for our trip with some gaiety.

This would be the first time Jinny had visited Helston as well as my first outing to town since my accident (for I still called my attempted murder 'the accident', even to myself) .

Gladys sat on the front seat of the trap with Will by her side, the reins slim and insubstantial in his broad hands, while I was comfortable in my chair which Will had wedged so that it would not tip over. I was wearing one of Gladys's frocks, drawn in with a belt and with an old shawl round my shoulders. My big painting hat served both to shade my eyes and to conceal my face, for I was nervous of meeting someone from my old life, some young blade who might have come to enjoy the various delights of the fair. Jinny sat on the narrow bench seat at the side of the trap, a pile of cushions and rugs at her feet for our homeward journey. She was ecstatic, twisting and turning in her seat, watching the passing countryside with eyes that missed nothing, marvelling and commenting on the costumes of the people we passed, for it seemed that all West Cornwall was on its way to the fair.

I caught the excitement and looked about almost as avidly as the child. The bal maidens were a sight to behold, having spent their hard won wages on skirts and bonnets of the brightest hue, red and orange and blue, green and yellow and crimson, so that a group of girls chattering eagerly together were like a clutch of exotic parrots - with screams and shrieks to match! The country-men too were resplendent in corduroy trousers, polished boots and gaiters, nankeen jackets and colourful neckcloths, their finery crowned by their high hats. Their wives were more quietly attired, neat in blue or brown pelisses. Only the matrons' huge bonnets revealed their need for audience and admiration, and the fruit and flowers that bedecked their headware cried shame to the rampant hedgerows that we passed between.

Will's sister Grace was already waiting at the end of the lane from Polbrean Farm and while he reached down an arm to help her aboard, I made a quick sketch of the charming farmhouse from which she had come. It had been added onto by succeeding generations until the thatched roofs reaching over to enfold the latest additions, looked for all the world like the outstretched wing of a motherly hen. But to Grace, the farm was simply a place of toil, a place where she must needs work until she wed, and today she was eager to be gone, to leave behind the farmstead which to my bemused eye, looked as if it always had, and always would, stand in its sunny hollow beneath the encircling elms and where raucous rooks would for ever fluster about their scribbled nests.

But there were to be no more dreaming, idyllic dwellings to catch my eye, for now the road became even more crowded and Jinny was forever clutching at my sleeve to point out new sights, chattering non-stop until a huge stage-wagon crawling along the road finally struck her speechless. We trailed along behind it at funereal pace, and I could well believe what we were told, that this huge vehicle, drawn by eight large horses would take three weeks to reach London, loaded as it was with goods and passengers. There were bells on the horses' necks to give notice of its coming, and the prodigious breadth of the great wheels were necessary to give some stability to the dangerously top-heavy wagon.

But finally, as we neared Helston, Will turned off the road onto a lane he knew and so we pressed on through the crowded by-ways until we reached the Angel Hotel where we were to stable Jem for the day, with the help of Grace's young man, Ralph Trezize. He greeted us and led us to a back room so that we might tidy ourselves while be and Will saw to the pony and then he would join us, having earned the time off by working half the previous night tending the horses of those who had come to watch the wrestling which was always such a feature of the fairs.

I was glad to leave the inn which was growing busier by the minute, for I constantly expected to see some old acquaintance burst through the door and stare at me aghast, for though we were separated by the length of Cornwall from my old home, the rich made light of the discomforts of travel and I had no doubt there would be many smart ladies and gentlemen from far afield in Helston today.

Ours was a gay little party as we set out from the inn and into the press of people who thronged the streets. Then Jinny clutched my chair and I looked up and saw sheer terror on her face for this was the first time she had been in such a crowd. But Gladys took her hand and Will forged a passage for my chair and soon the child lost her fear, distracted by the stall holders crying their wares, the displays of fire eaters, bearded women, two-headed goats and sellers of potions guaranteed to cure all manner of disease. Gladys and Will took turns escorting Jinny into the various tents while Grace and Ralph stayed beside my chair despite my protests that I would be quite happy to wait on my own, for the crowd itself was sufficient entertainment for me. And presently, when they saw me happy with my pencil and pad, both young couples were content to go with Jinny, leaving me to enjoy myself, for the colour and vigour of the mass of people was a moving canvas waiting to be caught. It reminded me of the markets of Rome and Paris and I felt a stab of grief for my father who had taken me there so long ago. All manner of people were to be seen, from the poorest urchins, begging for a share of the delights, to young squires and their ladies, deigning for once to join in the fun. I even saw two faces I recognised; two young men swaggering through the press of people, but though I watched them cautiously from beneath the brim of my hat, they cast no second glance towards the shabby woman seated in a wheelchair.

But presently the others returned, Jinny pink-cheeked with delight. The morning flew, until our hungry stomachs reminded us that the day was advancing. Ralph and Will went back to the inn to fetch the basket of provisions Gladys had prepared and Jinny pushed my chair towards the banks of the distant pool where we planned to eat in peace. At length we were settled in the shade beneath the trees, along with many other revellers who had the same idea.

The food was set upon with vigour for it was a long time since our breakfast. I watched Jinny's expressive eyes widen at the sight of the cold chicken, the fresh bread rolls, white and brown, the wedges of cheese wrapped in lettuce leaves, and the light pastries which Gladys had made. The two young men had brought jugs of lemonade and cider from the nearest public house (never had I seen so many inns selling so much alcohol!) and we set about our repast in true holiday spirit, with much laughter as we reminded one another of the morning's events.

Afterwards, we rested for a time in the shade, until Jinny anxiously reminded us that there wouldn't be time to see everything if we didn't make a start. Smiling at her fervour, we stirred ourselves and the young people rose to their feet. 'Why don't you four go off on your own? Jinny and I can take our time and we'll meet you back at the Angel at six o'clock.' And I saw their eyes light up at this suggestion.

So Jinny and I set off, her hand firmly holding my chair. We saw a dancing bear and Jinny's wonder was mixed with sadness at the great beast's present plight and she plied me with questions about the forests where he once had roamed. But soon the blare of trumpets cut through her grief and we were at a booth where a short, stocky man challenged all comers to a lifting contest, flexing his huge muscles as he bellowed his feats; he could lift not one man, not two men, and so on until he reached the total of five! And after that there was a conjuror of no mean ability, convincing the more gullible members of his audience that he could read their minds and knew exactly how much money there was in their pockets, and woe betide them if they did not give him his due, for was he not Magroy the Magnificent! But there was a good natured mood prevailing and I enjoyed myself as much as did Jinny, only wishing that Theo was here beside me and wondering fleetingly how he fared, with that familiar twist of guilt and longing.

But at length I told Jinny that no, I had no wish to see the Hall of Horrors, but she could go inside if she wished. I gave her some more coins and waited by a low wall where there was room for my chair, for though my whole body ached, the infinite variety of the crowd still enchanted me. So Jinny ran off with a swirl of her striped skirt, her small face bright and animated under the becoming boater. I watched her join the group of people waiting to be admitted, saw her respond to some chance remark with laughter, and was glad we had come, glad that she could so unreservedly enjoy all the fun and gaiety of the day.

Slowly they filed into the tent and I sat on in the sunshine, imbibing the cheerful atmosphere and mentally constructing a picture of the scene, the orange and yellow tent brilliant against the sky, the motley crowd flowing past. . .

But suddenly Jinny was there before me, and the look in her eyes made me hold out my arms and the next moment she was shuddering against my shoulder.

'My dear child! What is it? What's the matter?'

She did not speak for a long time, but gradually the rigidity left her body and she sank down onto the wall beside me, still clutching my hand.

Presently, after another shudder, she spoke. 'It was a man. Standing beside me in there.' Her arm jerked towards the tent. 'He stood close and I moved as far as I could. And then he put his hand on me.' Her own hand moved as if to cup her budding breast and then recoiled in revulsion. And now she was weeping, tears streaming from her eyes. 'Why are they like that, Miss Millbrook?' she sobbed. 'I wish I hadn't got no new clothes. I wish I hadn't come. I wish I was dead!' And she slid off the wall and sank to the ground, burying her face against her knees.

With difficulty, for I was stiff from sitting, I leaned forward to touch her. 'They're not all like that, Jinny. Think of all the people here today, it was only one man. Only the one. We've been having such a good day, don't let him spoil it for you. Come on,' I drew her to her feet. 'Where's your handkerchief? There, that's better. Let's go and get some sweets from that funny stall down the hill. And we can have another look at the bear if you like.' And so I prattled on, inwardly cursing my banal inadequacies and meekly she came along with me, pushing my chair where I willed. But all the pleasure and fun of the day had fled, for me as well as for the child, for I knew my words were meaningless, that she was reliving those nightmare years of abuse. And as I glanced at the remote and unchildlike eyes in her set face, I wondered with anguish if she would ever escape her horror, if she would ever be able to experience the wild pulse of passion in her veins, ever be able to melt into a man's arms with mutual love and desire. And as we made our way through the crush, back towards the hotel, I knew all she could see was a fat boy's face near to her own and smell his breath and dread his inevitable, blundering weight upon her small form.

Somehow we reached the inn, I cursing fluently as she pushed me, for once regardless of heads turned in my direction, and we made our way to the stables at the back where we found Jem in his stall. He whickered gently at us and Jinny went to him and pressed her face against his neck. After all the noise and heat of the day, the dim coolness of the stable enveloped us with an almost church-like calm and gradually I saw the rigid stiffness lessen and the fingers which clutched the horse's mane, unbend. She gave a long, shuddering sigh and then turned to me.

'Sorry, Miss Millbrook. I 'specs you want to see a bit more. I'm all right now. You say where to go.'

I smiled at her and looked round for somewhere for her to sit. 'Look, there's a bench by the door. Let's wait there until the others come. They won't be long now anyway, for Will wants to be well along the road before it gets too dark. And I certainly don't want to go out there again, you've already worn me out!'

But though she was calm now, and striving for normality, her gaze slid away from mine as though any human contact was to be avoided. I cursed again in my native French and she looked at me sharply for here there was no noisy throng to drown my words.

'What's that you said, Miss Millbrook?'

I was surprised at the sudden interest in her voice. I smiled down at her. 'I was being rude, in French, my dear Jinny, so you would not know what I was saying.'

'Can you teach me some? Please!'

So Jinny's first lesson in French began, with Jem swinging an inquisitive head towards us now and then while the busy toings and froings of the stable yard went on behind us. Jinny sat, safe for the moment in the little stall, colour and interest coming back into her pinched face as I coaxed her in the delights and difficul-

84

ties of my native tongue.

By the time Grace and Gladys arrived, Jinny was much more herself, and she told them her name, her age, and asked after their health in her new tongue with glee. Gladys recognised the last sentence which she had seen many times on the lips of both Guy and myself, and she replied in careful sign language.

'That's three languages I can speak now! I can speak English and French and I know a lot of that sign stuff!'

I was grateful that my rough curse had brought about such a transformation in the child in a short hour, but realised, perhaps for the first time, what a brittle shell protected her from the ever threatening past.

Then Will and Ralph came, talking enthusiastically of the wrestling they had watched when their young women had wandered off on their own. Ralph fetched us some refreshment from the inn, saying it was now much too full and too rough for us to enter and we drank our lemonade while he hitched up the trap, and Jinny ran to help buckle all that harness which was within her reach. Gladys and Grace packed their several purchases into the back and Jinny and I were settled for our journey home, Gwen and Ralph exchanging a discreet kiss of farewell before we left. By the time we had travelled a mile, I could see Jinny's eyes begin to close and she needed little persuasion to lie down on the trap floor, cocooned in a rug against the jolting of the trap and the sudden cooling of the evening air.

Chapter Eleven

It was a long, slow trip home for there were many others making their way along the road. Several times we were brought to a halt, and each time Jinny stirred uneasily. We dropped Grace at the end of her lane once more and she walked off towards the farmhouse with little reluctance, looking forward no doubt to her small white bed under that undulating thatch. And then at last we were trotting along the track across Goonhilly Downs and I was thankful that our journey would soon be over.

But it was not to be. Just after we turned off the road and onto the narrower track which led to Polwerris, we came to a standstill behind several other vehicles. Will climbed down and went to see the cause of the obstruction, and I told Jinny to go back to sleep, we would soon be moving again. She settled back readily, for she had risen early and the day had been full of incident.

Will came back with a young man at his side whom I recognised, one of the sons of Mary Penrose, a woman whom I had once painted, a tall, strong woman who had walked gracefully upright bearing a huge basket of laundry upon her head. I had heard her story, of course, for there was not one village drama which had not been relayed to me several times. This son, Jack, was the reason Mary had not wed Lambeth Weekes to whom she had been pledged, for when she was raped by Reece Penrose, Lambeth would have no more to do with her and from what I saw with my own eyes from time to time, there was no doubt that marrying the father of her child had led to little but poverty and violence at his hands.

Jack Penrose smiled up at me. 'There's a wagon ahead lost a wheel and it's blocking the road. If you go back a bit, you can go across Mr Hocking's fields. He won't mind. And then you can pick up the track again past our place.'

Will was nodding. 'It's a bit further, but we might be stuck here for hours, the way they're goin' about things up there.'

Will had to back the horse until there was room to turn and Jack opened and closed several gates as we drove across the fields, dry and cushiony beneath us after the rough roads. Gladys gestured to Jack to sit beside her, despite his protests that he was wearing old clothes for he was on his way home from the mine. I was surprised for his clothes, though old, did not look as if he had been working underground in them all day.

He laughed when I said as much. 'Ah, but we keeps our oldest rags for down below, Miss Millbrook. 'Tis so warm down there that you don't need much on, only to save 'ee bein' cut to ribbons, like, on the rocks. We got plenty hot water too, in the Dry, tha's where we change our clothes and clean up a bit 'fore we go 'ome. If we went straight out in the winter, we'd be dead o' cold 'for we got home.'

We all lapsed into silence for a time, the chink of Jem's bridle and the trundle of our wheels drowsily comforting as we wended our way home.

'Here we are,' Jack grinned as we emerged onto a narrow track. 'There's our place down there. Will b'longed to come here a lot when we was boys, we got good fishing down under Hogback Point, habben us Will?' Looking where he pointed, I could just make out the smudge of a cottage outlined against the sea where the last of the light clung to the shimmering water. 'I hope Faither 'idden there yet. Though if he is he'll be too drunk to move. He's bad enough any time, but fair days he's like a man possessed.'

'Do 'ee ever hear from Gerald?'

Jack shook his head. 'Tidden easy when you're at sea. He do come and see Mother when 'e get the chance, but it must be near a year since he come last time. He said then t'would be eighteen months or so 'fore he come home again.' He swung himself down from the trap and went to open and close the last gate.

Just as he was about to turn and make his goodbyes, the cottage door opened and a figure stood silhouetted against the lamplight; a woman's figure. But there was such a wild desperation about her that we all paused, staring down at the cottage. Then she screamed. My scalp prickled and Will gave an involuntary curse while Jack stood frozen beside the trap. As we watched, Mary Penrose raised her hands and tore at her hair. Will pushed the reins into Gladys's hands and bounded down the track towards the cottage and Jack followed more slowly, as though in dread of what lay ahead. The woman turned as she heard the stones rattle beneath their feet, then she dashed from the doorway and started to run towards the cliffs a hundred yards away.

I gripped the arms of my chair in terror at the woman's anguished cry and Gladys flung me the reins before she too, raced down the path after the others. From where I sat, helpless in my chair, I could just make out the fleeing form of Mary Penrose in her white apron, and then Will had grabbed her. I bit my lip as they struggled violently, perilously close to the cliff edge. Then Jack was there too and it seemed that they had overwhelmed her and were leading her back, each holding her close, away from the danger of the cliffs. I strained my ears to catch what was being said down there, but the endless roar of the sea on the rocks drowned their words until, clear in the darkness came her voice, harsh and flat, 'They shan't hang me! They shan't!'

And I guessed then what deadly drama had so lately been played out in that cottage kitchen, and my heart went out to the woman who had stood in the doorway, rending her very hair in her despair. Then Will's voice came, clear and hard.

'No one shall hang for that bastard.' And then Gladys was with them and they were leading the woman back to the house and Will's voice was now a gentle murmur of reassurance while Jack's arms enfolded his mother and his head drooped close to hers.

I watched it all from my vantage point in the pony cart at the head of the track. I saw Gladys go to the stable and fetch the cob. Saw Will and Jack drag a limp body out through the door. Watched them both struggle to hoist their burden across the horse's back. Held my breath when Will led the horse away along the cliff path and out of my sight, Jack walking alongside like a sleepwalker. Then I saw Gladys come out and dip a bucket of water from the barrel by the back door and vanish into the house and soon return to throw the water away. Twice she did this before the two young men returned and stabled the horse once more. I waited in growing anxiety when they all disappeared into the cottage, my teeth chattering with fear or cold or both, for I was apprehensive that some other traveller might chance upon the detour we had taken. Several times I peered down at Jinny, but the child slept undisturbed in her nest of cushions.

But at last Will and Jack emerged from the house and I could see Gladys standing in the doorway, looking into the house. The two men came up to the trap, Will's face like chiselled granite in the dimness.

'You saw nothing, Miss Millbrook. You were asleep in your chair.' And I marvelled at Will's incisive tone, and even at this moment, part of me was glad that I had been wrong; for though he might appear to be slow in both speech and movement he could be both swift and decisive when the need arose. Now I leaned forward in my chair, murmuring my assent. Then I reached across and touched Jack's hand as he stood, still dazed beside the trap. 'Did I not hear Mary call up the track to us that the cob had come home an hour ago with a broken girth and no rider? And did she not ask us if we'd seen her man along the road?'

Both men turned their faces towards me, then Will gripped Jack's shoulder. 'That's it, boy. That's what happened, right? You stay here with her tonight and come down the village tomorrow and ask if anyone else has seen him. Right?' he said again.

Jack nodded his head, dumbly and Will shook him a little. 'Wake yourself up, pard. Did you hear what we said?'

'Yes. Yes. I heard. I'll go back in there with her now. P'raps Gladys can come over in the morning, so's I can leave her to go down the village like you said.' And his gaze turned to my face.

'Of course. Don't worry Jack. Go and look after your mother.'

He turned and went slowly back towards the cottage door and Gladys moved aside to let him through, giving one final glance behind her before she closed the door gently and made her way back up the path to where we waited.

We completed our journey without further words. Jinny stirred when Will lifted her down and woke sufficiently to drink the milk Gladys heated for her on the fire which was fanned to a welcome glow. And while Will stabled Jem, Gladys went up the stairs to see to Jinny's bed and I set about preparing a hot toddy for Will to share with us when he returned, for I knew both Gladys and I shared his grey pallor.

But just as Jinny put her foot on the bottom tread to follow

Gladys up the stairs, she turned to me and spoke.

'Will's right, Miss Millbrook,' she said, 'there's no one should ought to hang for bastards like that.'

And I looked back into her face, trying to control my expression. 'You've been sleeping, Jinny. Run along up, Gladys is waiting for you.'

She gave me a little smile. 'Right, Miss Millbrook.' She turned away and then back again. 'Hadden it been a lovely day, though. With the bear and that. 'Tis been the best day of my life, and no mistake.'

And I watched as her little figure trailed tiredly up the stairs and wondered how much the child had heard, out there on the darkening clifftop; and how much of the black drama would be real to her, how much of it part of her own nightmare, a nightmare so horribly reawakened that afternoon at the fair.

And long after Will had returned and drunk his toddy, silent and grim, had said goodnight to Gladys and gone to his home; long after the cottage was dark and still, I lay in my bed and heard her words in my head, over and over again.

'Will's right. There's no one should ought to hang for bastards like that.'

It was a week before Reece Penrose's body was seen floating off Hogback Point. Before that, Jack had played his part well; making enquiries at each of the many inns from Helston to Penzance which his father had been known to frequent, and asking the parish constables to let him know if there was any news of his whereabouts. So by the time the body was discovered and identified, there were few questions asked. I did not have to attend the inquest, for when I told the magistrate's man who called at the cottage what I thought I had heard that night, he nodded his head and said, yes, that bears out what the others said. Gladys too, was exempted from attending because of her disability. So the inquest became a brief formality, and the verdict was given of accidental death.

Mary Penrose continued to fetch and carry laundry from the Red Lion, but now she would stop and have a cup of tea with us. The village was surprised at her mien, astonished that the widow of such a brute of a man should show such signs of bereavement, for she moved like one in a trance, her face pale and set. If I was not engrossed in a painting, I would join them in the kitchen and I noticed that her hands, strong and work-reddened, were never still; they rubbed the edge of the table before her, or pleated her apron into folds or leapt together in a quick, wringing motion.

One day I could stand it no longer and leaned forward and took those restless fingers between my own. 'Don't Mary. Don't torment yourself so. Your husband is dead and buried. It's over. Now you must turn your back on it and look to the future.'

She looked at me. 'You don't understand, Miss Millbrook. 'Tis me I'm worried about, not him.' And there was venom in the final syllable. 'I keep thinkin' they'll come for me one day. One day they'll come and take me and there'll be a trial and then they'll hang me. Judges and juries don't let a woman like me get away with killin' whatever the man has done.'

I shook my head. 'But they won't do that Mary. They have no suspicion. Will and Jack supported your story and they hardly bothered to ask me what I knew. There's no need to worry about them. And your own conscience is clear; you said he was trying to throttle you when you both fell. It could just as well have been your own head that struck against the fender as his.'

She looked away from me and I released the hands that sought to escape from mine. And for a moment I wondered if she had told us the whole story of Reece's violent end. But she picked up her cup and sipped the tea and seemed to relax somewhat. I could understand her doubts about the justice she would receive if she had told the true story, for it was not done to allow a woman to take the law into her own hands and she would not be the first to suffer the death penalty after striking out at a violent husband in defence of her own life.

She put down her cup. 'That Lambeth Weekes. He've been round to my place. Asked me to marry him, would you believe. And him not a week in his box.'

I looked up, startled and curious as to what she had said to her old suitor.

'I told him if he ever set foot near my door again I should have that dog onto him, that hound Jack brought me for company when I said I was goin' to bide there still.'

I tried to prevent my lips from twitching at the picture of Lambeth Weekes paying court to this implacable woman.

'Oh, I sent him off, right enough. But he called back to me that one way or another he was going to make me change my mind. What do you think he meant by that, Miss Millbrook?'

'Why, that he was not going to take 'no' for an answer. That's all he meant, Mary. It wasn't a threat, he has no evidence and no witnesses.'

'There's the child. He might get to work on her. That child do worry me. She looks at me . . .'

'Come now. Jinny was asleep. I promise you there is nothing to fear from her.' And she looked intently into my face as I spoke and at last she turned away with an involuntary sigh, as if she had laid down a heavy burden. Our talk turned to normal matters and when she left, even with the weight of the heavy basket on her head, she seemed to walk with an altogether lighter step and something of the grimness had left her lips.

Chapter Twelve

But my sympathies for Mary Penrose were suddenly swept away by my own concerns, for a couple of weeks after the inquest, a time when I had seen little of Theo, he called on me one morning. Standing just inside the door of my room, he came straight to the point.

'I thought I would tell you before you heard it from someone else. I'm walking out with Gwendoline Matthews.' His eyes met mine, his own bruised with emotion.

For a moment my body suspended movement, heart, blood, breathing, all stilled. Then, with a dizzy rush, the blood pounded and breath left my throat in something of a gasp. I swallowed and closed my eyes to compose myself.

'Sit down.' I managed the invitation in a low voice.

He drew a chair from the table and pulled it near to where I sat before my easel. I put the brushes into a pot, wiped my fingers on a rag and turned to him, straightening my shoulders.

'Gwendoline! Of course! How right for you Theo!' I could not believe the cheerful voice I heard, for my whole being was crying out 'Don't! It's me you love! I am bereft without you . . .' But I knew it could not be. Could not be.

'I've told her I want a child. A family.'

I nodded, unable for the moment to speak. I knew the girl, for I had done a portrait of her earlier in the year, a happy picture which showed her tying up the boots of her three-year-old son, her tawny hair fiery in the sunlight, laughing down at the face of the child who was solemnly attempting to button his jacket into the wrong buttonholes. It had made a good composition, the momentary relaxation of the young woman's normally stiff manner, the rapt concentration of the child. I admired her, for the child was illegitimate, the result of a brief involvement with a builder from Helston who had been working on the reinforcement of the harbour wall; a married man who had promptly washed his hands of responsibility when learning of her pregnancy.

Yes. She would make a good wife for Theo. Young. Attractive. Hardworking. And she had courage and tenacity and pride. It was that which kept her head high when she came to the village from her father's smallholding to buy fish from the boats at the wall, and the snide glances of the village women had changed in time to a guarded respect when they saw how the girl was coping with her life.

'I still want to see you, Elizabeth,' his eyes were hard, trying to conceal the passion that blazed behind. 'I've been trying to keep away, but . . .' his voice trailed off.

My heart leapt. I did not care that he was to marry someone else, I did not care that it was wrong, unfair to the new bride, that it would cause gossip. As long as I could see him, as long as he would call, as long as we could talk, and smile and let our eyes meet . . .

So I nodded again and if my smile was slow and my cheeks pale, it was not because my heart did not pound and boom within my breast, driving the blood to my cold limbs.

'Oh God!' The anguish in his exclamation brought up my head and I looked at him again. 'This is madness. I shall see her, tell her I've changed my mind.' ·

'No, Theo. No!' I was surprised at the firmness of my voice. 'No, you must do no such thing. She's right for you, the very one. She has a mind of her own. And courage.' And my words gave me a sort of courage of my own. 'You want a family, a home, a future. I can give you none of those. But yes, come and see me. I shall wait for that. I shall look for you when I am on the quay painting, listen for your step and the sound of your voice. I never expected anything more. And it will be so much better than . . . nothing.'

He took my hand and absentmindedly set about trying to rub away the smudge of vermillion on the end of one finger. With his head bent so, I could look down on the back of his neck and I had to bite my lip to stop my free hand from leaving my lap to caress the thick dark hair. And the silence which fell between us was charged with all the things we could have said, would have said,

94

had fate but dealt us a different hand.

So after a while he raised my stained finger to his lips and stood, not meeting my eyes for which I was glad. He muttered something I did not catch and then he was gone.

Mechanically I extracted a brush from the pot and turned back to the canvas. But though my eyes were dry I could see not a thing but the dark head which had bent so close to my breast. . .

At last I shook myself. For what had changed? Always I had known there was no future between us. And what had we shared that now we must lose? A mild flirtation, chance meetings, laughter and the exchange of thoughts. And he said he wanted that to continue. Ah, I thought, but that cannot be. Now we had acknowledged the strength of the feelings between us and they must either be brought to fruition or to an end. He must know that too; why else should he be so broken when leaving just now. So I accepted that in a little while, if we should meet in the street, he would call a cheerful greeting but his eyes would avert themselves from mine. And if he came to return a book, he would bring her with him. And thus the flames which had grown between us would slowly he smothered.

Gladys came. With her acute sensitivity to my moods, she chivvied me into putting away the work I so obviously was not doing, and coming out with her for some fresh air. Too dejected to argue, I allowed her to collect a shawl and some provisions. We would go for a ride in the trap, she insisted. I had not been out of doors for several days and now the rain had stopped and the fresh air would do me good, she signalled, especially away from chattering people. Gladys had no high opinion of most people's power of speech! And the pony was too fat, she added, and needed the exercise. She would go and harness up right away. And with a swirl of her grey skirt, she was gone.

In my numbed state it seemed no time at all before she trundled down the road past the window. I went to the door and watched as she turned the trap down by the quay and brought it up the street to halt by our front door. From the top of the steps she could help me board the trap with comparative ease and I settled myself into the seat which ran across the front of the trap for Gladys did not want to take my chair.

And so, we clattered up the road out of the village, exchanging brief pleasantries with our neighbours as we passed, Gladys by

95

means of a her beaming smile and jaunty wave. My dull heart began to lift for the sun shone warmly and the breeze was gentle and the summer flowers tangled the hedges, foxglove and campion, red and white valerian, herb robert and lady's bedstraw; a massed bank of colour on every hedge, so that as we progressed along the narrow road we seemed to be moving through a sea of colour.

When we reached the top of the steep hill from the village, Gladys shook the reins on the pony's fat back and he began to trot briskly along the bumpy road. The cushion on which I sat absorbed some of the shock, but I still felt every jolt along my battered spine. I looked at Gladys. She stared at the road ahead and I knew that although she understood my discomfort, she knew it was not my body's pain that so oppressed me. What had Theo told her? Nothing, I expect, in words, but she could read a person's mind and heart with uncanny skill.

So we clattered along the road while I hung on and gritted my teeth and then we had left the hedges behind and were out on the open moorland of the cliffs. The track now ran across patches of grass, for it was little used, and what with the wind of our movement singing in our ears, and the sun and the vast expanse of sky, blue as azure above our heads, the ache beneath my heart began to fade.

I could see the sea now, on our left, darker than the sky with here and there a flick of white, and the fringe of surf that marked the base of the headlands that curved away, mile after mile into the haze of the distance. Gladys stuck up her thumb with a grin and indicated we were almost there. The ground sloped down towards the sea and presently she slowed Jem to a walk as the track became stonier and more uneven where the earth had been swept away by the rain of many years. Near the bottom I had to hold on with both hands while Gladys walked at the pony's head, for the steepness of the hill and tilt of the road made me fear the vehicle would overturn. But just as I was about to question Gladys's judgement, we turned the last corner and were on a beach of flat white sand where great tumbled rocks lay beneath the hot sun like stranded whales.

She helped me down, and with no eyes to watch, it did not matter that I stumbled and fell about until my legs began to obey my brain's commands. And while I limped about on the hard wet sand, Gladys unharnessed Jem and took from the cart the basket of provisions and rug and cushion which she spread in the slight shade of a smooth upright rock where we could sit and watch the breakers cream over the white sand. Gladys released Jem and let him roam where he would; his fat nosebag lay on the cart, and she knew he would not go far from that!

Then Gladys threw off her shawl and sat down beside me, stretching her arms luxuriously in the sun. She wore a grey calico skirt and a white blouse with a pintucked yoke and full sleeves gathered into deep cuffs, pretty yet practical. I regarded her with some surprise. My Gladys was becoming a good looking woman: her tall stocky body had fined down in the last year and had a certain grace, her thick straight hair was wound into a shining bun, and her eyes were very blue in her fresh-complexioned face. It was time I made a new portrait of my friend for she had changed from the friendly puppy of a girl I had always known. And I thought with warmth of Will, whose gentle love had brought about these changes. And selfishly, my bruised heart sank still further within me for how could I manage without Gladys! What should I do when she married?

Suddenly she leapt up, flashing me her wide grin, and hitching her skirt up into the waistband, she pulled off her shoes and stockings and ran down the beach to where Jem trotted to and fro, recoiling in distaste from the pools he sipped. She caught him by the mane and led him to the stream which trickled down the cliff beside the track, and let him drink from the shallow puddle which had formed in the rocks until, refreshed, he wheeled about and she ran at his side down to the sea. I watched them sport in the waves which broke and rushed endlessly as the tide lowered. Gladys's skirt was drenched by the spray as Jem galloped to and fro, his movements comically slowed by the weight of the water. I found myself laughing at their antics, glad of Gladys's happiness, and the sun on my back warmed away some of my fears of the future.

I pulled myself up and limped over to explore the pools which lay between a string of rocks nearby. Most were shallow fissures in the great rocks, teeming with small fish and lined with anemones and mussels and limpets, a strange, alien world beneath the green water. I hobbled on, and there before me was a great pool, deep and still and limpid in the sunlight. I was hot, and

e

without further thought, I threw aside my big hat, stepped out of my shoes and pulled off my clothes, blouse, camisole and pantaloons and dipped my toes into the water.

It was not as cold as I had expected, not as cold as the fresh-water lake where I had swum in France as a child, for this pool had lain beneath the summer sun for hours as the tide receded, warmed by the heat of the rocks. I slid into its depths and found I could swim a dozen strokes before reaching shallow water. At first I was tentative, using my arms rather than my legs to propel me, fearing the affect of this movement on my damaged spine. But gradually I found that here in this element, I felt no pain, and soon I was swimming to and fro across the sunlit pool with the energy and vigour I once had taken for granted.

I paused, breathless, turned onto my back and floated, my body suspended. Gladys had tired of her play and came to stand beside my pool, beaming down at me. I gestured her to join me, but she shook her head; to reveal her legs as she was doing was quite far enough to go against the ingrained taboo of nakedness, though she accepted my own unclothed body with the equanimity of a true lady's maid. I swam again until I was tired, and when I came out of the water, Gladys wrapped a shawl round me and helped me back to the rug where I dressed, using the shawl as a towel.

Gladys busied herself setting out our picnic while I lay and dreamed, both exhausted and refreshed by the events of the day. Presently she tapped my shoulder and I sat up. We moved the cushions and sat in the shade while we ate, for the sun was now fierce overhead. Gladys had done us proud as always; there were marinated pilchards, their bones dissolved in the aromatic juices, crusty bread freshly baked that morning, lettuce and spring onions from her garden plot. The air and the exercise had sharpened our appetites and we both completed our meal with chunky saffron buns, full of currants and lemon peel and Gladys produced with a flourish a bottle of good French wine.

One of the luxuries I had never gone without was a plentiful supply of wine, for the fishermen would meet with French fishing boats at sea and exchange oysters and crabs for barrels and bottles of country wine, the war their politicians fought forgotten in this simple barter. It was on a scale too small to be thought of as smuggling; instead it was a small bonus to the fishermen amongst all the hazards of their lifelong toil. And I was paid for my charcoal sketches of harbour and ships, small miniatures of wives and children, with a bottle or two of wine of my choice. Only for work which was commissioned did I charge, and then just enough to cover the cost of my materials; I had to live with my neighbours so it was the gallery in Penzance that must pay for our simple needs.

Jem came to stand in the shade beneath the rock and Gladys pulled the nosebag over his head while he whickered with anticipation. And I dozed again, and dreamed, and remembered with wonder how all the pain in my mind and body, had floated away in the cool waters of the sunlit pool. And it was not until the sun began to drop towards the sea that, at last, we slowly journeyed back to Polwerris Cove, refreshed and comforted, our skins taut with sun and salt.

Chapter Thirteen

I expected Lambeth Weekes to call early the following week but he was as unpredictable as he was reticent about his affairs; about anyone's affairs, for although he was insufferably inquisitive, I never heard him talk about anyone else, which was remarkable in the village where gossip was the lifeblood. But I was not surprised when the days ticked by until it was Thursday before he appeared.

He came into the room and stood beside the table and fished in one of the pockets of the voluminous great coat he wore despite the warmth of the day. Slowly, he brought out a leather purse and from this he counted out the monies he said Mr Swain from the Penzance gallery had sent me. It seemed to me that my receipts were diminishing each month and I said as much to Lambeth.

'Ah, but 'tis the framing, see Miss Millbrook. That do take up some lot of money, the framing do.'

'Yes, well I think I'll get David Carter to make the frames in future. He did a beautiful job with that painting of his children. And not being able to work any more since losing his leg, I'm sure he'll jump at the chance to earn good money making frames.'

Lambeth Weekes' face changed.

'I don't think Mr Swain would like that at all, Miss Millbrook. Very particular he is about his frames. Gets them made up to his exact requirements. No, I don't think that would be a good idea. I'll tell you what, I'll see if I can't get you a little extra next time, seeing you'm such a good and regular customer.'

It was so glib and so rapid a response that it served to confirm my suspicion that I was being gulled over my receipts. However, until now the money had not greatly concerned me though

Lambeth Weekes would shortly be finding changes made. But not yet, for I had a proposition to put to him. I was just about to begin when be lowered himself onto a chair and he himself began to talk.

'I bin to see her, Miss Millbrook. I bin to see Mary.'

I did not let him know that I had already heard of his visit but merely looked up at him with curiosity, for my interest in this one-time romance was not pretence.

'I asked her to marry me.' He looked away. 'She sent me packing. Just like that. No time to tell her what I felt. No chance to say she would be a wealthy woman.' His gaze came back to my face, defiantly. 'I knows you won't abuse my confidence, Miss Millbrook. 'Cos I got means, you know, plenty of money in the bank. All these years I been hoping Reece Penrose would come to a bad end. I thought 'bout helpin' him on his way too, but . . .' he held his long arms out before him, contemplating their thinness and remembering no doubt the burly strength and dangerous reputation of his rival. Then his dirty hands with their bitten nails returned to playing with the great yellow buttons on his drab green coat. 'I aren't downhearted though. I didn' expect no more'n I got from her, not at first, not after the way I let her down, and the life she've led ever since. But I'll make it up. You see if I don't, Miss Millbrook. You see if I don't.' Then, with an obvious effort, he brought his attention back to the business of my painting orders and while he drew from his pockets the scraps of paper that were supposed to be my accounts, I remembered that day when he had called, soon after he had begun to market my work.

He had been standing in my room when his wandering gaze fell upon a recently completed portrait of Mary Penrose, a picture which had, I thought, captured her graceful carriage as she walked with one upraised hand supporting the laundry basket upon her head. She appeared to be glancing at the viewer, her strong features softened and the large dark eyes interested as she turned. Lambeth Weekes' face had stilled when he looked at the painting and when he spoke his voice was croaky with emotion. 'I'll buy that picture, Miss Millbrook,' he said. 'I don't care how much it d'cost. I got to have it.' I had looked at him with astonishment, at where he stood, gazing at the portrait, cap in hand and with yearning in his eyes.

101

'I'm sorry, Mr Weekes. It is not for sale. I am building up a collection of such informal portraits. I want a record of daily life in this village, of people going about their work. . .' My words tailed off for the constriction in my throat. I could not tell him it was to be a legacy for my son, for Guy; a record of the years of my life after I had lost him. . . Some way of sharing with him the time he could never know with me. . .

Then he had turned to me with desperation and told me at first hand the story I had heard once or twice before, the story of his betrayal of the woman he loved, and watching his tormented face as he spoke, I had no doubt that his unfulfilled passion was still the driving force in his life. As he finished, he had turned back to the picture. 'Let me 'ave it Miss Millbrook.' And he went over to the table and pulled out a handful of sovereigns from the depths of one of his pockets. 'For you 'tis only a picture of a washer-woman. To me . . .' his voice trailed away. Then he thrust his hand into his pocket again. 'More. I'll give you whatever you ask!'

'Stop! All right. You can have the picture.' I hardened my voice. 'I'll take what you've put on the table because that painting was important to me.'

'Not like it is to me, my dear.' His voice had dropped almost to a whisper and he lifted the picture, unframed as it was, and held it before him.

'I'll need to wrap it.' He looked round anxiously for something to cover it and picked up a folded tablecloth which Gladys had just placed on the table. 'This'll do. I'll bring it back dreckly.' And before I could protest he was on his way to the door fearing I might change my mind and not let him have her portrait.

At the door he turned. 'Don't say nothin' about this to no one will 'ee Miss Millbrook? I don't want they to know,' and he jerked his head to indicate the village at large. 'I would'n like it to get back to . . . she.'

'I'll tell no one, Mr Weekes. Don't worry.' My voice was curt. It was hard to be sorry for such a man, but he had paid dearly for his cold pride and would go on paying for the rest of his life.

But all that had been more than two years ago. Now it was my turn to call on him for a promise of secrecy.

'Mr Weekes. I have always found you to be a man of discretion. I need someone to take a letter to a place in North Cornwall. It has to be done in the strictest confidence and I think you are the man for the job.'

His eyes glittered and I could sense the relief that I was not going to pursue the matter of the payments from the gallery.

'Well now, ma'am. North Cornwall. Tha's a brer way, Miss Millbrook.' I noticed that Lambeth often stressed his Cornish accent when talking to me; perhaps he thought it would make me feel he was stupid and gullible. Far from it; I had recognised his sharp intellect long ago. 'That means I won't be able to do my usual work for a while. My customers won't like that.'

'I realise that. But if you go to Plymouth on the *Heart of Gold* or *Araminta*, you can hire a horse for the rest of the journey. It's only about fifteen miles from there. The whole trip should take you no more than three or four days at the most.'

'Well, I'm not so sure I can do it my dear. I'd like to oblige you, but I do have my other people to consider, if you get my meaning.'

'I get your meaning all too well Mr Weekes. I can see it will be an expensive trip. But never mind, you're the first person I have asked. There are plenty of young men in the village who would look forward to a jaunt to Plymouth and beyond on my behalf.'

'Well I 'speck I can manage it, to oblige a lady like yourself. You'd better tell me what I 'as to do.'

I sighed and wished I did not have to depend on this man; the only reason I chose him was for his undoubted discretion but when I spoke my voice was confident and steady. 'No one is to know your destination beyond Plymouth, Mr Weekes. You'll have arrangements to make no doubt. Come and see me when you're ready and I'll tell you then what I want you to do.'

He nodded his head. ' 'Tis Thursday t'day. I 'speck 'twill be early next week,' his eyes met mine. 'Somethin' on account 'fore I go and the rest when I gets back?'

'Very well. I'll ask about the passage money myself. I'll see Captain George.'

His face changed. 'No need for you to bother yourself, Miss Millbrook.'

But I interrupted him. 'No trouble Mr Weekes. I'll see you next week.' And I turned back towards my painting easel in abrupt dismissal.

*   *   *   *

I thought hard about my plan over the weekend. I fully understood (who better?) the danger in my scheme. And I also realised
with a wry smile that the idea had been in formation ever since
the previous winter when I had seen the announcement in the
Cornishman: 'To Sir Charles and Lady Iris Trelawne, on 4th
November 1812, the gift of a son, Claude Percival, brother to
Mary Louisa Stephanie.'

At the time, I had smiled maliciously, imagining the furore that
would come about if it were to be known that Lady Francoise
Elizabeth Trelawne was still alive and living in the same county.
And that the little Trelawnes were the fruits of a bigamous
marriage! I had shown the item to Gladys and we laughed
together, and then I had tossed the paper aside as of no relevance
to me in my new life.

Now however, I went over my scheme again and again. There
must be no mistake. When Charles discovered my existence, I
was well aware that he might try once more to kill me for now I
would be an even greater threat to his security. I sat back and
imagined the thoughts which would run through his mind; the
threat of a charge of attempted murder, the certain charge of
bigamy. The scandal . . . for that is what would concern Charles
more than any moral issue; scandal. Talk that would besmirch the
great name of Trelawne. Snide looks from his workers at the
mighty landowner who had been brought to heel at last. And
Society women who would no longer took warmly at him, at the
man who had broken just too many of the laws designed to
safeguard their privileged way of life. Oh yes. I knew the way
Charles's mind would work, even though I had been brought
close to death before accepting the truth about the man I had
married.

So I sat and thought. A frisson of fear ran over me as I
imagined his face when he received my letter; when he saw once
more my seal on the back of the envelope. . .

The fear woke me to reality. I drew a deep breath, took a sheet
of paper and began to draft the letter, a letter which would
rebound either to my benefit or to my undoubted death. And the
awareness of danger cleared my mind and I sat and wrote with a
careful hand.

I had to bear in mind that Lambeth Weekes would most certainly read the letter, for his devious mind would have to discover the contents of a missive important enough to be delivered by hand in such secrecy. I gnawed at the end of my pen with irritation and tore up what I had so carefully written and began again. This time it seemed right.

Sir Charles,

My congratulations on the birth of your son. I expect your good wife and little daughter are equally delighted at the increase in your family.

You will, I am sure, be interested to hear that I was ill for a long time but am now much recovered and would dearly like to hear news of your other son, Guy. Indeed, it would give me the greatest pleasure to get into contact with him once more. But I feel it necessary to seek your permission before renewing an acquaintance that has been so greatly affected by the course of events. Perhaps one day when you are in Plymouth we could meet to exchange news? Either at Pettigrew's or at Woodlands, you remember, the school I once attended. It you care to give a note to the bearer of this letter saying when, in the next week or two, we might meet, I shall be able to send you my confirmation and the venue by post. Should you, however, not wish to resume our acquaintance, I shall take your silence as permission to write directly to Guy in France.

I await your response.

I was about to scrawl my signature, 'Francoise' at the bottom of the page when I remembered Lambeth Weekes. After a moment's thought I decided to leave the letter open on the table when he came to collect it, to give him plenty of opportunity to read it, then sign it quickly and fold it up. I was sure he would not bother to re-open the letter once he had already seen its contents. I particularly did not want the seal interfered with; the seal of my signet ring, the 'C' of the Curvoisier family encircling the bunch of grapes and I smiled grimly at the thought of Charles's face when he recognised my mother's family seal.

I looked at the letter for a long time. There was enough detail to convince Charles of my identity but the contents were innocuous enough for the eyes of Lambeth Weekes. I was still uneasy at having to use his services, but I knew he would keep his counsel. I knew too that Charles's subtle mind would try and discover my whereabouts from the messenger, but Weekes would stick to the story I planned to brief him with; how a manservant had approached him as he left a Plymouth inn and offered him good money to deliver this letter, his instructions being to return to the same inn, the Golden Hind, and stay there until someone called for the reply.

How I wished it was Theo who was going as my envoy! I had in fact, toyed with the notion of telling him my story but the troubled emotions between us forbade that luxury. And besides, his ship was nearing readiness and he was much involved with all the work entailed in starting his business.

No. It had to be Lambeth Weekes. I would warn him most strongly of the risk of an indiscretion; that he must on no account mention my name or my whereabouts. I knew the expedition was fraught with risk but I felt the covert threat in my letter that I would write to Guy if I did not receive a reply, would guarantee the safe return of my messenger.

And of course I showed Gladys the letter and told her of my plan. For her safety too was at risk if it should fail.

And so it was that on the following Wednesday, Lambeth Weekes stood on the deck of a fishing boat bound for Falmouth from where he would take passage on the *Araminta* to Plymouth, the next stage in the journey to Trevingey; a journey that was to cause momentous changes to both our lives. . .

Chapter Fourteen

A day or two after Lambeth Weekes left on his commission for me, the early morning haze promised later sunshine and I asked Gladys and a boy from the village to push me along the clifftop paths for a full day's painting. We found a place beside an outcrop of rock from which there was a dramatic view of the fissured cliffs, with mile after mile of mighty headlands lapped by a sea of moving, dancing blues. When Gladys was satisfied that I had all I needed, they left me, she planning to return with a picnic lunch at noon and the boy, Jathan, would come and help to take me back at the end of the afternoon.

I was glad when they had gone and I could be alone with my thoughts. And I smiled to myself that the only reason I was here and not in the village was because I knew Theo would be away all day in Penzance. For he had not stopped seeing me as I had feared. True, our meetings were brief and unplanned, but I lived for those snatched moments, for conversations, so light on the surface, yet so charged with feeling, for the exchange of looks and the proof I saw in his eyes that nothing had changed between us, despite his betrothal to Gwendoline.

It was a beautiful summer morning and the sun was already warm. I pulled on the hat I needed to shade my eyes and set to work. The breeze sang through the clumps of long grass that interspersed the carpet of heather and low gorse at my feet and the sun danced and glittered on the shifting sea that heaved and pushed against the foot of the cliffs. Now and again a bigger wave would climb slowly up the cliff face in a cloud of spray, pause in a moment of suspense then slide back with a crash and roar and I turned to my canvas excited by the challenge of the beauty all about me.

I painted. All my senses were alert and I worked with a buoyant delight. I could hear men working somewhere below the cliffs towards the village: Jathan had told me they were repairing a boat which had grounded there. It was lucky, he said that its bottom had found a piece of shingle beach, rare enough on this section of coast. The thump of hammers and clang of metal and the wild laughter of the gulls all added to the vigour and excitement of the scene.

Then, breaking through my concentration, there came a desperate cry.

I put down my brush. Could it have been a gull? No, for there it was again! A cry for help! The sound seemed to come from the headland beyond the bay!

I picked up the telescope which I liked to bring with me on these trips and with it I scanned the distant cliff. There! A boy was clinging to a ledge on the cliff face, half way between the top and the fringe of surf. Through the glass I could see his terror-stricken face. He seemed to be looking straight at me! But of course he could see me, for my chair and light clothing would stand out clearly in that barren place.

I pulled off my shawl and stood up and holding on to the chair, waved the shawl above my head. Then, through the glass, I saw him point down to the foot of the cliff. I tracked his pointing arm with the spyglass. Oh God! A crumpled figure lay amidst a fall of scree only feet from the breaking waves! After a moment's frozen shock I waved again.

I must fetch help!

I dumped my painting gear and took hold of the chair. Without it for support I would not be able to walk far on this terrain. But after the first few yards which I covered easily, the wheels became stuck in a rut and I could not move.

I thought of the boy, watching my distant figure with desperate hope. I could not let him down. So I released the chair and lurched forward. There were only a few yards to go before the path turned a rock and I would be concealed from the boy's anxious vision. He was expecting me to bring help. And so I must. But it was only will power which kept me on my feet along those few yards of path. Rounding the rock, I collapsed against its side and caught my breath.

The pain in my back, always present in some degree, stabbed

a tattoo of warning against this exertion. I thought of the mile-long path back to the village, of the stony track with its steep undulations and I prayed desperately for strength. Then I took a deep breath and pulled myself upright.

And as I did so, the noise of hammering from the cove reached my panicking brain. Of course! If I could get a message to the men working on the beach below, they could quickly reach the boys. But how? From my feet the moorland sloped gently for a short distance, then the incline steepened abruptly until it reached the edge of the vertical jagged cliffs. I looked at the heather and gorse which covered the slope, seeking a narrow animal track I might follow but there was none visible in the dense blanket. And I looked at my silly satin shoes. Thought of the boys. And set off.

I had covered no more than a dozen steps across the first gentle slope before I tripped and fell. I rolled painfully and sat up, my head spinning. But as I clutched the ground to stem the dizziness, I knew that this was how I must traverse the steep slope towards the cliff edge.

I pushed myself sideways and met the first prickles of gorse with my back. The myriad of needlepoints seared my skin through my smock and blouse and thin knickerbockers. It was agony. Too much to endure. But I was on the slope. Surely it could not get worse. And there was no alternative. So I pushed myself off again.

It was no more than twenty yards to the cliff edge, but despite the acute angle of the ground, the low clumps of heather slowed and stopped my descent many times. Each time when I paused, I sat up to see how near to the cliff edge I had come. And as I drew nearer, I had to pause and wait until the spinning sky slowed enough for me to get my bearings.

Then, at last, I rolled clear of the torturing cushion of prickles and was on the rabbit-cropped grass of the cliff top. When the dizziness had passed, I crawled cautiously forward and found myself peering down an almost sheer rock face to where an outcrop at the bottom blocked off all view of the beach. My heart sank with sick disappointment. I could actually see the stern of the ship on which the men were working, could hear their incessant hammering, but it was impossible to shout and wave to draw their attention.

I dropped my head onto my arms in defeat. What could I do?

How long could the boys last? The tide would soon reach the lad on the shore. And the other one, the boy on the cliff; he had seen me go for help. He was depending on me, counting on me!

I raised my head and looked down again. What chance would my voice have over the crash of the waves and the clamour of the men's hammering. But it was my only chance: the boys' only chance.

I screamed. A long primaeval scream that sent the gulls hurtling from the cliffs in panic flight.

But as the echoes died away, the hammering continued unabated. I screamed again, with desperate urgency.

And this time there seemed to be a pause in the pattern of hammering. Into the pause I shrieked once more.

The hammering stopped.

In the sudden silence when even the gulls were hushed, I yelled 'Help! Help!' until I heard an answering shout. Then I dropped my head onto my hands again and sobbed with wild relief. But soon another shout brought my head up and I peered over the cliff edge once more.

There were two men in a boat coming round the stern of the beached ship. One man was rowing, while the other looked up towards the cliffs, his hand shading his eyes.

I cupped my hands round my mouth and shouted slowly, spacing the words so that they could be heard over the surf.

'Boys . . . over . . . cliff . . . round . . . rocky . . . point . . . Second . . . cove.' And I gestured wildly in the direction they must go.

'Right!' The word came back to me on the wind, terse and grim and I watched the dinghy go back round the stern knowing they would soon reappear. And more quickly than I had dared hope, two boats came into sight, three men in the first, two in the second. I could see coils of rope at their feet and blessed their forethought and watched them rowing hard against the tide. Soon they rounded the first headland and were lost to my sight.

And then I became aware of my body, burning all over from the myriad of scratches and imbedded thorns. The thin sleeves of my smock were ripped and the stuff of my blouse was stuck to my skin with sweat or blood. I tried to sit up, tried to find a position that did not exacerbate the pain of the prickles. But every movement seemed to make matters worse so I slowly lowered myself face down once more.

I wondered how long it would be before they reached the boys. Would they be in time? How long to get them both into the boats. Then back to the harbour. And I tried not to work out how long it would be before someone could be sent to the clifftop for me, for my body had the strength to make no further movement.

Gradually the world seemed to shrink into the place where I lay. My back was burning, whether from the sun's heat or from the thorns I did not know. I allowed my head to collapse onto my arms, and closed my eyes to stop the whirling of the cliffs and then I spun away through a dark, roaring tunnel into blissful oblivion.

When next I opened my eyes, I found I was in my own room with Gladys sitting at the side of my bed, anxiously watching my face.

I tried to speak to her, tried to smile. But I seemed not to be in control of my body. Half of my mind recognised that I was in the laudanum induced state of blurred reality that I had so often sought after my accident. Part of me wondered at Gladys for having administered to me a dose, remembering her fear and reluctance to touch it. But most of all I was grateful for the other-world respite it gave my body. So I floated off on its magic carpet of sharpened image and blurred reality; off into time and space and temporary freedom from pain.

My next consciousness was of women's voices in the next room. I opened my eyes and waited for my mind's confusion to clear. Then the door opened and Gladys came over to the bed. Mrs Snell and Mrs Fisher wanted to know how I was. Gladys's face was clouded with anxiety so I smiled reassuringly and told her to bring the women in. She looked at me a little doubtfully but turned to the door and beckoned to my neighbours.

They approached the bed with some caution, but took the chairs Gladys offered and beamed at me. They chattered brightly. How was I? One of the boys, Toby, the boy who had slipped down the cliff, had a broken leg and the doctor was worried about his back but 'we 'specs he'll be all right. Lucky you was there Miss Millbrook. Lucky there was a boat so near.'

'Lucky you was able to walk that far, Miss Millbrook.' Mrs Snell had a glint in her eye that did not match the sweetness of her remark. 'Raymond Johns said you was in some state when he found you. He said you wouldn' be able to move for days.' I read the challenge in her eyes. You're just a sham, she was thinking. Nothing wrong with someone who can cross the pathless moor. Nothing wrong with this little madam.

Mrs Fisher also recognised the insinuation for she began to prattle rapidly about the fish her grandson had brought home that week. And did I know there was chicken pox in the village again.

My skin burned. I could feel places where prickles were working to the surface and I had a sudden desire to see what my body looked like, and fuelled by anger at the other woman's snide remarks, I interrupted the chatter.

'Do you want to see for yourself why I can't walk? Is that it Mrs Snell?'

She reddened and started to bluster but I took no notice. I pushed back the bed covers until there was nothing over me but the old sheet which Gladys had wrapped round me to prevent the salve from rubbing off onto the bedlinen.

'Light the candle.' As I spoke to Mrs Fisher I became aware that it was evening already and the curtains were drawn against the lowering sun. Then, when the candle had flamed, I peeled back the sheet.

My body looked as if I had a bad case of scarlet fever. My skin was nowhere free of reddening, but there were patches which bled and wept where the thorns had torn away the skin. Gladys had done what she could when they brought me home and removed all the prickles she could see. But there were many more, small and sharp, just under the skin. For these she had smothered my whole body in a yellow ointment and this added a ghastly sheen to the burning rash. I myself stared in some astonishment, but I was childishly glad there was so much visual proof of the tortured burning I suffered.

'Oh my dear love!' Mrs Fisher exclaimed. 'Oh my 'andsome!' Mrs Snell was biting her lip and the look in her eyes when they met mine was of shock and remorse. But I had not finished.

'And now you can see my back. You can see what stops me walking.' I spoke through gritted teeth as I struggled to turn myself. They both protested, told me not to move, but I turned anyway.

There was a gasp from Mrs Fisher, and a choked sob from Mrs Snell. My back, of course, was covered with the same scratches

112

and contusions as on the front of my body, but I knew it was not that which so shocked them, but the livid scar which crossed my lower back from side to side, an inch wide and jagged like a fork of lightning. That much I had seen for myself whenever Gladys held up a mirror at my insistence. And where it crossed my spine the scar was further pitted and ridged. 'A quarter of an inch deeper and you would not be here,' the doctor had said. And I had wept with frustration for that elusive quarter of an inch, for the blessed relief from pain that so nearly had been mine. . .

The women began to speak, both at once and none of us heard the door open. I was suddenly aware of an abrupt silence and I looked over my shoulder. Theo stood beside the two women, staring down at me, his lips tightly pressed together and his face pale.

I tried to move and could not. Then the sheet was drawn gently round me and he laid me back on the pillows with infinite care.

'Has the doctor seen you?' His voice had a rough edge to it.

I shook my head. 'I'm all right. I told Gladys. In a day or two it will all be healed. The scratches, I mean.'

Both women were now talking, saying that yes, I did ought to have the doctor, that I was in some state, my lore, the poor thing.

But Theo turned a flinty glance on them.

'She should not be having visitors. I'm going now. I only called to say that Toby is much better. He can move his toes. His leg is broken but his spine is all right. And the other boy, the one on the ledge, he's only got a few scratches.'

I closed my eyes in relief, selfishly glad that my pain was not for nothing.

The women were carefully replacing my blankets, and then they went, with promises of help, anything we can do, anything. And I knew that now they meant it.

I looked up at Theo who was still standing beside the bed.

'I did knock. No one heard. Gladys nodded me to go inside.'

'It doesn't matter.' But it did. Not the nakedness which he had seen. I had painted too many models when in Paris with my uncle to be embarrassed by nudity and I knew too that my body was still good. But for him to have seen the scratches and the blood and worst of all, that hideous scar. . .

'I shall get the doctor for you now. He's still with the boy. No!' he held up his hand to stem my protest. 'Those thorns will be weeks working themselves out. He can make you comfortable in an hour.'

I closed my eyes against the tears that were suddenly near. To be taken charge of, to be over-ruled, to be made to feel fragile. . . All emotions against which I had fought so hard for most of my life! But now as I lay back on the pillows, the pain of my body subsided beneath a warm wash of pleasure. I felt too weak, indeed I was too weak for protest. I wanted only to escape into sleep. And to take with me the image of the man who stood over me, his face reflecting those same conflicting emotions which swept me whenever the thought of him crept into my heart.

The outer door closed behind the women and Gladys entered in some confusion for they had indicated to her what had happened. She seemed reassured to find Theo standing aloof from my bed, and I myself so composed and still. Then he bent over me and cupped my face briefly in his hands, nodded a farewell and was gone, the door closing gently behind him.

And I lay back against the pillows, drugged with laudanum and pain and the sweet languorous image of my love, and with the touch of his hands still warm upon my face.

Chapter Fifteen

It was not old Doctor Morrison who knocked briskly on the door half an hour later, but a stranger, a younger man whom I had never seen before.

'I'm Doctor Lawrence,' he announced as Gladys brought him into my room. 'I believe I have to take a look at you Miss Millbrook.'

I tried to sit up as I replied to his greeting but be waved me back. 'Lie still, lie still.' He put his bag on the table as he spoke and turned to the bed and drew back the sheet.

Gladys had put on some more of the salve but the redness and irritation looked, if anything, worse than before. Certainly the discomfort was intense for whichever way I turned there were shooting stabs of pain from another hidden barb.

'Hm. Yes. Well, this is going to take a little while. Get your girl to hold my glass for me, will you?' He turned to take several pairs of tweezers from his bag, and a large magnifying glass. 'She'd be better on your other side, out of my way.' So Gladys climbed across my body and knelt on the bed, holding the glass where he directed.

It took a long time. His fingers feathered themselves across my skin, sensitive to the slightest thorn, using the tweezers with deft precision. I did not mind the pain; it was infinitely preferable to the irritation of the spines. So while he worked, I lay on my back, teeth gritted, and studied this Doctor Lawrence whom Theo had sent to me.

He was a man of middle age and his skin had the sheen of good living. Perhaps too much good living for there was a hint of jowl at his jaw and his brocade waistcoat was tightly stretched across his chest. His clothes were smarter than one would expect in a country physician with his carefully folded neckcloth and well cut breeches, and there was a vanity and complacency in his studied movements. But his face was jovial and kind and when Gladys lit a candle and held it in her other hand, the eyes which glinted in its light became concentrated and intent on the work and his hands were gentle as a child's.

It was not long before he paused and pulled off that elegant neckcloth and soon his jacket too was flung across a chair. The light from the candle washed across the plains of his face, deepening the shadows of lines and contours. Upward light has always intrigued me and indeed, was a hallmark of my paintings and I presently found that by trying to commit his face to memory for a later portrait, I was able to escape some of the effects of his ministrations.

Presently he straightened up.

'A cup of tea, I think, before we start the other side.' He smiled at me with unexpected warmth and Gladys went off to get the tea, glad of the chance to stretch her cramped legs.

He flexed his fingers and turned his head from side to side to relax his neck. Then he looked about the room in frank curiosity and when he saw the half-finished painting that stood on the easel, he crossed to examine it.

'Why this is very fine!' he exclaimed, standing back the better to view my picture of two old ladies making lace.

'Thank you. I enjoy working on portraits.' Encouraged by his interest, I went on, 'I'd like to paint one of you.'

'A portrait of me!' There was no mistaking his vanity, but in him it was a likeable trait. 'Well, well! I won't have much time to sit, you know. Polwerris Cove doesn't see my presence very often.'

'That's all right. No doubt you will come to see young Toby once or twice more. I will only need a short sitting later on.'

Just then Gladys pushed open the door and entered carrying a laden tray. The doctor's eyes brightened when he saw the slices of saffron and chunks of hevva cake on the plate which she offered him and he set about the food in a way which brought a smile of pleasure to Gladys's face.

Between them they helped me to sit up and I sipped my tea with relief. If Doctor Lawrence could remove as many barbs from my back as he had done on this side, I should at last be able to

116

find a comfortable place to lie and sit and the dread of an endless night of discomfort began to recede.

'Right then, on with the good work!' he exclaimed when he had finished his second cup of tea and several pieces of cake. And with that he helped to turn me over. 'We'll bring the pillows down and put them under your chest, like that. Then you can rest your arms on them so that I can reach. And you'll be able to breathe without having to turn your head. Good. So off we go again.'

I was more comfortable than I had dared to hope. Gladys took up her kneeling position opposite the doctor and held up the candle. There was a moment of silence and then he spoke.

'How did that happen?' His voice had an edge to it and I knew it was the scar to which he referred.

I drooped my head over the pillow which cradled me. 'I was shot,' I replied tersely.

'Shot!' There was a moment of silence. Then he went on. 'Oh well, that's not on my agenda for today, is it?' And he picked up a pair of tweezers and continued his painstaking search.

I lay quiet. I knew I should be more forthcoming. He was a doctor after all, and his curiosity was professional. But my self-imposed secrecy was hard to break. So the clock ticked on and the little dish on the bed received more slivers of thorn, some the size of a pin head, others thicker, dark shadows drawn from under the skin.

At last I spoke.

'The shooting I cannot talk about because of the others involved. But afterwards I almost died.'

'What is the degree of paralysis?' For he had noticed my wheelchair.

I paused. 'At first, for about two months, I could not move my legs at all. But one morning I felt sensation in my feet and after that I was able to move a little. Mrs Perry, that was Gladys's grandmother, worked miracles on me. It was she who made me move, forced me to get up, forced me to take my weight.'

'And how is it now?' He had not paused for my reply and I could feel the hands moving across my shoulders.

I sighed. 'Sometimes, like now in fact, my back is almost painless. Sometimes I can walk about for quite a time. I limp, of course,' I added. 'Then, suddenly, there is such an intensity of pain shooting down into my legs that they simply fold under me.

117

Hence the chair.'

'Go on.' His tone implied that I had more to say.

But what more was there to tell him? 'That's all there is to say. Two men in the village made the chair. I used to shuffle along with a kitchen chair for support and sit on it when I must. But sometimes I could not get back. Twice they had to carry me home. After that I would not go out. So Jack Symons and Percy Kellow made the chair.'

No need to tell him of my gratitude and delight. Of the freedom they gave me with that chair. And they had been so reluctant to take payment. 'It's all made of bits and pieces, nothing bought,' they insisted. A cane armchair they had acquired, wheels from an old pram, an extra wheel at the side with which I could propel the chair on level ground. I called it Pegasus, my magic steed. . .

'How long ago was this, Miss Millbrook?'

'Three years.' No harm in him knowing that.

Until now I had not flinched as the doctor's hands drew out the spines. But as he approached the area of the scar I became more and more tense.

'Relax, woman, for God's sake!' he suddenly exclaimed in irritation. 'How can I get this damn prickle if you keep jumping away!'

'I'm sorry.' I spoke through clenched teeth.

The hands continued their work, soft as a woman's, but each touch in the vicinity of the scar was like a burning brand. I clutched at the pillow beneath my arms and buried my head into it, trying not to scream at the man to stop, to leave me alone, to forget the thorns. Just to stop and give me peace. But I knew if I opened my mouth to speak, a choked scream would burst out.

I could feel the perspiration on my arms now and the pillow in which my head was buried was damp. Time was suspended. After you count to fifty, I told myself, he will have finished. But I could not complete the first count to fifty, nor the second. So I stopped counting and ground my teeth and burrowed deeper into the pillow, turning my head when I must to gasp a mouthful of air.

At last, at last, his voice came.

'There. That's it as far as I can see. Let's get you comfortable.'

And with Gladys to help, Gladys with tears wet upon her cheeks, they helped me to sit up, propped upon fresh pillows. I leaned back gingerly, but found that the needle sharp pains of the thorns had largely gone.

'You will probably find a few more working out in the next day or two. I will call again next Tuesday when I come to see how Toby is getting along. That will give you a little time to heal and I will be able to see how many thorns I have missed. All right?' His voice was brisk and businesslike as ever, but the bright blue eyes were kind.

I nodded my thanks, suddenly too weak for words. I think Gladys gave him more tea, but I drifted off into a light sleep and when I aroused myself, Doctor Lawrence had gone.

Theo came. It was late, very late, but our lamp still burned. Gladys was just about to go to her bed but she ushered him into my room with a smile. He came and stood by my bed as he had done earlier, but this time I was modestly clad in a fresh nightgown, my hair had been vigorously brushed and most of the traces of the day's ordeal had been washed away. Or so I thought.

'God, you look terrible! How are you?'

I gave a wry smile. 'About how I look, I think,' but as the concern in his eyes deepened, 'No, I'm much more comfortable. Your Doctor Lawrence is a ministering angel if ever there was. Thank you.'

I did not know then that Theo had waited for him on the hill above the village, and that he had ridden with the doctor for a couple of miles along the road towards Helston, discussing my condition freely, without fear of being overheard by the ubiquitous ears of the village.

Now he stood looking down at me with that disturbing intensity.

'Let him do whatever he suggests, Elizabeth.' He rarely used my Christian name. It was not the name with which I had grown up, being the second of my Saint's names, an English name to please my English father, and never used by my French mother to whom I was Francoise unless I behaved badly. Perhaps that was why, when I recovered from the shooting and all that followed, I had subconsciously reverted to my 'bad girl' name, knowing that it was my own recalcitrance which had brought me to this pass.

I smiled. I was too weak, too tired to dissemble. What I felt showed in my eyes. I knew I showed too much, saw the reaction on the man's face. Saw how his eyes became aware and responded to the look in mine, until the joining of our gaze was tangible as an embrace.

But this was all wrong. Something must be done, something must be said, to bring an end to this forbidden intimacy.

So I asked, 'How is Gwendoline?' His face changed, the smouldering passion in his eyes fled, leaving them bleak and despairing and he muttered something I did not catch. I closed my own eyes lest they should betray me, should show how I longed for him to kneel down beside me and take me into his arms. I thought of his first wife, an invalid for so many years. I could not, must not, draw him to the bed of another frail and sickly woman. And anyway, there was Gwen to whom he was pledged. . .

So I groped for some words where we could meet in safety. Thought of the boy, of Toby, who lay in another cottage in the village with his badly broken leg. Asked of him. Shut my eyes. Summoned Gladys. Said I was sorry, but I feel so tired, it must be that draught from Doctor Lawrence. Thanked him again for his concern and help. And sent him away. . .

And then I lay back of the pillows, my body forgotten and my mind in torment while I went over and over those moments when our eyes had met and our hearts were open to one another.

But not for long. Gladys came back into the room after closing the door behind Theo, and she busied herself about me, settling the pillows, smoothing the sheets, and I could see that she understood my hurt and gradually her small ministrations calmed me. And she did not question or refuse my plea for another dose of laudanum to help me through the coming night.

I rose next morning only a little later than usual, astonished at how much better I felt; the salve which Gladys reapplied cool and comforting and the redness of my skin was already fading. As soon as I had breakfasted I set up a new canvas and started on the portrait of the doctor while his image was still so sharp in my mind.

There were numerous interruptions for Toby Pearce's mother came to give me her thanks and a rooted cutting of the rose that had rambled over their cottage for generations. I was pleased, for the plant was flourishing in an earthenware pot and together we decided against which wall it would be happiest. Mrs Pearce was pleasantly surprised to see me up and working for she had been told by the men how they had found me in a state of collapse.

'Oh, I'm better now, Mrs Pearce. The doctor removed the thorns and I slept quite well. Better than Toby did, I'm sure.'

And while she spoke of her son and the tide that had begun to wash over his feet before the boats arrived, the other lad, Jack came to see me.

He told us how the pair of them had been collecting gulls eggs when Toby had fallen. Jack had climbed down to him and made him as comfortable as he could before trying to scale the cliff to fetch help, but he had found himself under an overhang, unable to go forward or back. And that was when he had seen my seated figure in the distance.

'I guessed it was you, Miss Millbrook, though 'twas too far to be certain. And I was that worried 'cos I didn' see as how you could go and get help. Not with your wheelchair and all.' And while he spoke I could see his fists clench in his lap, and his eyes were dark with remembered fear.

But we shared some of Gladys's lemonade and when my visitors left I went on with my work, knowing there would be more interruptions but glad of the happy outcome of the affair.

When Doctor Lawrence next called, he found me seated before the easel working on his portrait, relaxed and smiling, a different woman from the one be had treated only days before.

Gladys came to help once more and the doctor examined my skin with meticulous care and was pleased to report that not many prickles had escaped his eye. Those few he dealt with and I did not mind the small discomfort. But when he began to examine my back and the area of my scar, I shivered with dread and clutched the pillow to my mouth. His fingers gentled themselves across my skin, but now and then they would probe and press and once his touch caused such a flame of pain that my legs jerked in spasm. At last, just when I was about to raise my head from the pillow and beg him to stop, he gave a grunt of satisfaction and drew the sheet over me once more.

'Make yourself comfortable, I want to talk.'

f

So Gladys helped me to pull on my clothes and presently we sat at the table and he demolished a plate of cold meat and pickles while I sipped at a tisane of camomile, drained by the onslaught of pain he had caused.

'I examined you like that because I think I can help you. As I expected, there are two causes for your disability.' He had pushed aside his empty plate, having finished his meal with a dish of apple tart and clotted cream. 'You have a chronic inflammation to the nerves of your lower spine which I can do little to relieve, but you also have a foreign body lodged just to the left of your spine. When you are at rest, this floats free as it were, but after standing or sitting for a while, it bears down and presses on the nerves, sending such spasms through your legs that it causes you to fall. I think I can remove that foreign body.'

I felt the blood leave my face.

'No! No, you cannot believe I would let you attempt any such thing! It's unthinkable! Just a touch is unbearable, how do you think I could lie there and have you cut and probe . . .' My words caught in my throat and I buried my face in my hands as if to blot out the very thought of such an operation.

He reached across the table and touched my shoulder.

'I understand. But this is where I can help. I have a friend, a brilliant young doctor who has been experimenting with a chemical which can induce unconsciousness at will. This can give a surgeon time to perform complex surgery while the patient is unaware that anything is happening. And after the operation, the patient wakes up and has suffered none of the shock that as you know, kills so many who ought otherwise to recover.'

I looked at him doubtfully. 'You said he has been experimenting. How many times has he used this chemical? And how is it administered?'

'He started using it on dogs and cats of course. At first he would use either too much or too little, but now he is confident of the correct amount to use. He pours drops of the mixture onto a pad and holds it over the patient's nose. When they lose consciousness, which takes a minute or so, the surgeon can then start work. My friend continues to drip the chemical onto the pad to maintain the same level of unconsciousness, watching all the time that there are no adverse signs. When the work is finished, the patient begins to come round.' He regarded me earnestly. 'I want you to give it some thought. The area where I should be working is very close to the surface and I could actually feel the obstruction with my fingers. I think it would take very little time to remove it.'

'How many times has your friend used this substance on human patients?'

Doctor Lawrence had the grace to look a little discomfited. 'He has used it with another surgeon three times, and with myself twice.' He gave a wry grin and went on. 'I must tell you that two of these patients died, but that was from loss of blood in complicated surgery. The other three came round and apart from a little nausea and sickness they made an excellent recovery.'

'So I would be experiment number six?'

'Yes, if you must put it like that. But think what you could gain, freedom from that chronic pain, and perhaps the ability to walk freely after a time.'

'After a time! Do you mean I might he bedridden for a while?'

'Oh my dear, certainly not! I envisage a day or two at most, the actual surgery would take very little time to heal. What I should have said was that the recovery to the nerves of your back might not be instant, the obstruction has been causing damage for three years now, and it may take some time for the area to repair itself after so long a time.' He took up my hand which was now pleating the edge of the tablecloth. 'I promise you I will not make matters worse. If I do not find it as simple a job as I expect, I shall leave well alone, I don't want to paralyse you.'

My breath caught in shock but then I gave a little breathless laugh. 'I should think not indeed! But you must give me time to think about this, Doctor Lawrence. I could not possibly make a decision right now for if I did, the answer would be no!'

'I understand,' he gave my hand a squeeze. 'I shall call again next week when I come to the village to see Toby. Until then, give it some thought. I would like to see you walking straight, a lovely young woman like you . . .' And he was suddenly lost for words.

'There's something else though,' I looked at him directly. 'How much would this surgery cost, with two doctors to pay?'

'My friend, Doctor Gerald Fitzsimmons, will ask no fee since he will gain more material for the medical paper he is writing. As for my own fee, Mr Pentire has told me . . .'

'No!' I interrupted him vehemently. 'Certainly not! I settle my own accounts, Doctor Lawrence. Just give me an idea of the total sum.'

'If you insist my dear. But I have been looking at that portrait of myself on which you were working when I came in. Will you sell it to me? For if you do, it is I who will be settling your account.'

I was surprised. I knew him to be vain, and this was a depiction of the man at work, eyes full of concentration in the candlelight as he leaned over his patient. Not a flattering portrait, for the subject's shirt was open at the collar, and the loose jowls were not disguised. But though the picture needed more work I knew I had captured what I had seen, a good physician intent upon his work.

'But it was not meant for sale, Doctor Lawrence, it is not the sort of portrait one would hang upon one's wall.'

'I know. But if I may say so, it depicts the better side of me for I am a rather shallow character away from my work.' He held up his hand as I would have spoken. 'I know! I know! I am too fond of food and drink, of playing cards with my friends, and of women, I must confess. But if that picture were to hang in my bedroom, when I rose in the morning I would see this other side of me that I had not before held to be of any great import. So may I purchase it from you?'

I smiled at him, a man who still had much of the boy within him but who recognised his weaknesses for all that. 'When it is finished we shall see.' But we knew the matter was settled between us and I was relieved that we would not have to further raid our funds.

And not long after the doctor had left, Theo called again and my heart leapt when I heard his voice at the door.

He came straight to the point. 'I've been talking to Doctor Lawrence.'

I smiled at him for he looked so stern and grave. 'And I suppose you have been discussing my case which is totally unethical! And you will have already decided what I must do, is that it?'

He gave a rueful grin and sat down at the table across from me. 'Yes and no. We talked, yes. But no, Elizabeth, I could not tell you what to do. It is a terrible thing to have to decide. If an operation would help you. . . But would it? This friend of his, he's just experimenting. He's had so little experience.' And I could hear the fear and worry in his voice.

While he talked I poured him a cup of tea and we continued to sit at the table in a dear companionship, going over the risks and possible benefits of the operation.

Presently I said, 'Let's leave it. I have a week to decide. And you have your work to do, Theo.' For I had learned from Mrs Snell that his ship was almost ready for sea.

His face lightened and he told me about his *Caroline of Quebec*, and I could see the ship was a greater rival for his affections than another woman could ever be.

But soon I hurried him away and returned to the canvas on the easel. I worked hard at the additions and alterations I had mentally planned during the doctor's visit and by lunchtime I was ready to lay down my brushes in some satisfaction.

Just then I heard someone fumbling with the cord at the front door which would agitate the chimes hanging in the kitchen, their movement letting Gladys know there was someone at the door, while their sound alerted me in my room. A moment later I heard the voice of Lambeth Weekes and my breath caught in a mixture of dread and hope. My emissary had returned and I sat frozen in my chair while Gladys opened the door and stood back to let him enter.

Chapter Sixteen

'Come right inside, Mr Weekes,' I called, and a moment later he stood beside the table peering at me with inquisitive eyes.

'I hears you been poorly, my dear. Are 'ee better yet?'

'Quite, thank you Mr Weekes.'

He gave me a complacent smile. 'Well here's what you want, Miss Millbrook,' and he delved into a pocket and withdrew a folded parchment.

'Thank you,' I said and I tossed it onto the table as a matter of no consequence for I would not open it in his presence. 'You made a quick journey. I did not expect you for another day at least.'

'Good following winds on the way to Plymouth, got there the same night. But coming back, 'twas slow makin' at sea what with the head winds, so when we put in to Looe, I found a carter making for Penzance, and I joined him. Cost a bit extra, but I thought you would be glad of the time saved.'

'I'm in no hurry, Mr Weeks,' my voice was frosty, but I was indeed burning to open the letter. 'Still, I'm glad the journey went well. So how much more do I owe you?'

Uninvited, he slowly drew a chair from beside the table and lowered himself on to it, stiffly, as one who has made a long and uncomfortable trip.

'Well now, 'tis difficult to say. Things have changed a bit, see, since I left. I think I had better tell you a little story.'

A chill of dread ran down my spine, for I could hear the sly threat in his tone.

'It was like this see. I made a good sea trip up to Plymouth, and spent the night at the 'Golden Hind', a clean enough place, used mostly by merchant men, better than the rough sailor's places.'

(Despite my fear, I smiled inwardly at the thought of his concern with cleanliness!) 'Then I hired a nag and covered the ground to Trevingey in spanking time. When I reached the house, I puzzled for a bit as to the best way to meet Sir Charles because you was most insistent that I gave your letter into his hands only. A groom came past leadin' a couple of horses and I asked him where I could find his master. He was very superior with me and told me Sir Charles leaves the likes of me to his bailiff who I would find in the long building yonder. But I said it was an important matter for Sir Charles only and we had a little argy-bargy like, voices raised, and this bailiff man came out from his office to see what was ado.'

(I quailed. I had wanted this matter handled in secrecy and here was a public fracas at the outset.)

'I told this other man that I had to see Sir Charles urgently and when he asked the nature of my call, I said it was none of his business and Sir Charles would throw him in the lake if he got to hear how he interfered in personal affairs. At this his manner changed. I 'specs he thought I was here on behalf of some young woman, not the first I should say by his look. "I'll go and see if Sir Charles is free," he says with a grunt.

'So I told the groom, who was listening to all this, to take my horse and give her a rub down. He was about to tell me what I could do with the mare when this bailiff man comes back. 'You're to wait in the games room,' he says, and leads me round the side of that left-hand block that sticks out and takes me into the games room. What a place! Leather cushions on the benches round the walls, a great table in the middle covered with green stuff, other tables with ivory chessmen. And pictures all over the walls.' Here he stopped and stared hard at me.

'Yes,' he said, as he watched my face change. I had not thought the picture would still be there! Not after the coming of the new wife! 'A very nice picture it is too, if I may say so.' And I remembered the painting, which I had not liked and had banished to the games room. The picture of a young woman on horseback, wearing a green velvet habit, her long skirt curving over the horse's flanks, the feathered hat curled over one eye; arrogance in every line of the body and in the curl of the smiling lip. I might have guessed he would keep it, I thought bitterly, for he had paid a handsome sum to the fashionable young artist I had so despised.

And so Lambeth Weeks had stood in the room, waiting, and looking about him until his shifting eyes had alighted on my portrait. I could well imagine how his narrow face would have changed, the surprise which would soon have given way to calculation. And I chilled with fear, for how had he used his sudden knowledge?

'Don't worry,' he went on. 'I told you I'm a good man for keeping his own counsel. When Sir Charles comes in, (I recognised him from one of the other pictures) he looked a bit nervous I'd say, wondering just what trouble I was bringing, and there I was standin' by the fire, warmin' my hands, real innocent. They had a fire in that big room, in July mind, 'cos there was a bit of a drizzle fallin' outside and they can't have the damp in there, can they? Anyhow, before he could speak, I takes out the letter from my pocket and says, "I got to give you this, Sir Charles, in private, I was told."

'He takes the letter, impatient like, and turns it over and sees the seal. His fingers was just about to tear it open, when he stops and looks at it, frozen like, his face hard. Then, slowly, he goes to a table and gets a paper knife and opens the seal without breaking it, like one who is going to look at it closer when he was on his own. Then he unfolds the letter and reads it. He says nothing. He reads it two or three times more, and by the time he finishes his face is white as the paper in his hands.

'I will say, Miss Millbrook, I couldn' help seein' the letter afore you folded it up, and I wondered then as how you didn't save your money and send it by the mail, but I hadn' seen the picture then. Side by side with the one of Sir Charles. Lady Francoise, that's what the groom said the first wife was called, the one who drowned down to Polmennor Court a few years ago. But I didn't know that then. I just knew I got to be careful because the look on his lordship's face was ugly and no mistake.

' "Who gave you this?" he blurts out, and I could see he was still tryin' to pretend to be cool and superior like.

'I was just as offhand. "I dunno," I says. "Some serving man was in the 'Golden Hind' where I'm havin' a little game of cards. He's watching me, and when the game is over he says 'Would you like to make two gold sovereigns?' 'What for?' says I. 'All you got to do is deliver a letter into the hands of Sir Charles Trelawne, down to Trevingey.' 'That means I got to hire a nag,' I says, 'and

128

that will make a hole in two guineas,' He 'olds up his 'and, 'The horse will be paid for,' he goes on. 'Alls you got to do is take the letter. But it have got to be Sir Charles himself, and no other, or you don't get the money when you comes back.' 'And how will you know,' I says, cheeky like, 'whether I gives it to Sir Charles or his butler man?' He looks angry now. 'I think I better go to someone more reliable,' he says. But when I laughs and says o' course I will do it, and put it into his Lordship's very hand, he makes the arrangements. But when I leaves, he says I won't get my money unless I brings a personal reply from Sir Charles, so's they'll know I done it right. So I hopes you will write a few lines for me, sir, for I done my job as stated, and I needs to be paid for it." He's frowning all the time he's listening to this. "You said 'The Golden Hind'," he growls. "I'll do better than that. My man shall go with you and vouch for you when you hand over the letter which I shall now write." "Oh no, sir," I goes on ('cos I'm enjoying this), "I got strict orders to return on my own. I got to leave the 'orse there and wait and the man will pay me the money when be comes. And I don't know when that will be."

'You could hear a pin drop, like they say. He bites his lip and goes over and kicks a log in the fire and it flares up and I don't like the look on his face as he's staring down at the flames. Then he looks up at me and I'm wondering if he's going to run me through with one of them swords on the wall. But while I'm backing towards the door to make a run for it, "Wait," he snarls, "I've got to write a bloody letter," (beggin' your pardon Miss Millbrook) and he goes over to a high desk and takes a sheet of paper and starts to write. Two or three times he stops and reads it and tears it up and goes over to the fire to burn it. Then, at last, he finishes this one, and very short it is too. He seals it and hands it over. "You better go," he says, still lookin' murder at me. So I takes the letter and doffs my 'at and goes out, innocent as a babe, but not happy till I was round the corner to the stables, because his eyes on my back was like daggers.'

Throughout this recital, I had sat at the table, cold with fear, but my mind racing all the time he spoke. I had to admit that he had covered his tracks well, sticking to our rehearsed story, but he had brought to life, only too well, the memory of Charles's cold fury and venom. What had I done? What Pandora's box had I opened?

'So you sees, Miss Millbrook, or should I say Lady Francoise Trelawne, I think it would be only proper for you to open that letter while I'm here, for you never told me I was putting my own life in danger for you in my innocence.'

'Nonsense man! I had made quite sure of your safe return by the wording of my note. You're here aren't you, and not a hair of your head the worse for your journey. I will pay you what we agreed for five days, plus a little extra.' And I opened the drawer in the table and withdrew the money and pushed it across to him.

He sat still, and his smile was a baring of the teeth.

'The letter first, my lady, don't you think? I know you're dyin' to open it. And it's in my interest too, to find out what he's offerin' to keep you quiet.'

My heart was pounding with uneven thumps, so loudly I thought he must hear its beat, but I made a conscious effort to control my breathing and my voice was quite steady when I spoke.

'Mr Weekes. You undertook to deliver a message for me, for which I agreed to pay you most generously. Here is that money. I am sorry you discovered matters that I had rather remained secret, but I have no intention to be blackmailed by you. Wait,' I raised my hand as he was about to speak. 'As you know,' I went on with some irony, 'my letter did not ask for money and I know this reply will not offer any. When I was married to Sir Charles I had a small income of my own from my mother's estate. This is now managed by Charles, and it is from this money that I shall be seeking a small annuity, small enough not to deprive my son when he comes of age.'

He sat, his eyes shifting from my face to the table where the coins lay before him and back to my face, not meeting my gaze, his large and broken-nailed hands encircling the money but not touching it.

'Then you needs advice ma'am, it seems. He would pay you whatever you asked to keep you quiet. I seen his face, remember. I know what your letter done to him. Think on, my dear Lady; you here in this li'l place and him in that great palace. And you his rightful wedded wife. Why, the man would pay you a fortune to keep silent. To keep you away from his new wife and children. And I would be your agent. I would go every month, if you liked, and collect your dues, and no one would be the wiser. For you know me, ma'am. Lambeth Weekes is not a man to pass on information. Lambeth Weekes keeps himself to himself. You chose right when you chose me my dear.'

'No. That is not to be, Mr Weekes. There will be no extortion. No blackmail. But I hope you will indeed, keep this knowledge to yourself, for I would be put in some confusion if it became village gossip. Good Methodists to a man. Already I am looked upon as different, a Roman Catholic, part French. Should they learn what you have discovered, I doubt I could remain here. I must then take myself elsewhere, and my paintings with me, which have been of benefit to you as well as myself these last three years.'

He was silent for some time, absorbing my words. But his roving eyes continually returned to the envelope on the table. I was surprised at his evident curiosity for I thought he would have found a way to discover its contents before now after what he had learned of my affairs.

But I was encouraged by the growing silence. 'After all, you know what our neighbours are like only too well when there is gossip to share,' I went on. 'Think what they would make of it should they learn of the portrait you hang above your bed!'

His head jerked up and the eyes that met mine were full of sudden shock. I felt a moment's pity for the man, for there was real anguish there, as well as rage and frustration. But my lancing words seemed to have done the trick, for he rose to his feet and scooped the coins into his pocket and made for the door. There he paused, however, and looking back, he growled, 'I'm off home now. I got to sleep. But when I'm more myself, I'll be back. We're no fools, you and me, Miss Millbrook, and you'll come to see things clearer in time, more my way. You think on, my dear, for I'll be back.' And then he was gone, the front door closing loudly behind him.

I sat staring at the letter as though mesmerised. The house was still and quiet, only the ticking of the clock breaking the silence. Gladys had gone into Helston with two neighbours in the pony cart and for once I was glad that she was not there; I wanted no one to see my tension and fear.

At last, I reached out my hand and picked up the letter. There was the Trevingey coat of arms on the seal. Intact. Trying to control the shaking of my hands, I broke open the envelope and withdrew the folded sheet within.

131

The loose scrawl was startlingly familiar, the message brief and to the point: 'Your letter has been received. Due to pressure of work, I cannot arrange an appointment in Plymouth at present. However, if you care to write and inform me of a date and venue after the middle of the month, I shall endeavour to comply with your arrangements.' And there was the scrawl of a signature beneath.

The middle of the month was two weeks away. Two weeks before a possible meeting! I wondered if he thought to use the time to try and trace me. But Lambeth Weekes had played his part well and if Charles sent a man to the Golden Hind, there would be little to discover; he might find that Lambeth Weeks had not played in any card game, had not even drunk in the bar for he was too miserly to spend his coins in such frivolity. He would discover that indeed the horse had been hired from that hostelry, but would they find the cheap boarding house where Weekes had in fact slept? For I knew he had merely called at the Inn to hire the horse. My mind ranged over Lambeth's story again and again, but I could see no way that Charles could trace him to the *Araminta*. And even if he should by luck get that far, Weekes had left the ship in Looe, telling the Captain he had business in the town.

My heart was once more beating a ragged tattoo. Two weeks. I had begun a dangerous game of chance. And the stakes were high; if I won, renewed contact with my son, financial security, perhaps even a new life in France when Gladys married, somewhere away from Polwerris Cove, where I would not have to watch Theo's children, who were not mine, grow up. . .

And if I lost? No doubt about that. If I lost, I knew only too well what to expect from Charles; if I lost, the stakes were sudden, violent death.

Chapter Seventeen

Although my scratches and lacerations were now well healed and few thorns remained to trouble me, I slept badly for the next few nights, my mind ranging to and fro like a hunted thing, and during the daylight hours I painted with grim concentration, churning out the sentimental cottages and cats that would sell so quickly in Penzance, and when I was calmer, working on the portrait of Doctor Lawrence. I went no farther than the ramp at the front door, ready to retreat into the cottage at the first sight of a stranger, the sound of a horse's hoof. I had already sent my reply to Charles, a terse note telling him that I would let him know where and when he was to meet me as soon as my plans were finalised. I folded it and sealed the envelope and then wrote a swift letter to Morwenna asking her if she would post the enclosed package which I wished to bear a Plymouth postmark. I could imagine her eyes widening at the impressive title and address on the envelope, her wonder at the background of her mysterious Miss Millbrook. But I knew I could count on her loyal compliance with my request.

On the third night I had such troubled dreams that at last I rose and stumbled into the kitchen to make myself a drink. I sat at the table shivering, though not with cold, for the night was mild and still. I cradled the cup in my hands, trying to still their trembling and trying to quell the images raised in my nightmares; Charles, as I had last seen him, seated on horseback, cloaked in black and with his pistol hand outstretched. . . Another dream where Mary Penrose walked tall with her washing basket upon her head, but when she turned, it was Charles's cold face that stared down at me. And in the last dream I opened the cottage door and found him standing there, his cloak flung back and the gun still in his

133

hand. . . It was some while before the normality of the quiet kitchen and the warmth of the tea restored me, so that presently I was able to make my way back to my bed for an hour's troubled sleep.

But next day it was Gladys who brought me some measure of release from the tension that still gripped me. I was sitting at the kitchen table trying to force the midday meal down my constricted throat when she suddenly put down her knife and touched my hand. I looked up at her signal and she gave me a small smile and began to communicate, using the mixture of soundless words and fluent hand signs that were so effortless between us.

It was most unlikely that Charles would trace us, she felt. The fact that Lambeth Weekes had left the ship at Looe would throw the scent. And who would find one carter out of the dozens that left the port daily? And I must not forget that Lambeth had a way of making himself so insignificant that it was likely the crew of the ship had already forgotten his brief passage with them.

I regarded her steadily. She was right, I thought. The man would have passed by on his journey like a shadow, leaving no trace; except on his dramatic arrival at Trevingey. And Charles could well have been convinced that Lambeth was indeed what he claimed to be, a casual messenger, hired merely to deliver the letter.

And also, she went on, no stranger could arrive in the village without everyone knowing, not even a seaman off a ship could set foot on the quay without one of the old fishermen finding out his port of departure and his destination!

Her grin was infectious and I felt relief seeping through me. I gave a huge sigh and smiled my thanks at her. And at last she had the satisfaction of seeing me turn to my meal with determination and enjoyment. And the following morning I was able to put the finishing touches to Doctor Lawrence's canvas so that I could show it to him when next he came to check on the progress of Toby's leg.

I showed Gladys the finished portrait and she grinned and raised her thumb to show her total approval. Then she took me down to the harbour and helped me on to the little beach that lay beyond the wall. Some children played there, paddling in the water and digging trenches for the sea to find and fill. The blue water was calm and flat, the sun warm and I made some pencil sketches of two tots seeking shells in the sand, serious and intent on their search. Some bigger girls sat near, keeping a casual eye on their charges, chatting to one another in the sunlight, their calico skirts hitched up above their bare legs; let one of the matrons catch sight of them and sparks would fly!

I let the sun seep into my bones, and as I relaxed the thought came to me of a way to draw Charles's teeth. I pulled a sheet of paper off my sketch pad and began to write another letter to Morwenna.

My dear Morwenna,

I was delighted, as always, to hear from you last week. Zeb seems to be making great progress with his engine. Even here, there is talk about it. Some of the men, like Theobald Pentire, say it is the way of the future, that ships will one day sail across the seas, powered by these engines, regardless of the wind and weather. Others say it is the work of the devil!

This is a brief note. I would like you to deliver the enclosed letter to a lawyer in town. Pettigrews is at the end of Armada Road, it's an old firm of solicitors. It is important that it is given personally to Mr Pettigrew Senior. I am sure you will do this for me - just hand it to him - you need not wait. Later a reply will be sent to you on behalf of a 'Miss Elizabeth Smith' and I would ask you to forward that reply to me as soon as you may. I will let you know what it is all about later on when I have more to tell.

Take care, my dear. We still miss the pair of you so much here in the village; it is not the same place without you.

Au revoir,

Elizabeth.

And then I drafted a letter to Jason Pettigrew which I would write more formally in ink later; a letter telling him briefly of my survival and my recent contact with Charles. A letter stating that I would be glad if he too, would contact Charles and let him know that I had been in touch and that there should soon be a meeting since negotiations must be made. I stressed that I had no wish to cause trouble, that all I asked was a modest annuity from my own funds to make my present life easier. And, of course, news of Guy and hopes of seeing him. (Tears fell as I wrote of Guy.)

I read the draft through. When the solicitor wrote to Charles, surely there would be no point in my husband trying to discover my whereabouts, for my secret would lie in other hands besides his own. And if anything untoward should happen to me, the scandal he sought to prevent would be blazoned from every news-sheet in the land, for I knew Jason Pettigrew's grim determination in a fight for justice, and so too did Charles.

Then I sat back in the sunshine and watched the children playing, relieved by the action of writing the letters, no longer a frozen rabbit, waiting in terror for the predator to pounce.

And so I dreamed in the sun, of a future which might yet be mine if Jason Pettigrew could bring himself, for the sake of our past friendship, to overlook what I had done. And I was sure he would not refuse my plea for help, for Guy's sake if not my own, for to Guy he had always been his dear Uncle Jason.

Later that day, when the letters were already on their way, Doctor Lawrence called again. I was surprised to see him so soon and he brought someone with him, a very tall, thin young man who stooped beneath the beams as he crossed the room.

'This is Doctor Fitzsimmons, Miss Millbrook. I brought him to see you to help you make up your mind about this operation we discussed.' Doctor Lawrence smiled broadly as be spoke.

I looked up at the newcomer who bent diffidently to take my hand. His appearance of extreme youth did little to encourage my confidence and I think my face showed my feelings for Doctor Lawrence laughed.

'I know, I know. He looks like an over-large schoolboy! But don't be deceived, madam, this young man was the best student in his college and has been qualified these five years. May we sit down?'

I waved them to the chairs with a smile of apology and the older man explained that they were spending the night up at the Manor where they had operated on two of the squire's dogs that day! At least, the veterinary had done the surgery, but the young doctor had administered the chemical and Doctor Lawrence had observed its affects. The squire now wanted them to remain overnight in case his dogs should need further care.

Doctor Lawrence laughed merrily. 'I had to beg permission to

136

take some air for an hour. That chemical gets into the blood and no mistake! He grudgingly let us take our own horses out for some exercise and we came over to Polwerris Cove to see you, Miss Millbrook. Because if you are agreeable to this surgery, we could perform it tomorrow.'

'Tomorrow!' I was appalled. 'I have not yet made up my mind. There is so much to think of. Should it go wrong, I might lose all movement! I cannot say . . .'

The young man reached forward a thin, gangly arm and took my hand. 'I know. And you fear the pain.' He smiled into my eyes, his own clear and steady. 'But I promise you, there will he no pain, my chemical will ensure that. When you regain your senses, there will no doubt be soreness from the operation, but if that obstruction of which Doctor Lawrence speaks, if that is removed, your recovery will be swift and your future, if not entirely pain free, then very much relieved. And as for fear of paralysis,' he went on as I would have spoken, 'Doctor Lawrence is far too experienced a surgeon to take risks. If he should find the foreign body too close to the spinal cord, he would let well alone, of that you may be quite sure.'

I stared into his face for a long time then I forced a smile. 'And how were the dogs, may I ask?'

Both men grinned and Doctor Lawrence replied.

'That veterinary was unable to believe his eyes! The young dog had a piece of bone wedged deep in his throat. With the animal limp and unconscious it was a small matter to extract. The older one, a spaniel had several small growths, better for the removal. But it is a savage little beast and normally would not let a man touch it. Both have come through well.'

The young man spoke, unable to hide the eagerness in his voice. 'I'm better able to assess the quantity to use now, having had quite a lot of experience. Too much leaves the patient, animal or human, deeply unconscious for too long a time, too little and the surgeon is aware that sensation is returning. But by dropping the liquid onto a pad, drop by drop, during the surgery, I am able to tell, with my finger on the pulse, just how much more or less is needed.'

Doctor Lawrence nodded his head. 'The only complication we have so far discovered, is the nausea and vomiting that can occur after the operation. That is why we would ask you to avoid food and drink for some time before taking the chemical. This means in your case, if you should agree to the surgery, nothing more to eat or drink, save for a mouthful or two of water, from now on. We would wish to start work in good time tomorrow, say eight thirty or thereabouts.'

I was frightened. I wished for Theo. For Gladys. For anyone who might advise me. Anyone, save these two men who had their own reasons for persuading me to agree to their proposal, for I was under no illusions that both of them had a far greater wish to further their experiments than to relieve me of my bodily discomfort.

And yet! And yet! To lose my limp. To be able to move without the constant fear of that savage spasm which robbed my legs of strength so that I would fall helpless to the ground. And the anxiety that the pain and numbness might one day spread and affect my arms and stop me painting. . . Thankfully that problem had not recurred since the frightening spell in the early spring, but the worry remained to haunt me in the small hours of the night.

I took a deep breath. 'All right. You may go ahead tomorrow morning. What will we need to provide?'

The two men smiled their approval and set about making arrangements: they would need to operate on the kitchen table which was large enough for their purpose. They would need several bowls, lots of hot water. . . I told them to find Gladys, sudden nausea sweeping me at the thought of what lay in store.

'Don't be afraid.' Doctor Lawrence turned from the doorway, recognising my fear. 'I promise you that this is a very minor operation. Normally I would perform this surgery without a second thought, and expect my patient to put up with the pain. But I appreciate that it is an extremely sensitive area and also the obstruction has been there too long; it should have been removed at the time of the injury.'

I knew he was probing for information but I was too full of concern for the coming ordeal to respond, and when he saw that, he followed Doctor Fitzsimmons into the kitchen. I was glad when they had gone for I was having to fight down nausea at their talk of bowls and dishes. . .

But presently I forgot my own concern in soothing Gladys. The fear eloquent in her blue eyes shamed me into giving her reassurance and gradually I too began to believe what I was saying;

138

that it was a trivial matter, that it might help to relieve my limp, that it would be over in an hour, so we might just as well forget it now and have some tea.

For once, however, that anodyne was forbidden to me and I had to smile cheerfully at Gladys while she held a large mug of the steaming beverage against her chest, drawing as much comfort from its warmth as from the occasional sips she took.

And when I asked that night for some laudanum, once again Gladys made no objection but went and fetched it. She kept the drug hidden in some secret place ever since the time when I had helped myself to so large a dose that she and her grandmother had watched me lie motionless in a deep trance for a night and a day. Now, however, she measured me a small dose and smoothed my pillow and settled me to sleep. And I did not hear Theo come and go, nor know until later that he, unlike myself, had spent the midnight hours in futile anxiety, tossing and turning until a pink dawn spilled itself across the sea.

I would like to pass over the details of my surgery, but since I am one of the few people to have been given this 'gas' as they called it, I had better recount what I can remember. The most important fact is that the two doctors were well pleased with their work. For myself there was the acute nervousness of the preparation and then, lying prone upon the table, the terror of suffocation as the chemical mixture seemed about to choke me. However, the struggle for air that overwhelmed me was of short duration and then I spun away into deep unconsciousness. When I returned to a muzzy awareness, they told me that Doctor Lawrence had removed a piece of metal which had come to rest near the spine. They both were sure that this was the prime cause of my difficulty in walking but there would continue to be a certain irritation of the nerves in the area since there was much scarring. They were united in their opinion of the doctor who had removed only part of the bullet after the accident; had he been more careful most of my problems would not have occurred. But they did not know, and I had not the energy to tell them, that at the time of the shooting I had not been expected to live the night; that the doctor had simply removed what lead he could find and had stemmed the bleeding and tried to prolong my comatose state in order to protect me from shock and pneumonia. I well knew that had it not been for his ministrations, however fallible, I would not have survived that terrible ordeal.

But instead, I sighed and closed my eyes. I was back in my own bed, face down and shored up on pillows, and Gladys sat nearby with a bowl in readiness should I need it. And indeed, the nausea persisted throughout that day, worsened by every mouthful of water I took to relieve my desperate thirst until, in fear of the consequences I turned my head away from the liquid that I so sorely desired. The young doctor stayed near me for much of the day, apart from taking short walks down to the harbour, inhaling the salt air in great gulps, they told me later, for he too was nauseated by the chemical he had administered. He told me he was designing a mask for himself as well as one for the patient for in an extensive operation he too might succumb to the gas and thus put the patient at great risk. He told me how he had checked my heartbeat throughout the surgery, his fingers upon my pulse, and had watched my responses minutely in order to minimise the amount of chemical he used. And indeed, he had performed well, because by evening I felt much more myself and was prepared to risk taking some sips of water which, to my great relief, caused no further reaction.

Doctor Fitzsimmons was well pleased at this, and decided he might now leave for his home in Helston, a long ride but the summer evenings were long and pleasant. And what a delight, I thought, to ride across the moorland under the paling sky, free from the sights and smells of the sickroom. His colleague, Doctor Lawrence, would call to see me tomorrow, he said. And just as he was about to leave, Theo came.

They stood beside my bed, the young doctor drawing back the sheet to show Theo as much of the operation as the dressing would permit. And while they talked about the surgery, I lay, with my head upon my folded arms, and my heart warm with the comfort of his nearness, for the way he spoke he might have been my husband. Indeed, later I learned that the young doctor had made that assumption, otherwise, he told me with great apology, he would never have permitted his presence in the room, let alone beside my bed. But his protestations lacked conviction, for he had seen the way Theo had taken my hand from under my cheek and held it to his own, and kissed the palm. And he had seen the way

140

I reached for Theo when the doctor said it was time I slept, and drawn him close for another gentle embrace.

Then they had gone. I sent Gladys away for she had not slept the previous night and I now felt much more myself. Yes, I assured her, if I need anything I would pull the cord. And I lay imbibing the quietness of the room, relaxed in mind and body for the soreness of the operation was too slight to cause discomfort, and I smiled and thought of Theo until gradually the ticking of the clock seemed to coincide with my heartbeat and I fell into a deep and refreshing sleep.

Chapter Eighteen

It was three days before Doctor Lawrence would permit me to rise from my bed despite my protests that I was quite recovered. And when I did get up, I was disappointed at the weakness of my legs and there was no way of telling whether the operation had made any real improvement. However, there was no searing agony when he removed the dressing and probed the area of the wound and I unclenched my jaw with a gasp of relief.

During the several visits he had made, Dr Lawrence's bedside manner changed greatly, for now he showed the much more human face which I had caught in the portrait which so pleased him; the kind heart that was hidden behind the veneer of self-satisfaction. On his visits he made himself quite at home, teasing Gladys, eating everything he was offered with relish and using stable language without apology.

Because of the shaking of my bedridden limbs, Gladys and the doctor helped me move about the room for a while. Then I attempted to cross to the window on my own, supporting myself as usual on the furniture. My heart sank as I progressed, for my limp was as pronounced as ever.

'Put your weight on your left leg, woman!' exclaimed the doctor in irritation. 'You're holding it like a dog about to pee on a gatepost.'

So, gingerly I stood still and with perspiration gathering on my forehead, I slowly allowed the leg to take some of my weight.

'Stand on it, go on stand on it for God's sake. I've not got all day to spend here. Toby down the road would be running round the room if his leg was half as good as yours.'

I stepped forward until my weight was evenly balanced and grimly set myself to cross the room. Right foot, fine. Left foot, don't anticipate the pain, take the weight. And the pain did not blaze through me! I took another step and another. My limbs were shaky with disuse and I had to force myself not to limp, but my legs functioned without that ever-recurring stab of pain that so restricted my movement.

'That's enough! That's enough for now.' Dr Lawrence nodded his approval of my walking. 'Go and lie down. You can lie on your back now, it's well healed. You don't have to wait until the stitches are taken out.'

'Back to bed? Nonsense! I told you I am well. I want to dress and go out into the sunshine. I want to show everyone what I can do.' And I smiled at him the thanks and gratitude I could not express without dissolving into irritating tears.

'Oh well, if that's your intention there's no point in my staying here to hold your hand. But you must use a stick at first. In fact, you may always need a stick. I did what I could but there has been damage to those lower vertebrae. In time there will almost certainly be arthritis. But the sunlight won't hurt you. I'll be off to see Toby while you get yourself dressed in those Persian courtesan things of yours.' But his tone belied the roughness of his words and I smiled, remembering the startled admiration in his eyes when he had first seen me in my eccentric but practical attire.

So as soon as he had gone, I put on a dark red blouse that matched the flowers in the black, baggy trousers and a pair of Gladys's wooden clogs for I had no shoes fit for the cobbles outside. And I needed not one, but two sticks for support. Then I went through the open door and crossed the ramp to the street. And some of the women who had been waiting for the doctor's departure came to watch my slow progress down towards the harbour. They followed along, and some children joined us, and with Gladys at my side we made a fine procession in the sunlight and I felt like a queen with my retinue around me.

The men who were working by the harbour wall turned to see what was going on, and their delighted grins at my new, albeit uncertain, mobility lifted my spirits still further.

When I looked to sit on the parapet, a coat was immediately placed for me as a cushion and I sat holding court for they had heard the nature of my operation and wanted to know all the details. I do not know who showed the most interest, the men who all their working lives faced the risk of terrible injury and the crude amputations where shock so often killed, or the women who could look for some relief from the pain of childbirth if this new chemical would indeed give such astonishing escape from consciousness.

'It's early days yet,' I concluded. 'Doctor Fitzsimmons tells me that several different methods are being tried out, but he feels his gas has much to offer. He needs a lot more experience yet, and a lot more people who are prepared to take the risk with something so new and untried. But he is sure that within a few years no surgery will be performed on patients without giving them the benefit of freedom from the pain of an operation.'

(And in time, of course, this would come about as the young doctor had predicted. But sadly, he did not live to see the common usage of his gas, for he died the following year from the affects of his constant experiments with dangerous chemicals and the world lost a great and good scientist. And although the papers on his work were never published, a door had been pushed ajar and the chink of light which shone through would encourage others to follow. But it would come too late for most of those friends and neighbours who stood before me that day, asking eager questions with a mixture of hope and apprehension in their eyes.)

Theo was not there. After checking on my health, he had sailed early that morning on his first trip round to Falmouth, a mixture of sea trials and business calls. But as I returned up the hill with Gladys, I caught a fleeting glimpse of Gwendoline Matthews, her small son by her side, disappearing into an alleyway. I wondered whether she had a call to make there or if she was simply avoiding a face to face meeting with me. Probably the latter. And I too was relieved at not having to pass the time of day with her when the words we ached to speak would hang between us in an almost palpable cloud.

But I soon forgot about Gwendoline, for leaning against the railing of our front steps was Lambeth Weekes, and the small smile on his face as he watched us approach reminded me how much I was in his power and I climbed the steps to the front door with considerable apprehension.

Gladys let us in and I was glad to sink into the armchair in my

144

room and let her assemble the stack of paintings for which he had ostensibly called. While she busied herself, he congratulated me on the success of the operation and asked several pertinent questions about it. But all the while I was waiting, for I knew there was something else he wished to say.

When Gladys left us, I braced myself for whatever was to come. However, his actual words were both astonishing and without threat. 'Mr Swain would like to come and see you next week.'

'Mr Swain? Whatever for?' But I think I smiled because I liked the idea of meeting the man who helped to keep our household solvent.

'He asked what else you paint. So I told him you do portraits of people going about their work. And he said he would like to see them. I hope you don't mind, but 'twasn't a confidence like, was it?'

'No, of course not. Yes. Tell him I'll he interested to meet him.'

He tightened the cord round the stack of small pictures and I thought with relief that he was leaving. But he had not finished, and now his words justified my earlier fears.

'What you said, that you wouldn' pay me to hold my tongue.'

'Yes?' My voice was icy and I forced my fingers not to clutch the arms of the chair.

'I got a better idea.'

'Oh?'

'I'm goin' to go and ask him, Sir Charles hisself, what it's worth for me not to let the cat out of the bag.'

Now my fingers gripped the arm-rests of their own accord.

'No! You must not! You don't know him! It is madness even to think of it!'

He laughed, a strange sound, wheezy and creaky from disuse.

'You think I abb'n worked 'un out don't 'ee?' His patently exaggerated accent grated.

'No, Mr Weekes, I'm quite sure you have made your plans very carefully. But there has been a development. The matter is now in the hands of a solicitor. I felt it prudent to go to the law.'

The shifting gaze flickered back to my face and I read the momentary consternation in his eyes. 'The law is it?' He pulled at his unshaven chin with a rough hand with those nails broken and

g

bitten. And the rasp of stubble as be rubbed his hand too and fro brought a rush of bile to my throat.

'Ah well, a solicitor is paid to keep quiet. And so I shall be paid too. And well paid what's more! When I tell him I shall go to the newspaper with my story, I don't think the high and mighty Sir Charles will have much choice but to pay up, and quick about it.'

'You're wrong! You don't know him. He won't pay you Mr Weekes. Believe me, he won't give you a penny. Can't you see what he will have to do? A man in his position, threatened by a stranger, a solitary man arriving out of the blue. You will never be permitted to leave the estate grounds.' I was leaning forward in my chair, my face bloodless.

For a moment the restless eyes met mine and I saw a flash of apprehension in the watery blue. But he shook his head. 'He won't dare to threaten me. I shall tell him I have left a letter behind, to be opened if I don't return.' He gave another wheeze of a laugh. 'You see, I'm not that stupid after all, Miss Millbrook.' He bobbed his head. 'Beggin' your pardon, My Lady, I keeps forgettin' who it is I been doin' business with all this time.'

I closed my eyes in desperate concentration, sought for words that would persuade this man to abandon his intentions, for only I knew the lengths to which Charles would go when his 'honour' was threatened. But there was such a rushing in my head that I thought I might faint and I cursed my weakness and my helplessness before this man and pounded the arms of the chair in feeble protest. He looked at me, uneasy at my reaction.

'I'll be off then. Mr Swain will call next Wednesday afternoon. I got a few more plans to make.' He grinned down at me, yellow teeth large and strong, wolflike. 'Don't you worry yourself about me, m' dear. 'Twill be no skin off your nose. He's the one should be shaking in his shoes.'

'Mr Weekes! Wait!' I pulled myself to my feet and took an unsteady step towards the door. But he had gone and the door to the street was closed by the time I reached it. I stood leaning against it, holding on against the movement of the room which swayed about me. Then Gladys was there and when next I opened my eyes I was lying on my couch looking up into her face which was full of anger and concern.

She tried to reassure me, to tell me that Lambeth Weekes

146

would change his mind after he had thought about it for a while, but I could see that she too was fearful. The summer day which had begun with such promise, was clouding over and I sat in the kitchen, grateful for the warmth from the ever-burning fire in the hearth, all my terrors returning. I poked restlessly at the turf which Gladys had carefully placed on the fire to keep it smouldering until it should be needed for cooking, watching the small flames flicker through when I drew aside the earthy covering. Gladys clicked her tongue and took the poker from my hand.

'Come on,' she indicated, 'I'll go and harness Jem and we can go for a drive. And you can practise your walking a bit more with nobody to watch.'

My heart lifted. Gladys was right. There was nothing to be gained by sitting indoors and brooding. And now that we were no longer encumbered with the need for the wheelchair, we could pick more varied terrain. I knew I was running ahead of myself, for my legs were still thin and weak from the years of inaction, but the simple fact that they obeyed my mind's messages, that movement no longer triggered agonising stabs of pain, encouraged me to hope that in time I might move about as easily as other people.

So now I collected a fat cushion and warm shawls for us both, and while Gladys went to fetch Jem and the trap, I put some bread and cheese in a basket with some fruit. I thought of taking some tea but as I was about to dip some milk from the can, I decided the ground was probably too dry to light a fire, so instead I fetched two stone bottles of homemade ginger beer.

Gladys collected our daily supply of milk from a widow who used the sales from her sole Jersey cow and eggs from her hens and ducks, to enable her to remain in the small cottage where she had spent all her married life and as I went about my preparations, I was forced to realise that the life Gladys and I lived was far removed from the subsistence level of many of the villagers. We had no rent to pay apart from the few shillings a year for the use of a field for Jem. The small but steady income from my paintings enabled us to buy regular supplies of firewood and logs so that Gladys did not have to walk miles along the beaches seeking driftwood to be dragged all the way home like so many of our neighbours. We were able to pay a man to cut and build the turf rick in the back garden so that the great open hearth did not devour all our supplies of wood and roast us out of the room. Both of us were good needlewomen and we had money enough to buy lengths of calico and muslin and linen for Gladys, and gay prints for my pairs of trousers, and wool for bright shawls. Our meals were simple and nutritious and the constant supply of fish was so cheap that I never ceased to wonder at the courage and tenacity of the men who toiled so hard and often in great danger, for such meagre returns. Eggs were plentiful, for few houses did not have hens running in the back garden. So as I covered our provisions with a fresh teacloth, I asked myself grimly why I had opened this Pandora's box with my letter to Charles. And I knew the answer was less the need for that extra cushion of income than the ever-growing yearning for news of my son.

At last I heard the trap rattling down the cobbles and a moment later Gladys came in. She looked pleased when she saw that I had forestalled her in preparing the basket, and she placed it in the trap and threw in a couple of rugs. Then I made my own way to the door and climbed the step to the seat with relative ease. Mrs Snell and a friend beamed their pleasure when we set off and when Gladys turned Jem in the open space before the harbour wall, two or three of the men gave a cheer just short of ribaldry! The incubus of Lambeth Weekes dissipated before their rough affection and encouragement, and as the pony hauled us up the cobbled street out of the village I found my heart was behind the smile on my lips.

Jem was fit and began trotting as soon as we breasted the hill and we bowled along the dusty road, the summer's growth of the hedgerows reaching out for us as we passed. Soon we were on the flat open moorland of Goonhilly where the frost never settled, warmed by the depth of the underlying peat, and where small flowers I had seen nowhere else, bloomed in profusion.

Huge clouds sailed across the high blue vault of sky and I watched the passing moor with rapture as the sunlight chased away the cloud shadows and the ground became a Persian carpet of colour. Tall marsh grasses, pale and dry, blew like hair in the light wind and the absence of hedges beneath the billowing sky was an intoxication of space and freedom. Here and there a low hump in the flatness of the moorland spoke of the ancient people who had used this land for their burial grounds many centuries before, and as my eyes sought for the tumuli, Lambeth Weekes and my own affairs became Lilliputian and I gloried in the rush of the wind as Jem began to canter and we laughed and clung to our seats as we bumped and rattled along the dusty track.

Gladys found us a place where the low gorse made a windbreak round a hollow of mossy grass and here we settled, a rug spread beneath us. We could have rested safely on the ground for it was bone dry, but Gladys would not permit me to sit until the blanket and cushions were arranged. I had been right not to think of making a fire out here on the moorland and when we settled to our picnic, the ginger beer from the stone bottles was splendidly cool, the bubbles harsh and prickly to the throat, spicily aromatic like the gorse itself; a drink which matched its surroundings to perfection.

We sat in pleasant companionship, and I wondered if the sadness on Gladys's face was because she, like me, knew there would be few more such outings for the two of us; when she married her life would be much more circumscribed than at present, since I cared nothing for routine and minded not at all if meals were late because Gladys had lingered overlong grooming Jem or if she had chosen to walk on the cliffs rather than finish the ironing.

Here on the peat moor, the warmth of the ground had brought some of the gorse so far ahead of the rest that I could hear the pop of the bursting pods and I revelled in the strong, coconut scent of the flowers. I stretched out on my back, luxuriating in the absence of pain and presently, lying on my back watching the clouds so far above I suddenly and sweetly floated off into a deep and dreamless sleep.

Chapter Nineteen

'If you were a man I would tell you to have a daily salt water swim to dry up that wound. And to strengthen those legs. My horses swim regularly. Nothing like it to build up the muscles.'

Doctor Lawrence was removing the stitches from my back. I gritted my teeth in expectation of hurt, but the site had healed well and I felt nothing.

'What a good idea!' I exclaimed. 'I have been wishing I could swim in the cove but the Chapel ladies would have me drummed out of the village. But if I say it's Doctor's orders, well!' and I laughed at the thought.

'You can swim?' the doctor looked at me in surprise.

'My father taught me when I was a child in France. There was a lake near our house and I used to swim with the village children when my parents were away travelling. As a matter of fact I swam a few weeks ago in a pool along the coast, but Gladys is too busy to take me there every day. But now that I don't need Pegasus,' and I nodded towards the chair which still stood in the corner, 'I could get someone to row me to that beach just round the point.'

The doctor looked enthusiastic. 'Marvellous. Just a short swim to begin with. Then build up to half an hour unless you feel cold. But I think it will take more than doctor's orders to mollify the old dames, my dear.'

'But I could wear my trousers and a blouse to swim in and change into dry things on the beach afterwards.' I was excited at the prospect for I now realised only too well how desperately weak my legs had become over the years, and I could walk only a short distance before they trembled with weakness and I had to sit and rest. 'I will ask their advice!' I smiled at the doctor. 'You'll see!'

'You're a conniving witch, that's what you are,' the doctor twinkled back at me. 'By the way, my wife loves the portrait. It's been moved downstairs for she wants our friends to see it when they call.' He was packing his bag. 'You, er, you don't give sittings on commission, I suppose.'

I bit my lip. 'Sometimes. Just occasionally, but only for people in the village.' I was being driven into explanations which I did not wish to give, and my heart began to pound as I recalled the threat to my present way of life that I myself had so recently put into motion. 'Perhaps later. Is it your wife who wishes to sit?'

He nodded and looked pleased. 'I would be most grateful. And I wish you would accept payment for my portrait, I know it far more than covers the cost of my attendance on you.'

I shook my head. 'If you are satisfied that I am not in your debt, we will not discuss it further. Do you want some tea before you leave?'

It was an unnecessary question, for Doctor Lawrence came, I felt, as much to enjoy Gladys's baking as to check upon my health. Toby, a few doors up the road, was also benefiting from these frequent visits and he too, was making good progress. Theo had insisted in taking responsibility for the boy's bill, since it was he who had sent for the doctor. Thinking of the lad gave me an idea.

'Would Toby benefit from swimming too?' I asked. Doctor Lawrence turned from his bag and regarded me. 'I said you were a conniving witch! But yes, that's a good idea! Swimming would do his leg the world of good. Two patients prescribed a daily swim! I think you may be able to get round those old dears after all!

So after the doctor had left, I sent Gladys with a message to two of the ladies who were stalwarts of the Wesleyan Chapel, the mainstay of the village. They came later that afternoon, suspicious and hesitant, for was I not a stranger and a Catholic besides. But one who saw neither priest nor vicar, nor, to the best of their knowledge, entered into any house of worship.

'Do make yourselves comfortable,' I settled them on the couch. 'I have a problem and I want to ask your advice.' They did not lose their look of suspicion immediately, but as I explained the situation they unbent somewhat. I recounted the process of the operation and they asked shrewd questions about the chemical used and about Doctor Lawrence. One of the ladies knew the family of young Doctor Fitzsimmons and was able to confirm that he was indeed a brilliant young gentleman. I think it was this factor that swayed them in my favour.

I explained the need to swim. During all my years in the village I had respected their views in most respects: my trousers were covered by a rug whenever I was outside in my chair, and they had seen for themselves that I could not manage a skirt whilst using both hands to haul myself up the steps to the front door. And when inside my house I was not corrupting the young women of the neighbourhood with my outlandish garb. My paintings too, were popular and they liked the idea of a record for posterity of their village life and work. So on the whole I had managed to fit into their way of life without too much friction. But I knew I was disapproved of by the more straight-laced members of the Chapel.

The two women sat with stony faces while I explained my need. 'I do not wish to offend anyone,' I concluded. 'But the doctor has said that both Toby and myself would benefit greatly from this daily exercise. And if we should be rowed round to Seal Cove, there would be no one but Gladys to see us. I know that Toby, of course, could swim here in the harbour, but I do not feel it would be seemly for me to do so. (And I had no intention of making myself such an object of curiosity!) What do you think?'

'Has it helped, this operation?' asked Mrs Jago, the less rigid of the two women.

'Oh yes. The doctor was able to remove the obstruction that had stopped my legs working properly.'

'How did you become crippled in the first place?' Mrs Bennets did not mince her words and I felt a spurt of anger as much at the crudity of her inquisition as at the question.

'I had an accident which it distresses me to discuss.' And they could see by the set of my jaw that I was not about to tell them more.

Mrs Jago looked uncomfortable at her companion's solecism. 'Well I do feel, Jane, that if the doctor says it will help her, we should not let our feelings stand in her way.' She turned to me and I saw a gleam of sympathy in her old eyes. 'You must understand, my dear, we old folk are set in our ways. We worry about the changes we see, the way our grandchildren question things that we think are right. But you have said you will be discreet in your bathing. I have heard that some ladies do swim from those bathing huts at Penzance though it don't seem proper to me. But I can't see 'twould be setting a bad example to our young maids, not when it's doctor's orders.'

Mrs Thomas's tight lips clamped tighter. She stood up.

'Well, seems you've made up your mind, the pair of you. I shall have something to say at Chapel on Sunday. I think the men will say they should have been consulted on this matter. But good day to you now, I have my duties to perform.'

She let herself out, the door not slamming, but closing with a clipped finality behind her stiff back.

Mrs Jago smiled comfortably. 'Don't take any notice of she, my handsome. She's a proper old maid. She don't take kindly to anything that's a bit different, not even a change in the weather!' She too stood up. 'You go on as you've been doin' all these years. You've never harmed no one yet.'

But at the door she paused and turned to face me.

'I see Theobald Pentire have offered for Gwen.' Her eyes were watchful of my expression. 'That'll be good. Right for them both.' She looked away and hitched her shawl about her shoulders. Then she turned back and her eyes met mine.

'You're a very attractive woman, Miss Millbrook. I can see why he comes here. But with him courting now, 'twould be better for all if you sent him away.'

My lips twisted. 'So they talk, do they?'

'Some do. I'm surprised Janey Bennets haven't picked it up, she don't miss much.' She smiled at me suddenly with unexpected compassion. 'I know my dear. I know what 'tis like to want what can't be yours. Oh yes.' She nodded her head slowly and I could see remembered pain in her eyes. 'But there. 'Tedden for me to say. 'Tis your life and you'm making the best you can of it, far away from all you're used to, that much is clear. God bless you, my dear.' And she tucked in her shawl and the front door closed gently behind her.

I sat for a long time sorting out my mixed feelings. Anger and irritation at the narrow confines of their beliefs, annoyance with myself for having asked for their approval of what I fully intended to do regardless of their views. But most of all at the cold realisation that she was right about Theo. Wasn't it what we had already decided? But how could I send him away? I told myself that nothing passed between us that could not be seen in public. But I knew that when our eyes met there was no disguising the strength of the attraction between us. Each time he called I waited for him to say that this was the last time; I knew it must come. And then I remembered the comfort of his presence after my operation, the wonder and love I had felt after he had gone. And I knew that although my lips might beg him to go, not to come again, in my eyes there would be a stronger plea. And one that would not be denied.

He would be back in a few days from his trip along the coast and I wondered fleetingly if Gwendoline Matthews counted the days, and watched for the sails of his ship as eagerly as I. And I knew she did. I thought of her without jealousy, with pity even. Because I knew that what Theo gave to her was a pale reflection of the flame that was between us. And for the first time I wondered how it would be if we allowed that flame to burn; to let its white heat flare and cauterise the pain and need that consumed us both. . .

I sighed. This would not do. Mr Swain would be here next day. I must sort through my work. A number of my earlier canvases were stored in the spare upstairs bedroom, the place where Gladys's grandmother had spent her last days, and these we needed to sort out in readiness for our visitor. So I stood up and walked about the room for a while and then went to the kitchen to see when Gladys would be ready to help me to prepare for next day's visit.

Mr Swain arrived promptly at two o'clock. He came in a smart gig driven by an elderly man in the garb of a manservant. He himself was a man in his early fifties, resplendent in a dove grey frock coat and striped trousers, white shirt with high collars and plain dark cravat, the whole topped off by a high beaver hat. He checked the hour on the splendid gold hunter which hung from a heavy chain across his waistcoat before descending with dignified calm to our front doorstep, smiling distantly at the eager children who stared open-mouthed at this elegant newcomer. The driver touched his forehead and steered the equipage away, presumably to wait in the yard behind the old inn along the harbour front.

Gladys opened the door before Mr Swain had reached it and a moment later I walked forward to greet him, suddenly and unexpectedly shy.

He stood for a moment regarding me then held out both hands as though greeting an old friend.

'My dear Miss Millbrook. What a pleasure to meet you at last.' His hands were small and firm and he beamed up at me, a small man who barely reached my chin, but a man of presence withal and one who would not be overlooked in whatever social gathering he chose to grace.

'I must confess you are not at all what I imagined.' He slowly relinquished my hands and I gestured him to the settle. 'I expected a much older woman. Mr Weekes was unforthcoming about my favourite client.' His blue eyes twinkled at me as he sat down.

'Mr Weekes is unforthcoming about everything,' I smiled back at him, devoutly praying that it might indeed be so. 'You must excuse my apparel,' for I felt disadvantaged before my meticulously dressed visitor. 'I have a difficulty in movement and find these more practical than skirts,' and I indicated the dark green and gold trousers which fell in baggy folds to brush the tops of my slippers. I was glad the blouse I wore, also green, was my newest, with sleeves which echoed the shape of the trousers and fell loosely over the narrow cuffs. My only decoration was the plain gold leather belt around my waist, a relic from Trevingey days.

'Mr Weekes had in fact indicated to me that you had a handicap which is why I called here instead of inviting you to my home in Penzance. But please make no excuses for your dress! I declare I have never seen such a becoming - and most practical - mode of attire. I am surprised you have not started a fashion in the village! I have always felt it must be such an encumbrance to be burdened with skirts and petticoats. I used to play as a child, dressing up in Mama's old frocks. And my dear! The falls I would have! How a woman can perform her daily tasks so cluttered with skirts, I never fail to marvel.' And he flicked an invisible piece of fluff from his immaculate trews.

'But there,' he continued happily, laying on the compliments with a trowel, 'I dare say you need to be young and exceptionally

155

beautiful,' and here he bowed his head towards me, 'to set off so completely your charming style of dress.'

I smiled back at him. He reminded me strongly of Uncle Pierre in his salon in Paris. Uncle Pierre, strutting round the fitting room, lavish with his compliments to the half dressed models who sold his brilliant designs to the new rich of the city; girls who need never fear unwelcome attentions from their employer. Indeed, though they had to work as long hours as he himself at times, they were well remunerated and if they had personal problems they turned naturally to him for his sympathy and advice. And I knew that there would be no wife in the background at the Penzance studio of Mr Swain, perhaps not even one of Uncle Pierre's smooth faced young men. Perhaps his busy life amongst his pictures was enough for him. . .

But I left my impressions for later musing.

'You want to see some of my other work, I believe. But first I am sure you would like some refreshment,' and I turned to introduce Gladys who stood patiently beside the door.

Mr Swain bowed over her hand with practised gallantry and she blushed rosily. But then he looked again at the splendid gold hunter. 'I would love a cup of tea, my dear. How did you guess? But later, later. First things first, I always say. And pictures come first in my world, my dear Miss Millbrook.'

So I stood up and made my way across the room to the easel, glad I could now control and lessen my ungainly limp, uncertain though my progress was. I turned the picture to face him, angling it so that the light from the smaller, sea-facing window would illuminate it gently.

It was unfinished, a painting I had begun after completing the portrait of Doctor Lawrence. Now I looked at it as critically as did my guest. It was a picture of two men at work, Tom Opie and Jim Snell, wheelwrights. They worked together, placing the almost completed wheel horizontally on to a prepared base where it would be held rigid for the fixing of the iron band which must hold it together. Nearby blazed the pyre of gorse in which the iron was heating to its full expansion. Buckets of water stood by in readiness and I could almost smell the heat and steam that would plume from the wheel as the iron band was cooled. It was a process I had watched many times, marvelling always at the skill and precision of the men's work. They had grown used to my presence, sketch-pad in hand, and worked as though I was not there, except perhaps they watched their language if a slip was made. Though they could hardly expect shock from me; my occasional outbursts were well reported, and I dare to say, fancifully embellished.

So now we looked together at the picture. The flare of the fire reflected onto the sheen of sweat on the men's faces and there was concentration and studied urgency in their movements as they approached a critical moment in the completion of the wheel. The tools and implements of their trade were near at hand on the beaten earth. I needed to finish the patch of shade beneath the background tree; shade needed to prevent the unworked wood from buckling in the heat of the sun. But the focal point of the picture, the men at their work, was complete and I was as satisfied with it as ever I would be with my compositions.

Mr Swain gazed at the painting for some time. Then he sighed and rose and turned the easel a little and walked back to stand and look again. He nodded. 'Yes,' was all he said but my heart beat unsteadily. I wished Gladys would bring some tea for my mouth was dry with tension.

'What else can you show me?'

I fetched Gladys then, and she went to bring down some more of the paintings from upstairs. Together with those stacked in the big cupboard at the head of my bed, there were over forty and we had to display them in batches. Paintings of women at the washtub, of men fishing or repairing nets and boats. Of rough seas smashing against the harbour wall, of calm sunsets. Of children searching rock pools, of a beggar sleeping in a patch of sunlight. . .

And there were a few of the 'different' ones, those pictures which I had found myself compelled to paint from time to time, portrayals of image rather than form, loose subjects set in swirls of colour that hinted at movement and feeling, that sought an instant response from the emotion rather than intellect. I had doubts about setting these out for my visitor but my artist's need for audience proved too strong and I was gratified by the time he spent poring over these novel depictions.

We took tea in the midst of a stack of boards and canvases and Mr Swain so far forgot himself as to smear his coat with dust. Some of the paintings had been completed when first we came to

157

the village, and I cringed over them for there was no doubt my work had improved over the years of daily practice. But Mr Swain seemed to find merit in a few of even the earlier canvases and busied himself making notes in a leather-bound book.

At last we sat down and looked at one another. He had long since lost his studied gallantry and even more did he remind me of Uncle Pierre, his eyes glittering with excitement as he patted the back of one pile of paintings. Then he turned to me.

'You have a small fortune here, Miss Millbrook. We could name our price in London! I have a friend who exhibits for me every five years in a small studio in Pimlico. I normally show about a dozen paintings from local artists, for it takes that long to get a few worthwhile pieces together. But these. . .' He encompassed the room with a wave. 'These! Well my dear Miss Millbrook,' he was beginning to recapture his normal manner, 'I can only ask you to forgive me for making you paint cottages and cats. How could you bear to do it?'

'Very simply, Mr Swain. For the money! They sell and I need to live.'

He shook his head in wonderment. But before he could say more I interrupted.

'But my collection is not for sale, Mr Swain.' I bit my lip at the look of consternation on his face. 'Perhaps I should explain. I live here because of an unfortunate accident which occurred some time ago and as a result I am estranged from my son. These paintings are my legacy to him for I am a woman of indifferent health. I know you will keep my confidence - no one else in the village knows so much about me. But then, you are the only one to have seen all of these.'

He regarded me with those keen eyes for some time, fingers rubbing the smooth surface of the gold watch. At last he nodded slowly and then bowed his head.

'I must accept your feelings. It has indeed been a privilege to see this work,' and his small hand again swept the room. 'But what a shame that it cannot be shared! You have given me an insight into the lives of local people that I am ashamed to admit is a new experience for me.' He turned in his seat and stared again at the picture on the easel. 'But think, my dear. Suppose your son inherits all these paintings? Too many to display, yet it would no doubt cause him feelings of great guilt to sell them. Why not select half a dozen or so to be your memorial, and sell the rest on his behalf. Those you retain would instantly be of greater value as your name became known. I won't say that I was not counting the commission I would make on your work, but you must believe me when I say that was secondary to the excitement of finding so rare a talent. Think about it, my dear. But while you do, will you at least let me send them off for an exhibition? I could ask my friend for use of the studio for one week for your work alone! "A Portrait of Polwerris." That's what it could be called!'

I turned away from his pleading eyes and as I did so my gaze fell upon the painting of a boat bobbing on a glittering, moving sea. It was the one over which Jinny had shown such response the first time we met, a picture at which most viewers gazed in confusion. And suddenly I needed to know if there were other Jinnys who might take delight in my imagery. . .

So I looked back at my friend, for so he had become in the course of the afternoon.

'All right, Mr Swain. You can take them all for exhibition. And I will offer for sale enough to cover the cost, and for reasonable expenses for yourself. For I should insist you travelled with the work.'

He let out a long-held breath. 'Splendid! Splendid! Give me a list of those you are prepared to part with. Not now! Not now! For I must go. George Peel has spent far too long in the tavern. Lucky for me that Prince knows his way home and is too lazy to take to his heels.' He went over to one of my experimental pictures. 'May I hope you will include some of this work in those you wish to sell? I think you will be surprised at the response they will bring. As for the rest, you have captured history in your work, Miss Millbrook. Later generations will look through the window you have opened and regard these toilers with admiration and shame. For they breathe and suffer and smile.' Then he blew his nose abruptly in the silk handkerchief which had hung so decoratively from his coat pocket, made his farewells, and went briskly down the road to find his driver.

Chapter Twenty

I swam next day with Toby. Gladys asked Will, who was working on a boat in the harbour to row us round to the cove. This he was only too pleased to do, smiling warmly at Gladys as he helped us into the dinghy. The sea was calm and it was a happy trio he later left on the small beach of white sand enclosed by the towering cliffs. When Will reluctantly rowed away, promising to return in an hour or so to take us back, Gladys spread our things on a rug well clear of the incoming tide and we helped Toby to unwind the wrappings on his leg. The bone was splinted and well secured; Doctor Lawrence had given orders to leave some ties round the splint, and after swimming to once more strap it up for support. The boy could not wait to be in the water and as soon as we had freed the final bandage, he took up his crutch and hopped down to the sea. Soon he was floating on his back, his crutch bobbing towards us on the gentle swell.

I was wearing nothing beneath my loose trousers and blouse and I had merely to drop my shawl and slip out of my clogs. I needed Gladys's support to wade through the shallow water, and she hitched up her skirts, then, gasping from the shock of the cold water, I let go her arm and was swimming. The buoyancy of the water soon made me forget the drag of the clothes I wore, light though they were, and the lift of the swell was an unexpected delight to me for I had never before swum in the sea.

I told Toby to swim without moving his bad leg; we could do some gentle exercises later for that. And so we swam about, revelling in the joy of independent movement. Soon, however, the coldness of the water sent us to the beach where we flopped onto Gladys's rug and soaked up the sun, for although it wanted an hour to noon, the heat would have driven us into the shade

160

were we not so chilled.

After a while, however, we ventured once more into the sea which did not now seem so cold, and this time we gave some thought to the simple exercises which Doctor Lawrence had devised for Toby's leg. Then I helped Toby back to the beach where Gladys rebound the splints. On my own now, I swam again, forcing my feeble body into a few minutes of fierce, fast movement, determined that my legs should obey my will.

Breathless, I returned to the beach, on my face a smile of triumph as I wobbled across the sand to flop down onto the rug. Soon the boat would return to pick us up and presently I took up my dry clothes and made for the cave where I changed, chilled by its dank shade. Toby had told me all about this cave, how it was used by smugglers who would hide their caches in the deep pools which lay against the cliff face within. I dressed in my lace-trimmed drawers and camisole, pulled on my trousers and fastened my blouse with fingers clumsy with cold, thinking with a smile that the cave had witnessed far stranger and darker sights than this in its long history.

By the time I regained the sunlight, Will's boat was rounding the headland. Toby wanted to row and persuaded Gladys, who was generally uneasy on the water, to help him. Will Thomas sat in the stern, an aimiable grin on his face as Toby coached Gladys into matching her stroke to his. Once, when she missed her stroke and fell in a tumble at his feet, he laughed aloud, but was gentle as he helped her back to her place. And as I sat watching them, I was glad for Gladys that she had found Will. And my pleasure was matched by the realisation that I was stronger now, and not so fearful of a future without my friend's constant support. Soon, as soon as I was further recovered, I would write to Charles to arrange our meeting, and here in the sunshine with the boat bobbing on the translucent water, the prospect did not seem so terrifying as before.

My mood of physical well-being was further enhanced when later that day a letter from Morwenna arrived. I opened the fat envelope with fingers that trembled a little and found, as I suspected, a long letter from Jason Pettigrew, the Solicitor. Morwenna's accompanying note was read at a glance for it simply said that here was the package I expected and she would be writing later and sent her love as always.

I sat at the table in my own room and slit the enclosed envelope which was addressed to 'Miss Elizabeth Smith' and withdrew the folded sheets, my heart beating unevenly. For was not this my first direct contact with someone from my old life, someone who might be prepared to help me or who might be telling me that for these last few years I had been in breach of the law of the land and must now face the inevitable consequences.

But his greeting reassured me as to where his sympathies lay and I read on with great relief:

My dearest Girl,

How can I tell you my emotions when I opened your letter? My joy to know that my lovely Girl still lived, that the sad ache I felt each time I thought of you would be no more. Suffice it to say that your letter took several readings for my old eyes were blinded by my tears of thankfulness to the Lord who watched over you in your danger. Yes, my dear, danger, for I never believed the story that you had drowned in the lake at Polmennor Court when your punt overturned as you returned from a day's painting. My Girl would never have come to such a feeble end.

Firstly, I wrote to Charles the day I received your letter for I, like you, had a fear of his reaction. I told him that I had incontrovertible evidence that you lived and that we must meet urgently to discuss ways to avoid a great scandal as the news-sheets would give much to get their hands on such a tale.

That was over a week ago - I delayed writing to you until I had seen him, but since I have still not yet received a reply, I write now because of the delight it gives me to pen my thoughts to you. I want to meet you face to face and therefore I write to ask your whereabouts so that I may travel to you, wheresoever you may be. So, dear Child, let me know soon what preparations I must make to journey over land or sea to reach you. My years fall away from me at the thought. I shall ride on a white horse like the brave knights of old. Perhaps not, perhaps not! A carriage then, or a ship if you are so far away.

Talk of ships brings me to Guy. From your letter you knew he had returned to France, running away from his school soon after that dreadful funeral Charles gave for you. I hear from him on occasions. He does well, a nineteen-year-old, running a vineyard which is growing in prosperity under his care. He continues his education with a tutor but tells me he has no need of Greek and History for his travels finding markets for his wine teach him far more than his old tutor can know! He has your Spirit my dear, and your Grace. I recognise your dilemma: to discover after weeks of delirium that you have been pronounced dead and buried, that your only child has fled from the country, taking his grief to be assuaged by your family in Normandy. Yes, my heart breaks to think of your despair but I give thanks to the Good God who strengthens us that your expectation of death receded and your health has improved.

I have sent for Guy! It may be some time before he receives my letter for he travels much in building up his business. But this news cannot be given to him in a letter; I must meet him face to face and then you will be able to see your son once more.

Pardon me, my dear, I weep at the thought and my tears have smudged the paper. [My own tears dripped down my nose throughout the reading of the letter and I rubbed them away on my sleeve, burning with impatience at the blurring of my vision.]

I will say no more just now. Write to me. Write to me swiftly so that I may make my travel plans. How well you have covered your tracks! I have tried to make discreet enquiries at Woodlands about the girl, 'Miss Elizabeth Smith' who must receive this letter, but I have made no progress. My hope is that you are indeed in this country so that a journey by sea may not in fact, be necessary. Ah me! What a feeble knight I make. Write to me Darling Girl. Your letter will make my blood run more warmly and swiftly through these old veins. Bless me! A love letter at my age! For that is what this is my Sweet. I see it all now! My urge to keep this news to myself and not consult the law is so that I may avail myself of your 'freedom' and marry you tomorrow!

Take no notice of my foolish ravings! Blame your lovingly remembered Beauty and Kindness and Affection for your Friend.

Always your Servant,
Jason Pettigrew.

I showed my letter to Gladys. How could I not when she had been at my side through all the travails which had brought me here to Polwerris, and she too wept at the thought of meeting Guy once more. For she shared none of my fear and doubt that my son might shun me, unable to forgive the wilful actions that had led to our anguished separation. Gladys put down the letter and danced round the kitchen stepping a hornpipe that Guy had taught her so long ago while I watched and laughed and cried at the same time.

But when I returned to my own room to read and re-read the letter, doubts of a different kind began to chill me. Why had Charles not replied to my friend's letter? I began to go over the sequence of events. Lambeth Weekes had taken the letter to Charles and returned at least a week before I wrote to Pettigrew. Then my friend had written to Charles demanding a meeting. Another week had passed before he wrote this lovely letter to me. Almost three weeks since Charles had discovered I still lived. What had he been doing in that time? And what of Lambeth Weekes? Had he, despite my warnings, gone again to Charles? Certainly I had seen nothing of him since the day when he had told me of Mr Swain's visit. But that need not mean anything for Lambeth worked to his own pattern, and in his own way.

The euphoria of the visit from Mr Swain and his enthusiasm for my paintings had so buoyed me up that I had briefly put aside my worries and fears. Now, after the wonder and excitement of the letter, they rose again and caught at my throat.

I took my sticks and informed Gladys that I would walk down to the harbour for a while and went out into the heat of the summer day. I made my way down to the small beach alongside the harbour wall and found some shade beneath its grey stone. It was strangely still for mid-afternoon, no child made sandcastles at the water's edge and even the sporadic banging from the men working on a boat in the harbour basin sounded muffled and distant.

I sat and let the sand run through my fingers while the conflicting emotions churned within my breast. It seemed all too much to bear. I wondered whether perhaps the chemical I had received during the operation was still working inside my trembling body for I had never in my life suffered such a disturbance of nerves. Fleetingly the thought came to me that it was in just such a state that people took that final desperate step to end their lives. Certainly the thought of death and calm and peace fluttered like a dove through my turbulent emotions.

I stood up and walked across the beach, to and fro, to and fro, keeping to the strip of pebbles where my sticks had better support. Presently the concentration required to keep my footing began to calm me. The hat with which I had covered my salt-stiffened hair gave welcome shade, and I continued to criss-cross the beach until my legs started to protest. People began to appear once more, children came running past me towards the water's edge, one or two women emerged from their houses; men's voices could be heard beyond the wall and the noise from the smithy up the hill rebounded off the cliffs. The strange hiatus was over; life went on. And my wild thoughts were calmed.

I set off home. And just as I climbed the steps to the front door, something made me turn, and there, sails billowing as they caught a slight breeze, was Theo's ship rounding the headland.

It was dusk before he came to me. Later he told me that there had been much to do with berthing his ship, removing some goods, discussing further orders with the local merchant who had interested himself in Theo's venture. But for me it was a long, impatient wait and Gladys would have been shocked had she been able to hear my petulant mutterings. And all the time I tried to convince myself that it was not me he would visit, but his bride to be, Gwendoline Matthews.

Gladys coaxed me to eat, thinking my mood was a reaction to the letter we had received. And in part it was. But so too was my burning need to see Theo. To be close enough to touch, yet not to touch. For he was not mine. Such a hunger there was within me but the food Gladys proffered so anxiously stuck in my throat and after a few mouthfuls I put down my fork. She removed the plate, clicking her tongue in reproach, and then, touching my hair, she informed me that she had lit the fire and filled the cauldron in the scullery so that I might wash away the salt from my skin.

I was grateful for the benison of the hot water. The scar from the operation had healed well and it was good to lie in the long wooden tub and for a while blank out all thoughts and worries and desires, for I now accepted that Theo would not call on us until the morrow.

Gladys brought me a choice of clothes but I decided to shorten this endless day by donning my nightgown and a long red damask wrap. She was going for a walk with Peggy Tresize, a freedom she was able to give herself now that I was so much more mobile and I smiled my appreciation as she took her light shawl and waved her goodbye. And if the two young women should happen to meet Will and Peggy's young man, their walk would last long into the sunlit evening.

When she had gone, closing the door softly behind her, I made my way to my room. The setting sun shone straight through the small harbour window, bathing the room in a red glow and I stood gazing out for a long time. I was still standing there when there was a light knock on the door and I turned and Theo stood before me!

I think I held out my arms to him. Certainly I remember that for a moment he leaned against the door, then his face changed. He turned the key in the lock behind him, crossed the room and at last, at last I was in his arms.

His lips tasted of salt and his breath was sweet as the sea breeze. He groaned as he held me, tipping back my head to receive his hungry lips. And my mouth responded to his need and when he moved his head and his lips travelled down my neck I shuddered with desire.

Then he lifted me in his arms and I pushed back the doors of my bed and he laid me down on the quilt. His seaman's hands, palms polished smooth by the ropes, slipped the wrap from my shoulders and drew the long nightgown over my head and I lay back watching with eager impatience as he pulled off his shirt. His chest and back were deeply tanned, the skin of his haunches startlingly white as he stepped out of his canvas trews. Then there was the sweet kiss of our skins as he drew me to him.

Ah, dear reader, perhaps I should not thus describe our coming together, but how can I not record the wonder and the passion of our love. Never before had I known such delight as when I felt his lips travel down my body. Never before had I anticipated and met, another's needs with such abandon and desire. Theo! Theo! His name was music, my heart a drum beat as the blood pulsed through my body. And then the wonder of exploration was not enough, was too much, and our urgent bodies met and fused and were one.

And the aftermath of our coupling was no less sweet. I turned my head on the pillow and looked at my love who lay beside me. I think he slept, totally relaxed against me, lips faintly smiling. I gazed at him with my artist's eyes, loving the width of his brow,

166

the strong cheekbones and jaw. Presently, I ran my fingers through his dark beard, liking the way the curls sprang back on release. There were curling hairs on his chest too, and these I pulled and teased and then he was awake and his hands found my breasts and I could not believe that the fire so newly quenched could blaze so fiercely once again.

When next I became aware of my surroundings the red glow of sunset in which we had met had died away. Now the room was pale with the clear grey wash of light that follows the setting of the sun. Theo kissed me and rose and pulled on the clothes which lay on the floor. I too, drew on my nightgown and robe and when Gladys came back half an hour later, her friend with her, they found us sitting at the kitchen table drinking cups of tea. Peggy Tresize looked askance at my dressing gown, but we appeared so casual and relaxed, (Oh! how relaxed!) that I could see she would have no suspicions to report to her mother.

I was careful, however, not to let my eyes meet his until Peggy had gone on her way. But when Theo stood up to leave I went to his side and briefly touched his hand. He gazed at me, his eyes so full of tenderness that my heart wrenched.

'I'll see you tomorrow, Elizabeth.'

So trite a remark. Such poetry and music.

'Goodnight, Theo.'

Of such banality are the words of lovers. Outwardly as commonplace and insignificant as grains of spice. Only the sharers of the conversations know the feelings aroused, like those who bite on the peppercorn, the sudden explosion of stimulus and heat. And such was our separation.

When he had gone I made my way back to my room and climbed into the bed which smelt of him. Of us. And I closed my eyes, my lips smiling as my hand traced the imprint in the pillow where his head had lain. And all the day's anxieties were gone, swept away on the tidal wave of our love.

Theo was back. Tomorrow I would see him again. Stray thoughts drifted through my sleepiness like clouds across a moonlit sky. And the last thing I remember before I slept was that it was time to tell Theo my story.

Chapter Twenty-one

But Theo did not come next day. We soon learned why. A Spanish fishing ketch had run aground at Galvin Point some way up the coast, a grim spot, inaccessible by land. Two men in a dinghy from the cove, lifting crab pots in the dawn light, had seen the stricken vessel and old Tom Hunter and his even older brother, Ezekial, had bent their aged backs and rowed urgently back to the harbour and roused Theo who was asleep aboard his ship. They gathered a crew in minutes. I had seen how the men responded to an emergency, the apparently unhurried manner in which they made their preparations, the way they seemed to steady themselves for whatever they might be called upon to do; men who would use every ounce of their skill and strength and ingenuity to save their fellows if it were humanly possible, and use those same strengths to claim their share of booty if there were none alive left to claim it.

Five men were still aboard the grounded ketch when Theo's party reached them, but the skipper's twelve-year-old son had been lost overboard when they foundered. Everyone worked together, and on the midday tide they winched the damaged vessel off the rocks and Theo took her in tow. The wind was kind and we were all there to watch as they rounded the headland and drew the listing ketch into the harbour. Two gigs had already gone to search for the boy's body, nets and ropes hidden beneath the thwarts from the Spanish captain's anguished eyes. And for once the grim underwater reef yielded up its prey, gently and unmarked. Theo himself went down to the gig and received the boy's limp body. And it was Theo who passed his burden to the arms of the boy's father and who knelt beside the man when he slid down to the deck, and Theo's tears which fell for this other

168

man's son, whom he had never known, and who now was lost.

The whole village shared in the Spaniard's grief. The women took the crew of the vessel into their homes for food, rest and dry clothing. The men took time from the immediacy of their own struggle for survival to toil over repairs to the damaged boat, for the skipper must urgently take his son's body home to his wife across the sea so that she might look upon his quiet face just once more.

And I went back to my room and did the only thing I could. I painted. I worked with urgency to record this other side of the life of my village; the humanity and compassion that flowed in so rich a stream from the meagre resources of these cottages, food that could ill be spared which was spread with generosity before these strangers, labour which asked no wage as the men hammered and caulked the boat's bottom while she lay heeled over on the beach beside the harbour wall. A series of water colours I began that day, perhaps my best, for while I painted this record of nobility and tragedy, my own tears flowed. For I knew that I must send Theo back to Gwendoline, for only she could give him the child his heart so much desired. And I accepted that my dream of a lifetime in his arms was not to be. Not to be.

And gradually I found a kind of peace. Gwendoline came down to the harbour that day, for she had heard of the tragedy by means of that strange osmosis in village life, whereby even the remotest cottage is fed news, and from my window I saw her holding her son's hand as she watched from the harbour wall. Theo saw her too and raised a hand in greeting. And I was glad she could not see the doubt and confusion which I knew would be there in his eyes.

He sailed as the sun set, accompanying the Spanish vessel part-way across the Channel to be sure she was not taking water. Then he would complete his planned journey to Plymouth, for his initial trip had been fruitful and he had promising business to arrange.

I did not let time hang on my hands. The paintings I had started the previous day needed more work, but not too much for I had learned that too much is worse than not enough. And perhaps that applies to everything in our lives, to food, to possessions, maybe

169

h

even to the very length of our allotted span. . .

And so I filled my days. There was my morning swim which did much to strengthen my legs, short walks to places which so lately had lain beyond my reach, painting and more painting. I wrote again to Uncle Pettigrew, thanking him warmly for his support and saying that I needed a little more time to regain my strength after my operation before arranging a meeting with Charles, and that my more urgent need was to re-establish contact with Guy. I asked him to bear with my secrecy for a little longer and to write once again to Elizabeth Smith at Woodlands if he should need to contact me urgently; otherwise to wait until my next letter.

Mr Swain sent his man with crates to collect my paintings for an exhibition which was to be put on in Pimlico as soon as could be arranged, and I watched the bulk of my work, carefully stacked in the crates, swaying in the back of the gig as the horse leaned into the harness and clopped away up the hill.

Gladys had to go to Penzance in the pony cart to purchase more painting materials, for there was no sign yet of Lambeth Weekes. She left early in the morning, with an old neighbour, James Opie, to do the talking for she was nervous with strangers although she could communicate on paper perfectly well when she chose. And after they had gone I prowled round the house, restless and troubled. The cottage had a hollow feel, like an empty shell. I had noticed this before in other houses when a woman had gone to tend a sick relative; that absence of the driving force which makes the humblest of dwellings into a home.

It was this lack of purpose that drove me out into the early morning sunshine. I would not swim today without Gladys as my chaperone for I was careful not further to offend the sensibilities of my neighbours. I walked up to the top of the headland, a good half mile and the farthest and steepest walk I had yet undertaken. I rested many times but when at length I dropped onto the rabbit-cropped grass on the clifftop, I was glowing with the pride of achievement. I knew I would never walk as freely as others, but the relative mobility I now obtained was a wonderful release.

I lay face downwards, watching the moving sea. Today it was of a blue so dark as to be indigo and purple, except where the small waves danced towards the beach and curled with swan-like grace in purest turquoise and purest white.

The harbour lay to my left, the cottages snug in the sun and I could see the movement of people, hear voices, words even, for the still air was like a lake through which the sound floated upwards; words and laughter and snatches of song. For these were the lucky ones, men and women who worked near their homes, in the fresh air, the men not deep in the darkness of the mines, the women not toiling in the clamour of the crushing yards, wielding sledges in air too thick with dust to breathe in summer, in winter worse than underground, so the men said, with the cold winds and driving drizzle and babies lying in baskets waiting to be fed. No wonder was it that women could lose their hold on life with such abruptness. And children too, young boys standing in the yards, ankle deep in the cold water of the streams, sorting the ore with their innate understanding of the rocky land on which they lived.

I seemed no longer to feel the sun warm on my back and I shuddered and thanked the gods that strangely shaped my life for the gifts I had and for the relative ease of my life. And presently I rose and made my way homeward. As I reached my front door I stopped to give the time of day to the miller who was turning his cart where the road widened before the harbour. He was a cheerful man, his big body enveloped in a huge smock the colour of wheat and it gave off a floury smell, warm and comforting. He turned his cart and plodded up the hill towards me, leading his horse to preserve the beast's strength for the steeper hills along the road.

'Looking well you is, my 'andsome. I been meanin' to come down Polwerris to see this 'ere mermaid they d' tell about, swimming round the bay like a fish.' His eyes danced and as he grinned small particles of flour rolled down his cheeks and off his nose. Close to, I could see the fine stitching on the yoke of his smock, a practical garment as I myself had found, with room to move in comfort and a great protector of the clothes beneath.

'Come down tomorrow Mr Polkinghorne,' I smiled. 'Go out to Pointer's Rock,' and I indicated the upthrust of rock that marked the end of the headland, 'and I will sing to you and lure you to join me in the caves.'

He threw back his head and laughed the great roar that matched his size. ' 'Tis almost worth drownin' for, my bird, Tha's the best offer I've had this day, nor likely to have no better I can

171

tell 'ee.' Then he looked up and down the street as if to be sure we were private and his face became as solemn as the upward wrinkles would allow. 'What 'av 'ee done with Lambeth Weekes, Miss Millbrook. His pony is eatin' me out of house and home.'

I had not known that Lambeth stabled his horse at the Mill when he journeyed away from home. My face must have registered surprise, followed instantly by shock and apprehension. 'I sent him nowhere, Mr Polkinghorne,' I replied grimly, 'but I think I possibly know where he went.'

'Then you best tell me where he is, my dear. For he told me as how 'e wouldn' be no more than a week at most, four days more like, he said. And now 'tis nearly three weeks gone by.' He looked left and right once more. 'You see, my dear, he left me a letter to be took to Lawyer Watters if anything should 'appen to'm. I dunno how long I'm s'posed to wait afore I do that.'

I bit my lip, thinking desperately, my body cold. If Lambeth had kept his promise to write down everything that he knew. . .

'Give me a day or two, Mr Polkinghorne. I'll make some enquiries first. You know how secretive he is. He wouldn't be pleased if he turned up in a few days and found that the lawyers were settling his affairs!' I forced myself to meet the miller's eyes, eyes that were suddenly keen and intent.

'Previously he went to North Cornwall on a personal matter for me.' I went on, 'And he thought he had found a way of making some extra money for himself. I warned him not to try. I thought he had taken my advice. But it seems not. I think it best if I write, before you do anything more, and find out if he did in fact go there again.'

'Well, all right my dear. I don't suppose another day or two'll make no diff'rence. But his old aunt down Falmouth stopped me last week. Some worried up, she is. Not 'bout Lambeth,' and here his face broke into his irrepressible grin, 'she's upset 'cos her rent is due, and he do always pay it. I must say I never knew Lambeth to put his hand in his pocket for any other soul. But my missus said tis 'cos he do want to keep the 'ouse for hisself when she's gone. 'Tis right down near the waterfront, ideal for all his dealin's.'

I forced a smile in acknowledgement of his wife's astuteness and he went on his way and I let myself into the cottage and sank onto the settle before the hearth. Gladys had banked the fire carefully and the turves would need only to be uncovered to bring to boiling point the great iron kettle that sat on the trivet at the edge of the fire box. My distracted gaze travelled over the implements she kept so neatly to hand on the granite slabs on the hearth, the skillets for fish, the saucepans, the small oven that looked like a shallow hat sitting on the stone to one side. My mind refused to leave the safety of the hearth and I remembered with what interest I had watched, first her grandmother and then Gladys, heating the small oven on the fire until it was hot enough, then lifting it off with the tongs. Then they would place their pies and pasties inside the 'hat' and put back the lid onto which they piled hot ashes. And within the hour the contents would be cooked to perfection. My gaze roved to the cloam oven in the wall at one side of the fire, the larger oven which was used just once a week for the 'big bake' of bread and buns and cakes, for it was greedy of fuel, consuming branch after branch of dry furze, the pale smoke billowing from the opening to drift away up the chimney, until the walls of the oven were heated through. Then the quick scrape out of the ashes and in went the food to be baked, the door firmly closed so that the bread would bake readily in the retained heat. And the saffron cake of the next batch would fill the kitchen with its rich fragrance.

Gladys had left food set out for me. But I sat before the hearth, unable to eat, recognising at last my guilt. For I had known all along what would happen. I should have told someone. Told Theo. Told Mr Polkinghorne. For though I had not known of the miller's involvement in Lambeth's schemes, I had made no effort to know, no effort at all to find out if Lambeth Weekes had indeed followed his threatened plan.

I had told the miller I would make enquiries of my own. Now I laughed grimly at the thought. For who could I approach? It was not a matter for the militia stationed at Falmouth and the local magistrates and the Parish Constables were notoriously cautious of offending the landowners whose favour had given them their powers. If they should learn the truth of my situation, the most likely outcome would be my imprisonment for knowingly deceiving my husband and he, rich and powerful, would be considered the innocent party. My suggestion to the miller that I would write to enquire about Lambeth was simply a play for time; Charles was the last person to whom I could write about

173

Lambeth.

There was no one to whom I could turn. No one but Theo. And he was not here and I did not know how long it would be before he returned. And the ache for him was physical, the longing to feel those strong arms round me, the warmth of his breath on my cheek, to hear his voice. . .

My whole body was shaking. I knew I should eat, or at least should stir the fire for warmth, for the thick walls kept out the heat of the summer's day. I forced myself to remove the turves and I fed some wood onto the embers. Soon the flames leapt and I held my trembling hands out to their warmth. Then I ate a mouthful of the cold chicken Gladys had set out and made myself a camomile tisane, and by degrees I became a little calmer.

It would be hours before Gladys returned. I could not paint, that much I knew without making the attempt. I could not concentrate on my copy of the local paper which came each week, and I put it back upon the kitchen table no wiser than when I had picked it up. And so I passed the long hours in unfruitful contemplation of the now glowing fire, huddled on the wooden settle with my feet outstretched to the warmth of the hearth, my thoughts an endless treadmill of guilt and apprehension.

And Gladys found me thus when she returned. She glanced at me as she came in, her arms full of purchases. She had already rubbed down and fed Jem and he was back in his field and she went to wash her hands and face before coming over to me. I roused myself from my torpor to ask her how her day had been and I put the kettle on to boil once more. Then I told her what the miller had said about Lambeth Weekes. She stilled for a moment, her face reflecting quick concern. Then her eyes cleared and she turned to me, hands flashing with the speed of their movement. They had met Theo in Penzance, she told me. Yes, Theo! and he would be back in the harbour before nightfall.

And all my good intentions, my plans to break with him, to send him back to Gwendoline freely and without reserve, fled away. For my need of him was greater than was hers. But even as I told myself that it was only to seek his advice and help, my body was filled with desire and happiness that soon he would be here and that once more we could be together.

And when it was almost dark, he came. We sat in the kitchen, the three of us in candlelight and fire glow, the curtains not drawn so that the curious could see us sitting and chatting, innocent and amiable. For I was concerned about causing scandal, not for myself, but for Gwendoline's sake. And an hour later when heavy clouds deepened the darkness, Theo went out of the front door and down to the harbour and Gladys, tired by her excursion, went off to bed. I blew out the candles and listened carefully but even before I expected, there was a light scratch on the back door and then it opened and he entered, closing the door silently behind him.

In the darkness we clung together, arms and lips fierce to hold. And then we made our stumbling way to my room and there was the deeper shadow of my bed, a welcoming cave for our reunion.

We knew one another now; knew each other's needs and responses more sensitively than many a long-married couple. For there were no reservations between us, only the recognition of our love and passion, all the sweeter because I at least, knew it soon must end.

So passed time. I do not know how long it was before we briefly slept. Then I rose and drew the curtains across the panes and lit a candle. Leaning back on the pillows Theo watched me and held out his arms, smiling, and I slipped back into the curve of his arm.

And in that firm embrace I found myself telling him about Lambeth Weekes and all that had gone before, all the strange events, acts wilful and wanton, both of my own and of others, that had brought me at length to the refuge of Polwerris Cove.

Chapter Twenty-two

It was because I was bored that I took a lover. Richard was the younger son of the Penhaligon's whose estate bordered Trevingey, its wooded acres encompassing, like ours, several of the streams which made their way from the moors to the sea, joining the River Tamar in their final reaches. He was twenty-six, and had just returned on furlough from India and he made me laugh, and surprised me with unexpected wit and cynicism about our acquaintances and flattered me with his persistent attentions. He called often, though always with propriety, so when we met unexpectedly one day in the grounds, it was quite without my foreknowledge.

I was with Gladys in her trap which was laden with stools and picnic basket and painting materials, for we had a day free of engagements and the sun shone warmly overhead. Suddenly Richard rode from the woods and swerved towards us across the rolling parklands of Trevingey.

He reined in beside us and leaned over to take my hand, his grey eyes dancing with mischief.

'I was told you drive about the estate sometimes, and this is the third day I've risked getting my head blown off by those game-keepers of yours. And just for the chance of this,' and he raised my hand to his lips.

Gladys had pulled up the pony and now sat, staring stolidly ahead. It was spring, and the park lay, sun burnished and green beneath trees which shimmered with the pink of bursting buds.

My heart, sore with missing Guy who had just returned to his hated boarding school, seemed to melt beneath the ardent gaze of the handsome young soldier. I was still a young woman, starved of affection for Charles had long since ceased to visit my room,

176

preferring his tumbles with the women of the night, one of whom had recently been given a cottage in the estate grounds.

Richard rode with us that day, and sat near while I painted and Gladys sewed. Though not much work was done by either of us for he entertained us both, amusing and cleverly satirical with his outrageously exaggerated accounts of his foreign exploits and the foibles of the men in high command whom he had observed with his cynic's eye.

And that was how it started. It was surprisingly simple for Charles never bothered to question our trips to distant parts of the estate; why should he, it was our habit of many years.

Only these days, Richard and I would leave Gladys with the trap, and I would ride pillion with my lover until we found a glade where we could tether the horse while we pushed aside the beech wands and made for ourselves a bed upon the bluebells, their crushed scent heavy in the air.

It was an interlude for us both. Nothing more. Neither of us pretended it to be a grand passion and we were careful not to meet too often or to a pattern that might cause talk. Richard was on extended leave to help with the running of the estate for his father had just died and his brother, the new squire, was on his back recovering from a hunting accident. And we both knew that when his help was no longer needed at home, he would return to his regiment without a backward glance.

And so our light-hearted assignations went on through the idyllic early summer but stopped for the long vacation when Guy came home, Richard impatient and wishing away the summer days. But it was something Guy said during those holiday weeks that sowed the seed in my mind of all that was to follow.

Charles had been his usual cold self, disapproving of Guy's every action and my every word, his sarcasm bitter and cutting even to me who had long since built a carapace of indifference to his cruel gibes. But when Guy said, 'Maman, why do you stay with him? Why do you not leave, go to Normandy! You could live with Grandmere and I could join you there and make the vineyard prosper like it did in your father's time,' I had stopped his words with my finger.

'And do you think your father would permit that? He would know my plans as soon as they were made and I would be dragged ignominiously back before I had even reached the coast.'

177

But when he had gone back to school and life resumed its routine of empty social visits to and from the same insular group of acquaintances, the thought grew. Richard and I once more began to meet and I made sure my paintings were half complete before I set out so that when I returned there would be something to show for the hours spent away in the park to those eyes curious enough to look.

Then came a formal invitation from Lord and Lady Tregale of Polmennor Court to the engagement party of her daughter, Georgiana. 'Come and stay for a week or two,' Lucinda urged in the accompanying note. Charles consented to go just for the party, when, he said, he might meet one or two men who mattered. But I could go on ahead and help the silly woman since that is what Lucinda wanted.

I thought and planned and when next I met Richard, I asked straightaway if he would escort me in flight to Normandy - while I was staying at Polmennor Court, for it was closer to the sea and I would be away from the eyes of Charles's henchmen. At first he protested at the thought of my going away, for at that time there was no one else in his life, but he knew as well as I that his brother was almost recovered and soon he must himself depart. 'Damn me!' he laughed, 'what a joke! Just imagine Charles's face when he finds out the bird has flown!'

His levity annoyed me somewhat, for my escape must depend on secrecy and careful planning. But he calmed down and pleased me with some ideas of his own. 'I will arrange the sea passage from Fowey Harbour. Just you be at the place of assignation on time and leave all else to me.'

So it was that a few days later I was standing in my bedroom at Trevingey helping Gladys to pack my things for the planned visit. Into one trunk she carefully laid the satins and silks of my evening gowns, into another the laces and lawns of the morning frocks and tea dresses, a froth of colour and ribbon, while I attended to a valise, small enough to strap behind the saddle of a horse. Into this I packed the cambric and silk of small clothes, a travelling gown in fine rose wool, and good walking shoes. I would be wearing my riding habit and skirt of smart green velvet and a hooded cape in which I could hide my face should the need arise. It was enough.

Gladys was full of concern at the thought of having to cross the sea again for she had accompanied us to Normandy when my mother died, and had suffered the sea malady most severely in the two rough crossings of the Channel. I reassured her. She could go back to her grandmother until the next summer when, I promised, I would send for her when the sea was smooth and calm as a lake. Her face lit up, for since the death of her grandfather she worried about her dear Gran, alone on the isolated holding.

So she too packed a trunk. And into it I threw some of my good clothes that she could alter for herself and her grandmother. And as an afterthought I packed my box of brushes and paints, for painting trips would enable me to meet Richard in secrecy so that we might complete our arrangements.

And so we left Trevingey in our usual style for Polmennor Court, Gladys following the carriage, driving her Jem in the trap as she always chose to do, my mare on a leading rein beside our surly groom. I would, by choice, have ridden the twenty miles between the two estates, but Charles insisted that I travel in the splendour of the new carriage, as a lady should. Our trunks were securely stowed, and safe in a corner of my valise lay the little suede bag with the sovereigns from my French allowance which would fund our escape.

It was on the third day of my visit that Richard told me the final arrangements had been made; that it was time to go. His grey eyes sparkled as he talked, and I could see that the thought of spending several days and nights alone with me was no small inducement to the making of his plans. We had met briefly in the grounds of the court for the house was overrun with guests and their servants, ears everywhere, as he put it. His brother was now recovered and Richard had already made his departure from his home, stating he would spend a few days with friends before rejoining his regiment.

There would be a full moon tomorrow night, he told me, a help for us when riding through the dark woods to Fowey where we would board ship for Cherbourg. Was he sure that no word had slipped out, that none of the servants had wind of our plans? Positive. Have no fear. But his easy laugh for once did not amuse me and doubts accompanied my lone ride back to the house. For if Charles should get to hear of my flight. . . And though he was still at Trevingey, his cold presence seemed to reach out in threat and a shiver of apprehension ran down my spine.

I sent Gladys off the next afternoon, telling Lucinda that I felt she should have a few days at her old home. A large trunk for a week's stay? Her expressive eyebrows shot up. Some blankets and clothing for her grandmother, I explained glibly. My valise was tucked away inside the trunk, together with my paints, and a net of hay and a bag of oats filled the remaining space in the trap. Off they went, Jem happy to be out with his easy mistress, heading along the road towards her grandmother's. But five miles along the way she would turn off into the woods and wait until all was clear before making for the crossroads near the old mill where we would meet that night. And I was glad I had given her a pony skin rug to use when driving for she would need its soft warmth during her long wait that night.

Back at Polmennor Court, the day dragged along its trivial course, the continual changing of dress made more onerous still because I had to use one of Lucinda's maids to help with the fastenings. At last I went down to dinner in one of the lavishly embroidered evening gowns which I myself had designed. I toyed with my food, and hoped that the suppressed excitement which had brightened my eyes and brought a flush to my cheeks, might be interpreted as incipient fever, for at eleven o'clock I pleaded a headache and left the card table. In my room, I wrote a brief note of apology to Lucinda, rumpled the bed and placed the envelope beneath a pillow. I did not want the note found until the next morning when the bed was made. (Much later I learned that when Charles produced my 'body', Lucinda said the regretful words must have indicated suicide and she was only too glad to give the missive to my husband for him to destroy.) I did not send for the maid and took off my silken evening gown with difficulty, missing Gladys's deft fingers. Then I lay on the bed for a while, watching the slow drag of hands across the face of the clock, but well before midnight I could wait no longer and donned my riding habit. It was a cold night for September and dark clouds scurried before the wind as I crossed the yard to the stables. I found my sidesaddle, new and light enough for me to carry, and I bumped it along the track to the field where my mare grazed.

How long it took for my cold fingers to fasten those buckles! I was ready to cry with frustration by the time Silver was at last harnessed and I cursed her pale colour as the moon briefly appeared between the skudding clouds. I waited at the far end of the field until another cloud spilled its welcome shadow and then I opened the gate and led the mare through, closing it behind us and climbing on to its bars in order to mount. Then I set off along the woodland track where the early fall of leaves muffled the sound of Silver's hoofs. I walked her for the first half mile, then, impatient for action, I kicked her into a gallop.

It was well that the track was almost as familiar as my own grounds at Trevingey. I have often thought of that midnight flight, and the shadows of the trees fleeting past, with the wind on my face tearing the hood from my head and loosening my hair so that it streamed out behind me. A wild, reckless ride, when any pothole could bring our downfall. But the god of fugitives was with me and I did not slow until the gleam of the river showed through the trees on my left.

Now I walked Silver quietly along the track until it met the road. Suddenly nervous, I pulled up my horse and glanced towards the bridge which crossed the river. All was still, the only sound the muffled roar of the water where it went over the weir and the clank, clank of the mill wheel, endlessly revolving.

And then the moon sailed out in splendour and every detail of the scene sprang into being, the distant mill, the water, black save for the white scar of the weir, the pale curve of the road. I strained my eyes for a glimpse of the pony and trap which Gladys was to have drawn in beneath the clump of trees beside the mill. I could see nothing, hear nothing apart from the water and the soft swish of the trees overhead.

At last, dry mouthed, I left the shelter of the woods and Silver's feet were slow drumbeats on the road as I made my way towards the copse. But it was not until I entered its welcome darkness that I was able to make out the shape of the trap and the next minute Gladys was helping me down from the saddle.

We clung together for a moment, no longer mistress and maid, but two friends who must part for an unknown span of time. A moment only, then I felt her stiffen. Profoundly deaf though she was, Gladys was acutely sensitive, always aware. And it was she, not I, who had seen Silver prick her ears and Jem turn his head towards the bridge.

Then I heard. A single horse at the gallop. Surely Richard would not ride to an assignation in such a manner! Then I heard the urgent thud of other, pursuing hooves. The moon still bathed

181

the road with silver light and I saw his urgent signalling arm. Gladys helped me into the saddle and the next minute I was alongside Richard, galloping towards the bridge.

'They're after us! I'll take you half a mile up the road and then draw them off. Stay with me, sweetheart!' And the laugh was in his voice, a reckless gaiety in his bearing even then, with pursuit so close behind. I caught something of his daring as we thundered towards the bridge, for he had already planned for such an eventuality as a soldier would. There would be another time, another assignation and another flight, for we had good horses and we knew our destinations; the advantage in the chase was ours.

The bridge was ahead and we swerved our horses into the narrow vee of its mouth, Richard a length before me. And then the dark woods ahead were split by a flash of light and the crack of a gunshot. Fear froze the echoes of the shot. For I had seen the tall horseman in that instant flash. Charles! Charles, rigid in his saddle, his pistol arm outstretched. And then, while the echoes still rebounded, he was urging his horse from the woods towards the far side of the bridge to try and cut us off!

There was another loud report and then it was that Richard lurched sideways, only to recover, and spur his mount onwards. My own horse reared in terror and there were more shots, from behind us this time. And as Silver wheeled on her hind legs I felt a sudden slash of fire across my back and I remember falling backwards through space and then there was the blessed darkness of oblivion.

Gladys saw it all from her hiding place. Saw Richard swaying onto his horse's neck as he raced away. Saw Charles wheel and follow close behind. Saw my horse, a rearing silver sculpture on the bridge. Told how I fell backwards to the river like a rag doll, with arms outstretched, my cloak a wide fan as it spread upon the surface of the water. And even as she started in desperation towards the river, two other riders, with their pistols in their hands, galloped past her hiding place. They reined in on the bridge and peered down at my body, still half afloat on the cushion of air trapped by the billowing cloak. She paused in the shadows, willing the river to send my body to her side of the bank, for she could swim not a stroke. Then all three watchers saw the river take me, saw the dark smudge of the cloak as it went over the weir. And just before another cloud enveloped the moon, she saw the men hesitate, and then turn and ride off to follow their master, and saw my body, now barely afloat, swing towards the nearer bank.

She plunged into the river, fighting to keep her footing in the strong current until she was waist deep in the cold confusion of water and darkness. Her straining eyes sought for my body, and a merciful shaft of moonlight caught the paleness of my face in the dark stream. Then her hands were clutching at the heavy cloak. She held my head above the water as she battled her way back to the bank and as she tried to pull me from the current, the very garment which had kept me afloat, waterlogged now, sought to drag me down. She wrenched open the fastener and let the current take the garment from her, down into the mill race whose thunder she would never hear, down over the sill to vanish beneath the great, rotating wheel.

Then, to her astonishment and relief, Gladys felt my body spasm and cough. She laid me prone on the ground and pressed urgently on my back and watched the water flow from my mouth. Again I coughed and retched and she knelt beside me and saw that I breathed again. Tears flowing down her cheeks, she dragged me to the trap and with desperate strength she heaved me up onto its floor. Then she grabbed the rug from the seat and flung it over me, all the while anxiously watching the bridge upstream for the return of my pursuers. For she knew they would soon catch up with the wounded Richard, hard on his heels as they were.

She dared not remain near the mill for they would surely return to seek my body, yet she could not take to the road for the fickle moon once more poured its light down through the trees. So she headed for the track up the hill opposite the copse, back to the place where she had waited in hiding for much of that long evening. Up the rough track she led the pony, the trap lurching behind and she groaned to think of me, so near to death and so ill used.

She urged the pony towards the small clearing from where she could see down into the valley and then she turned her attention to me. Her sewing scissors were in the trunk and she swiftly cut away my wet clothing, catching her breath when she saw the jagged wound across my lower back. She bound it tightly to stem the bleeding which the cold wet garments had suppressed, and then she pulled some hay from the net to make a rough mattress. She laid me on my side, face downwards in case there was yet more water in my lungs, wrapped dry clothing from the trunk about me, and covered me with the pony-skin rug. On this she spread the rest of the hay, both for concealment and extra warmth. And all the while she kept glancing down at the bridge over which she knew the men must soon return. They were longer than she expected and she had stripped off her own wet clothing and pulled on some dry garments before she saw them ride back across the bridge. Three riders leading two horses, one with a body slung across the saddle, head down, and limp.

One of the men gestured from the bridge to the place where I had fallen, another pointed excitedly at the wheel and they rode quickly down to the mill, and Gladys was glad that in their urgency their own horses trampled away the signs of our presence that we must have left.

Then she realised that the dark shadow which showed up on the wheel each time it revolved, was my cloak! They were a long time before they retrieved it, losing several branches in the process until at last one of the men found a pole and hook in one of the buildings and she saw them wrench the garment from where it clung. She clasped her hands in gratitude, for after having buoyed up my head when first I fell, now the cloak bore mute testimony to my death. They would not now watch the roads for their victim, but would make their way downstream, searching the banks for my mangled body.

Gladys wasted no more time. She led Jem out of the clearing and set off on her long journey home.

Chapter Twenty-three

Theo drew me gently to him as I came to the end of my story. I buried my head in his shoulder, tears pouring from my eyes. Tears for Richard who had died so needlessly, tears for the young woman who never again would ride with the wind in her hair, most of all, tears for my son who had so brutally been parted from his mother.

Presently Theo released me and got out of the bed. He went off to the kitchen and came back bearing the bottle of wine we had opened at the table, and two glasses. I was grateful, for my throat was tight and my voice husky from recounting all that had befallen on that autumn night three years ago.

Theo resumed his place beside me and we lay against the pillow watching the candle burn low in its socket. Presently he gave a deep sigh, shaking his head.

'How did you survive, my lovely, lovely girl?'

I closed my eyes for a moment, overwhelmed by the love and sympathy in his voice. Then I too shook my head in disbelief. . .

. . .It was Mrs Perry, Gladys's grandmother, who pulled me through. It was dawn when Gladys arrived. Her grandmother had helped to carry me into the kitchen and they laid me on the settle. I was deeply unconscious and my skin cold to the touch but Mrs Perry pressed her ear to my chest and heard the slow, weak pump of my heart. While Gladys, weeping with exhaustion and despair, described with her hands the night's events, Violet Perry filled two stone hot bottles and sorted through her collection of dried herbs for the makings of a poultice.

Together they pulled a truckle bed into the room and set it up near the fire and laid me on it. Presently the heat of the fire and the warmth of the bottles raised my body temperature and Violet checked the wound on my back and found that as she feared, it had begun to bleed again. She told me it was a ghastly wound, laying bare the bone on my pelvis. She staunched the bleeding with a compress and an hour later, seeing that I still breathed, she left me with Gladys and rode her old horse to fetch the doctor who had attended her own late husband. Grim faced, she had taken some of the sovereigns from the purse for she knew he would not ride a ten-mile round trip for nothing.

When he came he probed out the bullet and drew the edges of the wound together. He sounded my chest with his trumpet and shook his head.

'I doubt she would walk again after that injury, the bullet tracked across the spine. But it's immaterial. She'll get pneumonia. Call me again if you must, Mrs Perry, but I should save your money, for there's nothing more I can do except remove those stitches if she lives that long.'

But Violet Perry had a lifetime's knowledge of the herbs and fruits that grew around her. She had nursed her own husband through years of chronic chest weakness and knew precisely how to fight for my survival. I remember nothing of the next two weeks, only the smell of pungent steam in the tent of blankets she had built around me. But at last I opened my eyes and called to Gladys. I was bewildered, frightened, unable to move.

Immediately I was given a spoonful of beef tea. Violet smiled at me. 'There, 'tis a lot easier getting that down you now you're awake. Don't you worry about those legs, 'tis only bruising of the nerves. You'll be all right, my dear child.'

And her voice went on, soothing, comforting, and presently I fell asleep and she knew she had won me back.

Even so, it was another week before I had the strength to question all that had happened. And then I realised that Guy would think I was dead! I became so distressed that Mrs Perry said she would go to a friend's house on the Polmennor Estate and find out what was being said about my disappearance.

And so it was that I learned of my funeral. Guy had been there, she said, white faced and silent, Sir Charles coldly composed. There was a body, Violet said, taken no doubt from some poor-house to Trevingey in state. The story was that I had taken the punt to the island in the lake at Polmennor Court. The boat was found overturned and when the lake was searched, the sluice gates which governed its depth were discovered to be mysteriously open so that my body had been borne away on the current. My cloak was produced at the inquest and Charles's two men gave evidence as to how it led them to find my body trapped between boulders a mile downstream, unrecognisable, they said, apart from the cloak, because the stream was in spate and the rocks were many and jagged. . .

I was wild with grief for Guy and struggled to rise and for the first time was able to move my legs despite the searing pain. But then I sank back in hopelessness. What would it avail me to contact him? I was still very ill, my whole body trapped in a deathly lethargy. If he came, it might well be to my death-bed and then he would have to suffer his loss once more. No, it was better to leave matters as they were, and to let nature take its course.

Then Violet told me Guy had gone to France. He had refused to return to his school and announced he would go to his grandmother in Normandy. Charles for once had been unable to coerce his son or bend him to his will. And for the first time since the shooting I felt a flicker of happiness. So Guy would do what he most desired. And Grandmere would feed him all her knowledge, and nurture him as she had nurtured me, with endless love.

I think it was this news of Guy, the knowledge that he was not alone, neither subject to Charles nor grimly accepting the horrors of his school that helped me on my slow recovery and to partial mobility.

And also there was the realisation that Violet Perry herself was very ill, wasting away before our eyes. She was quite matter of fact about it.

'When I'm gone my dears, it won't do for you two girls to stay here. You got to be where there's people. I been thinking for a long time about goin' back down Polwerris Cove where I used to live before I married George. I wrote to one of my cousins just after you came because I had to make plans for my Gladys. Martha do take her time, but she'll write when there's a place coming empty.'

And two weeks later the letter came. A nice cottage, a bit big perhaps, two bedrooms, but nice and sunny and not too much of a pull up from the harbour. Violet wrote back to rent it on her behalf and we would arrive next week. What a bustle it was to sort and pack and discard! The neighbouring farmer would buy the livestock, and we would take the bedding and kitchen utensils in the trap while Violet took a few pieces of furniture and her bed piled on the cart. She would sell her old horse when we arrived, she said. He had a few years work in him yet and did not like to be idle.

We took two nights and three days to make that slow journey to Polwerris. For the first time in my life I slept beneath the stars, and the wonder of the night sky seeped into me and I saw that my little life was of no great account; I must simply take the days as they came and do what I could to repay my friends for their love and care.

Within a month of arriving we bought the cottage. Violet was speechless with gratitude when I gave them the pile of sovereigns and said the house must be bought in Gladys's name. Then we set about making it comfortable, buying one or two pieces of furniture that were needed from a widow who was moving into her daughter's house. All this gave me an interest and I found I was getting stronger and with much more movement in my legs. But despite all my efforts, walking was limited to a few paces and then my legs would collapse and I would fall ignominiously to the ground. Then one day I took up my paint brushes and before long Lambeth Weekes suggested selling my work in Penzance. Thus we had a small income and Violet passed her last four months in comparative comfort, happy in the knowledge that her dear Gladys was secure in a home of her own, a blessing known to few of the working people amongst whom we lived. . .

. . .'And we could have remained like that, safe and sound, had I not sent Lambeth Weekes to see Charles.' My voice broke again and Theo tightened his hold on me.

'Don't fret. I'll go to Falmouth tomorrow, well, today I suppose,' and there was a smile in his voice. 'I'll soon find out where he went, all the boatmen know Lambeth. Then, if he has gone to Trevingey, I'll go and see this Charles myself.'

'But you have your own business to attend to,' I protested.

'It couldn't be a better arrangement - I'm taking my ship to Saltash, to the boatyard to have one of Zeb's engines fitted. She'll be there for a couple of weeks. I was intending in any case, to go along the coast and sound out some trade while the work is being done. My call on Charles can be a business one - to see if he needs lime for his fields, or if he has timber to sell.'

188

And so I eagerly told him of the great parks and woods, of the river which was tidal for many miles, almost up to Trevingey itself, ideal for shipping timber.

'How did you meet him, Lizzie?'

I sighed. 'He saw me when I was at school in Plymouth. Maman had sent me there when she thought I was being badly influenced by Uncle Pierre and his friends in Paris. Before that I had never been to school. When I was little, Grandmere taught me, and I ran wild with the village children while my parents went off on their travels. Grandmere thought that it was time barriers came down between classes; she could sense the way things were moving in France. But Maman was aghast when she came home unexpectedly and found me consorting with the peasant children. That's why they took me with them on their next journey which was to Italy.'

Theo smiled. 'I can imagine how much you loved that.'

I smiled in return, remembering the excitement of Rome and Naples, the tremendous architecture, the vibrant people.

'Yes, I did indeed, but Maman was possessive of Papa and resented the time he gave to me. So the following year I was taken to Paris and enrolled at an Academy and left in the care of Uncle Pierre. I did not care for the school at all and many times I stayed home at the Salon. It was there that I learned to draw and paint. Two wonderful years I had before my parents arrived to find me sitting in the dressing room working at my easel, surrounded by the young models in various stages of undress! Maman was shocked when she saw my series of nude studies although Papa said they were brilliant in form and design. But Maman won the day and I was sent to Woodlands in Plymouth, for Maman had known Madame Giselle (whom we pupils called Ma Mere) since her childhood.'

'How old were you then?'

I sipped my wine and then nestled my head back against Theo's shoulder.

'I was fourteen when I arrived in Plymouth, eighteen when Papa died very suddenly and I returned to Paris to be with Maman. It was the very worst time to be in the city, for the Terror was at its worst. Charles had met me at Woodlands at one or two Soirees which Miss Roberts arranged so that eligible young men might meet her young ladies suitably chaperoned. When he heard

I had returned to Paris and all its dangers, he followed me. Uncle Pierre was urging Maman to go to Normandy to Grandmere who was living quietly in a farmhouse on the estate. She had abandoned the Chateau to the Revolutionaries who were violent even so far away in the country. And Charles was pressing me to marry him, and Maman refused to leave Paris unless I was safely out of the country. And so, before I knew it, I was Lady Francoise Trelawne, living in state at Trevingey. And Guy was born the following year.'

We were silent for a long time. And then, saying he must go before the village stirred, Theo drew me to him and once more our bodies touched, heart to heart, mouth to mouth, skin to skin, until we were one, fused together, melting together, in such a transport of passion that even now the memory can send a spasm of delight through my body.

And after he had gone, I lay back on the pillows and slept, a sleep untroubled by memories of the past or fears of the future, or threats to this new life of mine; this life into which Gladys had drawn me that moonlit night three years ago, when she had pulled my limp body from the chill waters of the dark stream.

Chapter Twenty-four

Theo sailed from the cove the following afternoon and I tried to settle down to my normal work, prey to emotions that seesawed from ecstasy at the consummation of our love, through guilt and despair when I thought of Gwendoline, and then to fear for my lover's safety at Trevingey. But work I did, both out of doors and in my room that seemed so bare now with most of my paintings having gone to London in the care of Mr Swain.

Theo had said he would probably be away for about a week, for he did not know whether he would return to Polwerris by sea or by road. And I was not to worry about him for he had legitimate business to attend to at Trevingey and would write from Falmouth tomorrow to the Steward, seeking an appointment with Sir Charles to discuss the purchase of timber. His enquiries about Lambeth Weekes would be incidental. Trust me, he had said, and I tried to quell my fears and do just that.

I wrote again to Jason Pettigrew saying that I was now much recovered and should be able to meet him at the Red Lion Hotel in Truro in perhaps two weeks time and would he inform Charles that his presence would be necessary at our meeting. I had chosen Truro as our meeting place because I still did not wish Charles to know where I lived, and also because it would be a somewhat shorter journey for my dear old friend, Pettigrew.

And with the letter on its way and Theo working on my behalf, my spirits lightened somewhat and I renewed my teaching sessions with Jinny whom I had rarely seen of late. She had been busy, she told me, picking gooseberries and raspberries which her grandmother turned into conserves to he sold in town. And soon she would have to help with the corn harvest, like all the other village children, when every pair of hands was needed to gather

191

the precious crops the moment the weather permitted. But for a few days she called daily and we spent several pleasant hours reading and writing in English and conversing lightly in simple French.

It was easy, living in this isolated corner of the land, to forget that battles were still being waged around our shores, though the war with France was nearing its end, with Bonaparte now captured and exiled on Elba. Already the fishermen were crossing the Channel more frequently and trading openly with the French boats. There was a general impatience among the men whenever they referred to the government; that it was time to lay down arms and start trading with Europe once again. And I listened to their talk, and heard them forecast that Theo had arrived at the right time, and that before long he would have a flourishing business because he had years of experience behind him, and new ideas of how things should be done. Take this engine, for instance. . . And while I painted, I listened to what they said about the man I loved, and my heart lifted and I willed that they might be right. . .

He had said give him one week. But six days after he had gone, I was alone in the house for Gladys was out, when something brought me to my feet. I had been painting, and now I stood with my heart rapidly beating, every nerve tense. Then I heard the familiar footfall on the steps, and even as I breathed the word 'Theo!' he was there. And once more my good intentions to stand aloof and quiet counted for nothing, for it was he who crossed the room and drew me into his arms and I was enveloped in his warmth and strength and could not prevent my own arms from holding him close, close to my hungry body.

'Let me look at you!' Theo took my face in his hands and held me a little away from him. 'Liz! Oh Liz, my love. You look like an oriental princess!' And he brushed his finger over my skin, darkened by my daily trip to the cove. 'No need to ask if you are well, sweet Liz, there's such a bloom on you! You look like a woman in love!'

I laughed and leaned back to look the better at him and saw the strain in his face. 'Come into the kitchen. Gladys is out. I'll make you some tea.'

'I'd prefer a hot toddy if you don't mind, my sweet. I've had a long day travelling by coach to Falmouth and I borrowed the Sanders' cob to ride home.'

I nodded my understanding, for though Helston was the nearer town, more coaches came daily to the busy port of Falmouth, and by crossing the ferry at Helford, the journey to Polwerris was considerably shortened. Soon the kitchen was filled with the warm aroma of cloves and hot rum. I turned to get food for him, but Theo caught my wrist and drew me over to the settle by the hearth.

'I've eaten on the journey down from Plymouth. But I have a great deal to tell you. Do you mind sitting here? I have memories of such a hearth from my childhood and the sight and smell of a turf fire eases my heart.'

And so it was that I joined him beside the fire as he told me his story.

Theo leaned back at an angle on the settle, half facing me.

'I found out in Falmouth that Lambeth Weekes did indeed take passage on the *Araminta* to Plymouth nearly three weeks ago. But the mate told me he'd disembarked at Port Poll.'

I nodded my head, for the tiny port was familiar to me being only an hour's ride through the woods to Trevingey.

'So I followed suit, and when I got there I tried to hire a nag. That's when I knew I was on his trail because the innkeeper told me the last person he'd hired the horse to hadn't come back. The horse had found its own way back a couple of days later with a broken rein and bloodstains on the saddle.'

I caught my breath. 'Yes,' Theo went on grimly. 'Until then I'd thought your fears were unfounded, my dearest. But now I could see you were right to be concerned and I determined to take the greatest care.

'I rode up the valley alongside the river, noting the quality of the timber and glad to see the river was still tidal so far up, but keeping a pretty keen lookout all the while. And soon I felt I was being followed. So I tethered the nag and waited behind an old oak. A heavily built man with a port-wine stain on his face suddenly appeared, with a gun gripped in his hands.

'I had the advantage of surprise and before he knew it, he was on his knees and the gun was mine. To cut a long story short, my sweet, I learned he was one of Trelawne's keepers and without mincing my words I asked what he knew of Lambeth Weekes. His

193

j

colour showed me he knew plenty, but he would not talk - even more scared of his boss than he was of the gun at his head.

'So I tied him up with his own belt and boot laces and stuffed his kerchief in his mouth for a gag, and went on.

'When I reached the inn you told me of, near the gates of Trevingey, I went inside and let the landlord know I had business with Sir Charles of buying some timber. There were several men lounging inside, and I had a feeling the steward knew little of what was going on behind his back.

'They wanted to know where I came from, and asked a lot of questions about Canada. And then, when they were unsuspecting, I said I had another errand, to find out the whereabouts of a man called Lambeth Weekes - that his old aunt had put up a reward of twelve guineas to find out what had become of him.

'Their faces! There was a prompt and united denial of having seen anything of Lambeth; of any stranger in fact. But I noticed they had looked sharply at me when I mentioned the reward and I was sure I would hear something before the day was out.

'And then, as some of the men got up to leave, I announced to the landlord that he had better get a couple of rooms ready, because the Magistrates and Sheriff's officers have been told of Weekes' disappearance, and unless I could give them a positive report, they'd be on their way next week to make their own enquiries. And then I caused another stir - I asked who was the man with the port-wine stain.

'One of the men, a lad in fact, let out a little cry. "What, Morgan Saul, you mean?" and was promptly scowled into silence by the others.

'I asked the landlady if I might have a room for the night and then I set off up the drive on the hired nag.'

(I tried hard not to interrupt as Theo talked, for I could see he had much to tell. But at this point I disentangled myself from his arm and stirred the fire for I was chill with terror at the danger into which I had sent my love.)

He smiled and drew me to his side again.

'It's all right, Lizzie. I'm here, safe and sound.'

And I took his hand in mine and nodded for him to go on.

'The Steward took me to the study and there was Trelawne, seated behind a great desk. The Steward, one Oswald Curtis, showed all the signs of a heavy drinker, but seemed not an

194

unkindly man. They had a map out on the desk and Trelawne pointed out a stand of timber he was willing to sell. It was close to the river bank, ideal for shipment.

'But while we were poring over this, there was a knock on a side door and when Curtis opened it, I saw a couple of men from the Inn standing there. They spoke to the steward and I heard the name Morgan Saul mentioned and guessed there was trouble ahead.

'Trelawne motioned them inside and when he heard I had been asking after Lambeth Weekes, he went mad with rage. He flew at me, knocking me on to my back across the desk, trying to strangle me and all the time shouting, "He's another! He knows! He knows where she is!" And in the middle of this furore, there was a tap on the door and in came an old man. "Get out!" yelled Trelawne, beside himself. But the old man stood his ground. "Lord Chambers is here, Sir. With his sons," he said.

' "Blast it!" he snarled Then he turned to the men from the Inn. "Tie him up. Tie him to the chair. And you get out Bailey. I'll be along in a minute. Just see no one else comes in here." The old man backed out, his face very pale. And then Trelawne straightened his jacket and cravat and watched grimly while the two men dragged me across to a chair the steward pulled out and they started to tie me up with some cord from their pockets.

'Well, Lizzie my sweet, I had an Indian friend who once showed me how to brace oneself so that binds that seem tight are really much slacker. And the two men were trying to show how strong and rough they were. And the steward seemed afraid they would go too far, so between them they did not make a very good job of it, although I played up a bit, looking as though I was on the point of collapse.

' "Now, Curtis. Go with the men and search for Morgan Saul. I'll deal with this Pentire when Chambers has gone." And a few moments later, I was left alone.

'It didn't take long for me to manoeuvre myself over to the desk and reach behind my back for the paper knife I'd noticed. And although I got a few scratches, I soon cut through the cords. And when I had freed my legs from the chair, I went straight over and pulled on the bell cord.'

'But Theo!' I cried in anguish.

'Ah but don't you see, Liz? Only Bailey would come. And

indeed he did. And the first thing he said was, "Is it true, sir? Do you know where she is?"

'And I learned from him that Lambeth Weekes had threatened Trelawne and Bailey had heard enough to suspect you were still alive. He didn't know what had become of Lambeth, but said he doubted whether the man still lived. And I told him that the less he learned about you the better, for the moment. But that all would be well. And tears ran down his face when I said that. . .

'I asked Bailey who was this Lord Chambers and he told me he was a very respected figure, a Magistrate and Member of Parliament besides.

' "That will do very well, Bailey," I told him. I think I'll go along and introduce myself to him. But first, I'd better tie you up." And I did. And a pathetic sight he looked too, gagged with his own handkerchief which had bloodstains from the cuts on my wrists. But don't worry, my dear. He wasn't hurt and gave me a wink as I left him.

'I wish you could have seen Trelawne's face when I strolled into the Salon where Bailey said I would find them! His wife was there, and Chambers with his two sons. I apologised for coming in unannounced but said I must take my leave of Sir Charles as a pressing business matter had arisen. The boys were intrigued by my accent, and when I said I was travelling to Plymouth next day, Chambers invited me to go with them in their coach as the boys found the journey tedious and he was sure they would like to hear something more about Canada!

'We arranged that they should pick me up at the Inn next morning at ten. And I felt my life to be a lot safer when I rode away down the drive half an hour later!'

I wept at the danger he had faced! But Theo just grinned and asked if there was a cup of tea to be had as talking was thirsty work!

Then he told me how back at the Inn no less than three people turned up during the course of the evening, offering information about Lambeth Weekes in return for the reward. And so it was he learned that Morgan Saul had killed him. It seemed the keeper was nearby when Weekes confronted Trelawne one day as he rode in the grounds. Angry words were exchanged; threats, and Trelawne was white with fury when they parted. He rode back to the house and ordered his coach to take him to Plymouth and Saul

196

had boasted in the Inn that night that he would gain favour now because he'd got rid of his master's enemy. He told how he had followed the man down the track towards Port Poll and shot him point blank. The horse had bolted and Weekes' body fell off and rolled into the marsh. Saul had dragged it farther out towards the bogs but with all the dry weather, the men doubted it had sunk far and were sure they could find the remains and claim the reward. And Theo knew that only the patronage of Lord Chambers had given these men the courage to come forward, reward or no reward.

Next day, Theo arranged for two of them to 'discover' the body and arrive at the Inn with the news just as Lord Chambers arrived. And so it turned out. And Theo had the unpleasant task of identifying Weekes by the old green overcoat with its yellow buttons and by a few wisps of grey hair. . .

Chambers arranged an immediate inquest and the verdict was given of murder by person or persons unknown, for Theo kept his word to his informants that only the position of the body should be revealed to the authorities. And when I protested that Saul had got away with murder, Theo shrugged and said he knew the men would deny all knowledge of the matter if they had to stand up in court. As it was, each of the three got the twelve guineas, Theo saying it was well worth it for the look of impotent rage on Trelawne's face on the day of the inquest.

We sat in silence for a while, I holding Theo's hand against my cheek, appalled at the risks he had taken on my behalf.

Suddenly he smiled at me. 'I met your friend Jason Pettigrew in Plymouth. He told me he is to meet you soon in Truro. He wanted to know all about you, about your health, how Gladys fares, everything. And he asked me to tell you how much he looks forward to your meeting.'

And just as he spoke Gladys's name, the door opened and in she came. When she saw Theo sitting beside me on the settle, her face for once did not break into a grin of welcome. She nodded a greeting and went rather stiffly to hang up her coat.

Theo too, noticed her reaction and he gave a small shake of his head as he remembered his dual responsibilities, his promise to Gwendoline and his commitment to assist me through the difficulties of the coming meeting with Charles. 'I must go. I have to see Polkinghorne at the mill and tell him Lambeth is dead. And I

197

must get hold of that letter he spoke of.' I gasped with fear. I had forgotten the letter! So Lambeth could still be our undoing!

'What can you do, even if he gives it to you?' I whispered.

He shrugged. 'It all depends on what he has written. It may be possible to do a little forgery. Don't worry. I'll take care of it one way or another.'

He stood up slowly and put on his coat and hat. Although he had taken some refreshment, the trying events of the past few days after the brutal encounter with Charles had taken their toll and he looked sorely in need of rest and sleep. He smiled his farewell to Gladys and turned briefly to me. He did not kiss me or take me in his arms, but the look in his eyes was embrace enough, and when the door closed behind him, I stood for a moment, hugging my arms to my breast as though they enfolded him.

After a while, I turned to Gladys, using my hands to emphasise what my lips were saying. 'Don't look at me like that, dear girl. He will go back to Gwendoline when this matter is cleared up.' And I drew her to sit beside me and went over the story Theo had told, and when I finished, she took my hand and nodded, understanding that I needed his support for the ordeal ahead of me. But she informed me that she had just seen Gwen and that the girl would be very upset when she learned that Theo was back and had come straight to our cottage rather than going to see her.

We had just finished our lengthy communication when there was the now familiar tap on the door and it opened immediately and Theo entered the room. His pallor brought me to my feet with a cry and Gladys too, leapt up. He came to a halt a yard from me and I remember crying, 'What is it? Oh Theo, my love, what has happened?'

My words brought a bitter curl to his lips and he shook his head in hopelessness. Then, with utter despair, he came and took my hands in his.

'It's Gwen. I've just seen her. She's pregnant.'

The words lanced my heart. I felt the blood drain away and I thought I was dying. Wanted to die. I sank down onto the settle behind me and Theo was beside me, as he had been just now, only this time his arms were not around me, and the hands that held mine were rigid with determination not to pull me to him. Never again! And while it was no more than I had always known must

198

happen, that I had vowed to my pagan god of love that I would let him go, soon, soon; now that the moment of truth had arrived I did not think I could survive this wrenching separation.

Gladys knew what he had said to me. I think she had already seen 'new life' as she called it, in the girl's face that day. It would explain her stubborn insistence that we were not being fair to Gwen; her strained reserve when she came home and found Theo seated beside me. Now she brought me a glass, but it was Theo's hand that steered it to my lips and the spirit which I swallowed burned a channel through the ice of my body. At last, a minute, an hour, an eternity later, I gathered myself together. A strange phrase, but one which expresses so exactly the recapturing of those elusive elements of pride and dignity, purpose and strength that are our very being.

'Then our path is chosen, Theo.' My voice sounded hollow, my words too starkly simple for their desperate import.

'Oh God!' Theo shook his head in despair. 'How can I marry her, feeling as I do for you, Liz!'

'Our love was stolen Theo. You knew that. I knew it. And now we have to give it up. Go to her. Now. Tell her you will be married within the week.'

He slipped from the seat onto his knees and put his arms round me, burying his face against my breast. And I drooped my face against his head, my fingers amongst those dark curls, and so we clung together oblivious to all but the anguish of our separation.

At last, Theo stood up and my hands slid emptily to my sides. He crossed the room, his back straight though his head was bowed, nodded thanks to Gladys when she opened the door, and then he was gone. My love, gone. Gone. And the door closed and the latch fell into place with a click, clear and sharp in the silence of the room.

Chapter Twenty-five

Theo and Gwendoline Matthews were married by special licence in a little church which neither of them had previously attended, by a vicar who was a stranger to them both.

He took his bride to a hotel in Falmouth for a few days while his housekeeper and her husband made ready for them their new home; the house he had so recently bought; the house with its pear tree and a flutter of doves about the low eaves and the sunshine glinting on the window panes. . .

We tried to follow our normal routine though I knew it was pointless to try to paint. Gladys was making her trousseau and so I helped her, trying to fill the empty hours with work. I plied my needles readily enough along the fine seams of a blue silk gown, but many times the sharp point pierced my finger and the physical stab of pain served only to remind me that soon Gladys too, would be lost to me. For though she might insist that this would always be my home, I knew that I must leave her to make her new life with her young husband.

Many times in those days following Theo's marriage, I read and re-read the only thing I possessed that was his; the letter he had sent me the day after our parting. It had come by special delivery from Helston, and as the young man on the doorstep in hotel livery handed it to me, I had recognised Theo's writing with a start of pleasure.

'Just a moment.' My hands trembled and I went into my own room for privacy, calling over my shoulder for the young man to come inside and take some refreshment. Jinny was in the kitchen with Gladys and as she led him to the table, playing the hostess, I closed the door behind me.

Inside the envelope was a single sheet of paper with the address of The Blue Anchor across the top.

'Liz. There is no need to worry. My attentions were not necessary, for the contents concerned other matters. I am sending this by messenger to reach you swiftly, for as you know I have other business to arrange and for the present need some time away from Polwerris. Always, Theo'

I held the paper to my lips, my heart bursting. The letter said so little and yet told me so much. First, that I need no longer worry about Lambeth's letter; whatever the 'other matters' were, they posed no threat to my safety. Then, by its brevity I knew Theo feared that prying eyes might read his note, for he had once told me of hotel managers who made a lucrative living from discovering the contents of clients' correspondence. I guessed the 'other business' he must attend to, would be his wedding arrangements, and my heart ached at his need to be away from the cove for a few days, while he came to terms with himself.

Oh Theo, Theo, I thought. Always he had longed for a child of his own, and yet, now that it was happening, he wanted only to be free again, free to choose, to follow his heart. For he had thought of settling a generous sum on Gwendoline and asking her to break their engagement; indeed it was one of my few creditable actions in this whole affair, that I had prevented him from doing so when first we had made love. For I had recognised his need for children, for a family. And, more selfishly, I had no wish to see the desire in his eyes turn gradually to pity as my body aged and became ever less mobile. No it was better thus; for this present anguish would lessen and I would always have my memories of him which no one could take from me. And he would have Gwendoline and her son, and soon, a child of their own. And so I stood, rocking to and fro, holding the letter to my face, and thinking of Theo's loneliness and despair as he sat writing this note in the impersonal hotel room in Helston.

Jinny came round every day when her chores were done and Gladys showed her how to hem and tuck the crisp, smooth fabrics that filled the room with the smell of their newness. But though she showed interest, it was clear her greatest enthusiasm was reserved for her lessons with me, whether in painting or reading and French.

And we busied ourselves and I smiled and sewed and let no one see that the wonderful, rainbow-coloured bubble that had encompassed me for so short a time, had now vanished, and my world, no longer protected by its radiant shield, was now a bare and empty place. . .

And so the days passed. I could not bring myself to touch my paints, for my eyes seemed no longer to respond to the stimulus of light and movement and colour. It would come back, I told myself. But there was a hollow fear within me that it might not flicker once more into life, and then, how should I fare. . .

Food tasted of dust. For a few days I ate nothing at all, but Gladys so scolded and chivvied me, that it became easier to force down a few mouthfuls than to resist. But my now shrunken stomach rejected all but the smallest portions and I could see the flesh fall away from my face and my clothes were looser than before.

A letter arrived from Pettigrew saying that he had booked rooms for Gladys and me, and for himself for the twenty-ninth, the day before we had arranged to meet Charles. It was clear he wanted us to be safely installed in the hotel well before Charles arrived. Ten more days to get through. . . But I found my fear and dread of meeting my erstwhile husband was dulled by the pain of losing Theo, and I was listless and unconcerned about the clothes I would need for the meeting, despite Gladys's attempts to make me respond.

There was one incident, however, which shook me out of my lethargy. Mary Penrose had called, as she did nowadays whenever she returned the laundry to the inn. She still wore her lost, haunted look, but sitting in our kitchen, she seemed able to relax and lose some of her tension.

On this particular day, the widow became quite animated as she admired Gladys's growing trousseau. Suddenly there was a knock on the door and I, being nearest, went to answer it.

There stood the aging Parish constable. 'I've come to see the widow of the late Reece Penrose. I believe she's here ma'am.' I turned back and saw Mary Penrose's hands clutch the edge of the table and her face grew white as a ghost.

'What do you want with her?' I countered, striving to shield the woman from his sight.

'I got to give her this 'ere letter from the lawyer down Helston,' and be pulled a long stiff envelope from inside his jacket.

I turned to the woman who sat beside the table, rigid as a carved image. 'It's a letter for you Mary. You'd better come and take it.'

And like a sleep walker she rose and came forward. The constable, a rough and uncouth man, gave her the envelope with scarcely a look, and left, heading briskly for the Red Lion down by the harbour wall and we both turned to Mary.

'Open it,' she whispered through whitened lips.

I picked up a knife and slit the seal and drew out the single sheet of paper.

'Read it! Read it!' she whispered intensely and I realised without surprise that she herself could not read.

The letter was brief and to the point and as my eyes perused it, my lips broke into a smile. 'Why, Mary, it's good news! Very good news indeed! This letter is from Lambeth Weekes' solicitor. He says that Lambeth has named you in his will as his sole legatee. Everything he owned is yours!' And I looked up in genuine delight at the woman before me.

'Lambeth Weekes! Him! No. No!' And suddenly she was on her feet. She snatched the paper from my hand, tore it across, flung the pieces to the floor and stamped upon the crumpled sheets.

Gladys and I stared in astonishment and I saw in the woman's face what perhaps Reece Penrose had seen in his last conscious moments; a woman driven to the edge and beyond. Then, her rage calmed perhaps by Gladys who drew her to sit before the hearth, she buried her face in her hands and broke down in tears, her bowed shoulders shaking with sobs.

I retrieved the shreds of the letter and presently she raised her head and asked a little nervously if it was true, or had she ruined it all with her temper, tearing the paper up like that.

I reassured her and pieced the letter together and read it to her again and I could see the import of the news had at last impressed her.

'Everything! That means I'll get his cottage.'

'The cottage, the barn up the road, and whatever money he has in the bank. You will have to go in to Helston and see Mr Watters at Messrs Barnes and Bailey's and he will tell you all about it. I think you should get Jack to go with you, as soon as you can.'

She blew her nose and nodded her head.

'He came again, you know, that Lambeth Weekes.' And there was undisguised venom in her low voice as she spoke his name. 'After that first time he asked me. . . Twice more he came. . . As if I could just forget what he did all those years ago. I'd like to be able to throw it all in his face. But he's gone, so there's no point, is there?'

'None whatever. Take it Mary. Take what he has left you. It's his way of making amends, of letting you know his regrets. So take it, and perhaps one day you may be able to think of him with a little kindness.'

And as I spoke I seemed to feel his presence in the room, in his old greatcoat with the huge buttons, and his wolflike grin. Yes, and too, those eyes that had gazed with such yearning at the portrait of the only woman there had ever been in his life; the woman about whom he had vowed, 'I'll take care of her, see if I don't. One way or another, Miss Millbrook, I shall take care of Mary.'

Chapter Twenty-six

And then, as though sent to rescue me from my depression, along came Mr Swain. For a moment I did not recognise the small, smartly dressed man who stood on the doorstep with his groom behind him. Then I welcomed him into my room, and Gladys and Jinny left their sewing to see to the kettle and a welcome tray.

The groom placed his packages against the wall and left for his own refreshment at the inn and Mr Swain sank down onto the couch with a sigh of contentment.

'Well, how did it go?' My voice was tight. In the desert of my existence I did not know how I could bear another rejection. I Then I looked again at the paintings standing against the wall. 'Where are all the others?'

His smile stretched until it seemed to reach his ears. 'Sold! All sold! A triumph, my dear, as I told you it would be.'

I sat down beside him, my hand to my heart.

'You mean . . .' But words would not come. That people should want to buy my work. . . Paintings and pictures of people and places so far away. . .

'Like I said, a triumph, my dear. Every picture sold apart from the half dozen you insisted on keeping. And at good prices, too. No more cottages and cats for you, my dear Miss Millbrook. You will be able to pick and choose your subject. And name your price.' And he stood up and went to the table where he opened the little satchel he carried and poured out a pool of sovereigns.

I thought of our depleted pouch, almost empty now since I had insisted that Gladys must have a good trousseau. I had been worrying about how to pay for the new canvases I must have if I were to continue painting, and how to replenish my paints, for since the death of Lambeth Weekes, I had become convinced that my attempt to get a portion of my mother's allowance, was doomed to failure. Already it had cost the life of my former agent, and I shuddered at the thought of how nearly it had also cost the life of the man I loved.

Now I swirled the golden coins around on the table.

'So much!' I turned to Mr Swain. 'You must take your commission. And your expenses for the journey and the cost of the exhibition.'

'All done, my dear. All done. See,' he withdrew a sheet of account paper from his satchel. 'Here are the figures. You will be especially pleased, I am sure, that your 'unusual' paintings sold as rapidly as the rest. And I told the buyers that in a year or two their paintings would double in value!'

I sat down, my knees weak, stunned by this sudden good fortune. It was like coming from a darkened room into a blaze of sunshine, and my body and mind, steeped in grief and despair shrank back, unable to grasp the full import of Mr Swain's words.

'Miss Millbrook! Oh my dear, where's that young woman?' And I was vaguely aware of him patting my cheeks and then rushing to the door for help. Then Gladys was holding a glass to my lips. She made me lie back on the couch and slowly the room revolved to a standstill and I was able to reassure my friends that I was better now.

Mr Swain left soon after, for despite his delicate manners he did not at all relish being in the presence of a woman in 'vapours'. But before he left, he went to the door and produced the package which he had left in the kitchen; canvases, paints, charcoal. . .

'Not so much a gift, dear Madam, as a casting of bread upon the waters. To return so wonderfully enhanced. So very wonderfully enhanced.' And he blew his nose again in a fresh dove-grey silken kerchief.

And later, in the silence of my room I lay and tried to fix my thoughts which revolved, much as the walls had earlier done, round and round, round and round, affording me no rest until at last I spun down into the whirling maelstrom of a sleep full of troubled dreams.

A few days later Mary Penrose called, accompanied by her son Jack, both of them aglow with excitement.

'We're rich, Miss Millbrook! That Lambeth, living like a miser! He've left a deal of money in the bank and he got houses rented out all over the place. That one his aunt do live in down Falmouth - 'twas his all along. And him telling her he was payin' the rent!' Jack Penrose shook his head as though he still did not believe their good fortune.

Mary Penrose had colour in her cheeks and had lost some of her aloofness. 'We're going to buy a shop in Helston! Jack and me will run it, and when Gordon comes home from the sea he shall have a share in it too.'

'Wonderful news!' I exclaimed. And we questioned them about the store they had decided upon; one which seemed to sell a vast mixture of goods, from tools to clothing and bolts of material. And watching the woman's sudden vivacity, I was sure they would make a success of the venture, for although she could not read, Mary Penrose had a sharp brain and was already talking in terms of profits and of expanding when his brother joined them.

'And when I've left here, I doubt I shall come back very often,' and I heard in her voice once more the shadow of the years of humiliation she had endured before the eyes of the villagers, caused by her husband's drunken idleness. I felt a prickle of the hair on the back of my neck, for though I tried to like the woman and admired the way she had coped with the rigours of her life, there seemed to be such a core of hatred within her, that I could not be sorry she was to leave the village.

Gladys seemed not to share my reserve towards her, and was now full of pleasure at their good luck. And I too, was unreservedly glad especially for Jack's sake, for now he would no longer have to walk the long miles to the mine each day, and toil in the danger and darkness below.

I could share too, wholeheartedly, in the release their new wealth would bring them, for I myself was experiencing the great relief of not having to worry about money; Mr Swain's windfall had arrived at a crucial moment in our lives.

I had seen nothing of Theo since his marriage. He had leased another vessel, we were told, for business was pressing and there had been a delay in fitting the engine into his own ship. But Gwen called one day when I was down by the harbour making a pretence at sketching and she told Gladys that Theo would be at our meeting with Mr Pettigrew and Charles, and that she too, was to accompany him to Truro. She was nervous, Gladys told me, at meeting strangers, and was dreading her visit to the hotel.

I felt a sudden sympathy for the girl. 'Tell her not to worry, Gladys. We'll be there. We can go shopping together if she likes.' And though I meant it at the time, later I buried my head in my pillow and doubted that I could be natural in her presence, for I was overwhelmed by jealousy and longing for Theo.

Sunday came. An endless day, for all work ceased, and village life revolved around the services in the chapel up the hill. Gladys went along to Chapel with Will, for though she could follow but little of the service, Gladys could feel the vibration of the music in the backs of the wooden pews. And from wherever I walked in the village, I too, could hear the singing that surged from the crowded building. Now, leaning over the harbour wall, and gazing down into the water that reflected the dull, slate coloured sky, I listened to them sing of the harvest, safely gathered for the winter months ahead. A good harvest, for this year the weather had been exceptionally clement.

For the first time in my life I felt a pang of envy for their faith; their belief that whatever befell them, whatever death or disaster came their way, and whatever pain and hardship they were called upon to endure, their reward would be tenfold greater in the heaven which was to be theirs. I had no such faith. I could see nothing ahead; no love, no companionship. Theo, torn from me. Gladys unconsciously but gently untying the cords that bound us, my son not responding to the letters Jason Pettigrew had sent. For I did not believe that he had still not received the letters. I felt he had simply severed all ties with his old home. I could not blame him, for the anguish I had caused him was too much for a youth to bear, and I could well understand him wishing to forget the past, and concentrate on the present with Grandmere and his French cousins.

Not far away, an old Mr Francis sat in a boat, splicing ropes and humming gently along with the music. Another man was sorting nets surreptitiously below the harbour wall so that no one should be offended by this Sabbath work and a young man walked down the hill towards the chapel, in Sunday best, a-courting. But he had misjudged the time and must wait a while yet before the congregation came streaming out. And he too, like we others, gravitated towards the harbour.

I looked down into the water once more. A sudden shaft of sunlight illuminated the depths, and the gentle swell rocked the boats and patches of reflected light played across the face of the weathered granite wall beneath me. My eyes followed the random series of movements, and my mind began to play with a picture of boats and lights tossed about beneath a broken sky. A 'different' picture, one that might help me at last to escape the misery and ennui which held me in thrall.

I felt the familiar shiver of excitement run down my spine. So my muse had not deserted me! I straightened and turned and in doing so came face to face with the young man who walked to and fro alongside the harbour. He stopped suddenly and stared at me with astonishment. And I too stared at the person who stood before me, hat in hand and with his jacket slung across one shoulder. Then he dropped the knapsack he held and his jacket slid to the stones. He made a sound that was something between a gasp and a sob and the word, 'Maman' and in that instant I saw it was my son who stood before me.

'Guy!' My cry was smothered as his arms enveloped me and we clung together, tears streaming from our faces and our lips were salt as we kissed them away and yet more poured from our disbelieving eyes. At last I managed to hold him away from me long enough to examine his face.

How he had changed! No wonder I had stared without recognition until he had spoken. Gone was the sixteen-year-old son I had known. This young man, near to twenty, had the bearing and confidence of a man, a stranger. And he too, held my shoulders and gazed into my face, seeking the mother he had lost. Then he sighed and drew me to him once more, stroking the hair that once he had liked to watch me brush, heavy dark braids that then had reached my waist.

'I can let it grow again, if you like,' I murmured against his cheek on which I could feel the prickle of young stubble.

'I like it so. It sets you apart. You have changed Maman, greatly, you have become so thin! But you are more beautiful than ever.'

I smiled and stopped his words with my fingers on his lips, but my vain heart swelled with delight. 'Come. We'll go home and talk there. They'll all be out of Chapel in a moment.' He picked up his things and waved gaily to the two men who had witnessed our reunion with open mouthed astonishment. And as we started to walk back to the cottage, the last hymn burst from the open windows of the building and the strings and the brass played with staunch conviction, so that we were buoyed up by the surge of music. And never have the words, 'Rejoice! Rejoice!' echoed and re-echoed so joyfully across the water, and the gulls took up the melody as they wheeled and soared above, their wings pink in the rays of the setting sun which had chased away the last of the heavy clouds.

Gladys came as we reached the front steps. She came flying down the cobbles, arms outstretched in instant recognition of her dear boy. And he swung her round in his arms, laughing and hugging her to him. And Will, standing back a little, frowned at the kissing on both cheeks that seemed would never stop. But at last Gladys pulled her man forward and Guy bowed and shook his hand and congratulated him with such sincerity that Will's displeasure vanished like a summer storm. Then it was Jinny's turn to be greeted. Her cheeks were already pink with excitement at the sudden appearance of this unknown son, and now as Guy took her hand and kissed first one cheek and then the other, the colour surged into her face and she hung back and would have slipped away had not Gladys opened the door and pressed us all to enter. The street was filling with people as they made their way home, all burning with curiosity at the extravagant greetings taking place before them and so we crowded indoors and Jinny immediately justified her inclusion in the party by setting the kettle to boil and helping Gladys prepare a supper for us all.

And so our simple Sunday evening meal became a celebratory feast and Guy matched Will in appetite as they fell upon the cold meats and the crusty bread. And Guy piled clotted cream upon the fruit tarts, swearing it tasted even better than when he was a child.

At last, Will left to take Jinny home, and Gladys went too so that they might stroll back through the soft darkness, their arms entwined, wrapping their love about them. And Guy and I sat before the kitchen hearth and talked and wept over the years we had lost and the future which was now so miraculously restored to us both.

210

Chapter Twenty-seven

It was one of my paintings that had brought Guy to me. He was on business in London and had just left a wine merchant's premises in Pimlico and was walking along a street nearby when a painting in a window caught his eye.

'It was of a woman churning butter. An old woman, intent on her work, and you could sense the coolness of the dairy and feel the heat of the sun beyond the small window. My heart was beating unsteadily. I could think only of you, Maman. It so reminded me of the studies you used to make of the maids about their work. I could just make out the signature, something Millbrook. But it was the C for Curvoisier that curled like a vineleaf round the initial that made my knees weak. I tried the door but they had closed for the night and the longer I stood at the window, gazing at the painting, the more I knew it was one of yours. I scribbled a note, saying that I would buy the work, and would they hold it until I returned.

'And when I reached my hotel, I lay on the bed for a long while, wondering about the painting, and who could have put the name of Millbrook to a work I knew to be yours.

'But when I walked into the studio next day, I was told that the work was not for sale; it belonged to the owner of the studio, one painting out of a number that had made up a recent exhibition, a very successful exhibition too, the man assured me. He showed me a catalogue with titles and descriptions of many such paintings; all done, I was assured, by the same artist. But when were they painted, I asked in bewilderment. And when he told me that some had been completed within the last few weeks, I sat down, unable to understand what I heard. The artist, I was informed, was a semi-invalid who lived in Cornwall. And rather

211

reluctantly, he agreed that yes, she was, indeed, a woman.

'I asked where I might find her, and I was told that a Mr Swain, who had arranged the exhibition, had set off to return to Penzance a day or two earlier with those pieces which the artist had not wished to sell. He, no doubt, would be able to give me more information if I contacted him. I was desperate to meet this Mr Swain and question him but it seemed that at every turn I was to be thwarted! The only thing to do would be to travel to Cornwall myself.

'I looked again at the owner's painting, and pored over the signature. Yes! There was no doubt in my mind that the work was yours, the signature was yours, the exhibition had been yours. You were alive! That ghastly funeral had been some kind of charade! I did not understand what would make you disappear as you had done, but I knew it would not have been your choice. I knew you would never let me grieve for you as I did if you could have prevented it.'

And here I clung to my son and our tears flowed again as I told him in a few broken sentences what had happened. And as we talked and filled in the background to those terrible days, I was overwhelmed because Guy never once held me to blame for my actions, understanding without reservation that I had, indeed been unable to prevent his grief and the reasons why I did nothing to contact him when I regained consciousness.

'But now, Maman, you are much better, are you not?' And he sat back to regard me. 'You are thinner, it's true, but you look stronger than I think you ever did.' And I assured him that, yes, I was much recovered and the doctor saw no reason now why I should not enjoy a normal span of life.

'But how did you find me, Guy?'

He smiled at my impatience.

'I took the stage to Plymouth. And perhaps because I was so impatient to arrive, we met all kinds of delays, a flock of sheep blocking the road, an overturned wagon and last of all one of our wheels collapsed! So it was late evening when we arrived. I went to see Uncle Jason to discuss those letters which had been following me about on my travels, pressing me to come to him. But a stable boy told me he was away for a week. Then I thought of Miss Roberts at 'Woodlands'; she was your friend, perhaps she could help me. And that is where I spent the night. She was so pleased to see her Francoise's son, Maman! And I told her why I was going to Penzance, why I had to find Mr Swain's studio and find out my artist's whereabouts.

'A girl brought us some refreshments, a very lovely young woman who looked at me and then glanced back at my face once more as she put down the tray. "Morwenna," said Miss Roberts, "this young man has a great interest in paintings. Would you bring us that portrait of yours?"

'The girl's mouth set. "My picture is not for sale, Miss Roberts. It was a gift from a friend."

' "I know that my dear, I only want Guy, who is French, to see that our country people are also talented." I thought for a moment that the girl would refuse, but reluctantly she went off and returned bearing a composition that I knew instantly was yours; a painting of a girl crouched beside a spring filling a pail of water, a painting full of light and movement and one which caught the very essence of the young woman who now stood quietly before us. And in the corner, the name of Millbrook.

' "Where is she, Morwenna?" I burst out.

'But the girl's face stiffened and her jaw set stubbornly. "My friend wishes to be private, sir." And I could see that it would be desperately hard to shift her from her stance.

' "Morwenna," Miss Roberts leaned forward in her chair and addressed the girl quietly, "Guy's mother was supposed to have died mysteriously some three years ago. None of us saw the body. Guy now suspects that she did not, in fact, die, and that the person who painted this picture is his mother. Look at him, my child. Look at his face. Could it be so?"

'And the girl turned those wonderful blue eyes to gaze at me and I prayed that she would recognise, as I did every day in the mirror, your mouth and chin, your brow, your eyes. And I remembered the sudden look of puzzled recognition she had shown when she had brought the tray. But instead of saying the words that would make it all true, her gaze fell and she muttered that she could not tell.

'Mistress Roberts looked angry but I could see the girl was trying to protect the artist for some reason of her own. So I said that never mind, I will go and see for myself. The girl would have spoken then, her face first reddened and then became very white and she stood, clutching her portrait and looking from her

213

employer to myself and back again.

'Miss Roberts spoke out then. "Morwenna," she said, "Guy's mother was one of my dearest friends. If there is the slightest chance that she is still alive, we shall not rest until we have found her. Obviously Guy will go direct to your village and seek word of her there. So if you know anything that can help him, and help her, please tell us."

'The words had their effect. The girl slid onto a chair as if her legs would not hold her and then she told us all she knew about you, about how very ill you were when first you arrived at the village with Mrs Perry and Gladys. And on hearing Gladys's name I cried out with joy and relief that my dear Gladys was still looking after you. And my knowledge of her deafness seemed to set the seal on the girl's trust and we sat for a long while as I hungrily discovered what I could of your missing years, even to your partial recovery since that strange operation.'

Then it was my turn to learn of Guy's life, of Grandmere, almost ninety years old and still able to oversee the running of the vineyard and the farm whenever Guy went travelling to seek new markets. 'Just like your father, she says I am, Maman!'

I asked him of his dealings with his own father, of Charles.

And he told me how Charles made it impossible for him to get any of the trust money from my mother's estate. 'He says I cannot touch it until I am of age. And we could do with that extra income, Maman, for we need new vats, a new and larger cellar. We see to it that our workers all get a good living.' He grinned. 'Grandmere has told me often how she got the place back after the Revolution. Of the chateau that was looted and burned and the lands taken by the peasants. But after a while they found they could not sell what they grew, that the land was too much for them. Grandmere was living in the old farmhouse and she had the chateau pulled down and the stone turned into decent homes for anyone who would work the estate for her. She found a couple of old men who were willing to rescue the vines and after a year or two, money started to come back to the land.'

I did not tell Guy that I knew all of this, having heard it from my dear Grandmere's own lips when we went to Maman's funeral, when he was still a boy. But it was good just to hear my son's voice and to know that the lessons my grandmother had learned had all been passed on and assimilated by my son. And it struck me for the first time, that I too, had profited greatly from her tales, that I had never taken for granted the rights of the rich to treat their workers as slaves. I was glad that during the years when I was mistress of Trevingey, I had ensured that tradesmen were paid on delivery, and that dressmakers and saddle-workers did not have to wait in penury until their lord and master deigned to settle his dues. I wondered if it was like that still under the new mistress. . .

And then I told Guy of our planned meeting with Charles and Pettigrew in Truro in four days time. 'So that's why Uncle Jason was away! He must already be in Truro.' And later we found that he had in fact travelled in short stages to reach the Red Lion days before us, so that he would be well recovered from the travails of the journey before the vital meeting.

At last I sent Guy to bed; to the bed which Gladys had heated with the stone bottles, and while he dropped instantly to sleep, I lay in my own room for long hours, wondering at the way my life was changing and knowing that for Theo and myself our final parting was not far away, for though it had not been spoken, both Guy and I accepted that I would return with him to Normandy as soon as we had settled our affairs in Cornwall.

Next morning the September sun shone warmly down and Guy rowed us in Will's boat round to the cove. There we swam for a while and then, dressed again, we sat absorbing the sun's warmth, enchanted by the beauty of the turquoise waves and the encircling cliffs. We let the fine sand sift through our fingers as we talked and laughed and cried, going over many of the happenings in the years we each had missed.

At last we came to where we must now begin again; to our coming meeting with Charles.

'Do you still want to meet him, Maman? Now that we have found each other you don't need him any more. The farm and the vineyard provide enough for us all to live in comfort.'

'Don't forget, there's the income from my mother's estate that he's been holding on to for the last few years. That must be yours. As for me,' and I smiled with unconcealed pride, 'I have found I can support myself with painting. In fact I've just been well paid for the work sold at that exhibition in Pimlico.'

But the thought of staying safely in Polwerris Cove while Guy and Mr Pettigrew fought for my birthright was tempting. However, with my son beside me I should be so much stronger. And Theo had promised he would be there. . .

Three fishing boats sailing from the harbour passed the mouth of the cove and one or two of the men waved to us as they went, for the news of my son's arrival in the village had spread like fire. Guy said something about the idyllic life they led, his eyes on the swelling sails as the small boats rose and dipped before the wind.

'They live at subsistence level, Guy,' I said flatly.

'But there seems to be plenty of fish - the carts were buying from the harbour wall at dawn today. I watched them from the bedroom window. And everything was sold. And as soon as the tide was right, off they went again.'

'I know how it must look. But the men have their 'sleeping partners' to provide for.' And I told him how most of the boats were jointly owned, and when a man died, the rest undertook to give his share from all the sales to his widow.

'Two winters ago, a boat went down and her crew were lost, all five men. So the rest of the boats are having to provide for those widows and children too until they can support themselves. It's a desperate struggle, fewer men and many more mouths to feed. The widows try to work, but with small children there is little they can do, some spinning, laundry, sewing. Some of the men have gone to work in the mines at St. Just. But that is a gamble too, a few come back with good money, others with their health forever broken.' And we sat side by side, Guy enigmatic, I thinking of my own days in Polwerris, when though poor in comparison with my past way of life, I had been infinitely better off than most of my neighbours.

Presently our conversation reverted again to the impending meeting and what we should say. For another hour we sat, working out our plans and preparing our case against Charles.

At last Guy stood up and reached down his hand to pull me up beside him. 'Come on. The sun has got to your face, you'll be looking like a gypsy soon!'

'I know!' But I was glad, for the glow would banish the pallor my face had acquired over the past dreary weeks since Theo left. 'You must help me choose what I am to wear at the meeting. Gladys has been pestering me to buy some new clothes but I

216

intend to go dressed in my present fashion.'

And Guy held me at arms length and laughed. 'You look wonderful, Maman. Great Uncle Pierre would have been able to sell your clothes to his wealthy clients for a fortune!' And I laughed too, remembering my dear uncle fondly, sad at having lost him, sadder still for Grandmere who had lost both her son and my mother within months of each other, twelve long years ago.

At home, with Gladys beaming her approval, we examined my wardrobe. It was not extensive, consisting entirely of baggy trousers and various tops, blouses and tabards and smocks. And the most recent addition, a couple of wrap-around skirts which I had made for wearing out of doors now that I was walking; a fashion which had won the approval of one or two of the Chapel ladies. Some of my clothes I had fashioned from French silk, bought at the door after dark of an evening, beautiful, lustrous material on which no duty had been paid, a fact that bothered me not at all.

It was this silk which caught Guy's eye, and it did not take long for him to choose a pair of plain dark red trousers and a top with the same background but swirled with jewel colours, glowing and rich. He admired the satin slippers I had stopped wearing when I gave my wheelchair to one of the crippled miners, and these I put aside to take with us for wearing in the hotel, keeping for the journey the heavy leather walking shoes I had recently bought.

Gladys ran upstairs and came back carrying a soft claret wool cloak I had made for her some time ago. She wore it rarely, having been teased by some bal maidens that her cloak was not the bright scarlet of the garments they wore with such pride. This she urged me to take. And then we delved into the trunk I had given to Gladys on the day of my flight, and in it we found a black velvet bonnet trimmed with ostrich feathers. I inspected it critically and found that with a little alteration it would serve well and with the wrap-around skirts and the cloak to cover my less conventional wear I would not draw undue attention to myself in the streets of Truro.

Guy pulled his own clothes from his knapsack and Gladys fell upon the bottle green velvet jacket with hands that could not wait to steam out the folds and creases. The clean buckskin trousers needed only the smoothing iron but the spare shirt must needs be washed again for it was not starched to her exacting standards.

217

k

She herself had plenty of clothes from which to choose, for her trousseau was now almost completed and her eyes shone with delight and excitement, all fear gone now that Guy had come to us.

The night before we were to leave for Truro I bathed and washed my hair with care, brushing the short locks until they shone like satin, liking the feel of the bounce and swirl when I turned my head, and glad no longer to have to endure the endless curling and crimping I once had accepted.

Jinny called earlier that afternoon and clapped her hands with excitement as we packed our clothes. But her face in repose was shuttered and fearful, for she knew that with Guy's coming and Gladys's wedding not far away, things were all to change. And as I soaked in the wooden tub that night, I wondered if the ideas I had for Jinny were less a favour to her than a means to my own selfish ends. And later, lying thoughtful in my bed, I still had not resolved the answer to that particular question. . .

Chapter Twenty-eight

We set off in the trap next morning in good spirits, Guy sitting with the reins in his hands, resplendent in his velvet jacket and tall hat. Will came to wave us off, watching Gladys yearningly as she smiled her goodbye. She was wearing the blue outfit I had made for her, the jacket with nipped-in waist and a matching skirt over which she wore a cloak and bonnet of darker blue made gay with clusters of small embroidered flowers. She had wondered whether it was right to wear this part of her trousseau but was happy to be reassured and smiled proudly, confident that she looked her best. Much of her wardrobe had cost us very little because I have always enjoyed designing and cutting good materials in the way my Uncle Pierre had shown me. The red cloak I wore, the one I had made for Gladys last winter, was fashioned from a piece of beautifully fine wool woven in a cottage near Goonhilly Downs. The weaver's wife had come one day and sat on my doorstep showing me her bag of samples, less interested in my compliments to her husband than in what I was prepared to pay for a length of the lovely cloth. (I had recently given her Mr Swain's address in Penzance, knowing his delight in good clothes and sure that he and his friends would soon become favoured and valued customers.)

And so it was a well-dressed trio which alighted outside the Red Lion in Truro later that day and I was glad that we had Guy to escort us, for the inn was a bustling place where passengers for the Mails waited and alighted, their friends sending them off with much noise and good humour, while those arriving sought familiar faces among the welcoming press of people. Pettigrew had booked the rooms for Gladys and myself, but Guy was lucky to find a small back room for himself, the only bed still available

219

in the whole of the busy hotel. He came with us to our rooms first, up the twisting stairs and along the narrow passage. My room was mostly taken up with a great four-poster, and Gladys's, which led from it, seemed the more spacious since it contained nothing more than a narrow bed and small wardrobe and stand.

We had barely discarded our cloaks when there was a tap at the door. Guy opened it, and there stood our dear Pettigrew, his arms held wide and with the tears running down his cheeks! Always sparely built, he was thinner than ever, and the years which had sat easily upon him now showed their full weight. But his affection for us had not dimmed; indeed there can be no more heartfelt reunion than when the parties meeting have long thought each other to be forever beyond their reach.

After our emotional greetings, Pettigrew led us all to the private sitting-room which adjoined his bedroom, saying that an old man must have his creature comforts and anyway, we needed to be private and comfortable for our meeting with Charles tomorrow. So we all sat over a welcome tray of tea and cakes and talked and questioned each other in the manner of dear friends who have much ground to cover after so long an absence.

Presently our dear friend shooed us away. 'Off you go! You young people will want to see something of the town. And I must have a little sleep. And after dinner tonight we must settle down and pool our ideas on how to deal with Charles.'

Nothing loathe, I took my stick, and with Guy on one side and Gladys on the other, we spent a happy time inspecting the goods in the shop windows and piled high on the stalls in the busy streets. But each time a carriage made its way along the cobbles, I flinched, and wondered if I should look up and find myself staring into the cold eyes of Charles Trelawne, the man who had been, and in the eyes of the law was still, my husband.

But we returned to the hotel without incident, both Gladys and Guy laden with our purchases, for it had been a long time since I had the luxury of such choice in my shopping - and money in our purse to spend! And in the hall my heart turned a somersault, for there was Theo!

He was standing at the desk with Gwendoline at his side and he seemed to sense my presence for he turned towards the door as we entered. And later, thinking about that moment, I was glad she had her back to us, glad she had not seen the look that passed between us; a look which told me, and told him, that nothing could change the passion which was ours, neither bride nor legal husband, not time nor distance, and that wherever we might meet in future years, this flame we shared would still leap in our hearts.

I sensed Gwendoline was about to turn and forced myself to look away from Theo's face. And when my blind eyes at last found focus, it was my son's face I saw, watching me with awareness and concern, and I knew he had learned much about me in that swift exchange of glances. Somehow I managed introductions and I was grateful that Guy flattered and flirted with Gwendoline so that I could have a precious moment with Theo, although under Gladys's stern eye it was no more than the brief pressure of our hands in greeting and the awareness of caught breath and parted lips that made the blood course through my veins. And perhaps Gwendoline might believe that my shining eyes and the glow on my cheek was because my son was there at my side. . .

We all dined together in style in Pettigrew's private room and Guy said the food was very good, praise indeed from the Frenchman he had become! For myself, I ate little and sipped my wine tasting nothing, for all my senses were directed at Theo who sat across the table from me with Gwendoline at his side. While we ate, the conversation was light, Guy using his flamboyant sign speech to include Gladys and he encouraged Gwendoline in the skill and there was much laughter round the table. And through it all, Theo and I sat, aware of each other's every move though rarely allowing our glance to meet for we both were painfully conscious of Gwendoline's presence.

I knew that Guy was doing his best to engage her attention and dear Uncle Jason joined in the gaiety and it was not until we were served with our dessert that the talk changed direction.

Guy was speaking. 'When Maman comes back with me she will stay in the farmhouse with Grandmere, of course. But I shall have one of the buildings that enclose the inner yard made into a studio for her, somewhere of her own where she can work undisturbed.'

From the corner of my eye I saw Theo's fork pause and remain suspended above his plate.

'What kind of pictures will you paint, back home in Normandy, Maman? Will you still do commissions for Mr

Swain?'

And I must have made a reply for the conversation went on about me, about us. I had not said the words my heart cried out at the thought of leaving him; Theo, Theo. I stared down at my plate and saw there the images of my love, of Theo.

Theo, smiling down at me when first we spoke as I sat painting outside the cottage, Theo's hands taking the sheet to cover my torn body as I challenged my sceptical neighbours, Theo, in my bed, raised on his elbows and gazing down at me with such wonder and passion in his eyes. Theo's face now, across the table, stricken with the awareness that I was soon to leave Polwerris for ever. . .

But so ingrained is our response to comply, not to make a scene that I smiled and nodded and made small talk when all I wanted to do was retreat to my bed and abandon myself to wildest grief. And yet, on the thought, I knew that I could not, would not, miss one moment of this sweet torture, so close to my beloved and yet so far apart. . .

And when the table had been cleared and we sat grouped round the fire, Theo sat in the chair beside me, and our arms at times touched and I could feel the urgency of his body, and of mine until the name of Charles Trelawne was spoken and chilled us both back to cold reality.

Pettigrew was speaking, dignified and incisive, no longer warranting the avuncular title I gave him in private.

'Charles is, unfortunately, within his rights to withhold Francoise's income from Guy until he comes of age. That is to say, he would be within his rights if Francoise were in fact deceased. Now everything has changed.' And I could see from his face that the complications were appalling to his legal mind.

'How would it be,' I closed my eyes for a moment while I rallied my mind and senses away from Theo. 'How would it be if we were to let things remain as they are, with me still 'dead'?' Pettigrew began to protest, but I smiled at him and went on, 'In return, Charles would have to release my mother's trust income to Guy, the monies from the past few years in a lump sum and then the normal monthly payment. I think the alternative of me reclaiming my title and making his young children nameless will be enough to bring him to our way of thinking.'

'But you, my dear Francoise, would then have nothing. Oh yes,

I know Guy my boy, that you would never see your mother in want, but as a lawyer I have come across too many instances of what can happen to overset our best intentions - a new wife who resents funds going to the mother-in-law, the expenses of a family, or even, God forbid, your own death, Guy, when under the terms of Francoise's mother's will, the monies would go to your children, or to the French cousins if you had no heir.'

Theo spoke, 'Trelawne has more than one attempted murder to answer for, and two actual killings besides; there was Richard Penhaligon whom he shot, and now Lambeth Weekes,' Theo's voice was cold and hard. 'We have him at our mercy,' and there was none in the implacable tone. And all of us remembered how he had fared and what he had learned so recently at Trevingey.

And thus it was that we shaped our plans. Pettigrew compromised his lifelong principles of getting the best possible settlement for his clients, for in this case his clients had no intention of claiming their rights. He told us he would at last retire from the business and leave his partners to carry out the instructions they would soon receive from Sir Charles Trelawne and his son, instructions which he, Pettigrew would instigate. Then the partners would not knowingly be parties to perjury. And for a man to whom the law of the land was sacrosanct, he revelled in checking out the fine print of the document that purveyed justice and fairness in every line, although it was all founded upon the false premise of my continued 'death'.

Then I put forward some ideas which I had been mulling over in my mind for the past few days, and after the initial surprise, everyone present added his or her suggestion. Even Gwendoline lost her diffidence and made a telling point and I at once asked for her to be named as one of the Trustees, the people who would put our wishes into practice, and the others agreed with pleasure.

It grew late. The day had been long and when at last we stood, I knew I had eaten too little food and drunk too much wine, for the room swam about me and the next moment I was falling. Guy caught me. But it was Theo who lifted me in his arms and carried me along the corridor to my room.

I kept my eyes shut, not just to keep at bay the swirling walls, but in case I should see Gwendoline's eloquent eyes watching me in her husband's arms. And too, because for this brief moment I was where my soul cried out that I belonged, resting my head on

223

his shoulder, his throat an inch from my lips, his beard soft against my cheek. There was an instant when his arms tightened about me and then I heard the door being opened and even as I breathed his name, he was laying me down upon the bed, relinquishing my body from his enfolding arms. I opened my eyes at last and saw Gladys behind him, concern and worry on her open face. He remained with Guy at the side of the bed until they were both reassured that I was myself again, and then Gladys shooed them from the room.

She made me drink the hot tea she sent for, and helped me out of my clothes in a way she had not needed to do since my recovery of movement. And as she busied herself about me, I could sense her growing worry at my renewed listlessness and from the tightening of her lips I knew she blamed it wholly upon the affair between Theo and myself.

Guy came to give me his fond goodnight kiss, and then I was alone in the four-post bed, listening to the unfamiliar sounds of the streets outside, for traffic still passed beneath my window. I sent Gladys off to her own bed and she left the door between our rooms ajar so that she would see my light if I needed her. With a great effort of will, I turned my thoughts away from Theo and tried to imagine tomorrow's meeting with Charles. I wondered if we would prevail over him or if he would call our bluff and damn me to make known my existence. For if indeed he chose that path, all our carefully thought out plans would be to no avail. Then my restless mind wondered how would fare his meeting with Guy, their first since the boy had left home after my supposed funeral, for Guy was his own flesh and blood and how could a man meet his first-born son and deny him what was rightly his? And I thought again of Theo, in a room not far from this, and of Gwendoline lying beside him and I wondered if he was seeking comfort with his arms about her body and his face buried in the mass of hair that was like spun sunlight. . . And I turned and buried my own face in the pillow and heard the striking of the slow hours from more than one clock tower during that long night. But at last, when the sky was lightening and there were the once familiar sounds within the building of the maids going about their work, the rattling of fire tongs and of doors being opened and closed, then at last, I fell into a deep sleep.

*   *   *   *

224

It was after ten o'clock when I awoke and Gladys insisted that I take my breakfast in bed. And to the surprise of us both, for the first time for weeks I fell upon the scrambled egg and the toast and conserves with a healthy appetite. And after I had completed my toilette and dressed, we made our way to Pettigrew's sitting-room and found Guy reading the paper and waiting to accompany us on a walk beside the river if so we wished.

We took some bread for the swans and made our way along the path which was sun-dappled beneath the trees. Once, looking back, I noticed we were being followed by two burly men and Guy nodded with a grim smile; they were our escorts, hired by Pettigrew in case Charles should have plans which were of a more sinister nature than ours. And while I felt safer for their presence, my mouth was soon dry and not even the sweep of the river at flood tide, its limpid surface reflecting the dense oaks of the further bank and the exquisite curves of the swans' necks and wings, carved white beauty offered back twofold by the water, could for long keep my troubled mind from our forthcoming meeting.

We turned to retrace our steps, and our escorts stepped aside with lifted hats for us to pass, and fell in behind with measured step and I suddenly wanted to giggle like a schoolgirl and I saw that Guy too was hard put not to laugh. Despite the sunshine, a cool breeze blew and the way back seemed longer than I remembered and I was thankful for my son's supportive arm. Presently we regained the streets, busy with people and noisy with the cries of vendors and the altercations of drivers frustrated by the mindless crowds which thronged the streets. And I was no longer smiling and was glad our burly friends were close on our heels, watchful and intent in the press of people, and gladder still when we gained the security of the hotel.

In the hall, Theo and his wife, cloaked like ourselves, were just returning from a brief excursion. He and Guy talked together quietly, and I turned to speak to Gwendoline, assuring her that, yes, I was quite recovered; the journey must have taxed me more than I knew last night. I sensed her diffidence within our group and when I suggested that she should accompany Gladys and me upstairs to my room to see our yesterday's purchases, she came readily enough, for with Gladys at least, she was comfortable.

We were barely halfway up the first flight when some sixth

sense made me turn and see who it was who had just come through the door. It was Charles! Tall and fair as ever, elegant in a grey cut-away coat, and with his beaver hat in his hand, he cast a glance of familiar arrogance around the hall as he entered. I paused, one hand on the banister rail. 'Ah Charles. There you are.' I called. And my voice had all the old authority and clarity which I remembered so well among my erstwhile friends.

He froze. There was a tense moment when we all seemed to lose movement, Theo and Guy, heads up, were staring at the newcomer, and Charles had paused, rigid and tense, his eyes fixed upon my face. And we three women, stood motionless upon the staircase, Gladys, so changed from the girl he once had known, comely now in her blue suit and with the bloom of love upon her, Gwendoline, elegant in a russet brown caped coat and with a tiny hat perched upon her burnished hair, and I, in my long red cloak and the hat with the ostrich feather curling to my chin.

I was suddenly aware that other people too were turning their heads with an instinctive awareness of the unusual, and as I felt their curious gaze, I waved a vague hand, 'Guy will tell you where to find us,' and I turned my back and the three of us proceeded up the stairs to my bedroom.

Inside the door I clung to Gladys, my legs shaking, and it was Gwendoline who removed my cloak and settled us both into chairs and fetched a small flask of brandy from her own room. Gladys was white to the lips, remembering the time when last she had seen Charles, the tall horseman outlined against the moon, with the pistol in his hand. The tumbler rattled against my teeth as I gulped the measure of spirit Gwendoline had poured and perhaps it was that, and not anger, that so burned within me. I passed the glass to Gladys, and she, who never drank spirits, accepted the brandy without demur.

A few minutes later there was a tap on the door and Guy's voice called and Gwen let them in, Guy with Theo close behind. When they had seen for themselves that our pale cheeks were regaining their colour, Guy laughed. 'Wonderful, Maman! You were magnificent! Never have I seen him so discomfited. There in public for all to see!'

'Yes, that was very foolish of me, wasn't it? Our whole case against him rests on preserving the tale of my death, and there I stand and publicly greet him. I cannot believe I could have been so foolish!' And I twisted my hands together with renewed anxiety.

'Don't worry. There was no one in the hall who might know you. I checked with the doorman. There were only a few yeoman farmers downstairs who have booked a room for a meeting.'

'I think it was a good thing he saw you the way he did, Elizabeth,' Theo agreed. 'Now he knows that you are not some poor recluse whom he can intimidate. He has seen you in a public place, well dressed, confident, surrounded by friends. He knows you would only have to go downstairs with your story and he would be ruined.'

I looked up and saw that he was gazing down at me with his mouth stern but in his eyes that hint of a smile that caused the blood to sweep through me once more. I looked away quickly, for the more I saw of Gwendoline the more I felt the guilt at my feelings for her husband; father of the child that soon would show its presence beneath the trim waistline of her gown.

'Come, it's lunchtime.' Guy pulled me to my feet and drew off the hat that I still ridiculously wore. Gwen and Theo went on ahead while I splashed water on my face and brushed my hair, and then we joined them in the sitting-room where Pettigrew awaited us.

It was too soon after my hearty breakfast for food to tempt me, but fearing a repetition of last night's weakness, I forced myself to take some soup and bread and toyed with some wafers. I declined the wine to Guy's amusement, but drank the good coffee and hoped my appearance would not betray my nervousness, for my stomach quailed now at the thought of the meeting which lay ahead. I told myself repeatedly that I was not alone; Guy, Theo and Pettigrew were with me, and also my most loyal Gladys and Gwendoline too, who was fast becoming both friend and ally.

A waiter came and cleared the table, wheeling the trolley quietly away, and as the door closed behind him the clock on the landing struck two and we all fell silent. And it was into this moment of silence that there came a sharp knock upon the door. Guy rose and crossed the carpet to open the door and then he stood back to let his father enter the room.

Chapter Twenty-nine

Charles paused on the threshold, nodded a greeting to Guy to whom he had briefly spoken earlier in the hall downstairs, (a meeting notable for its lack of emotion on both sides,) and then his gaze travelled round the room. I was already seated at the table beside Pettigrew with Gladys on my left and Gwen next to her. I could see the cold rage in his eyes when he beheld Theo standing at the window with his back to the room. Guy closed the door before crossing to the table where he drew out a chair for his father opposite me. He then continued round the table to sit at Pettigrew's other side. Theo was the last to come to the table where he took a chair next to Guy, so we six were on one side of the table, with Charles isolated on the other.

'Well, Charles,' Pettigrew broke the unnatural silence. 'These are serious matters we have to discuss.' He moved the papers which were neatly stacked before him on the polished surface. 'Most serious. It is fortunate for you that Francoise does not intend to charge you publicly with the actions which brought her to this pass.'

The man who was once my husband raised his eyebrows. 'Indeed? A wife who runs away with her lover will not receive much sympathy from the magistrates, especially if she compounds her felony by abandoning her only child.' And he lounged back in his chair, on his lips the curl of sarcasm and contempt that had once the power to reduce me to a jelly. But that was a long time ago, and that young bride had grown into a very different woman, a woman whom Charles grew to hate as she became one of the few people in his life whom he could not control and order at will.

'You forget, Charles,' and my voice too, was contemptuous, 'I have witnesses. Witnesses not only to the gunshot that so nearly killed me, but witnesses to the fact that I was close to death for weeks thereafter, far too ill to prevent that travesty of a funeral you arranged. You over-reached yourself when you buried some other poor soul in my place, for more than one is prepared to testify that it was not I who lay in that coffin. The face may have been rendered unrecognisable, but the hands were not mine, with nails bitten down to the quick.' (And I was grateful to my dear Bailey who had lately confessed to Uncle Jason that he had opened the coffin when it lay in state in the great hall of Trevingey and had known as soon as he saw the hands, that this was not the body of his young mistress.)

Charles's pale skin whitened further. 'Then why was I not told at the time? I, the bereaved husband who buried the woman found in the river in all good faith as my wife.'

'Because they feared that I was, indeed, dead by your hand. That their protestations would have met with ridicule. But now that they know I have survived, matters have changed and they have written depositions which Jason Pettigrew has here in his case.' (And here I lied freely, for there was only one witness to this fact, Bailey, whom I feared might become yet another of Charles's victims if he knew the truth of the matter.) And my dear friend Pettigrew nodded and tapped at the pile of papers before him. And I saw his hand, the skin mottled brown, the veins swollen and dark about the fragile bones, and my heart went out to him and I wondered how much toll the long journey and this stressful meeting would take upon his health.

Then Gladys began to use her expressive hands, mouthing words that even Charles could read: I saw. I was there. I saw you kill Richard Penhaligon. I saw you shoot my lady. I saw you send the men to get her cloak from the wheel.

At last his arrogance faded and though he drawled, 'The evidence of a deaf-mute. Hah! What is that worth?' we could hear the sudden lack of conviction in his voice.

'There is my evidence too, Trelawne,' Theo spoke quietly, his voice cold and clear. 'My evidence, backed by Bailey. Oh yes, your butler is at last prepared to speak against you. And yes, when he recently left Trevingey, it was at our suggestion and to a place of safety. But others too, from the estate are ready to tell more about the death of Lambeth Weekes now that I have the ear of

Lord Chambers. He already holds suspicions about you, that much I discovered when I shared his carriage ride to Plymouth and back, discreet though his queries were.'

'What did you tell him, damn you?'

'I told him nothing. Not then. I only mention the fact lest you think you can bluff your way out of this matter, like so many others in the past.'

Pettigrew stepped in. 'The purpose of this meeting, Charles, is to arrange compensation for Francoise and to press you to release to Guy the monies that should be reaching him from his maternal grandmother's estate.'

'He is not of age. I can use that income as I see fit until he comes of age.'

'Ah yes,' Pettigrew's old voice was smooth. 'But matters have changed. Francoise is alive, so the monies are in fact, hers. But she has generously suggested that it would, perhaps, be better to let matters stand and not to make an official reappearance.'

The white, chiselled face across the table moved not a muscle. But I saw his eyes, saw in them the dread of public knowledge, the frustrated fury and then the glimmer of hope that there might still be a way out of the corner in which he was trapped.

'What do you mean?' The clipped voice was guarded, the arrogance barely subdued.

'Guy, against my strongest advice, has stated that he will disclaim his inheritance of Trevingey in favour of your young son Claude Percival.'

'What!' I could see the disbelief in his eyes.

'In return, of course, for a settlement upon him.'

'Now much?' The voice was harsh.

'One thousand pounds a year for twenty years.'

'One th. . . You're mad! You know Trevingey cannot afford to give away a thousand pounds a year! And for twenty years!'

'If my memory does not deceive me, Charles,' and Pettigrew spoke with a cold anger that I had not suspected in him, 'your new - wife - your own cousin's widow, has brought with her, besides his large estates, no less than three productive tin mines, left to her by her father.'

'Those are all entailed to my son.'

'Well, the choice is yours.' Pettigrew straightened the papers before him and made as if to bring the meeting to a close. 'I would suggest that you take your new wife into your confidence. I am sure she will appreciate, even if you do not, that twenty thousand pounds is small compensation indeed for the loss of an ancient title and the great estates of Trevingey. If, however, you decide to comply with our demands, the monies from Francoise's mother's estate must be paid monthly into the bank for transfer to Normandy - and there are over three years arrears, don't forget. And the annual sum of one thousand pounds for the next twenty years will be paid into a bank in Penzance, into a Trust Fund to be run by the nominees of Francoise and Guy. The alternative is for Francoise to return to Trevingey with her son. I am sure she will be generous to your new 'wife' and her children and will do what she can to live down the scandal of your hanging.'

'Don't be ridiculous!' And in his voice was all the arrogance of the aristocrat, who believed himself to be far above and beyond the reach of the law.

'Times have changed, Charles.' Pettigrew's voice was almost merry. 'Times have changed. Across the channel we have seen what happens when the poor are pushed too far. And there are many revolutionary pressures here in our dear land today. The establishment would not be prepared to bend the law to save your neck in such a blatant crime. And for whom? For a man who has lost the respect of all about him to a degree you cannot imagine, my poor friend.' Pettigrew paused and scribbled some note on a piece of paper and then looked up again. 'If you decide to comply with these terms, I have papers already drawn up for your signature. If you need more time to think, then I shall have to send one of my staff to Trevingey. Personally, I feel that a matter as delicate as this would best be settled here and now, far from the eyes and ears of your staff.'

He gave in then. His stiff shoulders slumped and his head bowed and he stared for a long time at the hands before him on the table, hands whose long fingers drummed a restless beat on the polished surface. At length he looked up, looked round at the silent group who faced him across the table. He looked first at his son, in whose jaw I could see the taut control as he gazed steadily back into his father's eyes, then he looked at Pettigrew, old and bowed but implacable, then at me. . . And I surprised a glimpse of guarded admiration as well as the tight-lipped fury. His look dismissed Gladys as it had always done, passed over Gwendoline with indifference and settled on Theobald Pentire with a cold, hard venom that brought a spurt of bile to my throat.

'There is just one thing you forgot, Uncle Jason.' They all turned to look at me. I clenched my fists in my lap, forcing my body to be calm. 'You forgot to say that should any sudden or inexplicable death overtake any of us now present at this table, the others will meet and decide whether to make public immediately the contents of these papers.' As I spoke I laid my hand on the pile of papers in front of Pettigrew, never taking my eyes from the face of the man who sat before me. Jason Pettigrew gave a sigh that sounded like one of pleasure, and his old hand rested on mine as Charles made his pledge. And then there were documents to be read and re-read, papers to be signed in the presence of the hotel manager and his assistant and then, at last, we were able to push back our chairs.

And Charles Trelawne stood and came and made a stiff bow to me, his eyes taking in my stick and my pantaloons and blouse of crimson silk, and for one disbelieving moment I thought he was going to touch my hair where it swung just below my mother's ruby eardrops. But his outstretched hand dropped back to his side and his look was unfathomable as he turned and curtly inclined his head to his son. And Guy returned his look, his own dark eyes as hard and unforgiving as the icy blue gaze that locked with his. Then, with a final chill glare at Theo, he turned on his heel and left the room.

And it was thus that we contrived to place us all, I hoped, safely out of reach and out of danger from those long, powerful hands, hands that had already done such damage to my life and to that of so many others besides.

We dined together again that night, a meal quietly triumphant. Yet for some of us it was an occasion made sad because it was to be our last shared meal. Gladys ate little for the date of my departure for France had been set and as she pushed the food round her plate, my own heart ached at the thought of leaving my dearest and most loyal of friends.

Guy was saying that I would leave Polwerris with him on one of the French fishing boats that regularly came across from Cherbourg despite the war which dragged on between our two

232

countries. Theo protested at the discomfort of the voyage; I should go in his ship, newer, larger and more comfortable, and with the added bonus of steam power, for the sea trials off Plymouth were proving highly successful.

'And a much better target for enthusiastic French gunners, Theo,' Guy grinned at him. 'It's quite comfortable in the Captain's cabin. It's the way I always travel from Cherbourg to Poole. He's a strange man, Mon Capitain, but when he gets my message, he won't mind sailing down the Channel to Penzance. Knowing him, he'll take the opportunity to find a few more markets for his merchandise.' And the nature of the Captain's trade was clear from the expression on Guy's laughing face.

Uncle Jason crumbled the bread on his plate. 'So soon. Only three weeks. My partners must go over these papers with a fine tooth comb. It's fortunate for us that Charles employed a new lawyer two years ago. At the time I was most upset, for I had been fighting for Guy's rights and feared the boy would never get justice done once authority was taken from my hands. Now it is most fortuitous, since I could not, in all conscience, have acted on your behalf had he still been my client.'

Three weeks. I could see the pain in Gladys's eyes, I dared not look at Theo except when he spoke to someone else. Guy alone at the table was full of enthusiasm, his dark eyes gleaming, his smile wide as his expressive hands kept Gladys wholly included in the conversation. Had I once glowed and effervesced like that? Long ago in my other life, maybe. And more lately perhaps, in the company of my lover. . . But I was glad to watch my son, and thankful that he had come back into my life at so opportune a time.

'You are very cheerful for a young man who has just been disinherited and lost your chance of title and fortune.' Uncle Jason had a tinge of exasperation in his voice for it had been against all his instincts to draw up the papers we had demanded.

Guy threw back his head and laughed.

'But my father is a mere forty years old, Uncle Jason. If he lives only twenty more years, by that time, with careful use of this income of my mother's, my vineyard will be thriving and I shall be a wealthy Frenchman. I prefer my way of life, old friend, the barriers have been broken down. True, things are still troubled, but when this stupid war if over, we can settle down and work at

233

making a fairer society, one where the rights of each man will be ensured.'

I smiled, remembering Uncle Pierre saying much the same thing when I was a child. I remembered how he had worked on at his salon throughout the worst of the Terror, saved by his known humanity to all around. And he, in his turn, had rescued several noblemen and women by passing on information of their danger, and overcoming their blind arrogance and insisting they must flee. My son was much in his idealistic mould and I wondered how many of these thoughts and ideas I had unwittingly passed on to him during his childhood years.

'Are you quite sure Doctor Lawrence will accept Trusteeship, Francoise?' Uncle Jason regarded me with some anxiety.

'I think he will. Guy is going to visit him as soon as we return. We have already agreed that someone from outside the village will be able to offer a more dispassionate view if there is controversy over a particular matter.'

'Good. And you say he is no more than forty-five years of age. Don't smile, my dear, we want to know we can expect a few years of service at least before other Trustees need to be chosen! But before I recapitulate, are you quite adamant that neither you nor Guy wish to benefit from this money you have won from Charles? For in truth, my dear, although a large sum by anyone's standards, it is still little enough compensation for what you both have lost.'

'We are both decided, Uncle Jason. We have given it great thought. Guy has told you his feelings and though you may think him too young for such a decision, I agree with him entirely. Between us we have more than enough. Guy has the farm and the vineyard and now he will also have my mother's Trust money. I have my painting to give me an independence. No. We want Charles's money to be used entirely for the benefit of Polwerris.'

He sighed again. 'Very well, so shall it be. I shall now draw up a Trust Fund to be administered by Theobald and Gwendoline Pentire, Gladys Spargo, soon to be Mistress William Thomas,' (and here the old man bowed to her) and Doctor Lawrence, (assuming he is in agreement). Sir Charles Trelawne has agreed to pay the first sum of One Thousand Pounds into Martin's Bank in Penzance on the Twenty ninth day of this month of September and each year thereafter for Twenty Years.'

234

One could hear the capital letters in Uncle Jason's old-fashioned speech, but I blessed him for his careful pedantry: Charles's lawyers would find no loophole in the papers Pettigrew was drawing up on our behalf.

He went on, going over our plans one by one. 'A school will be set up using some of these funds. Mr Pentire has volunteered to install a Master whose salary will be his personal responsibility, while the running of the school and expenses of books and other materials will be funded by the Trust.' (And here Theo put in that he had just arranged with Jack Penrose to rent Lambeth Weekes's old barn to be the school premises.)

Pettigrew nodded his approval at this arrangement and removed his pince-nez and polished them with his silk handkerchief before resuming. 'The Trust will also take over responsibility for the 'Absent Partners' share in profits from the fishermen, thus relieving them of a burden fast becoming unsupportable with the loss of the *Mary Jayne* and her crew of three family men the year before last. The Trustees will arrange to meet from time to time to discuss the payments they have made.' He removed the pince-nez once more and looked round the table. 'Have we covered everything?' Gwendoline looked as though about to speak.

'Yes?' I encouraged her with a smile.

'I was just wondering,' she bit her lip and glanced at Theo for reassurance. And when he laid his brown hand on hers and smiled at her, my heart chilled and I briefly closed my eyes. 'I know this is so well meant, but I wonder if it will make the other villagers, the ones who don't benefit from the Trust, jealous, if it will cause endless ill-feeling in Polwerris.'

Gladys, who had been following the conversation with a little help from Guy who sat opposite, nodded her head vigorously and I was glad of the down-to-earth commonsense of these two women, for often, when I had seen dreadful need in some family in the village, I had wanted to give them money from our pouch. And Gladys had always insisted that instead we take them some ready-cooked fish or a hot pie. Other neighbours did the same and so the spectre of starvation was held at bay. A gift of money from us, Gladys had insisted, would upset those women who were so quick to share their own meagre food; would set us still further apart from the villagers.

'What do you suggest then, ladies?' Guy was looking discon-

235

certed for the first time that day.

Gladys produced a sheet of paper and handed it across the table to him.

Spreading it out before him, Guy studied it for a while and then looked up and smiled broadly at his old companion.

'Perfect, Gladys, ma cherie!' And he passed the paper to Uncle Jason who fumbled his glasses back on to his nose and perused the paper while Gladys reddened with embarrassment at being the centre of attention.

'Very good, my dear Gladys, very good!' He turned to us and read out Gladys's succinct suggestions.

'Theo to decide how much to be given to families of dead fishermen now being supported by the rest, since he knows the market. Doctor Lawrence to provide names of patients not able to afford treatment he considers necessary. Gwen and myself to report cases of need we get to know about in the village. Luxuries, that is, music, violin, painting lessons, (and here I smiled for Gladys had shaken her head at my enthusiastic plans for the children of the village), all these to be provided through the school, for any who are interested, regardless of their family background.'

'Excellent!' Theo beamed at Gladys. 'That will mollify any well-to-do farmer who is too mean to pay for his child's music lessons! Well done, Gladys.' And she smiled shyly back at him, and Gwen reached over and squeezed her hand. I felt another twinge of jealousy, this time because Gwen was usurping my place in Gladys's affections as well as taking Theo away from me. But in the general congratulations Gladys was receiving, my own silence went unnoticed.

I concentrated on my glass of wine, gazing down into the ruby depths shot through with candlelight, but when the chatter had ceased, I looked up and smiled at Gladys and said simply, 'You are wonderful, my darling girl.' And I cared nothing for the tears which glittered on my cheeks as I looked into the face of the girl who had saved the lives of both Guy and myself, at the stubborn jaw and the innocent blue eyes hiding the steadfast courage which had enabled her to become such a warm and clear-sighted woman.

A few more suggestions were made, and other ideas would come besides, but the basic purpose of the Trust Fund had been

236

set out. It was to be called the Millbrook Trust and it was to that fund that Charles had assigned our compensation for relinquishing our claims upon Trevingey. Pettigrew decided to remain at the Red Lion for a few more days so that the document could be drawn up and signed by its Trustees without delay.

And as he placed the papers in a metal deed box, Gladys and I looked at one another again and smiled, I remembering the dark rushing water below the bridge, slashed by the white scar of the weir, she thinking perhaps of the woman she had pulled from the dark millbrook, so near to death on that never to be forgotten night, beneath the great moon that sailed through the clouds, majestically unaware of the drama being played out on the river bank so far below.

Chapter Thirty

We left the Red Lion next morning, Guy, Gladys and myself, with
Jem between the shafts, eager to be on his way. We were bade
farewell by the landlord, Mr Stevens himself, for he had been
greatly impressed by Uncle Jason and extended his respect to the
rest of the Pettigrew party. Uncle Jason himself was to begin
his own journey a few days later, when his task was complete,
travelling only a dozen or so miles before resting at Mitchell, and
so proceeding slowly back to Plymouth. His home there was
being run in his absence by Bailey, our old butler, who had been
quietly spirited away from Trevingey at Pettigrew's behest,
during the inquest on Lambeth Weekes. There Bailey would live
out his final years, glad to be among friends, for he had begun
service in the same big house as Pettigrew's faithful Judd, and his
acquaintance with the Pettigrew family went back over many
long years.

Uncle Jason came to the pavement to say goodbye and we
wept as we embraced, for we both knew it was unlikely that we
should meet again. But presently he drew himself up and chided
me, 'Come my dear, people will talk. And I have not lived this
long to give cause for scandal at such a late stage in my life!' And
so we laughed as we parted, there on the cobbles outside the old
inn, and from the trap I waved goodbye, blinded by more than the
sun's rays as Guy steered Jem through the already crowded
streets. I threw down some coins to the gaggle of ragged children
who ran behind us with outstretched hands, astonished and
disturbed by the meanness and poverty in the side streets of the
town.

Gladys pointed with horror at the detritus she saw floating in
the leats which ran alongside the road; water which was used by

238

many of the cottages along its course and we all wrinkled our noses at the stench of the tanners yard which was sited in the midst of other lowly dwelling places. I was glad when at length we left the town behind and regained the open countryside once more, but we all remained subdued and troubled for several miles along our way; appalled that such conditions were permitted in so large and important a town.

Before long, the September sun vanished behind a bank of clouds and we became chilled where we sat, high up in the trap, and were glad of the pony skin rug behind which to huddle. Guy gave me a questioning glance as we tucked it round us, and I smiled.

'Yes, it is the one from Trevingey, the same rug that Gladys covered me with when she took me to her grandmother.'

'It has served us well,' Guy muttered, and I could hear the emotion in his closed throat. We said little more during the long drive, each of us busy with our own thoughts.

At last, stiff and cold, we reached Helston and Guy drove into the yard at the Angel Inn where I spotted Ralph Eva, one of our companions on our trip to the fair. He crossed to us with a smile and Gladys was glad to leave Jem in his safe hands and we went inside. While a meal was being prepared, the three of us sat before a huge fire, enjoying the bustle of activity about us. But when Guy suggested we rest there for the night, both Gladys and I shook our heads, wanting to get back to Polwerris as soon as we could.

Two hours later, rested and restored by the hot food, we set off on this last part of our journey. Gladys had worried that this break was not long enough to rest Jem, but Guy and Ralph both assured her that the horse was quite fit and fat enough to enjoy a leisurely trip that would total a mere thirty miles in one day. And indeed, when we remounted the trap, Jem tossed his head and whinnied his pleasure to be back in familiar country and set off at a spanking pace.

Before long we were travelling across the downs of Goonhilly, under a darkening sky as the day closed in. But there was light enough to see our way when we at last turned down the narrow track that led to Polwerris Cove, and to the cottage that would be my home for such a little time longer.

The neighbours were on their doorsteps to greet us as we came down the street, and Gladys permitted Guy to stable Jem while she lighted the fire she had prepared before we left; the first time in our years at the cottage that it had not continued burning, day and night.

And when it was well alight, we sat on the settle before flickering flames for a long while, going over the events of the past few days, for tired though we were, I for one, knew that sleep would not come until my muddled thoughts could find some peace. But at last, as the clock on the wall struck one, we said our goodnights and, glad to be in my own bed once more, I fell into a welcome sleep.

We had all decided to say nothing to the people of the village about the new Trust Fund until it was properly sealed. I had no doubts that Doctor Lawrence would willingly become a Trustee, for he had radical views of the society in which we lived and would be pleased to see this life-line put into being. And my confidence was proved well founded the following day when Guy called on him to acquaint him with the terms of the Trust. In fact, so eager was he to help, that he himself made the journey to Truro to see Pettigrew without delay.

Guy used his spare time to help Gladys prepare the house for her wedding which was to take place the following week. First he moved his things to the loft over the scullery where he was able to make himself more comfortable than Zeb had done, in those days when he lay in hiding while waiting for Tom Spinks to arrive. Then, despite her protestations, he helped Gladys to move the heavy furniture in her grandmother's old bedroom and set about lime-washing the walls. When the room was finished, I climbed the stairs to inspect their work. And how charming they had made it, with the dark furniture gleaming against the white walls, woollen rugs on the polished floor and her grandmother's patchwork quilt, jewel bright upon the matrimonial bed.

Apart from the wedding, there was much else to arrange. Mr Swain came over from Penzance as soon as he received my letter telling him of my plans. He was full of consternation that I was to leave Cornwall until I reassured him that I would still send him my paintings. 'You are sure your son will do this for me, will bring your paintings across the Channel when they are ready?'

'Of course I will!' Guy grinned at him. 'I come across to London twice a year. I'll bring you some good claret as well, if you like.' And the pair of them fell to discussing wines, for as I had suspected, Mr Swain was something of a connoisseur.

I showed him the painting which was to be my wedding present to Gladys and Will, a happy picture of the two young people on a beach, pulling a boat up the sand, Will's back a strong curve, and Gladys, head back in laughter, more concerned with keeping her skirts out of reach of the playful wave than lending her strength to the task in hand.

'What a present! If I were to marry, would you do one like that for me?' But he laughed and shook his head as he spoke. And our farewell was sad, for though I had met him so few times, I liked him, and appreciated that he would still be the means of my retaining my independence.

Uncle Jason returned to Plymouth and both Guy and Theo made trips to see him and to meet the other partners at Pettigrew & Pettigrew's. The complicated papers regarding the Millbrook Trust were duly signed and witnessed, and returned to the safety of the firm's vault. And while in Plymouth Guy met Zeb and learned that he and Morwenna were hoping to get her father's consent to marry.

Without letting her know my ideas, I tried to find out from Jinny if the plans I was shaping with her future in mind, were feasible, but she came so infrequently to the village these days that I was beginning to feel concern for her. Then, one day I glimpsed her passing and sent Guy to ask her to come in. But before I could properly begin to sound her out, the child forestalled me.

'I won't be able to come for no more lessons, Miss Millbrook. So it don't matter much that yore goin' away. My Auntie Sophie is havin' another baby and I got to stay home and help. And Gran says to say thanks to you for the new cape you got for me in Truro.' The child's voice was tight with tears and thus I could not, must not say anything that would add to her despair. So I made some light remarks and after she had gone, I shed tears of my

241

1

own, both for myself and for the child and we saw no more of her in the village in the following days, apart from a glimpse of her outside the Chapel after Gladys's wedding.

It was a simple wedding, the marriage of Gladys and Will. Guy walked her up the aisle and I sat near to the front as the young couple exchanged their vows, and I was glad to see the minister had troubled to acquaint himself with some sign language, for although she could follow the service quite well, it seemed to emphasise the gravity and import of the promises they made.

The Chapel was full and the volume of the singing voices took me by surprise since this was the first time I had been inside the building. Wonderful singing, heartfelt and sensitive and imbued with the unquestioning faith of the singers. And moved by the music and the gentle simplicity of the service, my tears fell once again and I found it hard to believe that soon I should be far away from Polwerris and Gladys, and all these people who had been part of my life for so long.

After the service our cottage filled with friends and neighbours and I was glad we had prepared so many tarts and pies and cooked meats. I missed Jinny's impish presence and Theo could not come for he was in Saltash again, where final tests on the new engine were being carried out. But Gwen was there and, strangely, I liked to be with her, for when she spoke of him it was as if he were close beside me and I could almost feel the warmth of his body, and the strength of his arms. . .

The feast, for such it became, went on for many hours. But at last, everyone had left and Guy and I made our goodnights and went off to our rooms.

It felt strange not to hear the boards overhead creak under Gladys's feet, for her old room was empty now, Guy having insisted on remaining in the little loft at the back saying it was not worth moving his things again for so short a time, but in reality not wishing to intrude on the privacy of the young couple who now had the upper floor to themselves.

I was glad to be alone after the crowded and emotional day, glad of time to think and plan. I undressed slowly and climbed into my cupboard bed, grateful for the cool sheets against my tired body, wondering whether I should light a candle and read for a while, for so many thoughts chased through my head that I knew I should lie awake for hours. But barely had my head touched the pillow than I was fast asleep and when next I opened my eyes daylight was already showing behind the drawn curtains of the cottage windows.

Chapter Thirty-one

But the following day, my plans were forgotten and the villagers were to need all their faith to sustain them against the coming events; for a great storm sprang up, a storm the like of which could not be remembered and one that would be spoken of with awe for many years ahead.

There was little warning. First the morning sky darkened and the wind freshened. A few of the men looked uneasy, and soon they were warning those who lived at the harbour edge to shutter their windows. Then the customers at the Red Lion helped to drag sandbags across the doorways, for it was not unusual for a wild sea to fling itself across the roadway and into the lower rooms, and as they worked they cast wary glances at the waves that were building beneath the rising wind.

By the middle of the afternoon it was almost as dark as night and the wind screamed with hurricane force up through the valley from the sea. We could not hear the crashes of falling slates because of the noise of the storm, but we could see the chunks of thatch which flew past the windows, torn from every roof. I peered seawards from my room, but could see nothing through the salt encrusted panes and Guy said that the water which poured through the roof of the back kitchen was also salt, snatched from the wave tops by the shrieking wind.

Together, Guy and Will went out to see what was happening in the harbour where all but two of the fishing boats were berthed. They staggered back a while later, white faced with shock. The vessels were damaged, every one, they thought, for they were being tossed and flung about, there within the shelter of the harbour basin, as if it was the open sea. But without the space of the open sea they were smashing against one another with every

244

new wave which surged over the wall, and masts were inter-twined and snapped and many of the furled sails had been ripped away and torn to shreds.

There was nothing the men could do about the boats, nor about the damaged roofs while the gale still raged, but they went off again to help where they could, to board up smashed windows, to carry crying children to safety from those houses down by the harbour into which the sea was flooding. Our kitchen became a shelter for one such family, and each time they returned from their forays, Guy and Will brought with them exhausted men who were grateful for the hot food and drink we provided, the drinks laced liberally with rum.

The storm raged on throughout the night. I did not go to bed, but dozed fitfully in a chair while the family from the flooded cottage slept in my room. And at last, I opened my eyes and found that day was breaking but the wind still showed no sign of dropping. An hour later, when Gladys was busy and the men had gone out again, I felt the need to see for myself what was happening to the village. I went out into the back lane which I felt might afford some shelter from the full force of the gale but I found that even here I could barely walk, and when I struggled to the corner from where I could see the harbour, the wind was like a solid wall against which I could make no progress.

I reeled back behind a projecting wall and found that I could see the harbour from this comparatively sheltered corner. And I gasped at what I saw. The whole of the bay was white, like a moving, surging snow-field. From it, great waves rushed forward to strike the harbour wall with a booming roar. The wall held, and fended off the battering waves, time after time, sending skywards curtains of water which the wind snatched and hurled at the cottages to fall as salt rain through the damaged roofs. Every now and then, a larger wave rushed along the wall, clawing its way up and up until it flung itself into the harbour basin, smashing into the herded vessels. I saw one large boat lying broken-backed upon the road before the inn, tossed there by some mighty wave at the tide's height. And when I looked up the valley behind me, I stared in bewilderment for some time at an unfamiliar space, until I recollected the pleasant copse which had stood there just hours before. And as far as I could see in every landward direction, thatching straw flew and caught, and flew on again.

Amidst the bedlam of the waves and wind and the grinding rumble of rocks dragged to and fro across the bed of the cove, there was a separate sound, like canon fire; a sound I had heard many times during the night and dared not speak of, for I had thought it to be the signal of a vessel in distress that we none of us could help. But now I saw the reason for the sound with relief and awe combined; great waves were driving into a blow hole at the foot of the cliffs and exploding outwards, sending a spectacular, rocket-like plume of spray across the very breadth of the cove, followed by that thunderous boom that shook the ground beneath my feet.

It seemed that I stood there only a few minutes, but when I turned and struggled back to the cottage, I was soaked through and bemused by the battering of the wind and the clamour of the storm. Gladys shook her head at my bedraggled figure, but was too busy to offer me her help, and as soon as I had changed my clothes, I too, set to preparing vegetables for a huge pot of broth for our swollen numbers.

Then, towards the end of the afternoon the wind dropped somewhat, and every able-bodied man helped to place layers of turf from the garden ricks on to the torn roofs to prevent further damage. And no one spoke of what was on everyone's mind; of the two vessels that had not reached Polwerris Cove before the storm broke.

Toby came to the cottage. He still needed his crutch and so was of little help to the men. He asked if he could borrow my spyglass, his face white and stiff, and I remembered that his elder brother was on one of the boats. He was going up to the cliffs, he said, to see if there was any sign of them. . .

We sent him off with heavy hearts, admonishing him to take care - as if he of all people would need to be reminded. And with this open admission of our concern, we spoke at last of the eight men who might have lost their lives.

But talking of it did not help. And so we worked steadily on, making more bread, more pies; glad of the store of salt fish and beef in the larder. We stoked both the hearth and the smaller fire in its brick box in the back kitchen where a cauldron of hot water bubbled and sodden garments hung from lines strung from side to side across the narrow room. Men came and ate and went, driven and preoccupied even while they ate, seeking only to restore their strength for the battle they fought, saying little, their eyes alone betraying their desperate fears.

And then there was a flurry at the door. A horseman had arrived, in the village, unheard in the noise of the wind. A horseman - one of the men from the missing vessels! Jacob Berryman was pulled into the room by eager hands while all eyes were on his face. They were safe, he told us. All safe in Falmouth harbour. And no, they had little damage, a broken spar or two. Nothing more.

People raced through the village with the news, running from house to house and the excitement and relief were so great that no one noticed that the wind had dropped away until one of the children suddenly clapped his hands and sang out, 'It's over! It's over! The wind is gone!'

And so it had. Soon the street was full of women and children who came to see for themselves the damage the storm had wrought. And fickle as we are, they forgot their recent great relief that their men had survived, and stood, stiff with shock at the sight of the damage to the village and above all, to the fishing boats in the harbour below.

I suddenly remembered Toby, and telling Gladys where I was going, I set off to climb the steep hill to try and find him. When I reached the brow, I paused and looked around, and presently spotted him, a small distant figure, peering out to sea through the spyglass. It was too far for me to walk and I took off my shawl and waved it to and fro as I had done once before in this place. And to my relief, he turned and saw me. I waved again, joyfully, grinning my delight, and he must have been looking through the glass at me, for he suddenly leapt to his feet and came hobbling along the headland with desperate speed.

By the time he reached me, he was too breathless to speak, but from my beaming face he knew his fears were groundless.

'All safe, Toby. They're in the harbour at Falmouth.' The boy put his free hand to his face so that I should not see his tears. And as he stood, chest heaving from his frantic run, I dropped my stick and put my arms about him, holding him and telling him over and over again that they're all right, Toby, they're all safe.

And presently we made our way back to the village, he with his crutch and I with my stick, laughing and teasing one another as we went. And no one who heard our silly prattle and our high laughter, would have believed we were returning to a village which had just been laid waste by the storm.

Despite the heartfelt relief that the storm had claimed no lives, there was a chill despair on the faces of the men next day as they toiled to make good the worst of the damage. They concentrated first on the houses, turning their faces from the splintered planks and broken masts which were being tossed about on the still heaving seas within the harbour, and only when the most urgent of the repairs had been seen to, did they go down to count the total damage to the boats. And their bowed shoulders as they later made their way to their homes, told its own story.

'We must tell them, Maman,' Guy announced. 'Theo and Gwen would not want us to wait until a formal meeting when he returns, and Dr Lawrence has already told me that we can do as we wish.'

So Will sent a boy to ask all the fishermen to come to our house that night, and when they filed in, their weather beaten faces were dark with strain and they moved like men bearing an unendurable load.

When they were all seated round the kitchen table, Guy asked them first what they thought would be the cost of the repair to their vessels.

Will's uncle spoke. 'Too much, boy. That much we know. We should have to borrow from the bank. And that we can't afford to do. 'Twas all we could do to keep goin' before, what with paying out for the *Mary Jayne's* crew and all. We don't know how we can go on, and that's a fact.'

Silas Jenkin nodded his agreement, his brow furrowed, for though he had his smallholding, fishing was the mainstay of his livelihood. 'If we use all that we can salvage from the wreckage, we might be able to make two of the boats sound. But two boats won't keep all our families. We're in a spot and no mistake, the worst we been in that I can remember.'

Guy cleared his throat. 'The reason we asked you here is to tell you that there is money you can use.' And as their puzzled faces turned towards him, he began to outline the purpose of the Trust. 'So if you need to borrow from the bank, the interest would be paid on your behalf from these funds, and you could pay off the capital in your own time. And as for the *Mary Jayne* dependants, one of the clauses in the deed ensures that they will be taken care of, and any other villagers who are left destitute through misfortune.'

From where I sat, beside the fire with Gladys, I could see the faces of the men across the table, and I watched the puzzled looks turn to disbelief and then to astonishment. And later, when realisation had sunk in, I saw them straighten their backs, ready to work with new vigour at the salvage of their boats and the rebuilding of their lives.

One of the men said eagerly that if they all took turns fishing from the two undamaged vessels that were right now on their way back from Falmouth harbour, the rest could work to repair the damaged boats, one at a time. They all agreed with this idea, and one of the older men, his eyes gleaming, said they could afford to lose one ship totally if it meant that using her planks would lessen the bank loan. For they all saw that the less the Trust had to pay out in interest, the more the villagers as a whole would benefit.

Gladys and I left them to their talk as the air grew thick with tobacco smoke, and from my room I lay listening to their rumbling voices from my bed long into the night. I was glad to hear the occasional burst of laughter, and glad that it was the spoils of our victory over Charles that would help these endlessly toiling men to free themselves from their hand-to-mouth existence and bring them some ease from their constant battle to survive.

Guy told us next day that the men had not inquired too deeply into the source of their good fortune, simply accepting that a Trust Fund had been set up which would run for several years, years in which everyone in the village would benefit in some way or other.

But if the men did not delve too deeply for answers, their wives were far less circumspect and they plied me with questions.

'Goodness!' I exclaimed, 'have you never heard the saying about looking a gift horse in the mouth? We have come into some money, Guy and myself, which we cannot take out of the country. So make the best of it.' I could see from their faces that this somewhat facile explanation did not satisfy them, but it sufficed to quieten them for the time being at least and they fell to talking excitedly of the new school and the opportunities their children would now have.

And so it was that Guy and I had the unexpected delight of seeing for ourselves how the Millbrook Trust would help the villagers, for wherever we went in those busy days of repair and renewal, there was excited talk about their astonishing good fortune and we could see that the Trustees would be hard put to making choices of how best to use the funds in the days and years ahead.

Chapter Thirty-two

After the storm, the weather changed and we had a few welcome days of stillness and sunshine, and the turf patches were removed from all the roofs and the thatches repaired at once lest the weather should change again. And the floating debris in the harbour was collected and sorted and stacked alongside the wall until it was needed. And to everyone's relief it seemed that apart from the boat which had been hurled up and broken upon the road, the others could all be made good by using the salvaged timber and taking out a relatively small loan for the new masts and such other materials as would be required. And it was good to see the spring in the men's step as they went about their work and the eagerness with which they set about the repairs now that so much of the burden had been taken from their shoulders.

The day before Guy and I were to leave Polwerris, Mary Penrose came over from Helston. Lambeth's will had been proved and she was now a wealthy woman and they had bought the shop of which she had spoken. She was driven to the village by her younger son who had gladly left the sea to work with his mother and brother. He smiled gaily and went off in the serviceable wagonette which she told us they used for making deliveries, leading the horse to the Red Lion where he could refresh himself and talk of his travels with the innkeeper and any customer who chose to listen.

Mary wore a smart navy pelisse over a pleated linen gown of the same colour, and she bore a wedding gift for Gladys; a beautifully crafted spice box, aromatic with the cinnamon and cloves it contained. I watched as she and Gladys examined the fine workmanship of the box. Gone was the distraught figure which had grappled on the edge of the cliff with Will and Jack on that unforgettable night; gone too, the woman who had sat at this same table, blanched with terror at the visit of the Parish constable, and in her place was a business woman who already wore an air of quiet confidence.

But even as I marvelled at her composure, she looked up and I surprised a sudden disquiet in her gaze. 'Where's Jinny?' she asked, glancing round the kitchen as if expecting to see the child about the place.

I bit my lip, my heart aching for the child who no longer followed at my heels, questioning and eager, and longing for the better life which she had so briefly glimpsed. And then I turned to this woman, this Mary Penrose whom I admired but found it increasingly hard to like. 'Jinny? Oh she's with her grandmother, making the most of the time she has left before she leaves for France with me.' And I heard my words with astonishment for I had sadly relinquished all thoughts of taking the child with us.

'Going to France with you! Good!' The words were heartfelt and I knew she still feared that the child would speak of what had happened that night. 'Good,' she said again and turned back to Gladys.

I sat, aghast at my words. Then I stood. I must see Jinny's grandmother without delay, before my thoughtless words were spread around the village and reached Jinny's home. I excused myself and left the two women over a cup of tea, the spice box still on the table before them, I met Guy as I walked up the street and was glad of his arm on the rough track outside the village. I told him what I had said to Mary Penrose and that it could not be, since Jinny had already told me of her grandmother's need of her.

'I'd ask the old lady herself if I were you Maman. Jinny can't be that much of a help, I see her roaming over the cliffs at all sorts of odd times. I think she made that story up because she couldn't bear to be near you when she knew you were to leave Polwerris so soon.'

'I hope you are right, Guy. Because it's not just for me, you know. The child could have a good life in France. She has talent.' I said no more and we continued on our way in silence, I regretting I had not worn my cloak, for a light drizzle had just begun to fall.

We found the tumbledown cottage nestled in its hollow with two small children playing outside, oblivious of the dampness in the air. I recognised little Sophie and Jack. They stared at us, eyes enormous in their grimy faces, and before I could speak they ran off shrieking, 'Visitors! Visitors!' Through the low doorway of the cottage, Jinny appeared, clad in her ragged old clothes with her grandmother peering suspiciously over the child's shoulder.

'Ah, 'tis you, is it?' Mrs Pellow's voice was hard and there was no welcome in her face.

I asked if I could have a word with her. Alone.

'Look after they little 'uns, maid. And mind that fire.' And with that she took a hessian sack from a hook behind the door, threw it round her head and shoulders and stepped out of the cottage, closing the door firmly behind her.

All my life, the smell of the camomile that our feet crushed as we walked to and fro over the rough ground, will take me back in time and place to that little hollow, where the low dwelling crouched out of the wind, surrounded by clumps of gorse and brambles, with the fine rain suspended in the air around us.

I told her what I had said to Mary Penrose; that I had had no right to make such a statement but for all that, I would indeed be happy if she could spare her granddaughter. 'I know you have these other, younger children to look after Mrs Pellow. I know Jinny must be such a help. I know I have no right to ask you.' And inwardly I cursed my stumbling sentences and my helplessness before this fierce old woman, and Guy too, was for once at a loss for words.

As I paused, she stopped in her tracks and turned to face us, her arms folded across her chest, clutching the sack close to her body.

'She might's well go with 'ee. She's no use to me these days, allus dreamin' and mopin' round the place. My youngest's maid have just married a sailor boy and she's comin' back here to live and have her babe. And by the time he do come back, if he ever do, then young Sophie'll be old enow to help. Come to that, she'm a more able cheeld now than our Jinny'll ever be, with her speakin' French and drawin' and the rest. Aise, you better take her with 'ee. I know you'll be good to the li'l maid.'

That was all she said. No haggling for money to compensate for the loss of her helper, no protestations of all that the child meant to her and the hurt of the parting. But I could see for myself the pain of loss in her sunken eyes.

'Thank you,' I held out my hand to seal our agreement and she released her sack with one band and accepted mine. Her hand was twisted with arthritis and calloused with toil and it closed on mine with a sudden, convulsive grip. 'She shall come back if she wishes,' I said. 'Whenever she wants. She has only to ask.' I wanted to say more but my throat was constricted with tears. Guy in his turn, took her hand and shook it, and then he raised it to his lips and kissed it and she stood still and watched us as we turned and walked away, she seemingly unaware of the drizzle which fell about us, collecting in heavy drops on our hair before trickling down our faces like the tears I tried not to shed.

When we regained the track, we looked back and saw the cottage door close behind her. Moments later we heard a familiar shriek and before we had walked many paces, Jinny herself came flying down the track to catch us up and make us tell her with our own lips that yes, it was true, we really did mean it, that she was to come and live with us in France and she must be ready to sail next day on the evening tide.

One other delightful surprise had been laid on for me, a pleasure of which I had no inkling; for early next morning, my last morning at Polwerris Cove, Guy called me to hurry and finish dressing for there was something I must see to urgently. My fingers became clumsy with haste and it was fortunate I had no buttons with which to struggle and I opened my door with anxiety.

Guy laughed. 'Maman! Brush your hair! You can't go out like that!'

Mystified, but reassured by his cheerfulness, I complied and even spent a minute checking my appearance. Since Guy's return, the dreadful lethargy and sickness brought on by losing Theo had left me, and the hollows in my cheeks had vanished; I looked fit and well, and it was only the parting from Gladys that I dreaded for though Theo would be there to wave us off, our real separation had already taken place; here in the cottage kitchen on that night when be had told me of Gwen's pregnancy.

'Come on! Hurry!' Gladys was smiling alongside Guy as he opened the door. 'There! Look at her!'

I turned to look where Guy was pointing. A ship was coming into the cove, sails neatly furled and a plume of smoke coming from a sort of chimney amidships. 'Theo!' His name was a whisper, but Gladys, completely deaf, turned and took my hand. There were already a number of people down on the harbour wall, and soon everyone who could, was making their way down to watch this steam-driven vessel negotiate the narrow harbour mouth.

And while part of me marvelled like the rest at the easy way the ship manoeuvred my heart was with the man we could just make out standing at the wheel. Soon they were alongside and tied up and then I turned to look for Gwendoline and was relieved not to see her for I knew it must distress her to see us together, try though we might not to let our eyes meet.

Gladys squeezed my hand and pointed. I looked at the ship again where a short gang plank was being placed. A tall girl stood waiting to step ashore, a girl who waved joyously and came bounding across the narrow bridge. Morwenna! She ran up and embraced both Gladys and me with a wide hug. Guy took off his hat and, very French, kissed her cheeks while she laughed and blushed for it seemed that the whole village was looking on.

'Enough of that, you Frog, you!' The grim voice made us all turn to where Zeb stood, face and hands blackened with coal dust. 'You leave my wife alone!'

'Wife!' Guy gave a great shout of laughter and released Morwenna to hug the grinning Zeb in his turn, regardless of both the dirt and Zeb's mock struggle to free himself, exaggerated for the entertainment of the onlookers.

Everyone was talking at once, about the young couple, about the surprise visit, about the wonders of steam power. I was glad of the hubbub for in the noise I found a moment of silence when Theo joined us. A moment when I saw again in his eyes that familiar struggle and anguish and a moment when my own heart was there in my eyes for him to read.

But a moment only, for the fishermen were eager to be shown the engine, and Theo and Zeb were pressed to go back on board with them.

At times like this, times of deep stress, I have found that one seems to live on two different levels, on the surface where speech and actions appear completely normal, and at a deeper stratum where emotions churn and boil like the inside of a volcano and where great reserves of strength are called upon to prevent that surface control from collapsing into the cauldron within. So it was with me as we walked back to the cottage with Morwenna at the centre of a cheerful crowd of friends and neighbours. And perhaps it was so for Theo as he let Zeb, his newly appointed ship's engineer, demonstrate the workings of his precious engine.

Certainly, when Guy and Zeb came later to join us in the cottage, there was a special concern in my son's eyes as he looked at me, and as he told me that Theo was still aboard and would be going straight home when all was secure.

Straight home. To his wife. And it came to me then that a part of Theo too, would be glad when I was no longer here in the village, when there would be no more chance meetings where every sense must be subdued, when no glance or word must pass that would cause hurt to Gwen. And I too, knew that this complete break was the better way, the only way, for us both.

Morwenna was speaking. 'Miss Roberts says I can work at the school as long as I like. Zeb says there's no need, but he'll be away on his precious ship most of the time! And I love being with the children.'

'When did you get married, you didn't elope, did you?' Guy chaffed them merrily, and I remembered that Guy had already met Zeb when Theo took him to inspect his ship after meeting the other partners at Pettigrew's.

'No. When Theo said he wanted the ship to come to Polwerris this weekend, Zeb said I must come too, and it was best if we got married first. Father came up and we got a special licence and have now been married exactly one week,' and Morwenna smiled her happiness. 'We told Father to keep it a secret so that we could surprise everyone!'

'Yes, and she's making eyes at a lousy Frenchman already!' growled Zeb.

'A lousy Frenchman is better than a filthy Blackamore! Look at the state of you! Gladys, will you dunk this fellow in a tub of water or shall I!' And while the pair went off together, Morwenna and Gladys and I sat and went over past events and mused about the present and wondered about what all our futures would hold.

'Will you stay in Plymouth, Morwenna?' I found my hands itching for a pencil, for the girl had become even more lovely in the months she had been away, her skin perfect and the brown hair a shining cluster of curls. Her hands too, were finer than before as she did little menial work, Miss Roberts realising that Morwenna was a natural teacher with the little ones.

'Maybe, if we have a child,' and here Morwenna blushed again, 'perhaps then we might come back to Polwerris. But for the moment we're better off as we are. We have found a nice little house to rent only half a mile from School. But tell me more about your plans, Elizabeth. I couldn't believe it when I got your letter saying you were off to France so soon.'

So soon! I glanced at the clock which hung on the wall. Only a few more hours and I would be boarding a French ship out in the cove, for it would not put in to the bay until dusk for fear of challenge. Guy had laughingly informed us that the only Excise vessel in these waters had sailed off to Fowey after a carefully placed whisper of planned activity in that distant port; a whisper which should give us a safe passage, for the local fishing vessels were more likely to seek trade than confrontation with a Frenchman in these home waters.

A few more hours. And then time began to drag, every slow minute underlying the finality of our parting. Gladys was pale and determined not to weep and I became brittle, my cheeks flushed and eyes too bright as I checked my trunk for the dozenth time; that same trunk which Gladys had placed in her trap on the fateful morning of my planned flight with Richard Penhaligon. Poor Richard, the lover whom I now remembered with compassion and shame at my part in his death.

I sighed, a tremulous sigh that threatened to become a sob and I turned over the contents of the trunk once more. There were the few clothes I now possessed, easily packed and light, for there were none of the boned corsets and stays that had once been an essential part of my wardrobe. There was my mother's jewel case in which the ruby drop earrings lay alongside the matching necklace and brooch, together with her other pretty trinkets, none of which I would ever have sold, no matter how desperate the need.

I gave to Gladys the valise into which I had packed my necessities for that ill-starred flight, but I kept the little suede pouch with enough sovereigns to keep me independent until I could start painting again, leaving the rest in a drawer with a note for my dear friend to find when I had gone. Gladys handed me my pillow and some sheets for she did not believe Guy's protest that the cabin the captain would have made ready would be adequately furnished. A separate box, fashioned by one of the men, contained all my painting paraphernalia, including some unfinished canvases which Guy would bring to Mr Swain on his next trip to England.

Throughout the afternoon, there were visits from neighbours, each bearing some little gift and it was these small mementoes, carefully made pincushions, a tea cosy, an embroidered cambric handkerchief, a new hand-carved walking stick, that finally made the tears trickle down my cheeks and I longed to be gone, for this drawn-out parting was too much to bear.

But at last, inevitably, the sun which had hidden behind the clouds for much of the day, showed its face low down over the horizon and presently a lookout signalled from the cliff top that our expected ship was in sight.

Gladys and I went into my room to spend a little time on our own; the room from which I used to summon her by the pull of the cord in those years of my pain and disability and I gazed with unseeing eyes at the splendid carving on the face of the cupboard bed. That would stay where it was; perhaps one day this would become hers and Will's bedroom, with the rooms above filled with their children.

Presently Gladys, sensitive as ever, left me alone in the room, closing the door behind her. And I stood, staring at the empty fireplace, at the chair and table where my sitters had spent long, patient hours, and I touched the door of the bed where Theo and I had shared our tempestuous love. . . Then, at last, I went to the little window which overlooked the harbour and saw the unfamiliar ship anchoring just inside the cove for she would not risk entering the harbour itself.

'Maman!' Guy's voice called from the front door. 'We must go now.' And so I left my home of the last four years and made my way down the cobbles to the little beach that lay beside the harbour wall. Jinny stood there quietly with her grandmother, a scatter of children around her, children washed and tidied for the occasion so that Jinny in her green skirt and the plaid cape and hood I had bought for her in Truro, did not look too out of place. And indeed, from the hugs and tears of the children, I wondered how soon before she would want to return to her family, and whether I was being wholly selfish in taking her with me. I turned away and then I saw Theo.

He stood alongside a rowing boat, ready to take us out to the waiting ship himself. We must go. I hugged Gladys one last time and turned quickly away, the faces of my friends and neighbours blurred by my tears as they shook my hands and offered me their farewells. I heard Gwen's voice, wishing me well, her own voice choked with emotion. And then Guy was shepherding me to the boat.

Theo helped me in and Guy swung Jinny over the side to sit beside me and willing hands pushed us afloat. The trunk lay on the floorboards in the bow with Jinny's small bundle of possessions alongside. Guy stood, leaning against the trunk, waving and waving as Theo pulled on the oars and took us into the red satin path of the setting sun. The water slid over the blades of the oars in falls of colour, pink and blue and mauve, dazzling me so that I had to close my eyes before I could clear my vision. Only then was I able to see Theo's face as he bent over the oars, pulling us smoothly out into the cove.

His gaze never left my face but my eyes roamed over his body, taking in the strength of his shoulders in that familiar jacket, the shape of the hands upon the oars, his feet, braced against the boards. . . At last I looked into his face and so we crossed those last few yards of water, our gaze locked in a silent pledge.

Guy said something and Theo reacted without taking his eyes from mine, shipping the oars as we glided alongside and bumped gently against the hull. Guy caught the short rope ladder and a sailor shinned down and threw a line round the trunk which was swiftly hauled on board. Then Guy took Jinny's bundle and with an encouraging grin, helped her scramble up the ladder.

Theo stood up and gave me his hand. I drew close to him, breathing the smell of the warm leather of his coat. Then he guided my foot onto the swaying ladder, and put his hand over mine on the rough hemp of the rungs.

'Goodbye, my love,' I breathed the words against his ear and then the motion of the ladder swung me away from him; from that last touch of his finger gentle against my cheek.

Guy reached down to clutch my wrist and draw me to the safety of the deck. And when I looked down, the dinghy had bobbed away on the silken water, Theo still standing, hand upraised in salute.

'Come,' Guy's voice was gentle but firm, 'they will be waiting to see you wave.'

And we made our way aft from where we could see the groups of people on the harbour wall and on the beach and in front of the old inn, people who waved handkerchiefs and scarves and whose voices called across the water. And then someone began to sing, a folk song, slow and sad, and it was taken up by other men, the purity of the tenors and the velvet of the baritones and bass, woven together with the sensitivity that never failed to surprise me in these men whose lives were an unending and often brutalising struggle to exist.

There was a jabber of French about us, strange to my unpractised ear, and then the anchor was lifted and the sails began to fill.

'We're moving!' Jinny clutched my hand. 'Oh Miss, we're really moving!' I smiled and squeezed her fingers, looking back to the shore. I could see Gladys, her face buried in her husband's jacket, and Gwendoline whose hair was a beacon in the gleam of the setting sun, and there was Theo, slowly rowing back to the harbour his gaze fixed on our departing ship. . .

And then, suddenly, abruptly, we had swung round the point of the headland and out of sight of them all, even of the boys who had run daringly along the rocks to be the last to wave us off. I stood, gazing and gazing at the headland which hid from view my loves. I do not know how long it was I stood there. Certainly the ship had tacked and turned, and now we were heading southeast and my beloved Cornwall was lost in a blur of low sunlight and tears.

Guy and Jinny had left me to myself and still I stared blindly across our wake, unable to rid myself of the after-vision of Theo's face as he stood in the dinghy with upraised hand and face bereft. . .

At last, my son appeared beside me, Jinny skipping excitedly behind him. 'Come up to the front with us, Miss Millbrook!' she cried.

'The bows, child. The bows,' corrected Guy.

And I let myself be drawn away from the stern rail, and as we made our way forward, the sails caught a breeze and filled with a loud crack and the ship plunged into the swell, the bow sending a shower of spray into the air. We stumbled and clutched one another as the sudden movement caught us off balance. I heard the wind sing through the rigging, heard the calls of the sailors as they trimmed the billowing sails, and felt the tremor of life run through the ship as she reared and fell, hitting the water with a resounding thump.

I tasted salt on my lips. Not the salt of tears for the time for grief was past. My son stood on one side, Jinny on the other, her small face alive with excitement. Gladys was settled and would be happy, Gwendoline would give Theo the family his heart craved. And I too must look ahead to my new life among the undulating hills of Normandy, with its mediaeval towns and castles, and to seeing again my dear grandmother, who was awaiting our expected arrival with great joy.

Jinny suddenly spoke, 'We'll see them again, won't we Miss Millbrook?'

I smiled, 'Yes, of course we will Jinny.' And I drew my cloak tight against the wind. Of course we would see them all again. And I smiled once more, for now I knew the reason for that anxious concern on Gladys's face these past weeks whenever she had looked at me. And I laughed suddenly with wonder and delight for only in the last few days had I discovered that I too, carried Theo's child safe beneath my heart. . .

For Gladys had known; known from the day of my first nausea and weakness. I, unable to conceive after Guy's birth throughout the barren years of my marriage, had given no thought to the possibility of bearing another child!

But now I felt young again, my thirty-eight years as nothing. I had sent Theo away because I did not believe I could give him his heart's desire, and although the irony of my condition had drawn bitter tears from my eyes that day when I had found out, now I was filled with thankfulness and joy.

I steadied myself once more against the movement of the ship and pointed over the bow, 'Look Jinny! Look Guy! Ahead there in the waves. Dolphins!'